READY FOR ANYTHING

Julian Thompson was born in Calcutta in 1934 and educated at Sherborne. Commissioned in the Royal Marines and parachute trained, he served in the Commandos in many countries round the world. He commanded 40 Commando Royal Marines from 1975 to 1978. He led 3rd Commando Brigade during the Falklands War in 1982.

He is now a consultant, and a research fellow at King's College, London.

JULIAN THOMPSON

Ready for Anything

The Parachute Regiment at War,
1940–1982

FONTANA/Collins

*To all past and present members of
the Parachute Regiment and Airborne forces
with affection and respect*

PICTURE ACKNOWLEDGEMENTS

The photographs in this book are reproduced by kind permission of the following:

Airborne Forces Museum 1*b*, 2*t*, 3*b*, 4*t*, 5*t*, 7*t*&*b*, 8*t*&*b*, 11*b*, 12*t*, 14*b*, 15*b*, 16; Hulton Picture Library 2*b*, 4*b*, 6*t*, 9*t*; Imperial War Museum 1*t*, 6*b*, 9*b*, 10*t*&*b*, 11*t*, 12*b*, 13*t*&*b*, 14*t*; Brigadier Pike 15*t*; Colonel Waddy 3*t*.

First published in Great Britain by
George Weidenfeld & Nicolson Ltd, 1989

First published in 1990 by Fontana Paperbacks
8 Grafton Street, London W1X 3LA

Copyright © Julian Thompson 1989
Maps by Terry Brown

Phototypeset by Input Typesetting Ltd, London

Printed and bound in Great Britain by
William Collins Sons & Co. Ltd, Glasgow

'D MINUS ONE'
BY THE REVEREND JOE DOWNING
(PADRE OF 4 PARA – 1942 to 1945)

Piled in the lorries
Down Route Seven,
Kit unloaded,
'Chutes to the 'ship' and
Picked up bedding;
An hour for eating
Bedding stacked
'Chutes all fastened?'
'Line up! Number!
Engines turning.
Engines roaring –
Now for the take-off –
Now we're airborne;
'No more smoking'
A bit of sleeping;
Nerves a bit tightened:
To France from Italy
Nearer and nearer –
Half an hour left now:
Whole stick standing,
Ten seconds warning;
Green light flashes
Parachutes open,
A few more seconds

Drove thro' Rome,
Out to the Drome.
Harness tried,
Safely inside
Over to tea;
Sleep for three.
Equipment on.
'Give a hand, John'.
Stick emplane!'
Switched off again.
Half-past-one:
Let her run.
Engines drone.
The Die's thrown.
Cramped a bit;
This is it!
On we fly;
Three hours gone by.
'Fasten your strop!'
Waiting to drop.
Red light on;
Now we're gone.
Air full of men;
And then, what then?

Contents

List of Maps   viii
Preface   ix

1 The Beginning   1
2 Jock Company and a Radar Station   32
3 Red Devils   53
4 By Air and Sea   93
5 Normandy   125
6 Operation Market – The Battle for Arnhem   195
7 Operations in the Mediterranean   266
8 The Ardennes – A Christmas Trip   281
9 Varsity – The Crossing of the Rhine   288
10 Peacekeeping – Java, Palestine and Egypt   309
11 Near East Operations – Cyprus and Suez   326
12 South Arabia   359
13 Confrontation in Borneo   386
14 Unfinished Business – Northern Ireland   406
15 South Atlantic – Falklands 1982   412

Glossary   457
Sources   460
Index   465

Maps

Page

15   Southern Italy, 1941–44

54   Tunisia

97   South east Sicily

131   Normandy

196   Operation Market Garden

211   Arnhem

234   The final attempt to reach Arnhem Bridge

289   Rhine Crossing

334   Suez, 1956

364   The Radfan

374   Aden, 1967

427   2 Para's battle for Darwin and Goose Green

442   3 Para's battle for Mount Longdon

451   2 Para's plan for Wireless Ridge

Preface

Why, many people have asked, should a Royal Marine write a full history of the Parachute Regiment? First, it is not a complete history of the Parachute Regiment. That is being written by someone better qualified than I. Second, having served near, alongside, or in the same theatre of operations as parachute battalions on a number of occasions and been privileged to have had two battalions under my command in battle, I have come to regard them with admiration and affection. If this brings a disbelieving smile to those who know the rivalry that exists between the wearers of the red and green beret, my answer is that a commander who had no affection for the men he commands, particularly in battle, is in the wrong business. However prickly and suspicious – and parachute soldiers, like Royal Marine and Army commandos, can be both to outsiders – I came to feel for the red-bereted men in my brigade the same affection and love as I did for the men who wore green. They have the same light in the eye, the same pride that admits no peer, the same wry sense of humour in adversity. There are differences, but not in the fundamentals. When things are going badly wrong, they will never let you down. Man proposes, God disposes; in action it is the other way about. Commanders may propose, but the plan is at the disposal of the soldiers. Their response will decide whether it will work or not. Parachute soldiers have, since 1940, been given plans to put into effect, from the excellent to the abysmal. I know, I gave 2 Para a rotten task at Goose Green.

So what is this book? It is an attempt to capture the spirit of the parachute battalions since 1940. In a book of this size there is insufficient space to cover every action, mention every name. That would take several volumes. I have given the lion's share of the book to the 1940–45 period. Those years saw most of the action and gave the Parachute Regiment the character it has today. There are many episodes in the period since 1945 that I have had to omit through lack of space. I do not wish to imply that they were unimportant. My shortest chapter is on Northern Ireland, the longest campaign in which the British Army has been involved since 1815. There will be many who may feel aggrieved that they are not mentioned. To them I apologize.

I have tried to write a book that is accurate, interesting and reflects some of the humour which shines through in even the grimmest moments. If this book does not achieve what I set out to do, it will not be the fault of the many serving and former members of the Parachute Regiment and Airborne Forces who have given freely and courteously of their time, putting up with endless questions and pestering by letter and telephone. I limited my reading of published books to the minimum I thought necessary to understand the outline of the events I describe, preferring to let participants tell the story, either directly, or through the medium of the excellent accounts in the Archives of the Airborne Forces Museum, King's College London, and War Diaries in the Public Records Office at Kew. Even so there have been problems. War Diaries, although extremely useful where they exist, can also be inaccurate. They are difficult to keep in the heat of battle. One officer described to me how he and his commanding officer in Tunisia used to sit down during a lull in operations after a period of up to three weeks hectic activity. To write their battalion war diary, the two of them started at either end of the period in question, and worked towards the middle, trying to recall what had transpired on the intervening days. Frequently they found they had lost a day! I was fortunate in being able to talk to so many who played key roles from the very beginning. Being a young regiment in British Army terms, many of the founders are still alive today. A full list of those with whom I spoke and corresponded is to be found on page 464. Most of them gave me at least half a day, some much more. They not only told me their stories, and read through parts of the typescript, but also gave me valuable advice, including suggesting further contacts. Many invited me into their homes, fed and watered me. However, I must make especial mention of the following, to whom I am particularly indebted:

Major Geoffrey Norton, the former Director of the Airborne Forces Museum, who gave me much encouragement and put me in touch with many helpful people; Jane Burrell, the former Director of the Airborne Forces Museum, who patiently found documents for me and allotted me space to work; Colonel David Mallam, the Regimental Secretary of the Parachute Regiment, for advice and valuable contacts; Mr Andrews and Mrs Blacklaw and the staff of the Ministry of Defence Library, whose collection of military books must be unsurpassed in this country, for their unfailing courtesy and forbearance; Patricia Methven, the Curator of the Liddell Hart Centre for Military Archives at King's College London; Michael Willis, the director of the photographic section of the Imperial War Museum, whose personal interest in my search for photographs was invaluable. The maps were drawn by Terry Brown, another ex-Royal Marine involved in the project! I am grateful to Her Majesty's Stationery Office for allowing me to quote from the Ministry of Information 1945 pamphlet, *By Air To Battle*, and to *The Guards Magazine* for allowing me to quote from Captain de Klee's article on Suez.

By seeking advice from General Sir Kenneth Darling

at an early stage, I was able to gain much valuable information about specific events, and the Regiment in general. I must thank Major General John Frost for his help with many parts of this book, particularly in assisting with the unravelling of what to me were the complicated events in North Africa in 1942/43, and for allowing me to quote from his book, *A Drop Too Many*. General Sir John Hackett, Major Tony Hibbert, Colonel John Waddy and Colonel Geoffrey Powell were most helpful in increasing my understanding of Arnhem, and I am grateful to Geoffrey Powell for allowing me to quote from his two books, *Men At Arnhem* and *The Devil's Birthday*. Major General Mike Walsh gave up much time to talk to me about Suez, the Radfan and Aden, and has allowed me to quote from his personal account of these events. Brigadier Paul Crook briefed me fully on 3 Para's Suez operations. Similarly, General Sir Nigel Poett gave up a whole day to talk to me about 5 Para Brigade in Normandy and the Rhine Crossing. Nigel Riley was most helpful in introducing me to members of 2nd Independent Parachute Brigade, and for allowing me to quote from his personal account, *One Jump Ahead*. Alan Jefferson, Lieutenant Colonel Allen Parry and Lieutenant Colonel Terence Otway were unfailingly patient in their explanations of the lesser-known events in the battle for the Merville Battery. Doctor Bobby Marquis, an eminent heart surgeon, allowed me to draw on his story of the experiences of 224 Field Ambulance during the first two weeks in Normandy in June 1944. In my experience the doctors in battle have an interesting perspective of events, and what they have to say is usually instructive.

Brigadier Alastair Pearson allowed me to use his personal notes; I found that the morning I spent with him one of the highlights of my research. Likewise Brigadier James Hill, who as well as keeping me entranced by his story, just as I was fourteen years before at the Staff College, was painstaking in his efforts to ensure the accuracy of my narrative. My afternoon with Brigadier Vic Coxen was equally fascinating. I count myself fortunate to have met three such distinguished fighting soldiers.

I would like to express my gratitude to Surgeon Commander Rick Jolly and Alan Jefferson for painstaking checking of my proofs; and to thank Martin Corteel, my editor at Weidenfeld, for his help and advice.

I have to thank many people, but most of all another prominent parachute soldier, Lieutenant General Sir Napier Crookenden, for generous advice, for allowing me to quote from his book *Drop Zone Normandy* and his personal accounts of the activities of the 9th Parachute Battalion, and for reading through and commenting on the whole of my typescript. Jane Harper read all the drafts; her support and incisive comments were inestimable.

Finally, I take total responsibility for the opinions expressed, and for all interpretations of events described in this book.

CHAPTER 1

The Beginning

Anyone standing on the banks of the River Rhine near the town of Wesel on the morning of 24 March 1945 would have seen over 1,500 Dakotas passing overhead, followed shortly afterwards by nearly as many other aircraft towing gliders, carrying the 6th British and the 17th United States Airborne Divisions to battle. This airborne armada was the outcome of nearly five years of training, planning, and much dearly-bought experience. The story starts in 1940, and there were moments when it seemed that nothing would ever go right. Fortunately for Airborne Forces, and for Britain, there were plenty of stout hearts to overcome the doubters.

'We are beginning to incline to the view that dropping troops from the air by parachute is a clumsy and obsolescent method and that there are far more important possibilities in gliders. The Germans made excellent use of their parachute troops in the Low Countries by exploiting surprise, and by virtue of the fact that they had practically no opposition. But it seems to us at least possible that this may be the last time that parachute troops are used on a serious scale in major operations.' *Air Staff paper, 12 August 1940.*

The Royal Air Force had been made responsible for the parachute training of the new airborne force immediately after the Prime Minister's directive of June 1940, which asked for 'a corps of at least five thousand parachute troops'. The Air Staff paper attempted to explain the difficulties encountered since June by the five-hundred-strong parachute force in training itself, let alone expanding to a force of five thousand. Events had moved swiftly between June and August. Manchester's civil airport at Ringway was selected for parachute and glider training and named the Central Landing School, for no other reason than that it was well away from areas likely to be affected by the forthcoming air battle over Britain. Flight Lieutenant Louis Strange DSO MC DFC, a First World War Royal Flying Corps ace and an ex-Lieutenant Colonel, was made responsible for the air side of training including parachuting. Major Rock, Royal Engineers, was sent to Ringway to take charge of the military organization of Airborne Forces, although he had no knowledge of aircraft except as a passenger. He was given no direction on which to base his training and was, in effect, just told to get on with it. The first instructors were volunteers from the Air Force and the Army – Flight Sergeant Brereton and eight fabric workers from the RAF parachute section, and RSM Mansie, Lance Sergeant Dawes and NCOs from the Army Physical Training Corps. Whereas the Army instructors were allowed to wear the distinctive and highly-prized parachute wings, the Air Force instructors were not. When asked the reason for this divisive ruling, a senior staff officer at the Air Ministry remarked: 'It is the duty of the Royal Air Force to remain in the air, not to fall out of it.'

The comment, although probably tongue-in-cheek, was an indication of Air Force resentment at their limited assets being diverted into what appeared to be a purely Army show. Another Air Force officer wrote: 'There are very real difficulties in this parachuting business. We are trying to do what we have never been able to do hitherto, namely to introduce a completely new arm into the service at about five minutes notice and with totally inadequate resources and personnel. Little, if any, practical experience is possessed in England of any of these problems and it will be necessary to cover in six months the ground the Germans have covered in six years.' He might have added, 'or the Russians,' who as long ago as 1929 had repulsed an Afghan invasion of Tadzhikistan by using a small but heavily armed paratroop force. In 1936 they dropped 1,200 men, 150 machine guns and eighteen light field guns on an exercise. General Wavell who was present said: 'If I had not witnessed the descents I could not have believed such an operation possible.'

None of this high-level inter-service bickering poisoned the relationships between the Army and RAF instructors at Ringway. Despite the total lack of practical knowledge of parachuting techniques, text books, special equipment, and in some cases, the basic ability to impart knowledge to others, the RAF and Army instructors of all ranks shared a boundless enthusiasm and great courage. They were to need both, because events moved fast and considerable difficulties lay ahead.

On 9 July 1940, B and C Troops of Number 2 Army Commando were the first pupils to arrive at Ringway. The Commandos had been formed after the fall of France, on the orders of Churchill in a minute to the Chiefs of Staff on 5 June 1940, to provide a raiding force 'for a vigorous, enterprising and ceaseless offensive against the whole German occupied coastline.' The wheels turned fast, because on 9 June and 11 June orders were sent out calling for up to 5,000 men for 'mobile operations'. One or two officers from each Army Command in Britain were selected as commando leaders. They selected five or six troop leaders, who in their turn found officers and men to form their own troop of about fifty or sixty men. Lieutenant Deane-Drummond was a signals officer in a corps medium artillery headquarters. On his return from Dunkirk he saw the notice calling for volunteers for commandos: 'My boss, who was a super chap and a proper

soldier, had strong views on the matter and let it be known
that he did not agree with this method of doing things.
He decreed that he would select the officers to go; one of
them was me.'

Commando officers and men were not quartered in
barracks or camps, but given an allowance to cover the
cost of accommodation and food. They lived in lodgings
selected by themselves, parading at a time and place
ordered by their leaders; a popular and jealously-guarded
privilege. Landladies were paid 3s 5d (17p) a day for each
man billeted, and for this they were expected to provide
bed, breakfast, a haversack lunch, tea and supper! Number
2 Commando, commanded by Lieutenant Colonel Jackson
of the Royal Tank Regiment, raised from the outset as a
parachute unit with volunteers from all commands
throughout Britain, moved into lodgings at Knutsford. All
volunteers were seconded, or lent, to the commandos.
They kept their own cap badges and idiosyncracies of
regimental or corps dress. Thus Number 2 Commando,
which was to become 1st Parachute Battalion, took the first
steps towards becoming Britain's first parachute soldiers.
Sergeant Lawley, who had been a driving instructor for
the RASC and volunteered for special duties, said: 'We
were a motley crowd, English, Welsh, Irish and Scots, and
belonged to all classes of life, ages running from eighteen
to forty years. But we had one burning desire, and that
was to have a go at "Jerry". The one thing that was
required to become a parachutist in those days was guts.
We were never medically examined beforehand, neither
did one's age matter.'

There were several soldiers of fortune among these
first parachute volunteers. Some had just returned from
fighting in the Spanish Civil War, and at least one had
the Order of Lenin from the Marxist Loyalists. All these
types wanted to do was fight. Commanding such men was

not easy, but they were superb soldiers provided they had a good, strong commanding officer.

Ten days after B and C troops had arrived, the school was told to train one complete commando of 500 men, followed as quickly as possible by a further 5,000, of whom a proportion would be foreigners. By this time garrison commanders and defence forces in the vicinity of Knutsford had received orders that friendly paratroops would shortly be training in the area, and that they were not to be shot! At this stage in the war a German invasion of Britain was thought to be imminent, and there were numerous false reports of enemy paratroops landing, even some, so rumours ran, dressed in nuns' clothing. The order was a wise precaution. A Dropping Zone, or DZ for short, was found at Tatton Park, the home of Lord Egerton. A supply of 28-foot parachutes, designed for the parachute training of aircrew, was sent from Henlow to Ringway. By 13 July all was ready for the first demonstration descents by the instructors.

The only people with experience of parachuting in Britain at this time were stunt men in films or at air displays, and aircrew who had taken part in the scheme to acquaint them with the art of parachuting in case they had to bale out of a damaged aircraft. It was for the latter purpose that the 28-ft parachute had been designed – to provide a softer landing than the 22-ft parachute normally worn by aircrew. This training scheme had been stopped some time before, so the 28-ft parachutes were now available for military parachuting. Both stunt men and aircrew under training had, in general, used the same technique, which consisted of climbing out on the wing of a bi-plane and, while hanging on to the struts with one hand, pulling the rip-cord so that the canopy deployed in the slipstream which pulled the parachutist off the wing. This was known as the 'pull-off' method. Parachuting was still thought of as a stunt and carried with it a dare-devil aura. Stunt men were individualists with their own techniques, and usually jumped from a greater altitude than was tactically possible for military purposes. This allowed time to sort out any minor problems on the way down and get into a good position for the shock of landing. If the main parachute malfunctioned, they usually carried a reserve parachute as a back-up. In these days of schoolchildren attending free-falling courses, middle-aged MPs and page three girls jumping for charity, and everyone, including parachute soldiers, wearing a reserve, it can be difficult to imagine what a dangerous business military parachuting was forty-nine years ago. Combined with much hard word on gear and techniques, there was also much experimenting, occasionally, for lack of time, of the 'suck it and see' variety, in the course of which a number of brave men were killed, and considerably more injured, some perma-nently. The first two descents at Tatton Park were by the 'pull-off' method from a Whitley bomber.

Captain Lindsay of the Royal Scots Fusiliers, who had been a polar explorer in peacetime, went on to command the 151st and the 9th Parachute Battalions. Among the first Army volunteers to jump, he described his first descent:

> We climbed into the aircraft and sat on the floor of the fuselage. The engines roared and we took off. I noticed how moist the palms of my hands were. I wished I didn't always feel slightly sick in an aircraft.
>
> It seemed an age, but it cannot have been more than ten minutes when the instructor beckoned to me. The Germans have a chucker-out in their aircraft for the encouragement of nervous recruits. Flight Sergeant Brereton, six foot two inches, would have made a good Absetzer. I began to make my way down the fuselage towards him, screwing myself up to do so. I crawled on my hands and knees into the rear-

gunner's turret, the back of which had been removed. I tried not to overbalance and fall out, nor to look at the landscape speeding across below me as I turned to face forward again.

I now found myself on a small platform about a foot square, at the very back of the plane, hanging on like grim death to the bar under which I had had such difficulty in crawling. The two rudders were a few feet away on either side of me; behind me was nothing whatsoever. As soon as I raised myself to full height, I found that I was to all purposes outside the plane, the slipstream of air in my face almost blowing me off. I quickly huddled up, my head bent down and pressed into the capacious bosom of the Flight Sergeant. I was about to make a 'pull-off', opening my parachute which would not pull me off until fully developed – a procedure which was calculated to fill me with such confidence that I should be only too ready to leap smartly out of the aircraft on all subsequent occasions.

The little light at the side changed from yellow to red. I was undeniably frightened, though at the same time filled with a fearful joy. The light changed to green and down fell his hand. I put my right hand across to the D ring in front of my left side and pulled sharply. A pause of nearly a second and then a jerk on each shoulder. I was whisked off backwards and swung through nearly 180 degrees, beneath the canopy and up the other side. But I was quite oblivious to all this. I had something akin to a black-out. At any rate, the first thing I was conscious of after the jerk on my shoulders was to find myself, perhaps four seconds later, sitting up in my harness and floating down to earth. The only sensation I registered was one of utter astonishment at finding myself in this remarkable and ridiculous position.

I looked up and there was the silken canopy billowing in the air currents. I looked down, reflecting that this was certainly the second greatest thrill in a man's life. Suddenly I realized that the ground was coming up very rapidly. Before I knew what had happened I was sprawling on the ground, having taken a bump but no hurt. As I got to my feet, a feeling of exhilaration began to fill me.

Captain Dawes remembers that he landed well away from the DZ on his first jump. RSM Mansie who had jumped before him was carried unconscious from the DZ, having hit the ground with his head.

'Take your time,' said Flight Sergeant Brereton. 'We'll make a dummy run first . . . we are almost over the airfield now.' With a great effort of will I dared to look down. To my horror I saw, 500 feet below, a tiny stretcher with a dark, motionless figure. Brereton must have seen it too, for he looked hard at me and said: 'There's nothing to worry about. If you like I'll pull the rip-cord for you myself.'

'I'm all right . . . just tell me what to do.'

'Watch my hand then, and when you see it fall, pull the handle upward and outward.'

'OK,' I said. 'You mean like this?'

'Not now, you bloody fool!' But it was too late. I'd gone. Three hours later the search party found me, six miles away from the dropping zone, hanging helplessly from the highest branches of a clump of trees.

The two jumps by pull-off were followed by six more through a hole cut in the bottom of the Whitley's fuselage. This method, like many features of parachuting in the early days, has a nastiness all of its own. The hole was small and three feet deep. Jumpers used parachutes modified by having the rip-cord connected by a static line to a fixed point in the aircraft. As the jumper left the aircraft, his rip-cord was pulled for him. Both RAF parachutes and American 'statichutes' were used for hole exits. American paratroopers jumped from door exits in Dakotas; their static lines were hooked to a wire which ran the length of the fuselage. As the stick moved aft towards the door to jump, their static lines pulled the hooks along the wire. The British were not so lucky. The Whitley hole was to be their lot until the Americans brought Dakotas over to England in mid-1942.

On the order, 'Action Stations' the first two jumpers sat opposite each other with their feet dangling into the hole. On the order 'Go' the number one launched himself through the hole while trying to maintain the position of attention. This was not 'bull' but an attempt to get the exit just right. Too hard a push-off ended in the jumper smashing his face against the opposite side of the hole; too feeble an effort caused the parachute pack on the man's back to catch on the edge of the hole and tip him forward, with the same result. Whatever the reason, this particular form of airborne head-banging was known as 'ringing the bell' and caused much laughter and beers all round for the rest of the stick of paratroopers. Number one was closely followed by number two, and in turn by the other members of the stick, who shuffled forward on their bottoms before dropping through the hole. With training and practice it was possible to drop ten paratroopers from the Whitley. A well-trained team could be out within nine to ten seconds. With the aircraft travelling at 100 miles per hour, this resulted in the ten jumpers being dispersed over 500 yards. With a Dakota the time and dispersal could be halved.

Deane-Drummond, having done a pull-off descent, found himself in a Bombay aircraft for his second jump. The Bombay was the only transport aircraft the Royal Air Force possessed in 1940. It was a monoplane, underpowered and lacking in range, but it was slow and had a side door; these last two features made it a good parachute training aircraft. For parachuting the door was lifted off its hinge pins and, to Deane-Drummond's surprise, the upper of the two pins was used as the strong point to which the parachute static line was attached with a couple of half hitches. The static line was thinner in those days, about twice the thickness of a rigging line or riser. It is a measure of the Royal Air Force's lack of preparedness for co-operation in the land battle that, unlike the Americans or the Germans, they possessed nothing to match the Dakota or the Junkers 52 transport.

During July more descents were made, some by pull-off, others through the floor. The School asked that the pull-off method be discontinued. But higher authority considered it a more gentle way to introduce men to parachuting. The men themselves considered it the most frightening thing that had ever happened to them. The School's view prevailed after some dummies dropped in a test pulled the steel bar off the back of a Whitley and fell to the ground in a whirling mass, still strapped to unopened parachutes and flailing static lines, all attached to the steel bar. The despatcher nearly went too.

After 135 descents had been made, Driver Evans of the RASC was killed when he became entangled in the rigging lines of his parachute. Evans's death caused a temporary stoppage of training while the accident was investigated. The American statichute, which their airborne forces used in a modified form throughout the war, was designed so that the static line pulled the canopy out of the bag on the jumper's back, followed by the rigging lines as he continued to fall. If the jumper made a bad exit, twisting and tumbling before the final tie connecting the canopy to the static line broke, he risked being entangled in his own rigging lines. At best he would then descend hanging by one or both feet to land on his back or head. At worst he would get wrapped up so badly that the parachute would not deploy at all. Even if all went well, the jumper always experienced a testicle-tweaking shock as he was brought up with a jerk at the end of his rigging lines.

Trials with dummies led to three more failures out of twenty-four descents. This was not good for morale. Over a period of five days Mr Raymond Quilter of the GQ Parachute Company, working with Irvin's Parachute Company, produced a combination Irvin parachute in a GQ packing bag. This X-type parachute, which was to be the standard parachute until the 1960s, worked on a different sequence of opening. As the man jumped, the parachute pack itself broke away from his back and remained attached to the static line and the aircraft. As the man continued to fall, his weight pulled first his lift webs, then his rigging lines, out of the bag. Finally, at the end of the taut and extended rigging lines, the canopy pulled out of the bag, a final tie broke, and the canopy developed. The opening shock was negligible and the danger of becoming entangled also greatly reduced.

During trials of the new parachute a canopy became entangled in the tail wheel of the Whitley. This combined with previous incidents caused Major Rock, not a nervous type, to refuse to allow any soldier to jump from a Whitley. Even the indomitable Strange agreed with him about the Whitley and reported that 'the Whitley fuselage is dark and gloomy with its hole in the middle, and it is bad for the nerves. The sight of other men disappearing through the hole is an unpleasant one, and the prospect of scraping one's face on the other side is not encouraging.' Despite his reservations, Strange then jumped with four Air Force instructors to demonstrate his confidence in the redesigned equipment. But Rock was adamant and suggested that the Bombay aircraft be used instead of the Whitley. This disagreement underlined the difficulties of dual Army/Air Force control of parachute training at Ringway.

The argument was elevated to Whitehall, where the War Office request that Bombay aircraft be substituted for Whitleys was turned down by the Air Ministry, on the very reasonable grounds that the Bombay was required to sustain the fighter squadrons fighting the Battle of Britain, with relief air crews.

The Air Ministry followed this up with a paper proposing that the Air Force should provide the paratroops, who would then be trained for the ground role, following the German example where airborne troops were part of the Luftwaffe. This alarmed the War Office into agreeing that the Whitley could be used for parachute training, which started again on 14 August 1940. Evans was not the last to be killed in these early days. Trooper Watts of the Household Cavalry was next when his parachute failed to function, after jumping from a Whitley.

However, some paratroopers had their first jumps from a Bombay, Sergeant Lawley:

After a few days of instruction at Ringway in the packing of chutes and how to drop through the hole of a Whitley, we were told that the next morning we would be making our first descent, what a thrill! We were all very keen to get the first one over. We arrived at the drome all raring to go; we noticed, however, that all the RAF personnel seemed very subdued and we were told that we would not be jumping that morning. We then paraded in the gym and amid a deathly silence we were told that a fatal accident had occurred in the first batch of drops, but were earnestly assured that it was 'one in a million'. After a week of expecting to jump, we arrived one morning and were told to draw our chutes, after which we were marched to a Bristol Bombay, into which eight of us were loaded. The door had been taken off and a handle had been fixed to the fuselage structure on the left of the door, to which the end of our static line was tied. I noticed after the first three had jumped the handle became very loose, but no one would say anything about it as they were all too scared at what would be said if they did – there were no jibbers in that stick.

By 21 September 1940, twenty-one officers and 321 other ranks had been accepted for parachute training, of which thirty had refused to jump, two had been killed and twenty badly injured or declared medically unsuitable. Those who refused were returned to their parent units. A fifteen percent wastage rate in two months with an average of only two jumps per man was discouraging, particularly bearing in mind the quality of volunteers. However, it was precisely this high quality which kept the morale of the instructors and of the majority of those under training high, so that by the end of 1940 2,000 descents had been made, and the soldiers of Number 2 Commando, now renamed 11 Special Air Service Battalion, were becoming impatient for action.

During this period a whole range of new kit and equipment was designed and tried. Some of it, like the airborne smock, was instantly adopted. It is still in service in a modified form today, and has proved so popular that non-airborne units have coveted them ever since. Others, such as spring-heeled boots to reduce the shock of landing, lasted only as long as it took to point out that the jump was only the means to an end: to get parachute soldiers into battle were they would march and fight on their feet – impossible in spring-heeled boots. The safety pin for the snap-hook connecting the static line to the strong point on the aircraft, or the strop hanging from the wire, was quickly adopted after Corporal Carter's snap-hook was twisted open on the edge of the Whitley hole and he plunged to his death in full view of instructors and pupils with his parachute pack still on his back. A scheme to drop men from very high altitude, each strapped to a personal autogyro whose blades, in theory, unfolded and started to rotate as the man plunged to earth, was quickly discarded when an inordinate number of sandbags were expended in fruitless trials!

In the autumn of 1940 Wing Commander Maurice Newnham joined Ringway to run the administrative side of parachute training. On rejoining the Air Force at the outbreak of war he was put behind a desk in the Air Ministry. He had won the DFC as a fighter pilot in the First World War and was chafing at not being able to do something more active in this one. He was to have a profound effect on the whole philosophy of parachute training, but a few months were to pass before he got his chance. He was not the only one seeking excitement. Throughout the war one of the problems that commanders of paratroop or commando units faced when there was no prospect of action was growing disillusionment, sometimes accompanied by indiscipline. The most adventurous spirits had volunteered for these units, and only the best remained. Most of the cowboys who had been attracted by the glamour were either weeded out, or voted with their feet and left when they discovered how much hard work and, on occasions, danger was involved in the training. 11 Special Air Service Battalion was no exception, and as the months passed with no prospect of battle, a trickle of good men started applying to re-join their parent units. Then early in 1941 the Battalion was told to provide a special party of seven officers and thirty-one NCOs and soldiers for an operation; their target, although they did not know it, the Tragino Aqueduct.

For some time the planners in Whitehall had been searching for an opportunity to demonstrate to the world at large, and the neutral states in particular, that Britain was still capable of aggressive action. The problem was finding an objective that would provide good propaganda

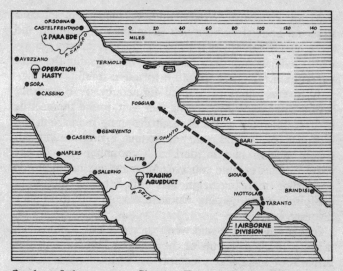

Southern Italy, 1941-44. Showing Tragino and operations by 1st Airborne Division and 2nd Independent Parachute Brigade.

and yet be cost-effective in terms of the effort expended. Italy seemed to offer the best prospect. Italian forces were busy in Albania and North Africa. The ports that supplied their forces in these campaigns were Taranto, Brindisi and Bari. Water was piped to these ports from the River Sele. Cutting this pipeline would serve both propaganda and operational purposes. One of the vulnerable points along the pipeline was the Tragino Aqueduct. Although it was considered too far inland for a seaborne raid and difficult to bomb from the air, it seemed an ideal target for airborne troops. The planners believed that, despite the distance, paratroopers could march to the coast on completion of the raid for a submarine extraction. Nevertheless, it was an ambitious project for a force whose largest exercise to date had been dropping twenty men from two Whitleys on Salisbury Plain.

Major Pritchard, Royal Welch Fusiliers, was selected from 11 Special Air Service Battalion to command the force, and Captain Daly, Royal Engineers, led the demolition team. It was decided to use Whitleys for the task, but without removing aircraft involved in training at Ringway. So the pilots of a force formed by 91 Squadron, commanded by Wing Commander Tait, found themselves with three weeks to learn about dropping men from 500 feet instead of bombs from 10,000 feet. Flying at minimum speed of 500 feet in dark and mountainous country requires considerable courage. Accurate navigation at this unfamiliar operating height was critical to the success of the plan, as was getting the men out quickly to avoid a dispersed drop.

Rehearsals for the raid were carried out at Tatton Park using a brick mock-up of the bridge. The training was marred by a fatal accident on 22 January 1941. Lance Sergeant Dennis drifted towards an ice-covered pond and plunged through. He stuck fast on the bottom and although a strong swimmer could not break free and drowned. The dress rehearsal on 1 February 1941 struck a farcical note when strong winds blew some men into high trees and they had to be rescued by the Knutsford Fire Brigade. Deane-Drummond missed the dress rehearsal. He flew out ahead of the main body in a Sunderland flying boat to Malta, the mounting airfield for the raid, taking with him the containers of explosives and other equipment that the Whitleys would not be able to carry on the long non-stop flight from England. During the three days the main body spent at Mildenhall, waiting to take off for Malta, they were taught a correspondence code to be used in case they were captured. Sergeant Lawley was later to find this 'invaluable'.

At dusk on 7 February 1941 the Whitleys loaded with paratroops left England, their route over German-occupied France. The first part of the flight was in darkness to minimize the chance of the lumbering, obsolescent bombers being shot down by enemy fighters. The aircraft flew as high as possible, so it was not only bitterly cold in the dark fuselages of the Whitleys, but the men found themselves short of oxygen and huddled semi-comatose. The trim of the aircraft was critical. 'I had to inform the pilot when any of us moved to the rear of the plane to answer a call of nature,' recalls Lawley. With the parachute force were two Italians, Picchi and Nastri, as guides and interpreters. Picchi, the pre-war banqueting manager of the Savoy Hotel, loathed Mussolini and loved Britain. On the outbreak of war with Italy he and a number of similarly-inclined Italians living in Britain formed the Free Italy Movement and offered their services to the British Government. Although Nastri had changed his name to Tristan and had lived in England so long that he spoke with a Cockney accent, both he and Picchi were taking a great risk because if captured and identified they would be shot.

The Whitleys arrived safely in Malta the next day. Final preparations were made and briefings given to the whole force, including the arrangements for their extraction on completion of the raid. The party was to march fifty miles to the mouth of the River Sele. Here they would find the submarine Triumph waiting to embark them on the night of 15/16 February.

At dusk on 10 February 1941 six Whitleys loaded with paratroops and two loaded with bombs took off from Malta. The latter were to bomb Foggia as a diversion while the para-drop took place. The drop was timed for 9.30 pm. The first Whitley carrying Deane-Drummond's stick arrived at 9.42 pm. Fifteen minutes earlier the stick had been warned to prepare for action. Suddenly the rear gunner appeared and shouted that they had less than a minute to go; the intercom between Deane-Drummond and the pilot had chosen this moment to break down!

There were no despatchers on operational drops in those days. The stick opened the doors and Deane-Drummond, looking through the hole in the floor of his aircraft, could see a village passing underneath. The red light came on, then the green. Deane-Drummond was last out because he wanted to land closest to the bridge over the aqueduct which was his objective. The rear gunner, who had returned to his turret just before the red light came on, reported to his pilot that the parachutes of the last two in the stick would not have time to deploy because the aircraft had not lifted high enough as it climbed out over the rising ground at the far end of the DZ. He was wrong. Deane-Drummond, his stick and two containers landed safely between fifty and 250 yards from the target; a remarkable effort after a flight of more than 400 miles, without beacons or other navigational aids. The next four Whitleys were almost as accurate, although one man landed three-quarters of a mile away. The sixth Whitley lost its way, was late and off course. It dropped its paratroops and containers in the next valley to the objective, and too far away for them to take any part in the action. Unfortunately this aircraft load consisted of Captain Daly, five engineers and two containers of explosives.

In the bright moonlight the aqueduct could easily be seen. Pritchard ordered Second Lieutenant Paterson, Royal Engineers, and Lance Corporals Watson and Jones, Royal Engineers, to carry out the demolition. Collecting the containers of explosives, scattered over the rough ground, proved difficult because the marker lights on some were not shining. To save time the paratroopers enlisted the help of some locals from a nearby farmhouse. Fortunately these Italian peasants were most obliging and did not demur at helping the enemy. When Paterson examined the two piers against which he was to place the explosive charges, he found to his dismay that instead of being made of brick, as he had been briefed, they were reinforced concrete. He had only 800 pounds of explosive because icing had caused two containers to hang-up in one of the aircraft, the containers from Daly's aircraft were miles away, and even with the help of the Italian peasants not all the containers could be found. While covering parties under Captain Lea provided protection, Paterson and his sappers placed all the available explosive around one pier and its abutment.

At 12.30 am the charge was fired, collapsing the pier and breaking the waterway it supported in two. Water began to pour into the ravine below. It was time to go. The Italian peasants who had assisted in collecting the containers were herded into a farm building and bluffed into believing that if they tried to leave they would be shot by a sentry posted outside. There was no sentry. Lance Corporal Boulter, who had broken an ankle on landing, was left in the care of a farmer. Having buried their heavier kit and all but one Bren, the force split into three parties and set off on separate routes to march fifty miles to the rendezvous with the submarine. They had four and a half days to get there. Much of the route was over mountains. Even the steepest slopes were ploughed and the para-troopers' feet sank into the wet clay with each step. Floun-dering through the sludge, sometimes on hands and knees, was an exhausting performance. The fields were inter-spersed with ravines, cliffs and huge rocks. Despite being so mountainous, the countryside was infested with farms and small villages; each house harboured at least one yapping dog.

Pritchard and Deane-Drummond's party, after march-ing for the rest of that night, lay up for the day in a ravine with sparse tree cover. Although worried that some children playing nearby might discover them, they were undisturbed. As soon as it was dark they set off, their objective a wood marked on their maps. At one stage, to make up time, they took a risk and walked along a deserted road and through a village. The inhabitants were probably all asleep, but hearing a horse and cart ahead they formed into file and Nastri called out in Italian: 'left-right, left-right' as though they were Italian soldiers. The peasant woman driving the cart was asleep! Approaching the wood in which they planned to lie up for the day they realized there was a farm in the middle. Dawn was close and the nearest cover appeared to be another wood marked on their maps on the summit of the Cresta di Gallo – the Cock's Comb. Making for this through the snow they discovered to their dismay that the trees had been cut down. There was nothing for it but to squeeze as many as possible into a small cave near the top of the Cock's Comb, while the remainder hid behind rocks and tree stumps and lay shivering and exhausted in their soaking clothes. Their footsteps, which stood out clearly in the snow, must have given away their position to a farmer, who stood looking at them for a few minutes before walking off. Pritchard sent Picchi after him to persuade him that he had nothing to fear. On his return from the farm, Picchi reported that they had also been spotted by women and children who had warned the local carabinieri. Soon the party was surrounded by a ring of spectators, consisting of children, their mothers, mongrels, some men, a few of whom were armed with shotguns, and, well to the rear, a handful of scruffy soldiers. Pritchard could not bring himself to order his men to fight their way out by throwing grenades among the women and children. After an anguished moment of indecision, he ordered his party to lay down their pistols. Somebody asked incredulously if they were not going to make a fight for it. Pritchard looked at the women, at the man who asked the question, and repeated the order. As they put down their pistols the peasants surged in. Deane-Drummond: 'I have never felt so ashamed before or since, that we should have surrendered to a lot of practically unarmed Italian peasants.'

Lawley remembers that they were all handcuffed 'in a chain-gang fashion and herded to the nearest village, the inhabitants of which lined the road and as we passed spat at us.'

The other two parties had similar experiences after leaving the aqueduct and were surrounded by large groups of locals, carabinieri and, in one other case, women and children.

Daly and his party got much closer to the rendezvous at the mouth of the Sele. They heard the sound of explosions not long after landing in the wrong valley, and without further ado, set off for the rendezvous. By dawn on 15 February they were within eighteen miles of it, very tired and hungry. As time was getting short they decided to move by day. Just before midday they were accosted by a group of soldiers and police. They tried to bluff their way out by posing as German aircrew on a special mission who had to reach Naples by two o'clock that afternoon, and demanded a car at once. The local mayor demanded papers from Daly, and as there were none he and his party were handcuffed and chained together. When they arrived in Naples, still chained together, they were threatened with death. Eventually they were all put into a prison camp – all, that is, with the exception of Picchi. He was questioned and shot. Nastri was saved by his Cockney accent and false papers.

HMS Triumph never made the rendezvous either. As luck would have it, one of the Whitleys sent to bomb Foggia as a diversion developed engine trouble. The pilot sent a message in code saying that he was about to ditch near the mouth of the River Sele. He chose this area because he was near it. He knew nothing about the submarine rendezvous. In Malta it was realized that because the code used was not secure, the area around the mouth of the Sele might shortly be swarming with Italian troops and police looking for the crew of the Whitley. After some agonizing, it was decided that the submarine and highly trained crew would not be put at risk by surfacing off an area in which all troops and police had been alerted. *Triumph*'s orders were cancelled. All specialist forces understand that every reasonable effort will be made to pull them out after an operation behind enemy lines. But when the price of doing so becomes prohibitive in terms of other men's lives and valuable assets, there may come a time when they will be abandoned to their fate.

In retrospect none of the paratroopers stood much chance of getting to the submarine RV. The distance they had to cover over such difficult going meant taking to the roads to have any hope of meeting their deadline. Nearer the coast, although the country was flat, the terrain was, if anything, even worse. It was devoid of cover and criss-crossed by irrigation canals, very difficult to transit even in daylight. It is hard to resist the feeling that it had been a case of 'big hands on little maps' on the part of those in Whitehall selecting the target and the route out. At least one survivor believes they would have done better to have stolen vehicles and driven to the coast.

The operation had little effect on the Italian campaigns in North Africa and Albania. The water supply of the ports supplying the campaigns was not interrupted for any appreciable time because the aqueduct was repaired before the reservoirs ran dry. But on the credit side the raid caused considerable consternation in Italy resulting, among other things, in additional troops being posted into the area, to sit in idleness until Italy was knocked out of the war two years later.

The paratroopers were eventually sent to Sulmona where the Italians had established a camp for British prisoners. Early in December 1941 Deane-Drummond and Captain Lea escaped by posing as electricians repairing the lights on the double ten-foot-high fence surrounding the camp. As Deane-Drummond was climbing a ladder they had made, towards a lamp overlooking their chosen exit, a sentry challenged them. Deane-Drummond shouted 'lampa', unscrewed the bulb and pretended to replace it. In the darkness, still carrying the ladder, they climbed out on to a ledge from which they planned to descend to the ground outside the wire. At this point the sentry who had challenged them came running up, screaming. Realizing they could jump down on the other side, Deane-Drummond threw away the ladder and they both dropped off the ledge, landing outside the wire, but not before the sentry had fired a round of disintegrating shot. A fragment grazed Deane-Drummond's cheek but unknown to him most of the pieces hit Lea in the leg. Their plan was to split up immediately on breaking free because each favoured a different escape route. Lea had been badly wounded but shouted at Deane-Drummond not to stop. The Italians left Lea bleeding profusely, whether deliberately or by accident it is hard to tell. Eventually the camp MO insisted that he was brought in. His wound proved so severe he nearly lost the leg.

Deane-Drummond walked the thirty or so miles to Pescara, where he bought a ticket on the train to Chiasso, near the Swiss border. He used money sent to him in parcels from England, hidden in the bindings of books. He spent some of the journey sitting between two carabinieri, but feigned sleep. He was eventually stopped by border guards who spotted his dirty shoes, and discovered his identity. His second escape in June 1942 ended happily. Having had a mastoid infection in his ear as a boy, he successfully wangled his way into hospital near Florence by feigning an ear complaint. After about three weeks he escaped, reaching Switzerland. Having passed along an escape pipeline via Marseilles and Gibraltar, he arrived in England where he was allowed five days leave.

In England events had not been progressing well for the airborne concept. In April 1941 Churchill decided to visit the School, and so a demonstration was laid on for him at Ringway. Wing Commander Sir Nigel Norman, the officer commanding the School and a great enthusiast, decided that the demonstration would be more dramatic and interesting for the Prime Minister if he could listen in to the chat on the ground-to-air-radio net. After asking the Prime Minister's permission to carry on, Norman spoke on the radio to the aircraft leader carrying the para-troops (who had been emplaned for some time awaiting the off): 'Hello formation leader – this is Wing Commander Norman calling. Are you ready for take-off? Over to you.' A moment's pause, and the reply came back loud enough for all to hear: 'No I'm not ready to take off – five of the blighters have fainted.'

Five minutes later a further message was received saying that the bodies had been removed and the formation was about to take off. Normandy was only three years off and the Prime Minister had just seen a demonstration by forty paratroopers, of whom five failed to jump, and five decrepit aircraft which were unsuitable for the job. The total fight-ing strength of 11 Special Air Service Battalion was 400 semi-trained paratroopers, and these were becoming pro-gressively disillusioned. Thirty-eight of the best men had been lost on the Tragino raid, and there seemed no further prospect of action. Men volunteering for parachuting were being dissuaded by their commanding officers from joining what was coming to be seen as a waste of time and effort.

Although the Prime Minister did not show his disap-pointment, and indeed his visit and the interest he showed did much to help morale at Ringway, he was clearly unim-pressed with what he had seen, and on his return to London he sent a note to General Ismay in which he said: 'Let me have this day the minute which I wrote in the summer of last year directing that 5,000 parachute troops were to be prepared, together with all the minutes of the Departments concerned which led to my afterwards

agreeing to reduce the number to 500. I shall expect to
receive the office files before midnight.'

Staff papers passed back and forth as a result of Churchill's note. But before he received an answer to it that
completely satisfied him, the Germans had invaded Crete
with parachute and glider-borne troops, thus proving
incorrect the senior Air Ministry commentator who, two
weeks before, had said that Crete would never be taken
by airborne assault. When the Air Staff answer on progress
with the airborne force reached Churchill, his reaction
was another note to Ismay: 'This is a sad story and I feel
myself greatly to blame for allowing myself to be overborne
by the resistances which were offered. One can see how
wrongly based these resistances were when we read the
Air Staff paper in the light of what is happening in Crete.
A whole year has been lost, and I now invite the Chiefs
of Staff to make proposals for trying, so far as is possible,
to repair the misfortune. The whole file is to be brought
before the Chiefs of Staff this evening.'

History does not relate who the unfortunate staff officers
were who had to produce the necessary briefs for the
Chiefs of Staff in the few hours between the Prime Minister's note arriving on their desks and the evening meeting.
However, the reply to the Prime Minister from the Chiefs
of Staff was more positive than the Air Staff note of eight
months before quoted at the beginning of this chapter,
although in fairness it was written when the Battle of
Britain was gathering momentum and the outcome far
from certain. In summary, the Chiefs of Staff told the
Prime Minister that by May 1942 there would be 5,000
paratroops, with the aim of producing one brigade in the
Middle East and one brigade at home. There would also
be sufficient gliders and tug aircraft to carry another 5,000
men and supporting arms.

To meet the targets promised by the Chiefs of Staff,
the training organization at Ringway would have to achieve

a far higher success rate than hitherto. Fortunately the man for the task was on hand, and on 9 July 1941, Wing Commander Newnham was transferred from administrative duties at the School to take charge of parachute training. The gallant Strange volunteered to fly Hurricanes catapulted from converted merchant ships. As each sortie almost invariably ended in ditching in the sea because the merchant ships had no flight deck and therefore could not recover aircraft, the life expectancy of these crews, particularly in northern waters, was not great.

Newnham realized that the key to reducing a wastage rate of fifteen per cent in two months from among the finest and most courageous volunteers was to make the training far less frightening, to develop the right attitude of mind in pupils, and to evolve a standardized drill that the average soldier could understand and carry out. But first Newnham had to find out what this parachuting business was all about. So obeying Sophocles's precept 'One must learn by doing the thing, for though you think you know it you have no certainty until you try.' Newnham made his first jump from a balloon on 28 July. He immediately realized the value of the balloon as a training aid. Although balloons had been asked for by Strange months before, one was not made available until April 1941. Jumping from a balloon seemed so cold-blooded that in the three months between its arrival and Newnham's first jump, less than 100 descents had been made and it was not included in the normal training syllabus. Newnham decided that the objection to its use was purely psychological and could be overcome. Ballooning was much safer and furthermore much quieter, which allowed the instructors to call out to their pupils through a loud hailer and give them instructions during the descent. This reduced accidents on landing dramatically. Before 1940 no techniques had existed for flying the parachute once the canopy deployed, for damping out oscillation, for steering and for kicking out of twists. Although these skills evolved and the men were trained in them, it was much easier to practise them in the calm and quiet atmosphere of a balloon descent rather than in the frenetic surroundings of an aircraft jump, with the combination of air-sickness, engine noise, buffeting slipstream and the roar of aircraft over the DZ even during the descent.

In the six months that followed, up to 6,000 descents were made from balloons each month. Newnham had arrived just in time. He also favoured the idea that parachuting must be made a normal activity and de-glamourized. He was thus very much in tune with Brigadier Gale, who was appointed to command the 1st Parachute Brigade and who preached that the jump was only the means to an end. What happened once the parachute soldier arrived on the ground was what really mattered. To produce the numbers required by the Chiefs of Staff for the two brigades, Newnham had to turn out 100 men a week. As the course lasted four weeks there would be 400 men under training at any one time. This took no account of training Allied troops and agents, who at times could push the number up to 300 trainees a week. To do all this Newnham had minimal facilities. Parachute packing was done in the airmen's dining hall between meals. He had a drying capacity for only 100 parachutes, each of which took forty-eight hours. There was little ground training equipment, six old Whitleys and one balloon. At the same time he realized that the moment had arrived to turn the whole business of parachute training over to the RAF, and that the Air Force physical fitness branch would produce the right type of instructors. After a small altercation with the Army he got his way, and by October the RAF physical fitness instructors started to arrive at Ringway. From the start they were inculcated with the Newnham dictum that parachuting was normal. There was to be no line-shooting about the dangers, but rather a quiet matter-of-fact approach, leadership by example and, above all, confidence and trust in the instructor. Newnham's philosophy survives to this day and the RAF Parachute Jump Instructors are among the finest and most highly respected of any military skill in the world. As Lieutenant-General Sir Napier Crookenden, a distinguished parachute soldier records: 'The RAF parachute jump instructors . . . have the knack of extracting maximum effort from their victims in a cheerful way; the whole parachute school has always been a sort of well-disciplined, dedicated fun-fair.'

When Gale was ordered to form 1st Parachute Brigade, he was told by the War Office to disband 11 Special Air Service Battalion and distribute the men among the four battalions of the Brigade. Newnham reported that, with the exception of one troop of about forty or fifty Grenadier Guardsmen under a Grenadier officer who all retained their regimental spirit and standards, the battalion was badly disciplined. It was thought that when the new commanding officer, Lieutenant Colonel Down, gave the battalion the option of staying in the brigade and giving up the commando privilege of living in lodging, or leaving parachuting, he would lose a large number of men. Such were Down's powers of leadership however that eighty-five per cent of the Battalion remained. Gale was so impressed by Down that he decided to ignore the War Office order and renamed the battalion 1st Parachute Battalion. For the soldiers it meant a complete change in their living habits. From billets in Knutsford it was off to barracks in Bulford. At first Down was hated and nicknamed 'Dracula' or 'Dracs'. He was ruthless and accepted nothing but the highest standards. His early talks to the battalion were frequently greeted by cat-calls and foot-stamping. But none of them was a match for his personality, and by the time he left to form the 2nd Parachute Brigade his men worshipped him and would have followed him anywhere. 'They realized,' according to one officer, a founder member of Number 2 Commando, 'That out of a somewhat undisciplined body of outstanding individuals, trained to fight in small parties, he had welded the finest battalion in the British Army.' Down was fond of emphasizing to his men how important each was in the overall scheme of things by telling them that they were all spokes in the wheel. One night, during a night rehearsal for an operation, the 1st Battalion's mortar platoon operator was twiddling the knobs on his set and suddenly the strains of 'Deep in the Heart of Texas' burst out over Salisbury Plain. A figure loomed up in the darkness: 'Who the hell are you?' it demanded. 'A spoke in the wheel,' replied the operator. 'Well, I'm the hub,' said the figure. 'Switch that bloody music off!'

The training at Ringway was moving into top gear. In October 1941 there were 2,250 descents at Tatton Park in one month. The RAF PFIs introduced the para-roll when hitting the ground on landing to replace the gym-style forward and backward roll taught by the Army PTIs. In November the men of 2nd and 3rd Parachute Battalions arrived for training and by the end of twelve days of the first course for these battalions they had completed 1,773 descents. There had been only two refusals, twelve injuries, and no one killed. Within two months 1,000 men had completed basic parachute training.

Despite this encouraging record, there were still some depressing days in the following months of the winter of 1941/42 at Ringway. Serious injuries were a daily occurrence, and in one span of sixty days five men were killed in full view of their fellows. February was a particularly bad month. Of 238 pupils, two were killed and forty-eight injured. There were only five refusals, but morale began to sag. Gale paraded the whole brigade at Tatton Park and gave what one officer described as 'a rather pompous speech' which evoked some disparaging muttering from the assembled soldiery. He finished by saying there would now be a demonstration drop by the Ringway instructors from three Whitleys, to show them there was nothing to fear. The Whitleys were an hour late, and chants of 'Why are we waiting?' arose. The drop soon became a farce. The exits were slow, the parachuting positions were bad and the watching soldiers began shouting: 'We can do better than that.' Morale rose visibly. When some of the instructors were seen to fall heavily on landing and were carted off on stretchers, the soldiers roared with laughter. The brigade was eventually marched off in high spirits. Gale had succeeded in restoring morale, but not quite in the way he intended.

Newnham, typically leading from the front, and three of his officers were among the injured. He had suggested the demonstration when he realized the injuries and deaths had been caused by bad twisting of lift webs and rigging lines which resulted in the canopy not developing properly and consequently not giving enough lift. He hoped to find the answer, but got bad twists himself and his canopy opened out properly when he was only about fifteen feet from the ground. The same happened to the other officers. The problem was never properly sorted out and men continued to be killed by twists throughout the war and afterwards. The wearing of a reserve parachute would have cut down injuries but was not introduced into the British airborne forces until the late 1950s, mainly because of prejudice.

By the autumn of 1942 the RAF had taken over the task of pre-parachute training from the Army and the whole training sequence took place at Ringway, avoiding duplication of effort and different methods of instruction. By this time it was decided to form parachute battalions from ordinary infantry battalions, so that they would arrive already imbued with regimental spirit and discipline, and thus be able to work as a team from the outset. It was highly successful, and men unsuitable for parachuting were soon sent elsewhere or volunteered out. Under the command of Major General Browning, the Parachute Battalions and airborne forces were taking shape ready for the busy days ahead. It was he who, in early 1942, recognized that an operation being proposed in Combined Operations Headquarters was just what the new force needed for good publicity and to prove its worth to the sceptics.

CHAPTER 2

Jock Company and a Radar Station

During 1941 a great deal of the British war effort had been going into the bomber offensive, mainly over Germany. From July 1941, the Russians, who were suffering enormous losses, constantly asked the British to do something which would force the Germans to ease the pressure on the Russian people; in short, invade the continent of Europe and open a second front. In 1941 this was a long way off, and until America entered the war in December 1941, an impossible dream. In the meantime the bomber was seen by Churchill and the Chiefs of Staff as the only way for the British to take the war to the Germans. This strategy accorded well with the apostles of air power. The most ardent preached the doctrine that the war could be won by the bomber alone. A massive bomber offensive, they argued, would cause mass destruction in Germany and sap the will of the German people to continue the war; the Air Force could win the war single-handed, without the assistance of the other two services. Events would prove the doctrine false, but it is not the purpose of this book to explain why.

As 1941 drew to a close Bomber Command was suffering increasing losses over Europe, which Air Force intelligence realized were caused by the efficiency of German radar. The Telecommunications Research Establishment (TRE) knew a great deal about one of the radars, Freya. They could jam it and 'spoof' it. But Freya was only part of the German system. It acquired incoming aircraft at long range and then handed them over to another radar, the Wurzburg, which had a very narrow beam and could be used to vector night fighters onto individual bombers to shoot them down. The scientists at TRE dearly wanted to get their hands on the workings of the Wurzburg.

Then the RAF Photographic Reconnaissance Unit brought back some pictures of the radar dish of a Wurzburg, situated on a cliff-top just north of a small village called Bruneval, twelve miles north of Le Havre. Mountbatten, then Chief of Combined Operations, agreed to a raid to bring back the parts from the radar for diagnosis by TRE. Browning told Gale to pick one of his battalions for the operation. He chose the newly-formed 2nd Parachute Battalion rather than the 1st Battalion which had been in existence for a year longer; he wanted to show that his whole Brigade was ready for operations.

The 2nd Parachute and 3rd Parachute Battalions shared a camp at Hardwick Hall near Chesterfield. After forming up in the late autumn of 1941, they were training hard for their new role under Gale's critical eye. He accepted only the highest standards of soldierly performance in the field and discipline in camp. One of the tasks of the Adjutant in each Battalion was, and still is, allocating soldiers to companies. Captain Frost, a Cameronian, the Adjutant of 2 Para, despite ten years as a regular soldier, was astonished to see the way in which commanding officers of units all over Britain had taken the opportunity of playing the old Army game of shunting off their naughty boys and misfits when the call had gone out for volunteers to parachute. Nearly half of those who presented themselves at the gates of the parachute battalions during this period were unsuitable for one reason or another. Some of them had conduct sheets (the papers that record misdemeanours) six pages long. There were few good NCOs because commanding officers often would not let them go. NCOs had to be found within the ranks of the volunteers. Some came forward of their own volition when battle appeared to be round the corner. Even these, excellent though they were in battle, sometimes overdid the celebrating when out of the line and were demoted, to be promoted before the next contest! At times it seemed that 2 Para would never be up to strength. Frost noticed that 3 Para were doing rather better. He discovered that the Adjutant of 3 Para had stationed a tout at the gate of Hardwick who directed all new arrivals to their guardroom. Here the RSM picked the best for his Battalion and sent the dross to 2 Para. Not to be outdone, Frost sent his own tout plus a truck further down the road to intercept the arrivals and take them straight to 2 Para's guardroom. When 3 Para caught on and sent their truck even further down the road, a truce was called.

The commanding officer of 2 Para, Lieutenant Colonel Flavell, had decided that C Company would be formed of men from Scottish Regiments. Jock Company, as they were known, were a particularly pugnacious lot. Frost has described them in his book *A Drop Too Many*: 'They weren't particular who they fought, and if there was no one else available as an enemy, then the English would do very well. This attitude of mind resulted in some unfortunate incidents in Chesterfield, where the trainees were apt to let off steam on Saturday nights . . .' However, having completed their parachute training, they were shaping up to be a very fine company under Major Teichman, a Royal Fusilier, and the only Englishman in the company.

Frost still had to qualify as a parachutist although he had already done two balloon descents, injuring himself in the process. His first balloon jump ended in a perfect landing after the usual misery of the ascent in the balloon car. 'We smiled at each other the learner parachutist's smile, which has no joy or humour in it. One merely uncovers one's teeth for a second or two then hides them again quickly lest they should start chattering . . . a quick agonized glance at the ground below, but in the main we stared upwards praying hard.' The second landing, full of confidence 'after laughing at the misery of the other two officers in the basket' put Frost in hospital.

On returning to his Adjutantal duties, he was about to take over Jock company when they were ordered to Tilshead on Salisbury Plain to prepare for special training, remaining there for five to six weeks. Frost was given a week to complete his parachute training or hand the company back to Teichman. As a Cameronian he dearly wanted to command that company. But Teichman was already qualified, and under his command they would carry out the mysterious mission for which they had been selected, unless Frost got his parachute wings very quickly indeed.

From the moment that Frost arrived at Ringway he discerned from his treatment by the RAF that his company were probably going into action soon. He was allowed to do his jumps with as little ground training as possible and was given priority over other trainees for a place on an aircraft. Until late afternoon on the second day he experienced that most frustrating feature of parachuting, waiting for the weather to clear. The tension on these occasions is bad enough, but in his case was heightened by the knowledge that if he did not complete the course in a week, C Company would go on their secret mission without him. He knew that the weather conditions at Ringway, combined with a shortage of aircraft, made it very difficult to complete the course in under two weeks. With five days to go the weather improved, and he did his last jump to qualify well before the deadline. Like most paratroopers, he found jumping from an aircraft much better than a balloon descent. The noise, sense of detachment from the ground, and other distractions in an aircraft were far less disconcerting than the silent, lurching balloon cage on the end of its wire.

When Frost arrived at Tilshead, Teichman told him

that the Company was to train for a demonstration to the War Cabinet, and that at present there was no operation in the offing. The day after the company arrived, General Browning, the commander of the Airborne Division, came to inspect them. Browning had fought for three years in the First World War in the Grenadier Guards, winning the DSO as a Lieutenant. He had been a ferocious Adjutant at Sandhurst between the wars, and had a reputation throughout the Army for demanding the highest standards of performance in everything, including turnout. C Company were very badly turned out. Their uniforms were old, tired, creased from travelling and now spattered with the ubiquitous clay of Salisbury Plain which dries to an off-white colour. Frost did not look forward to the occasion. The General spoke to nearly every man, taking a long time going round. When he had finished he turned to Frost and said; 'I think you have got a good lot of men but I have never seen such a dirty company in my life!' He then told his staff that the company was to have all the clothing and equipment it wanted, and a generous allocation of transport and ammunition for training.

The following day Frost was told by a liaison officer from the Airborne Division that training for the demonstration would take place near Alton Priors, close to Devizes. Here some steep hills would represent cliffs by the sea. The company was to land behind imaginary defences, destroy an enemy headquarters, and move down a gully to the beach to be extracted by naval craft. The site for the demonstration to the War Cabinet had not yet been chosen, but was likely to be near Dover or the Isle of Wight. Rehearsals with the Navy would be at the place selected for the demonstration. To Frost's surprise and irritation he was also told exactly how the demonstration was to be conducted. The normal company organization of three platoons and a small headquarters to command them was to be broken up into four parties of different sizes, each to drop separately and each having a different task. This was a departure from the normal military way of doing things. The man in charge of the job is usually given his task and left to make his plan and ask for any additional assets he requires to complete the mission, which he may or may not get. His superiors may monitor his plan, and may require him to amend it to fit in with what other units are doing, or to meet certain objectives. Frost did not like the organization that he had been told to adopt, which seemed to lack the flexibility to cope with unexpected events. These could almost be guaranteed, since practically no operation or exercise ever goes as planned. He made his own plan and took it to Divisional Headquarters to see the General.

The General was away and a senior staff officer, hardly listening to what Frost had to say, kept pushing the four-party plan. Frost left, absolutely determined to keep to his own scheme. The next day the liaison officer told Frost that the demonstration to the War Cabinet was a cover for a raid on the coast of France to bring back the parts of the latest German radar. Royal Engineers would be attached to the company to dismantle the equipment. The operation had been designed as a result of information about the enemy dispositions gleaned from air photographs and, although Frost was not told this at the time, from the French resistance. Finally, if he did not like the plan someone who did would replace him. Frost's objections evaporated, particularly when he learned that one of the most experienced bomber squadrons in the RAF would be dropping them, so there was a good chance that they might land in the right place.

Frost was now faced with the problem of keeping the mission a secret from the Glider Pilot Regiment at Tilshead, from his own company, and particularly from his Company Sergeant Major Strachan of the Black Watch. Like all company sergeants major he liked to know what was going on, and as he was responsible for the arms and ammunition for the demonstration he kept asking awkward questions. The company was organized into four parties. The sappers arrived, and training began. This included a phase at Loch Fyne in Scotland to practise embarking in landing craft in the dark. They did not find this as easy as expected, particularly as the coxswains of the craft were not always able to find their way to the exact position for the pick-up. In the end the company never achieved a satisfactory embarkation in training. The prospect of being left stranded in enemy-held France was not encouraging.

During the training period in Scotland, Admiral Mountbatten, the Chief of Combined Operations, announced his intention of visiting the company aboard *Prinz Albert*, the parent ship of the landing craft flotilla. The Captain, mistaking the Admiral's purpose, took the fairly typical step of asking the rough soldiery with their nasty dirty boots to go elsewhere. The company hid in the hills surrounding the loch until *Prinz Albert*'s siren hastily recalled them so that the Admiral could speak to them. After Mountbatten had addressed everybody, and the Navy realized for the first time what was required, co-operation improved considerably.

On their return to Tilshead the company did a practice drop from the aircraft of the bomber squadron taking them on the operation. This squadron, commanded by Wing Commander Pickard who had played a leading part in the highly successful film 'Target for Tonight', had never dropped parachutists before, and this was the last opportunity before the operation. Even at this stage in the war there were no operational squadrons dedicated to supporting airborne forces. Given this situation, it is astonishing that time was allocated for only one full parachute rehearsal. However, it went well, which is more than can be said for the rehearsals with the Navy. The seamanship of the young landing craft officers, many of them RNVR, was just not up to the task. The remainder of the available time was spent brushing up the embarkation drills with the Navy off the Dorset coast. This phase seemed fated to go wrong. During what should have been the dress rehearsal the weapon containers were dropped miles away from the company, who had been taken to the area by truck, the Navy came in to the wrong beach, and the company ended up in a defensive minefield. There were only two days to go before the first possible D-Day.

The Navy insisted on another embarkation rehearsal, on 23 February, the night planned for the actual operation. This 'final' final dress-rehearsal was perhaps even more of an 'opera bouffe' performance than any of the others. The weather was perfect, but because of an error over the tides the landing-craft grounded about sixty yards offshore. C Company waded out to try to push them off. They remained stuck fast. There were now only four possible nights when the conjunction of moon and tide was favourable. A fairly full moon was needed to give sufficient light for the company to operate, and the landing craft required a rising tide at the pick-up time. The four days were 24 to 27 February 1942.

Throughout the rehearsal period, final adjustments were made to the plan. The aim of the operation was to get the key parts of the Wurzburg back to England. Any immovable bits would be photographed. Flight Sergeant Cox, an RAF radar expert, and a section of 1st Parachute Field Squadron Royal Engineers under the command of Captain Vernon, had been trained for these tasks. Everything in the plan was designed to ensure that these key men got to the radar station, that they were protected while they dismantled the bits they needed, and got safely away with the photographs and the parts. There were thought to be between 170 to 200 enemy in the vicinity: about thirty radar operators, signallers and guards at the radar station, which was on the cliff-top near an isolated

villa, about 100 off-duty operators, signallers and coast
defence troops in Le Presbytère, a group of farm buildings
approximately 300 yards north of the radar; and forty men
garrisoned in Bruneval, about a third of a mile south-east
of the radar station, who were responsible for manning
the pill-boxes on the cliff-tops and on the beach. A narrow
road ran up a steep-sided valley from the beach, through
Bruneval and then inland.

The parachute force was to drop in three waves, starting
with 'Nelson' party of forty men under Captain Ross and
Lieutenant Charteris. Their job was to clear or capture
the beach defences so that the beach could be used to
evacuate the whole force. The second wave under Frost
consisted of 'Jellicoe', 'Hardy' and 'Drake' parties, and
included the sappers and Flight Sergeant Cox. The third
wave, 'Rodney' party under Lieutenant Timothy, was the
reserve and would be used to provide a covering force
against an enemy attack from landward during the operation, including the withdrawal. The planned DZ for the
whole force was about half a mile due east of the radar
station. The force was briefed on an excellent model.
Everyone was to get to his position as silently as possible,
and when all were ready, Frost at the front door of the
villa would blow four blasts on his whistle as the signal
for action to commence. 'What will you do, sir, if the door
is locked when you blow your whistle?' asked one man at
the briefing. 'Ring the bell,' replied Frost.

On Monday 24 February, C Company packed their
weapon containers ready for the operation. At 5 pm there
was a twenty-four hour postponement because of adverse
weather conditions. The same happened on Tuesday,
Wednesday, and Thursday, the last possible day for the
raid. It was very depressing. A month's postponement
looked on the cards. On Friday Frost expected instructions
to send everyone on leave, but instead was told that they
were to wait for one more night. For the fifth day running

containers were packed, but rather listlessly and without enthusiasm. The only cheerful man was Sergeant Major Strachan, who was sure that Friday was the day. He was right. At tea-time General Browning came to wish them luck. The operation was on.

Frost was going round his men at Thruxton while they fitted parachutes, sang and drank tea, when he was summoned to the telephone. At first he thought it was another cancellation, but instead it was Wing Commander Norman to wish him luck, tell him that there was snow on the other side, and that the 'flak was lively'. The company marched out to the twelve aircraft in their sticks, while piper Ewing played everyone's regimental marches, cheered on by them all. Ewing was going on the drop, but without his pipes. Wing Commander Pickard went up to Frost. Pickard was in Frost's words, 'already a public figure in those days, the survivor of countless bombing raids and an inspiration to all he served with'. He was particularly uninspiring on this occasion. Drawing Frost aside, he said: 'I feel like a bloody murderer!' An odd way for such an experienced leader to behave. But perhaps a feeling of guilt overcame him when he realized that he was about to drop these young and inexperienced soldiers into enemy territory with little prospect of coming back, knowing that he had a better chance himself. Frost was not flying with him, which was fortunate. Pickard was leading the first wave, which included Lieutenant Charteris's party.

The period before battle can be the loneliest for a commander. All that he can do has been done, and he waits for action which will take his mind off the doubts and fears that start edging in at such moments. Frost has described his thoughts as he sat on the cold, aluminium floor of the Whitley: 'This was no grand armada. We were so very much by ourselves. We knew so little in fact that it was only at the last minute that I had told the men our destination. At this period of the war the Germans were to us a terrible people. Their armies knew no halting and despite reverses in front of Moscow, they seemed formidable in the extreme ... I almost longed for a last-minute cancellation.' The cramped fuselage and aluminium floor of the Whitleys soon numbed their buttocks and legs. In the bitter cold they wrapped themselves in sleeping bags and sang. Flight Sergeant Cox sang two solos by popular request, and 'filled that gloomy fuselage with ringing cheery tones. So have we sung many times since on long flights over other countries when the engines seem to play the music of some unseen band.'

Frost was the first out of his aircraft, and as he descended he saw that they were right over the DZ. He landed softly in snow about a foot deep. His first action on getting out of his parachute harness was to have a pee because he was bursting after quantities of tea at Thruxton. It was also a gesture of defiance. As his party started towards the villa he saw the parachutes of 'Rodney' party, the last wave, coming down. The countryside was bathed in moonlight. Landmarks stood out against the snow. As the aircraft droned off it became uncannily still. There was no wind and the snow seemed to carry sound over considerable distances. The bad news was that two aircraft loads, Charteris's half of 'Nelson' party, were missing. Ross, who had arrived, was told to do what he could about the beach defences without Charteris. Frost and his party set off towards the villa. When everyone was in position, Frost walked towards the door. It was open. He was so surprised that he nearly forgot to blow his whistle before going in. The villa and radar station were soon cleared, and the work of dismantling began. By now fire was coming from Le Presbytère and increasing every minute. It was mostly inaccurate, but killed Private McIntyre as he was leaving the villa. While the work of tearing out the workings of the radar was in progress, Frost tried to find out how the other parties were faring. The radios would not work and he began to wish, not for the first time that night, that he had a proper company headquarters. It had been turned into an assault group for the attack on the villa, and his signallers, runners and sergeant major were doing other tasks. There was considerable confusion and he felt that he was not fully in control.

Frost ordered Vernon to start moving towards the beach. As they moved, Sergeant Major Strachan was hit in the stomach. He was pulled into cover and given some morphia. It then became plain that the beach was not clear. A machine gun position in the main beach pill-box was the problem. No sooner had he learned this discomfiting piece of news than it was reported that the Germans had re-occupied the villa and were putting in a counter-attack. Frost personally led the party to deal with this new threat, which fortunately was quickly snuffed out. Again he found the unorthodox organization that had been forced on him a disadvantage. By the time he returned from this diversion, he found Charteris by the main beach pill-box and the beach taken.

Charteris and two sections had been in Pickard's aircraft and the one following it. They had been dropped in the wrong place, about a mile south-east of Bruneval instead of at the main DZ nearly a mile north-east of the village. Fortunately they were able to orientate themselves by seeing the stream of Whitleys carrying later waves flying over the correct DZ. Charteris led his men at a jog trot alongside the narrow road leading through Bruneval to the beach. As he skirted the village his party fought a battle with a German patrol. Later a German joined the rear of the party by mistake, an error which cost him his life. Finally arriving at their objective, Charteris's party charged in and were able to turn the flank of the machine gun position.

So far, so good. Now what was required were the landing craft to take the Jocks home. They tried making contact

by radio. There was no reply. Verey lights were fired.
There was still no reply. Finally, as Frost was making
hasty and desperate plans to defend the beach, the landing
craft were seen approaching. They had been delayed by
having to lie doggo while a German destroyer and two E
boats cruised by in the moonlight. They then vectored on
to the beach, having seen Frost's Verey lights. As they
closed the beach, Bren gunners in the craft opened fire
on the cliff-tops where some of C Company were in positions to defend the beach against attack from the land.
Only when the company yelled at them did the fire stop.
The embarkation was chaotic as the paratroopers waded
out in the surf. On the falling tide the craft could not risk
coming in too close. By 3.30 am all craft were standing
out to sea, towed by motor-gunboats. At about this time
a message was received from two missing signallers who
had lost their way and reached the beach too late to be
taken off.

Years later, Frost met the German parachute officer
who interrogated paratroopers taken prisoner after the
raid. He said that they refused to give any information.
The Germans, as a gesture of comradeship, invited them
to carry out a jump from their aircraft, using their equipment. When the British paratroopers were introduced to
the German parachutes and technique they were so horrified that they became very talkative, in the process explaining the British methods – exactly what the Germans
wished to hear!

C Company returned to a heroes' welcome in Ports-
mouth after a brilliantly conducted raid. They had taken
off from England at 10.30 pm and five hours later had left
the coast of France, having achieved complete success.
On his return Frost told Browning that the plan and
organization he had been told to adopt had nearly scup-
pered the operation, particularly splitting up the company
into unhandy groups, and the requirement for him to take

part in the actual assault on the villa instead of controlling his company as a whole. Browning replied that if Frost had only told him, he would have altered it. This may be so, but as Frost recalls: 'Browning was an almost mythical, aloof figure to us. He was an Olympic hurdler, married to the novelist Daphne du Maurier, and moved among the rich and influential.'

The raid could not have come at a better time for the morale of the British people. The war had not been going well. The battleships *Prince of Wales* and *Repulse* had been sunk two months before, Singapore had just fallen and only two days before the raid the Battle of the Java Sea had gone disastrously for the Allies. The scientists of TRE were able to work out the way to defeat the Wurzburg by using 'Window', strips of tinfoil which fooled the radar. Almost immediately after the raid the Germans surrounded all their radar stations with barbed wire. The grass grew long under the wire, so that in a few months the radar stations stood out like molehills on a lawn. Before the Normandy landings all Freya and Wurzburg stations were taken out by rocket-firing aircraft. Finally, airborne forces were put firmly on the map. There were busy times ahead for the Parachute Battalions.

There is not room in this book for more than a passing mention of the part played in parachute operations by gliders and glider-borne troops. But they became such an important part of the airborne divisions that it would be churlish not to give a short account of their formation, early problems, and include mention of them from time to time. It was realized very early during the formation of airborne forces that if paratroops were to be used for more than just in and out raids, and were employed in advance of the main army or on its flanks, they might become involved in heavy fighting. In this case they would need support in the form of more infantry, artillery, anti-tank guns and so forth. The only way of getting heavy equipment to the scene of an airborne operation at this time was by glider. Gliders could be towed by bombers or transport aircraft from the launching airfield to a point near the landing zone (LZ), where they were released by the tug aircraft to glide down to a landing. That was the theory. It was not so easy as it sounds. 'It is equivalent to force-landing the largest-sized aircraft without engine aid . . . there is no higher test of piloting skill,' wrote the Deputy Chief of the Air Staff.

The Air Force could not spare pilots for gliders, so volunteers from the Army were called for. Once the glider had landed, assuming it was not a write-off, there would be a long period before it could be salvaged, repaired and used again. Similarly, the pilot would probably not be recovered for days or weeks. Rather than sitting about twiddling his thumbs, waiting to be removed from the battle, he could play a useful part. So it was decided from the outset that the glider pilot would be the total soldier, a man who could fly and also fight on the ground with any weapon with which airborne troops were armed; who could take his part, if necessary, with any body of troops travelling in his glider in any action they might fight; who was a trained signaller and liaison officer. They were to do all this and more in airborne operations from Sicily onwards. Lieutenant Colonel Rock was selected as the first Commanding Officer of the newly formed 1st Battalion Glider Pilot Regiment. He was killed soon after on a training flight. It was a great loss. He had been one of the founding fathers of airborne forces, a courageous and innovative man.

The infantry for the glider-borne role were found by converting standard infantry battalions. This proved very successful. Many of them were well-disciplined, regular pre-war battalions with excellent *esprit de corps*. Although to the uninitiated their method of riding to battle lacked the glamour of the paratroop battalions, in reality it was sometimes far more dangerous, and always unpleasant. Most soldiers were sick within a few minutes and often the floor of the glider would be awash with vomit. Like their paratroop brethren, on landing they had the prospect of finding themselves surrounded by the enemy and cut off from all resupply except by air while they defeated, or at least held off, a more heavily-armed opponent before being relieved by ground troops. The glider infantry needed to be fit, hard and well-trained. The air-landing battalions, to give them their official name, became outstanding units. It seems a pity that they were not accorded the title Glider Battalions as were the American glider infantry, rather than the low-key 'air-landing' which somehow does not convey fully what they did. As airborne operations became more ambitious they became a vital part of the team, and for this role the most heavily armed infantry in the British Army at the time. They were 800 to 1,000 men strong, organized into four rifle companies, and equipped with twelve three-inch mortars, eight medium machine guns and a six pounder anti-tank gun platoon. They were far stronger than parachute battalions with a jumping strength of 600 men, organized into three rifle companies, and with only four three-inch mortars, four medium machine guns and no anti-tank guns (until gliders arrived).

The risks for both parachute and air-landing units are illustrated by the rule throughout the war that, when planning an airborne operation, one third of the force would not be expected to arrive in time, if at all. This was because of the problems of bad weather, technical failures in aircraft and gliders, loss of direction, the difficulty of recognizing LZs and DZs, enemy action en route, and landing losses.

The Airborne Division, under Major General Browning, consisting of 1st Parachute Brigade and 1st Airlanding

Brigade, was taking shape and training hard. Browning chose for his Division sign Bellerophon astride the winged horse Pegasus, in blue on a maroon background. It soon became the symbol for all British airborne forces. Browning also chose the maroon beret for his soldiers. There are a number of versions of why Browning chose blue and maroon for Airborne Forces. Some say these were his racing colours; others, that while watching the filming of his wife's novel *Frenchman's Creek* he noticed that the hero wore a maroon beret to enable the cameraman to pick him out in crowd scenes. It was not universally popular to begin with, particularly with those who came from regiments which already had distinctive head-dress such as Glengarry and Balmoral bonnets or Irish corbeens. Some independent spirits stuck to their cherished hats as long as they could. It was highly popular with paratroopers from English line regiments and Corps, who at this period of the war were condemned to wear that military abomination, the side cap, known to paratroopers as a crap hat (a title which has now been transferred to the service-dress cap). The red beret has subsequently been adopted by parachute units in nearly every country in the world. In the summer of 1942 the 2nd Parachute Brigade was formed under Brigadier Down, lately Commanding Officer of 1 Para, and then joined the Division. The new brigade consisted of the 4th Parachute Battalion, transferred from 1st Parachute Brigade; the 7th Battalion Queen's Own Cameron Highlanders, who became the 5th Parachute Battalion; and 10th Battalion Royal Welch Fusiliers, who became the 6th Parachute Battalion. These two battalions were the first to transfer to the parachute role as complete battalions. They were followed by others when 3rd Parachute Brigade was formed consisting of the 7th Parachute Battalion (formerly 10th Somerset Light Infantry), 8th Parachute Battalion (formerly 13th Royal

Warwickshires), and 9th Parachute Battalion (formerly 10th Essex).

The conversion of a standard infantry battalion in this way was not just a question of issuing an edict. The men had to be asked if they wanted to parachute. Many did, but some were then found to be medically unfit. By this time selection and pre-parachute training was considerably more formal than in the days of Number 2 Commando. Medical inspections were rigorous; men who had previously broken a leg, had false teeth or wore spectacles were weeded out. The three weeks at Hardwick, which preceded parachute training at Ringway, ended in seven tests, including running two miles in sixteen minutes in full battle order. Failure resulted in a man being posted elsewhere. The organization of the battalion had to be changed, and it had to be re-equipped and re-trained. But it was highly successful, and in no way were these battalions one whit less effective than the units consisting of volunteers from all over the Army, as their performance in Normandy, Italy, the Rhine Crossing and elsewhere would show. They retained a core of good officers, and, more important, first class NCOs around which to build a structure capable of enduring the tough times ahead. Key people, like the Adjutant, Quartermaster and specialists, often stayed. In the all-volunteer battalions there was sometimes difficulty in filling these vital but less glamorous posts from the ranks of those who had volunteered, in some cases, to escape just those sort of jobs.

At about this time American jeeps began to arrive. They made a vast difference to the mobility of an airborne force once it had landed. Among their varied tasks, jeeps towed trailers, anti-tank guns and pack-howitzers and carried the heavier radio sets, ammunition and casualties. There were never enough of them, so an array of folding bicycles, mini-motor bikes and even two-wheeled hand-carts or trolleys joined the transport of the airborne units.

The major problem was still lack of suitable aircraft. Indeed 38 Wing Royal Air Force could not find enough aircraft to lift 1 Para in one wave for the Dieppe raid without borrowing from Bomber Command. Fortunately for the Battalion, their part in that abortive raid was cancelled. The inability of the Air Force to provide aircraft was to dog the steps of all those who were trying to form and train the new force. But for the persistence of Field Marshal Alanbrooke, the Chief of the Imperial General Staff (CIGS), their efforts would have been in vain. Predictably, perhaps, the chief guru of the bombing offensive on Germany, Air Marshal 'Bomber' Harris, poured cold water on the airborne idea, saying 'parachute or glider operations are not a practical operation of war . . . the weather in Europe is unsuitable to airborne operations . . . airborne troops could not be employed with any prospect of material contribution to victory . . . the only alternative (to using bombers to drop parachutists and tow gliders) was to set up a separate transport force,' which he dismissed as 'fantastic'. Despite his scepticism, a separate transport force was eventually formed, using the splendid American Dakota (C47), and the poor cousins, the obsolete Stirling, Halifax and Albermarle bombers, the best the British could manage. Meanwhile Harris pursued his private and, towards the end, fruitless war. His bomber offensive, fought with matchless gallantry and self-sacrifice, cost the lives of about as many young British aircrew as officers killed on the Western Front in World War One, a devastating loss of leaders. Some of these aircrew would have been more gainfully employed as officers and NCOs in infantry and armoured units in the battles to come.

The argument between the Army and the Air Force was put to the Prime Minister for arbitration. The outcome was awaited impatiently by the Airborne Division who had already started training together. The Chief of the Air Staff tried to exploit the uncertainty by suggesting that the

Air-landing Brigade be broken up, but was seen off by the CIGS. Fortunately Browning did not allow the unsettling effects of this inter-service manoeuvring to interfere with the arrangements for getting 1st Parachute Brigade to North Africa. This was not before time. By now the problem of boredom was beginning to raise its head again in 1st Parachute Brigade. Lieutenant Colonel Hill, who had taken over 1 Para from Down when he went to raise the 2nd Parachute Brigade, was given a series of operations that never materialized.

First we were going to capture Alderney and hold it for a short time. That was cancelled. Then we trained for the Dieppe raid with the Canadians on the Isle of Wight. Security was abysmal; several Canadians told my chaps that the objective was Dieppe. We got as far as being loaded in the aircraft when a front came in and the operation was postponed for a month. Mountbatten decided to simplify the operation by eliminating one of the weather-dependent factors, so we were out and the commandos were given our task. I nearly had a mutiny on my hands; it was a hell of a job keeping the men happy.

Our next job was to capture Ushant and hold it for 48 hours, being taken off by Hunt Class destroyers. Again, we were in the aircraft at Hurn airport, with engines ticking over, when that one was cancelled! The reason – a group of American Flying Fortresses, despatched to bomb airfields supporting Ushant, got caught in a front, losing their way and formation. They were escorted by a squadron of Spitfires who were ordered to tail them. The Fortresses had the fuel capacity to find their way back, the Spitfires did not and were forced to land in France and as far away as Spain. I took the battalion to Exmoor and we did an exercise with live ammunition.

I then marched them back to Bulford, saying that anyone who fell out would not go on the next operation. We did the 112 miles in two and a half days, carrying sixty pounds per man. Some people failed to make it. They had to pay the price.

Despite shortages of aircraft, parachute exercises were laid on as often as possible. During one night exercise a commanding officer landed on the roof of a house, slid down, and was brought up with a jerk by his parachute hooking itself over the chimney. He found himself dangling opposite a first floor window. Pushing himself away from the wall, with his feet in the approved manner, he swung forward and burst through. He was greeted by scrabbling sounds. In the darkness the local vicar and his wife, searching for their false teeth, had succeeded in cramming each other's into their mouths. Having calmed them down, the commanding officer assured the vicar that the War Office would pay for all the damage. As he was taking his leave by the front door, promising to send men from his battalion to make repairs that very morning, an aircraft on the same exercise dropped a container, demolishing the greenhouse!

CHAPTER 3

Red Devils

Once again it was General Browning who was responsible for getting British paratroopers into action. He was adviser on airborne forces to Commanders-in-Chief in all theatres of war and when he learned that only 2nd Battalion 503 United States Parachute Infantry was earmarked for the forthcoming North African campaign, he suggested that this was insufficient. He foresaw tremendous opportunities for airborne troops in a theatre of operations that was spread over great distances where the enemy would be likely to be dispersed, at least until surprise was lost. Accordingly 1st Parachute Brigade was placed under command of General Eisenhower, the supreme Allied Commander for the North African campaign. He put them under the operational command of First British Army. The United States Army Air Force (USAAF) with their Dakotas enthusiastically took over responsibility for the airlift of 1st Parachute Brigade and their training before going overseas.

At first there was some individual training. Lieutenant Colonel Hill was allocated three Dakotas at Netheravon. He sent a company to jump and went to watch. To his horror he saw a Dakota fly over the DZ with one of his men hooked upon on the tail wheel. The static line was too short on the British parachute and did not guarantee clearance. Longer static lines were fitted, and Hill led the first stick to jump. Thereafter 2 Para carried out the first drop as a complete battalion from Dakotas. There were four deaths. One man fell with his parachute streaming

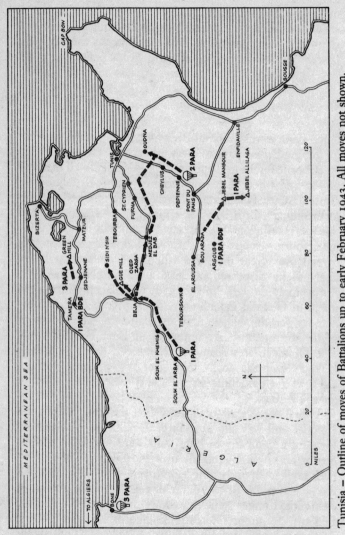

Tunisia – Outline of moves of Battalions up to early February 1943. All moves not shown.

out above him unopened, known as a Roman Candle. A second soldier's static line twisted so violently that the safety pin on his snap-link broke, and it was forced open, freeing the static line, so he fell with his parachute in its bag. One young officer leapt upwards as he exited instead of straight out, his parachute tangled in the tail-plane and as he swung back he hit the next man out. They fell to earth wrapped in a tangle of canopies and rigging lines. During the ensuing investigations all further practice drops were postponed. This resulted in a large number of the brigade, including many of 1 Para, leaving for North Africa without ever having jumped from the Dakota door, their only experience being the Whitley hole. But despite the accidents, most paratroopers found the Dakota a pleasant change. They could all look out of the windows, stand up, walk about, talk and even smoke if they liked. The Dakota carried twenty paratroopers compared with ten in the Whitley. But the most welcome difference of all was leaving the aircraft like a gentleman, through a door. Once techniques had been perfected, the exit was far quicker and safer. The Dakota became the most popular of all aircraft with the British paratroopers, and was the parachuting work-horse for the rest of the war, and several years after.

Because there were insufficient aircraft to lift even one battalion to North Africa, the whole brigade, except the headquarters and two companies of 3 Para, went by sea to Algiers. Once there, the Brigade was held ready for parachute operations ahead of First British Army as opportunities presented themselves. The initial seaborne landings on the coast of French Algeria and French Morocco were completed before the Parachute Brigade arrived. The vast majority of Frenchmen at this stage in the war were neutral, only a minority having joined the Free French to fight on the side of the Allies. German reaction to the invasion of North Africa was swift. They overran Vichy

France and started taking steps to occupy Tunisia and in particular the port of Tunis. About 1,000 miles to the east of Tunis, Rommel was retreating in front of the Eighth Army. If the Allies could forestall the German occupation of the port, Rommel would be trapped. British First Army was nearest to Tunis, albeit 500 miles away. There were plans for the 1st Parachute Brigade to drop at Tunis, a bold idea. If mounted early enough, it might have denied the port and airfield to the Germans, preventing them moving substantial forces into Tunisia. However, the Germans had greater numbers of well-trained paratroops who would have been dropped to retake the airfield or forestall the Allies once their intention became clear. The plan was deemed too risky. The opportunity was lost; the Germans began dispersing fighters forward to desert airstrips. Slow-moving transport aircraft attempting to fly all the way to Tunis would have suffered heavy losses. On 10 November 1942 General Anderson, commanding first Army, decided that the port and airfield at Bone, some 120 miles short of Tunis, would provide a handy stepping-stone on the route to his goal. Lacking an airborne adviser at head-quarters 1st Army, neither Anderson nor his staff had much idea about getting the best value out of 1st Parachute Brigade and even less notion about the planning required for an airborne operation, if such an expensive asset was not to be frittered away. In retrospect, Browning should have ensured that an officer of sufficient seniority was attached to 1st Army.

On the same day, 3 Para arrived at Gibraltar in USAAF Dakotas, expecting to fly on to Maison Blanche near Algiers, where they would sort themselves out for their first mission. They had already been briefed to seize the airfields at Djidjelli or Bizerta, and carried air photos and models of their targets. At Gibraltar the commanding officer, Lieutenant Colonel Pine-Coffin, was greeted with an order that his Battalion was to arrive at Maison Blanche with the aircraft combat loaded for an immediate parachute operation. This was not easy to achieve because the Battalion was flying in fewer aircraft than they would need for an operational drop and were carrying much heavy kit. To add to the problem, two aircraft failed to arrive at Gibraltar. However, the Battalion set to, and having restowed the aircraft arrived at Maison Blanche on 11 November. Pine-Coffin was immediately summoned to Anderson's headquarters and briefed personally by the General to drop on Bone airfield at 8.30 am the next day. He was told that a German parachute unit was about to capture the place.

The drop the next day, from 400 feet, was scattered over three miles and some containers fell well short. The ground was stony and every man was loaded with small arms ammunition in addition to the heavier weapons and ammunition in the containers. There was only one death from the drop when a man accidentally shot himself with his sten gun on the way down. Thirteen men were injured, including an officer who lay unconscious for four days, and from time to time was heard to murmur, 'I'll have a little more of the turbot, waiter!' But 3 Para had beaten the Germans to it. With Number 6 Commando, they held the airfield for a week until they were withdrawn. Here, for the first time, the British paratroopers encountered the thieving habits of the Tunisian Arabs who, on the whole were an unfriendly lot. They not only looted the containers, the wounded and the dead but on occasions sold information to the enemy.

While 3 Para was seizing Bone, 1 and 2 Para arrived at Algiers. When 1 Para was still at sea, Lieutenant Colonel Hill was told by signal to open sealed orders for the forthcoming operation. His mission was to seize El Aouina airfield at Tunis. If the enemy got there first, he was to capture the airfield at Setif. With the orders were detailed maps, air photos, and even a model of El Aouina airfield.

Excitement mounted as the Battalion, under the enthusiastic leadership of Hill, prepared a detailed plan, including load tables for each aircraft, the latter done with difficulty, because the Battalion had never exercised with Dakotas. Everybody was in high spirits after two years of waiting to get into battle. Then, while they were still at sea, they heard that the Germans had captured El Aouina. Disembarking at Algiers, the battalion marched out of the city towards Maison Blanche airfield. After dark they were pulled off the road into what looked like a park. The next morning, Captain Coxen, the second-in-command of T Company, woke up and 'saw over my head a huge bunch of bananas. I remember saying to myself: "This is not so bad, I can stand this sort of country." I think they were the only bunch of bananas that grew in North Africa. We were in the botanical gardens!'

During the night they were soaked to the skin by a rainstorm. On arriving at Maison Blanche, they were told to take off in forty-eight hours time for their alternative objective. They had to unload the ship themselves, and transport the equipment to the airfield twelve miles away. The only transport was a handful of dilapidated requisitioned French trucks, minus their drivers. Maison Blanche was bombed each night and blacked out, so half the work was done in total darkness. After twenty-four hours Hill was ordered to prepare for a new operation in twenty-four hours time in the Beja area, some fifty miles west of Tunis. Hill judged that it would be impossible to complete the unloading of the ship and sort out the equipment in the next twenty-four hours, so he asked for a postponement. This was refused. With the prospect of his Battalion fighting a battle after little or no sleep for forty-eight hours, Hill ordered his second-in-command and 100 men to remain behind to help get the remainder away in time. Hill had four tasks: to seize and hold the key road-centre of Beja; to bring the French Army, who were still dithering

under the command of Admiral Darlan, in on the side of
the Allies; to harry the enemy wherever they found him;
and to report by radio whether the strip near Souk el Arba
was suitable as an advanced landing ground for fighter
aircraft. 'It was a splendid task for a young Lieutenant
Colonel to be given.'

One of the problems before take-off was that the American Wing of thirty-two Dakotas had never dropped parachutists before, and there was no intercom between aircraft
or within the aircraft. The only map available of the Beja
area was a quarter-inch-to-the-mile motoring map. Hill
decided to sit in the front seat of the leading aircraft with
the wing commander. When the two of them reckoned
they had spotted the best DZ in the area of Souk el Arba,
Hill would go back, hook up and jump. This would be
the signal for the rest of the battalion, travelling in aircraft
in line astern, to do the same. The flight went to plan at
first, and the troops were able to watch a battle between
the four American Lightnings (guarding the Dakotas) and
Messerschmitts, which were driven off. Unfortunately,
when heading over the Atlas mountains near the Tunisian
border deep clouds were encountered and the Dakotas
had to turn back. General Anderson was furious at the
battalion's return and he did nothing to conceal his dislike
of paratroops, about which he knew little. He instructed
Hill that in the event of weather preventing the drop the
next day, he was to land as near to the enemy as possible.
Hill decided that in that event the battalion would drop
on the sandy beaches north of the route to Souk el Arba.

The postponement was a blessing, because they were
able to sleep that night and most of the rear party, including second-in-command Major Pearson, could go with
them on the following day. During the flight the lavatory
door in Coxen's Dakota opened and out came Colour
Sergeant Cooke who had been detailed off to remain
behind with the rear party. Cooke had acquired a para-

chute and dropped with Coxen's stick. Typical of some of
the types in the 1st Battalion, he had served in the French
Foreign Legion, had two sons serving in the British Army,
and had false teeth. Coxen, reporting to his company
commander on first joining the battalion, had been astonished to see a head coming round the office door at door
knob level, a pair of false teeth go 'chatter-chatter-chatter',
and the head disappear. No one took the slightest notice.
It was the Company Quartermaster Colour Sergeant
reporting. Cooke was captured later in the campaign,
escaped to the Vatican, and after the war joined the Australian Army to fight in Korea.

The weather was good and the drop on the outskirts of
Souk el Arba, the planned DZ, went without a hitch.
Luckily take-off was earlier than the previous day because
only one hour after the drop some German fighters and
bombers appeared on the scene. Airborne equipment was
so scarce that the battalion was told to salvage as much of
it as possible for use in the next operation. The whole
town turned up at the burial of the one fatal casualty of
the drop, much to Major Pearson's dismay. As principal
mourner he had to shake hands with 3,000 people. Meanwhile Hill and the battalion were advancing on Beja with
all speed, having requisitioned some French vehicles. With
525 men he had to take the road junction which was held
by nearly 3,000 French troops. The Germans had made
it clear that drastic action would be taken against the
French if the British were allowed to enter the town. Hill
decided that bluff was the best way to achieve his task.
He took up a position on a hill outside the town and
opened negotiations with the French commander. He
spoke of the armoured divisions that were moving rapidly
to their support, made mention of the secret weapons that
all parachutists had to defeat the German armour and
which so alarmed the French, and multiplied the number
of troops he had.

Hill's bold approach succeeded, and it was agreed that the Battalion would take over from the two French battalions. To avoid having his bluff called, Hill arranged for the relief to be carried out at dusk when, with luck, their few numbers would not be spotted. During the day before he marched the battalion through the town twice, once in helmets and once in berets, well spread out on each occasion to disguise their real strength. He also had the battalion stores and medical equipment disguised to look like the new weapons he had mentioned to the French. The bluff succeeded and the relief went without a hitch. The Germans had announced that if the French let the British into Beja, they would dive-bomb it. They were as good as their word. Some Arabs took advantage of the chaos to loot. Within half an hour the French had seized and shot the ringleaders. There was no more looting.

Hill learned from the French that a patrol of German armoured vehicles used to come up to the French at Sidi N'Sir station at 11 am each day, exchange cigarettes with the French and drive back to Bizerta. After some haggling with the French, Hill persuaded them to let S Company commanded by Major Cleasby-Thompson through their lines. The company spent the night in a farmhouse near Sidi N'Sir. The next morning four large eight-wheeled armoured cars, preceded by four scout cars, motored up the road past the concealed soldiers of C Company. They allowed the Germans to drive up to the French post. Round a bend, out of sight, the company laid anti-tank mines in the road. On completion of their bartering, the Germans reversed away, armoured cars leading. The first passed over the mines without mishap, the second blew up, the leader returned and he blew up, followed by the other two. The eventual bag was four armoured cars knocked out and four scout cars captured with prisoners. Hill had the scout cars driven through Beja with the prisoners to show the French that the Germans were not invincible.

Hill, realizing that the bridge at Medjez el Bab was a key point, decided to call on the French divisional commander there, taking with him most of his battalion, leaving only one company at Beja. After discussions with the French general, with whom he struck up a rapport, he became uneasy about leaving so small a force at Beja. His orders were to hold it in strength. He returned to Beja, leaving a platoon and an officer who spoke fluent French. The German Minister to the Bey of Tunis, hearing of the British presence in Medjez, visited the French divisional commander to inform him that he would be sending troops across the bridge. After some argument the French general summarily dismissed the German minister, who shortly afterwards sent in the troops. A battle ensued, which brought the French in the area onto the British side.

Having achieved three of the tasks he had been set. Hill proceeded to harry the enemy. One evening an Arab appeared at battalion headquarters in the Beja abattoir with the information that the enemy laagered their tanks each night on Gue hill, nine miles up the valley to Mateur. Captain Whitelock, the Adjutant:

That night, battalion headquarters, the mortar platoon, a party of sappers, two rifle companies and a contingent of Senegalese set out along the valley. In bright moonlight the mountains on either side seemed deserted, the only sound the barking of dogs. We crept along a rough path in single file, James Hill's and my batmen acting as scouts, followed by James and I, the Arab informer, and the remainder of the force. When we had gone about six miles we could see, in the moonlight, the hulls of the tanks. Leaving Alastair Pearson with the mortars and a company, James and I and the sappers crept on around the enemy. We tried to get the sappers to the rear of the position to mine the track, thus hindering their retreat.

As Whitelock and a platoon crept up the hill, led by their commanding officer, an engineer carrying a fused mine on his back slipped. The mine exploded, killing him and initiating a sympathetic detonation which wiped out the whole sapper party less two men. At the sound of the explosion, the tanks revealed their positions by firing tracer. Whitelock:

As we neared the top of the hill, James sent me to give a message to the company commander behind us. I rejoined James just as the fun started. He advanced on the first tank, pushed his pistol through a port in the side and fired, to the consternation of the crew, who promptly surrendered. He rapped with his stick on the turret of the second tank, whose crew surrendered. As he rapped on the third tank, the occupants came out firing and throwing grenades, James was shot three times through the chest and a grenade exploded at my feet. Shrapnel went through my nose, into my head, arms and legs; we were both in a pretty poor way. By this time the enemy were surrounded, and after a fierce little fight, bayonetting etc, they all surrendered. There were six light tanks, and about thirty to forty men.

James and I were carried down Gue hill to the railway line. We were laid on a motorcycle and side-car combination and pushed slowly down the line to Beja, the Senegalese doing most of the pushing. Halfway back, at dawn, we were visited by Messersch-mitts and machine-gunned. Mercifully they missed. But I felt very isolated, the medical staff and the Senagalese wisely having dived for cover. At Beja we were operated on by a parachute surgical team, who saved our lives.

Major Pearson took over command. Before the war he had run the family bakery firm in Glasgow and been an officer in the Territorials. He was twenty-seven years old. Within a period of two weeks he was awarded the DSO and the MC. He was to go on to win three more DSOs and to become one of the most decorated commanding officers in the British Army. 1 Para patrolled in the vicinity of Medjez el Bab and held a defensive position at Sidi N'Sir for about ten days before going into reserve in Algiers, where they were joined by 3 Para.

2 Para's first experience of war in North Africa was perhaps the most hair-raising of all. For several days after their arrival the battalion was kept in reserve on the outskirts of Algiers with nothing to do. Frost, who had taken command just before the battalion sailed, started to worry that if a task was not found for them soon they would be used as ordinary infantry. Suddenly he found himself very busy indeed. He was told to fly over Sousse, have a look at the place and find a DZ nearby from where he could capture the town. He had a frightening trip, culminating in being shot at by the American Parachute Battalion when he called in on them on his way back. Leaving his bullet-ridden aircraft with the Americans and hitching a lift in a Dakota, he arrived at Brigade Headquarters to be told that the Sousse operation was off. He was to drop on Enfidaville. On his return from that air reconnaissance, he learned that Enfidaville was off. The battalion was getting very restive by now and working off its energies by fighting with American and French parachutists in the town.

On 28 November Frost was briefed to drop at Pont du Fahs the next day and destroy any enemy aircraft he found. He was then to move twelve miles to Depienne to deal with the airstrip. This was to be repeated at Oudna airstrip another twelve miles away, followed by a link-up with the First Army at St Cyprien. This would involve carrying at least five days' food, ammunition and radio batteries. Frost's main worry, however, was that their only anti-tank weapons were the obsolete Boyes rifle and the Gammon bomb. The latter required the user to get right up to the tank before throwing it! The battalion was to use the same Dakotas that had dropped the other battalions. The emplaning on 29 November was chaotic. Each aircraft arrived marked with two different sets of chalk numbers. The chalk number should correspond with the number on the manifest prepared by the battalion, so that sticks of parachutists and containers are loaded onto the right aircraft. If all goes well, the battalion then drop in the tactical sequence required by the commanding officer. Heavy mud did not help the sorting out, and as tempers became frayed the air was filled with the soldiers' favourite four-letter expletive.

The battalion was almost loaded when Frost was told to change the plan again and drop at Depienne, march to Oudna, deal with any enemy aircraft and then link up with First Army at St Cyprien. Everyone in the battalion had been briefed for the previous plan, and there was no time to re-brief them or find a suitable DZ from the map. The pilots were hastily told the new destination. Frost decided that he would pick the DZ from the air.

The flight over the mountains was awe-inspiring, but not everyone appreciated the scenery. The Dakotas rocked and slewed in the turbulent air, many soldiers were sick and started the operation with empty stomachs.

Frost stood in the door of his Dakota, and as soon as it passed over Depienne he jumped. He rallied his battalion on the DZ by sounding his hunting horn. Because the drop was scattered, and most of the battalion had expected to find themselves at Pont du Fahs, considerable confusion reigned. Six men were injured and one killed in the drop because of heavy landings. Some Tunisians appeared and started looting the containers. Only shots aimed to strike near them seemed to deter them. Later that afternoon three British armoured cars from 56th Reconnaissance Regiment appeared. This was most encouraging, boding well for a link-up with the leading armour of 1st Army the next day. At last all seemed to be going to plan, despite the earlier chaos. At about midnight the battalion set off for Oudna, less part of a platoon of C Company under Lieutenant Buchanan left to salvage parachutes and look after the injured, who could not be left to the mercies of the Tunisians. These men were not seen again for weeks, years and, in some cases, ever. The route to Oudna took the battalion over rough tracks through hilly country. There were no arrangements for air-dropping supplies in North Africa, so everything that the battalion required had to be carried on the backs of marching men, or on the few mules and carts requisitioned locally. Including food, ammunition and personal weapon, each man was carrying approximately 120 pounds. They marched for most of the remainder of the night, over appalling going, stopping for a brief rest at 4.30 am.

The battalion was roused, shivering in the pre-dawn chill, and ate a cold breakfast of dry biscuits and chocolate before continuing along the crest of a long ridge running north-east towards Oudna. The surface improved as they progressed and soon the sun rose to warm them and lift their spirits. Suddenly, as they crested a rise, the plain lay before them, and there about ten miles away lay Tunis, dazzling white in the sunlight.

At about 2.30 pm that day, 30 November, the battalion captured Oudna airstrip, having cleared the German opposition. The enemy were not using the airstrip. An hour later five German tanks supported by Messerschmitts attacked the battalion but were beaten off. Two hours later the area was dive-bombed by Stukas, but they did not find

the paratroopers, who were skilfully camouflaged in their
para smocks and face nets. This was not the last time that
they were saved by their skill in concealment.

'Now as the whole object of the mission,' said Frost in
his report, 'had been to destroy aircraft at Oudna, and as
there were no aircraft to destroy, I made plans for moving
westwards to link up with First Army.' Frost withdrew
from Oudna at dusk and moved his battalion into a defensive position on high ground at Prise de l'Eau. The following morning, having ambushed one enemy column that
was probing the battalion position, Frost received the welcome news that friendly armour displaying the First Army
yellow recognition triangles was approaching. Support was
at hand, the wounded would be taken care of, and the
battalion could be re-supplied with ammunition. Relief
and joy soon turned to bitter disappointment. The Germans, using triangles picked up from the Depienne party,
had deceived some of the paratroopers into approaching
them and had captured them. They then sent one prisoner
forward with a message that the battalion was surrounded
and was to surrender at once. As this galling ultimatum
was being digested, a radio message arrived, the first and
only received by the battalion during the whole operation:
the armoured thrust on Tunis was postponed!

The battalion was in a precarious position, having been
dropped miles ahead of First Army and about fifteen miles
from the Germans' main base at Tunis. To sustain them
against an enemy who had now located them, had local
air superiority, and was moving in strength with armour
to destroy them, they had only the ammunition and food
they had dropped with. There was no prospect of re-
supply or reinforcement. They were on their own until
they could rendezvous with First Army thirty or forty miles
away. Frost decided to move at once to higher ground
where they could shake off the Germans in the dark.
While they destroyed equipment that was no longer of any

use, such as radios and their flat batteries, a party was sent to attack the Germans to show that the battalion had no intention of surrendering. They destroyed two tanks and immobilized two others, thanks mainly to the actions of Private Wilkinson, but at the cost of his life. Frost made the distressing decision to leave the wounded behind with Lieutenant MacGarvin RAMC of the Field Ambulance section; there was nothing else that could be done.

Heavily laden and tortured with thirst in the noon sun, the battalion struggled on up over the steep, rough ground, sometimes on hands and knees, while the enemy harried them with shell and mortar fire, causing more casualties. Finally they took up a defensive position at Sidi Bou Hadjeba, two hills near a well, about five miles south of Oudna Station, and waited for the enemy. They were not long in coming, and for the rest of the day the battalion was subjected to repeated assaults by infantry in half-tracks supported by tanks. Just as it seemed that they could hold out no longer, Messerschmitts appeared. The battalion unable to respond to this new threat, lay still, hugging the ground, invisible from the air. To their astonishment the Messerschmitts proceeded to attack the only troops they could see, the Germans, causing such mayhem that their assault withered away.

After nightfall on 1 December the battalion withdrew in company groups. Lacking radios, the signal for the withdrawal was blown by Frost on his hunting horn. By this time they had suffered 150 dead and wounded since the drop. Again there was the agonizing problem of what to do with the wounded. They left them with heavy hearts, knowing that lacking adequate drugs, blankets or shelter, many of the more severely injured would not survive the night. Frost decided to leave Leiutenant Playford's platoon behind to collect them in and protect them from the attentions of the Tunisian looters. He knew that this platoon would almost certainly be captured. The Germans did not follow up, and the battaltion scrambled down onto the plain. During the night it was noticed that Major Teichman, the second-in-command, and Captain Short, the Adjutant, were missing. They marched until shortly before dawn, exhausted, their throats aching from thirst. By now they were so short of sleep that most nodded off at every halt, and getting going after each stop became more and more of an effort. Some men who left the column to relieve themselves were not seen again. Sergeant Johnstone of A Company:

> We found the going down the side of the precipitous gully very tough . . . when we got down on the plain it was no better. I do not exaggerate when I talk of the agony of stumbling in a vineyard. It was like marching over a coal heap. It became a supreme effort to climb over a low wall or slight bank such as divided the fields . . . I was so exhausted I was staggering and I remember the Major's voice behind me, just piercing the fog of exhaustion, urging me on with 'keep it up lad, keep going'. I must pay tribute to that gallant man for the way in which he encouraged and cajoled his utterly exhausted and almost demoralized remnant of a company. That night was the testing point of all of us. I think it taught us that while you are conscious you can keep going, and things never seemed so bad again.

Just before sunrise, Frost and his headquarters, who were with B Company, found a farm surrounded by a thick cactus hedge. This made an ideal lying-up position for the forthcoming day. At about mid-day they were joined by Major Ashford's A Company, who had taken cover in a neighbouring farm, and were sent for by Frost to join him. Of C Company there was no sign. Reports were received from local Arabs that there were Allied troops at Furna, about ten miles to the west. Lieutenant

Charteris, who had done so well at Bruneval, was sent with two men to make contact with the Allied force and to return at all costs before dark.

During the day the enemy started to bring up more and more men until the farm was surrounded. Although they outnumbered the battalion by about four to one they seemed rather cautious. Perhaps they were mystified by the lack of movement in the farm buildings; the paratroopers kept silent and out of sight. During the afternoon the Germans intermittently mortared the farm, gradually increasing the volume of fire, with other weapons joining in. Frost decided that the battalion would break out as soon as it was dark and charge through what appeared to be the weakest part of the enemy ring around them. Just as darkness fell the Germans mounted an attack in strength, which the battalion beat back with withering concentrated fire at point-blank range. In the pause that followed, Frost blew on his hunting horn: the signal for the withdrawal to begin. This was their last chance. There was not enough ammunition to fight another battle. What was left of the battalion charged, breaking through the enemy. When clear, they rallied on the sound of Frost's horn. Charteris had not returned, and was never seen again. Frost decided to abandon any idea of making for Furna and head for Medjez el Bab instead. During a short halt at a farm for rest and a brew-up just before first light, Frost was told by the French inhabitants, who were extremely helpful, that a pro-German Arab had gone to betray the paratroopers to the enemy. The battalion moved at once on to some high ground nearby. From the summit, to their delight, they could see Medjez el Bab in the middle distance. A moment later an Arab approached with the news that the Allies were in town. Moving through some orchards, they reached the road leading to the town. In the early afternoon, as they marched along the road, they met up with an American armoured car. They had made the link-up after five days on their own.

This fighting retreat, which had started on the day after the drop on 29 November and ended on 3 December, cost sixteen officers and 250 other ranks. First Army had sent the battalion out into the blue to destroy enemy aircraft that did not exist. There was no excuse for this, because air reconnaissance could have quickly established whether or not the Luftwaffe was using Oudna. Having launched the operation, First Army made no attempt to find out what was happening to the battalion. The whole episode was the result of abysmal planning by all commanders and staffs above the battalion, right up to and including the First Army Commander himself. Only Frost's leadership, and the courage and initiative of all ranks prevented the whole of a highly trained parachute battalion going into the bag on a wild goose chase. The battalion, without artillery, air support, armour or transport, had fought and eluded the grasp of 1st Battalion 5th Fallschirmjäger (Parachute) Regiment, the Reconnaissance Squadron from 10th Panzer Division, and a battery of Italian artillery.

By 11 December another fifty of the missing had turned up. Corporal McConney dislocated his shoulder on landing, and after having it put back was taken with other injured men to a schoolroom at Depienne on 29 November, the day of the drop. The injured were being evacuated to hospital at Pont du Fahs, under the direction of Lieutenant Buchanan, who had been left at the DZ with two sections.

The last man to be taken was suffering from a broken pelvis, and as he had to lie full length in the car there was no room for me. The doctor said he would return for me at 15.00 hours. That left Mr Buchanan, his batman, and myself in the schoolroom. At 13.00

hours we started to make a meal. By the time we had cooked the food we heard the sound of tanks and armoured vehicles on the road leading north. In between each AFV (tank) were a number of motor-cycle combinations. The three of us lay down in a ditch facing the road. The crews of the tanks were Italians. Shots came from the direction of Mr Buch-anan and his batman, so I too opened with my sten. The range was approximately fifty yards, and I got off five good magazines with good effect on the motorcyclists. Mr Buchanan gave a cry and rolled over on his back, and the batman lay face down with arms outstretched. By this time the tanks had traversed their guns round and were raking the build-ing with fire. Seeing it was useless to continue firing. I crawled to the lavatory, put my sten and three mags on top of the wall to avoid detection, and hid behind the half closed door. About thirty Italians entered the yard and were very excited when they saw that a meal had been in progress. A heap of parachutes in the corner of the yard aroused suspicion, and several shots were directed at them. Then they lifted them up to see if anyone was hiding underneath. Then they began a systematic search of the out-houses. A few shots were fired. Luckily none touched me. Three of them walked in and were greatly alarmed at finding me. One officer addressed as 'Capitano' apparently gave orders regarding me, and I was taken out and put on top of an armoured vehicle and taken up the road they had come from. After three or four miles they stopped at a small wood and I was assisted off. One Italian was left with me and the vehicle went back. I at once set about a plan for escape. They had failed to detect my fighting knife which was concealed in a pocket, and my right arm was in a sling. To the sentry I must have appeared a very poor spectacle, for he did not seem to worry a great deal about me. I think he thought there was a chance of an attack by the battalion. As dusk approached he seemed to get more nervous, and whenever he turned his back I loosened the knife. At last I got it out and put it in my left hand trouser pocket. When he next presented his back to me I whipped out the knife and stuck at his back under the left shoulder. He gave a cry and fell forward on his face. I must have lost my head, for I struck again and again at the inert form.

I decided then to go back to the school and try and collect my arms if they were still there. I got there at about nine o'clock, for I was sick several times. The village seemed devoid of troops, so I made my way to the lavatory. I found my sten and mags still on top of the wall, but all the equipment in the schoolroom had gone except two small tins of cheese. I listened outside the door of the house and could hear only the voice of the schoolmaster and his wife. They had been very good to us so I knocked on the door and asked if they knew where the English soldiers were. They said they were at Pont du Fahs, gave me bread and water and told me to go as the Italians might return. I went and lay down in the ditch and started to eat and drink. I had nearly finished when I heard the tanks entering the village. It may have been the same lot as before, for I heard the words 'mon Capitano' several times. They came into the school and seemed to use it for a headquarters. I thought it was time to get out and crawled along the ditch. Several times I was only a few feet from some of them. At last I got clear of the village and made off in the direction of Pont du Fahs with the aid of a compass, part of the escape kit. After walking for a few miles I felt very tired, so went to sleep in some hay. Next morning I set off again. I stopped at a

French farm and they gave me sausage and eggs and then they told me that Pont du Fahs was in the hands of the enemy. This was rather a setback. I had heard that 1st Para Battalion were somewhere near Medjez el Bab, so I changed my course for there. The going was very hard over those mountains and the sun was very hot. On the morning of the next day I made contact with the 56th Recce Regiment.

Others had narrow squeaks of a different kind. Lance Corporal Cadden, who had fought at Dunkirk and at Bruneval, was captured:

A staff car drove up, a high ranking German officer stepped out and walked over to the first Italian officer. From what was said we knew we were to be shot as agents and saboteurs, even though we were easily reconizable as regular soldiers because of our uniforms. We were lined up against a wall and a machine gun was set up in front of us. We put on our berets, raised our fingers in V signs, and took our leave of Lieutenant Buchanan. The German officer ordered the machine gunner to fire but he did not react, and at that moment an armoured car pulled up. Down from it sprang Oberstleutnant Walter Koch, commander of Falschirmjäger Regiment 5. Sizing up the situation at a glance, he immediately strode across and kicked over the machine gun. After a heated argument between the two officers. Koch turned to the prisoners and said: 'You are paratroopers, and you put up a brave fight. You are prisoners of war and will be treated as such.'

For the next eight days the batallion was sent hither and thither to carry out a number of defensive tasks in the vicinity of Medjez. Then after being relieved by the Coldstream Guards they were sent to Souk el Khemis where they could rest. While the battalion was at Medjez, Frost was offered 200 anti-aircraft gunners as reinforcements. He was so understrength after his heavy losses in the Oudna operation that he accepted them with alacrity. These gunners were very put out suddenly to find themselves as infantry. However, they were very intelligent and responded to Frost's leadership. They were ordered to wear red berets so they would not feel outsiders, and were taught to shoot with rifles at petrol cans placed out in front of the defence positions the batallion then occupied in a quiet part of the line. Many of them stayed on in 2 Para.

So ended the last parachute operation in North Africa. Although Flavell, the Brigade Commander of the 1st Parachute Brigade, asked that his Brigade be brought up to strength and re-trained ready for further airborne operations, it was not possible at the time. Daylight parachute operations onto ground overlooked by the enemy in strong positions would be too costly, and the Dakota pilots were not trained to fly at night. But even more important, the Allied advance on Tunis had run out of steam and ground to a halt. The Allies had made one last effort to take Tunis before Christmas, and 1st Parachute Brigade were warned that they would pass through 1st Guards Brigade after they had taken a feature known as Longstop Hill, but in the end they were not needed. The German reaction had been so fast and violent that in some sectors they had not only contained the advance on Tunis, but their counter-attacks had broken through the Allied positions. Some units, notably the Americans, had been badly shaken by these unexpected reverses when all seemed to be going so well, with Tunis almost within their grasp. Much of the American army in North Africa was in a poor state at this stage in the war. 'It was,' recalls Frost, 'very depressing to see their low standard. The one question they were asking was "when do we go home?" ' They were different from the splendid US airborne divisions, and the American formations that fought later in the war. The Germans clearly had a low opinion of them too, because on one occasion a prisoner said to Coxen: 'We Germans have the Italians, you British have the Americans.' The three parachute battalions were desperately needed to plug gaps and to re-take lost ground. From December 1942 to April 1943 they were in the thick of this bitter campaign that swayed to and fro in the rocky hills and the mud, rain, sleet and snow of the Tunisian winter and spring. It would take a complete book to describe every battle in which they were engaged. But it was this fighting that established the high reputation of the parachute battalions, setting a standard for all to follow.

In January, 3 Para was placed under command of 36 Infantry Brigade and was heavily involved in attempts to take a feature known as Green Hill. On 4 January, Major Terrell's A Company, attached to the 4th Battalion The Buffs for a night attack, got to the top of the hill but were the only attackers to do so. They were unable to hold the position on their own and had to withdraw. On the following night a further attempt was made by two companies of 3 Para and the Buffs. The orders were issued late, and the mortars and other supporting weapons could not keep up because of the difficult terrain. Eventually Major Dobie's B Company of 3 Para found itself alone on top of the hill, having captured some concrete machine-gun posts on the summit. After wiping out the first enemy counter-attack by at least two companies charging *en masse* chanting war songs, B Company had run out of ammunition. They were forced off the hill by a second, stronger attack. Following this battle, the battalion rejoined their own brigade.

On 7 and 8 January, 1st Parachute Brigade, without 2 Para, were taken back to Algiers to prepare for a parachute operation on Sfax in conjunction with an American armoured force. The aim – to prevent Rommel, still retreating in front of Montgomery, joining up with the enemy forces in Tunisia. Subsequently the operation was cancelled. Meanwhile 2 Para were moved to several blocking positions, to plug gaps, or on one occasion to the extreme right flank of 1st Army. Here they were briefed by the brigadier under whose command they were operating to expect an attack by 100 tanks and ten battalions! He added that the Corps Commander expected them to take very heavy casualties. Fortunately this gloomy prediction never happened. On 8 February, 2 Para returned to 1st Parachute Brigade, who had arrived in the Bou Arada sector about two weeks before.

The Corps Commander had decided that the best way to protect his exposed right flank was to attack, Pearson and his Intelligence Officer accompanied a fighting patrol led by Coxen up onto Jebel Mansour. They had some information on the going provided by a French Foreign Legion officer attached to the battalion. It was very rough country, and it soon became obvious that the Frenchman had never made the reconnaissance he claimed to have done. Coxen, a German speaker, made the first contact: 'On being challenged, I replied: "Das ist Willie, dumkopf." He threw a grenade at me so obviously my German was not all that good! I got some grenade splinters in my back and hand. The reaction by the leading platoon was immediate. They deployed on each side of me and over-ran the position, taking about fourteen prisoners including the grenade thrower.'

The feature was held by a German mountain battalion. It was obvious that Mansour was not tenable without also taking Alliliga, which dominated the route to Mansour and enfiladed the feature. Having moved to the base of Jebel Mansour during the night, they had captured it and patrolled forward to Jebel Alliliga by 7 am, after very heavy fighting over difficult country. There were many acts of great bravery in this, the battalion's first and probably finest major engagement. They discovered that the Germans did not care for close quarter battle. They kept firing until assaulting troops got within a few yards and surrendered, by which time it was too late – they were killed. Jebel Alliliga was very strongly held. By 9 am having taken over 180 casualties and with ammunition running short, the battalion was forced to abandon any attempt to capture Jebel Alliliga and concentrate on Jebel Mansour. The next day one company of 3rd Battalion Grenadier Guards assaulted Jebel Alliliga. The company arrived on top of the feature commanded by the company sergeant major. All the officers had been killed or wounded. The enemy counter-attacked in great strength, forcing the depleted Grenadier company off the mountain. The Germans got so close in the course of repeated counter-attacks that the 1st Battalion found it difficult to bring down artillery and mortar fire without hitting their own troops. The paratroopers and the Grenadiers were short of men and ammunition, which could be re-supplied only by mule train over very exposed tracks. Unless Alliliga was taken, Mansour could not be held, so Pearson was given permission to withdraw under cover of a smoke screen. At the end of this battle, 1 Para had only seven of its original officers and 169 other ranks were killed, wounded or missing in action.

One of the officers killed at Jebel Mansour was Lieutenant Mellor, a piratical figure who wore a black patch over one eye. Coxen, who commanded all three rifle companies in 1 Para, remembers Mellor 'as the bravest man I have ever met. He regarded war as something that was made difficult by senior officers, whereas in fact it was extraordinarily simple! The men would follow him anywhere. He was one of those chaps who it is very difficult to keep alive. At Mansour he had most of a leg blown off and was last seen sitting up shooting at the advancing Germans with his pistol. They filled him up, killed him.'

After this battle the brigade remained in the Bou Arada sector, but fighting was limited to patrolling. 3 Para took up a position near Argoub, which became known as Happy Valley as life was suddenly so much quieter, although not for long. During this period, Lieutenant Street of 3 Para went out at dawn to visit his forward section positions. Hearing movement, he called out to what he thought were his men to keep quiet because there were Germans near. On being challenged he shouted at them again. The next moment he felt a sub-machine gun jab him in the midriff and a German ordered him to lead him and his patrol to battalion headquarters. Street, realizing that they intended attacking the headquarters, led them to the nearest company strongpoint which fired on them. Luckily Street was not hit. A moment later, lying in a fold in the ground alongside the German patrol commander, he distracted his attention, smashed him on the head knocking him unconscious, and made off to re-join his battalion. For this and other actions he was awarded the Military Cross.

The parachute battalions had a policy of patrolling vigorously. Officers did not spare themselves. Lieutenant Bentham of B Company, 3 Para:

Tom Gotts (platoon commander), was sent out one night on his first patrol. He only covered 500 yards having crawled all the way. David (Major Dobie – company commander) was annoyed. He was sent out two nights later and his men came back at 02.00 hours, said that he had stepped on a mine, and had sent them back because he was dying. Giles (Lieutenant Bromley-Martin), immediately went out with a stretcher party but could not find him in the dark. David took out another party in daylight. Although the Germans were only 1,000 yards away they did not shoot. They found Tom very badly wounded and brought him in. He was conscious when he reached

our lines and looked up at David and said; 'Did I
make up for it, sir?' He died in the ambulance, a loss
felt by all.

The Germans were gearing themselves up for a major
attack on the brigade at Argoub. On 26 February it started.
Bentham again:

A German patrol hit my platoon area, almost reaching
my headquarters before they were seen. I was out of
my dug-out in a flash and started throwing grenades.
My sergeant, MacDonald, slipped round the back
and took Guthrie's section behind the Germans and
took them in the rear. There were about twenty of
them with a machine gun but they fled. We killed
three and took two prisoners. I had a listening post
consisting of a lance-sergeant and three men at the
bottom of the hill, and could not understand how
they got up. Six days later I was awakened at dawn
to hear firing, and dashed outside. Guthrie was there
and shouted: 'OK sir, only another patrol' and without awaiting orders, dashed down the hill with
another man to try and get a prisoner. Poor Guthrie,
he realized too late that it was a big German attack
on the whole front. He ran into about twenty of them,
but bravely charged and was killed. I realized now by
the amount of firing that the whole of the battalion
was being attacked, and I was facing a company
attack. They were coming up the same way as the
patrol. They had murdered my listening post, consisting of one man on duty while the other three slept.
We found them dead afterwards, three men still with
their blankets wrapped round them. I decided to visit
my sections and ran from one to another with a
German machine gun following me around. That
chap was either a bad shot or nervous. When I got
back to my headquarters I received the most awful

shock; there was Giles (Bromley-Martin) lying outside dead. He was my best friend I had in the battalion and the sniper that got him, nearly got me.

After three hours of fierce fighting we got the upper hand, and finally counter-attacked and drove them off. The company killed fifty, wounded ninety of them and took 120 prisoners. Our casualties were two officers and nine other ranks. Leslie Wilson was the other officer killed leading a counter-attack. It took us two days to bury the dead.

2 Para, holding reverse slope positions on a very wide frontage, were attacked by Italian Alpini. Thanks to the excellent work by the French artillery in support, and the battalion's mortars and machine guns, they inflicted 150 casualties on the enemy and took eighty prisoners for the loss of one man dead and two wounded. When Frost reported this resounding success to brigade headquarters who were totally pre-occupied with the attack on 3 Para, they commented: 'Oh, have you been fighting too?' 1 Para had also done well, from reverse slope positions, with cunningly-sited machine guns. However, a neighbouring brigade position was penetrated by armour which, hooking behind 1st Parachute Brigade, reached their administrative area twelve miles behind.

After fighting on the right flank of 1st Army for nearly a month, the Parachute Brigade was moved on 5 March at very short notice to Tamera, on the other flank. The brigade was positioned astride the vital main road in the northern sector. Pearson found himself with only 300 men taking over from a full strength Guards battalion. His task – to hold Tamera station and the cork forest above it, overlooked by the large feature Jebel Bel. Realizing that with so few men he could not hold every yard of front, including Jebel Bel, he decided that he would fight a mobile, flexible battle. In company with his fellow commanding officers, he had learned that the Germans would attack in daylight, at last light and at first light, but hardly ever, in full strength, at night. So he ordered an intensive programme of patrolling as far forward as possible every night to harass the Germans and keep them awake. By day, he covered his front and flanks with standing patrols to watch for enemy attacks. The rifle companies were held back in company areas, and company commanders were responsible for finding routes forward to reinforce their fellow companies or to take the enemy in the flank. Once an attack was seen, Pearson would move his companies to hit the enemy where he least expected it.

It was here that the parachute battalions encountered their toughest adversaries, German parachute engineers under the command of Colonel Witzig. He was so formidable a foe that he was known by name in all British battalions that faced him. This is not common in war. Few officers below very high rank are known to the other side. For the next ten days, starting on 7 March, the Germans kept up an almost continuous series of attacks on 1 and 2 Para's positions in the cold and the pouring rain. The attacking force consisted of four German regiments, each about the size of a small brigade: the Barenthin Regiment, the Tunisian Regiment, Witzig's, and 10th Panzer Grenadiers. On 9 March Brigadier Down paid 1 Para a visit. Just before he arrived, the battalion was attacked rather half-heartedly. Down, who expressed disappointment at missing the battle, was assured by Pearson that he would get a battle on the morrow. Sure enough, the next day the Germans attacked in great strength. At a critical moment in the battle Pearson, without turning round, handed a message for Coxen to his runner standing behind him. The message was snatched out of his hand, and it was a second or two before Pearson realized that the runner racing off to deliver the message, heedless of enemy fire, was Down! The enemy pressed hard and broke through as far as battalion headquarters. All seemed lost until Sergeant Clements, gathering up a group of cooks, signallers and other HQ bottle-washers, all shouting 'Waho Mohammed', charged in with bayonet to restore the position. Pearson earned the second of his four DSOs at this time. He was a remarkable man by any standards and, like Witzig, came to be known by name by the opposition. Frost, no mean performer himself, wrote of him: 'Alastair had a wonderful flair both for planning and leadership. The battalion had a great technique through experience, and their battle procedure was as good as could be, but it was the almost uncanny instinct of their leader that so often brought them success when others failed.' Coxen: 'Alastair had a feel for battle, rather like a good scrum-half can read a game of rugby.' He also had another quality: 'Whenever he was about you stopped feeling so frightened. Because he was there, it would be all right,' remembers Major Mitchell, an Argyll and Sutherland Highlander, then one of the youngest private soldiers in 1 Para.

By 13 March the Corps Commander, realizing that the Germans were throwing the equivalent of a division at 1st Parachute Brigade, sent forward the Sherwood Foresters to take Jebel Bel and relieve the pressure on 1 Para. They almost reached the top but were beaten back with huge losses. That evening 1 Para were taken out of the line for a short rest. On 10 March, 2 Para were attacked by armour from 10th Panzer Division. The battalion was saved by the Luftwaffe, whose Stukas dive-bombed their own tanks.

Lieutenant Bentham of 3 Para, the brigade reserve, watched these major German attacks, in which he lost a number of good friends:

A few days later we left our positions and crossed over the valley and relieved a company of the 1st Battalion. This was an entirely different kettle of fish, as the positions were in the middle of intensely thick scrub which I could not even see over. On top of all this we were overlooked by the Germans, who could shell or mortar us at will. We lived in wet clothes and stood in trenches with a foot of water in the bottom. No one suffered as a result.

A week later a battalion of a county regiment relieved us, and we were out for a rest. Our rest lasted two days! The Boche had waited until we had gone to bed and then put in his attack. Our relief had withdrawn and we had to go up and cover their withdrawal. This we did successfully after a miserable day, the Germans pushing hard all the time, and we did not get out until midnight. My platoon went out on another sweep, collected four prisoners, and identified them as Panzer Grenadiers. We went back to a previously prepared line, but the county battalion had lost us fifteen miles of very valuable ground.

Under increasing pressure from the Germans, the British in the north pulled back. 1 Para covered the withdrawal in their sector. Coxen had a platoon of Irishmen from the Royal Ulster Rifles who had been sent forward to replace his losses after the Jebel Mansour battle. He promised them a battle on St Patrick's Day. On 17 March, his company was sent forward to the 2/5th Leicesters who were in a tight spot on the point of being outflanked during the general withdrawal. Coxen relieved the pressure on the Leicesters by ambushing the next German attack. He stopped it in its tracks by massing his brens together in a stop line, and while the enemy milled about, hit them in the flank with the rest of his company. Having offered to stay to cover the Leicester's withdrawal, provided they told him when they were about to go, he ran a telephone line back to their headquarters. Coxen takes up the story:

After a while, getting no reply and thinking that the

line had been cut, I sent back my signals corporal,
Platt, to investigate. He was a man with a limited
vocabulary. My telephone rang:

'They've f . . . d off!'

'Who have?'

'Those f. . . . rs.'

'Come on Platt, what are you talking about? '

'I'm in their f . . . ing HQ, and there's f . . . all
here. They've all f . . . ed off.'

And they had!

As 1 Para withdrew, a medical orderly Lance Corporal
Hewitt, was helping Company Sergeant Major Richards
who was badly wounded. Without warning they came
under mortar fire from the Leicesters. The battalion took
cover; Pearson saw Hewitt dragging Richards into a hole
in the ground and throwing himself on top. Hewitt was
killed. Richards survived. Pearson tried to get Hewitt
awarded the VC, but Hewitt was a conscientious objector
and debarred from promotion or awards. 2 Para, who were
last away, had a grim withdrawal, wading and swimming
down the River Oued el Medene under shell and mortar
fire all the way.

The last battles fought by the Parachute Brigade in
Tunisia were in the northern sector. On the night of 21
March, 3 Para captured Sidi Bou Della, known as the
'Bowler Hat', which had been lost by a battalion from
another brigade. By first light the following day 3 Para,
having exhausted their ammunition, were forced off the
hill. Pearson was in reserve. The Corps Commander,
Lieutenant General Alfrey, came forward and told him to
have a go. Pearson, who did not mince his words, even
with senior officers, replied, 'I am very tired, my soldiers
are very tired, and two battalions have failed. I will take
it, but not hold it because I do not have enough men.'
Pearson thought the BGS, Alfrey's chief of staff, was going

to have a fit at his Corps Commander being addressed thus! But Alfrey agreed, and 3 Para were ordered to follow up as soon as 1 Para had seized the position. Pearson decided to do it that very night.

Coxen's company was to lead the attack. The River Oued el Medene ran round two sides of the steep hill. Coxen spent the day looking at the objective from his side of the river. The hill was convex with a succession of false crests at about twenty yard intervals, therefore the enemy would have very short fields of fire. That night his company swam across and moved up the hill. He deployed his two leading platoons across the ridge leading up to the summit, taking care to avoid the natural tendency when attacking a hill to converge and present a bunched target. He walked along his leading platoons, and told them that when they came under fire they were to charge straight in because the range would be so short.

Coxen had arranged with Pearson that the German positions on the top would be shelled every hour at five minutes to the hour until midnight, starting at 7 pm. At midnight his company would follow up. He reasoned that being Germans, and battle-wise, they would take note of the timings, and after the first couple of times would get their heads down at about five minutes to the hour. That is exactly what happened. Coxen's company received only one burst of fire and only one of his men was wounded. The enemy ran, or were found asleep in their trenches. Pearson had one tense moment when the engineers dropped a heavy steel girder they were using to bridge the river for the two follow-up companies. The loud clang reverberated through the stillness of the African night, but there was no response from the enemy.

The other two companies moved onto the hill while Coxen's company advanced again. He decided to see if there were any enemy to his front, and went out with his batman. It was a bright moonlit night. After a while the batman whispered that they were being stalked. Coxen, taking a chance that they might be a patrol he had sent out earlier, challenged. He recalls: 'A voice said: "Glory be to God. I was just about to throw a grenade at ye!" It was Sergeant Birmingham of the RUR platoon. As they withdrew together, Birmingham said to me:

"What shall I do with the grenade, sorr?"

I replied "What do you mean?"

"Well," said Birmingham. "I've pulled the pin out!"

I said: "Don't bother me with it man, throw the bloody thing away somewhere?"

"Yes sorr," replied Birmingham, and he just turned round and threw it. We were out in the open, I shouted "Down!" and we all threw ourselves flat. The base plug whirred over me. For two pins I would have knocked his head off.'

On the reverse side of the feature was a cliff about thirty feet high bordering the river. Enemy shells could hit the top of the cliff, or the far side of the river, but not the water or beach under the cliff. After being relieved by 3 Para, all Coxen's men calmly went for a swim in the river while shells landed on the far bank.

The final series of attacks by 1st Parachute Brigade started at 10 pm on 27 March; but the next morning, 1 and 2 Para, with 3 Para in reserve on 'Bowler Hat', had captured their first objectives. Pearson had sufficient information about the enemy position to plan his attack, to hit the boundary between the Germans and the Italians. He had a long approach march at night. With Pearson's headquarters was a half-Arab half-Maltese Tunisian stationmaster who had attached himself to the battalion some time before. Pearson paid him, totally against regulations, out of the regimental institute funds. Pearson told the stationmaster to persuade a local Arab to lead the way for 500 cigarettes – 250 down, and 250 on arrival. At the first sound of gunfire the Arab disappeared, forfeiting his cigarettes! However, Pearson was right on course, and the Italians fled. When he reached his objective he swung to his right, going to the assistance of 2 Para who were in a tight spot.

German parachute engineers, under the redoubtable Witzig, put in successive counter-attacks against 2 Para. They held but took heavy casualties. Later in the same day both parachute battalions pushed on towards their second objectives. The fighting continued to be heavy, and A and B Companies of 3 Para were put under the command of 2 Para to reinforce them. Bentham:

> We were told that the company was to support the 2nd Battalion in a big attack. The idea was that we were to follow them up and hold the ground that they took. The night arrived and in we went supported by the fire of eighty-four guns! We were waiting in a railway cutting for a signal from the 2nd Battalion to come up, and who should come down the line but Dickie (Lieutenant Dover 2 Para). He had stepped on a land-mine and received a bad wound in the leg. I had a chat with him and saw him off back to the medical people – I was rather glad he was out of it as the fighting was very severe. Shortly after he had gone we received orders to go up the hill. The fighting was intense when we arrived, and we found ourselves in the thick of it. I was acting as second-in-command of the company and ensconced myself with the signallers in the mouth of a small cave, so that we could do our work without much threat from the many shells and mortar bombs that were flying about. The situation was rather critical, we were fighting parachute engineers under Colonel Witzig, and they were not giving ground.

At one particularly tense moment during this battle, when Witzig's paras were putting in yet another counter-attack, Frost ordered everybody to fix bayonets. At this point one humorist started handing round a box of Italian grenades, crying: 'Cigarettes, chocolates.' 2 Para, although down to the strength of one company, captured their second objective that night. Bentham again:

> We made one final assault led by Colonel Frost and broke through. The company pushed through the 2nd (Battalion) and followed Jerry up. The Germans went right back, we took many prisoners and at the end of two days had beaten them back twenty miles, a great achievement for a brigade that had been in almost continuous action for eight weeks. We finished up by taking Sedjenane, and then stopped for a breather. By now we were all in high spirits and were all for going on to Bizerta, only twenty-five miles away!

The Parachute Brigade was well ahead of the brigades on its flanks. At one stage in the advance, 1 Para, having secured its own objective, sent patrols onto the objective of the neighbouring infantry brigade to establish contact. There was no one there, neither friend nor foe. At that moment Alfrey appeared, riding on the pillion of a motorbike. He told Pearson that the infantry brigade was still on its start-line, which they should have crossed forty-eight hours before. The Parachute Brigade halted and dug in. By now the soldiers were weary, and having survived so far, with the end of the campaign in sight, less enthusiastic about taking risks. Alfrey ordered Pearson to capture a prisoner; always a dangerous business, however competent the battalion. Pearson told Coxen to take two platoons for the task, adding that he would go as well; unusual for a commanding officer, but Pearson was no ordinary commanding officer. He reckoned on taking several casualties on this enterprise. Having made their preparations, Pearson decided to delay going out until a standing patrol under Lieutenant Anderson came in. To his delight, Anderson walked in with a German officer who had been supervising a wiring party, unbeknown to him under the interested gaze of Anderson and his patrol. It was a lovely sunny day, the German went some distance from his men and fell asleep. With great skill Anderson and his patrol crept forward and collared him without alerting the wiring party. It would have been all too easy for Anderson to have done nothing on the basis that it was very risky. He was awarded a well-deserved MC.

In mid-April all battalions were moved back to Algiers for a rest. They had each completed a parachute operation and had fought for five months as infantry. They had captured over 3,500 prisoners and fought in every British sector in Tunisia, suffering 1,700 casualties. Somewhat to their chagrin, their presence in the hottest fighting and their remarkable achievements went unreported at home. for security reasons reporters were not allowed in their parts of the battle area. A far cry from the 1980s and the ever-present TV camera! Their enemies were only too well aware of their presence, and bestowed upon them the title of Red Devils, some say because of the colour of their berets, and some because the red mud of Sedjenane stained their faces so they looked like Red Indians. Whatever the reason, 'Rote Teufel' they were to the Germans, and, as General Browning said in his congratulatory signal to the Brigade: 'Such distinctions given by the enemy are seldom won in battle except by the finest fighting troops.'

The title was soon applied to all British parachute battalions. The battle cry 'Waho Mohammed' was taken up by the whole brigade, copied, it is said, from the Arabs when relaying messages to each other from hill-top to hill-top. The Arabs in their turn referred to the parachute soldiers as 'the men with tails' because the tail of the airborne camouflage smock kept breaking loose from its press studs and hung down behind the wearer, which amused the Arabs but infuriated the more dress-conscious!

The entry for 22 April 1943 in the 2 Para war diary records the pride in the battalion's achievements:

Train arrives at Chardimeau on the Algerian/Tunisian border, and with its arrival the Tunisian story comes to an end. It had started nearly five months ago when the battalion had dropped at Depienne, and since that date, with the exception of six days rest at Tabarka in mid March, the battalion has never been out of the line. It had fought under different commanders, in almost every theatre of the central and northern Tunisian fighting. It had suffered heavily on several occasions, and on like occasions dealt heavily with its opponents. It had fought as infantry with none of the amenities such as carriers, transport and anti-tank guns which an infantry battalion expects. On occasions it had attacked with success, but more often it had carried out a singularly aggressive form of defence, often against heavy odds in the Tunisian mountains; and for its labours, earned with the 1st and 3rd Battalions the name of the Red Devils among the Germans. It came out of the line with a total strength of fourteen officers and 346 other ranks, out of an establishment of twenty-four officers and 588 other ranks, having already absorbed some 230 reinforcements in January; a total casualty percentage of eighty per cent of establishment.

Pearson, Coxen and two others were the only four officers in 1 Para, out of the twenty or so who had dropped at Souk el Arba, to remain with the battalion without a break from the beginning to the end of the Tunisian campaign.

As the train carrying 1 and 2 Para on its way to Algiers was slowly trundling past one of the prisoner-of-war camps

outside the city the German prisoners, seeing the red
berets on the men leaning out of the windows, turned out
in their thousands. They ran towards the railway line,
cheering and throwing their hats in the air. 'That,' said
Frost, 'was the tribute that I liked best.'

CHAPTER 4

By Air and Sea

While 1st Parachute Brigade had been fighting in Tunisia, the 4th Parachute Brigade was forming at the other end of the Mediterranean under Brigadier Hackett. His battalions were 156 Parachute Battalion and the 10th and 11th Parachute Battalions, 156 Parachute Battalion had formed in India as the British Parachute Battalion, in the Indian Parachute Brigade, and was originally numbered 151 Parachute Battalion. The battalion had been raised in 1941 by Lieutenant Colonel Lindsay, the first soldier to parachute from the back of a Whitley. There was a flood of volunteers from British battalions all over India, many of whom, before the Japanese entered the war, saw little prospect of action. The aircraft available for parachute training were ancient Vickers Valentia biplanes, and with fourteen parachutes to train a battalion, progress was slow. Other equipment was in short supply, and they parachuted bareheaded for lack of helmets. In India until about 1942 it was a chargeable offence for any British soldier to appear out of doors without a topi for fear of instant sunstroke! To begin with, 151 jumped with their topis stuffed into the front of their jumping jackets. Bulging like pregnant mums, their bizarre appearance was enhanced by parachuting in shorts. Lindsay, who was a stimulating trainer and was to prove an outstanding battalion commander in battle, was unconventional. The Australian bush hat eventually replaced the topi. He also caused muttering among British officers outside the battalion by ordering his men to wear their shirts outside their trousers to reduce prickly heat rash.

When it was decided to form another parachute brigade in the Middle East, 151 was chosen to be the nucleus and changed its name to 156 Parachute Battalion in an attempt to confuse the enemy. The brigade they left consisted of one Indian and one Gurkha battalion that became the nucleus of the Indian Parachute Division, which never carried out a parachute operation as a division. When 156 arrived in the Middle East they immediately became subject to the theatre rules for repatriation, which meant that NCOs and soldiers with more than a certain length of unbroken service overseas were sent back to England. 156 Para's loss was 6th Airborne Division's gain. 156 recruited in the Middle East and their newly-joined men included some with battle experience in the desert and elsewhere, so on balance they did not do too badly out of the arrangement.

The 2nd Battalion The Royal Sussex Regiment, chosen to convert to a parachute battalion, produced a mere one hundred volunteers, so it was decided to use these men to form the 10th Parachute Battalion under Lieutenant Colonel Smyth and leave the majority of the 2nd Royal Sussex to go their own way. A recruiting drive had to be started all over the Middle East to find men to replace the repatriations in 156 Para and build up 10 and 11 Para. After a slow start volunteers started coming in from places as far afield as Khartoum and Malta. There was less incentive for men in the Middle East to volunteer as there was already fighting to be had. Most of the training in the early days was done in Palestine and Cyprus. During a demonstration to the Emir of what was then Transjordan, C Company of 156 Para 'captured' a fort belonging to the Arab Legion and the Emir presented the flag to Major Powell, the company commander. It was carried by the company in Italy and at Arnhem. It even accompanied the

company second-in-command Captain Bell into captivity
after Arnhem. He brought it to England after the war.

Many members of this brigade had a frustrating war.
Having volunteered for parachuting as a way of getting
into the fight, some as early as 1941, they found themselves, except for a short period in Italy, training, and
waiting for operations that never materialized, while to
their chagrin many of the units that they had left were in
action before them. Many were pre-war regulars. When
151 formed about ninety per cent of the other ranks and
all the NCOs were regular soldiers. Even just before
Arnhem, the Commanding Officer, the Adjutant, all rifle
company commanders, some captains, and all warrant
officers were regulars, an almost unique situation in the
British Army at the time. Their moment came at Arnhem,
after which the brigade ceased to exist; a long overture to
a short and devastating finale.

However, Arnhem was fifteen months away when in
June 1943 4th Parachute Brigade travelled the length of
the Mediterranean to join 1st Airborne Division at Sousse
in Tunisia. They left 11 Para behind in Palestine. This
battalion carried out a number of minor parachute operations in the Eastern Mediterranean between August and
December 1943 before sailing to join 4th Parachute Brigade in England. 156 Para were still wearing their bush
hats, of which they were rather proud, when they joined
the 1st Airborne Division, commanded by Major General
Hopkinson, a glider enthusiast. Hopkinson ordered them
to parade for his inspection wearing red berets. After much
searching, the Quartermaster found them stuffed away at
the back of his store. The battalion duly paraded wearing
them like pancakes! Hopkinson spoke to them, stating that
the first thing they should learn was to wear their berets
properly. A voice at the back was heard to say: 'We don't
want the f . . . ing things!'

The 1st Airborne Division was complete in North Africa

by early June 1943. During the fly-out of the Division, Air Commodore Norman was killed in an air crash, and as the Official Account says: 'So died Nigel Norman, to whose vision and steadfastness of purpose the Airborne Forces owe so much. "Why must you always want a hundred percent?" a high ranking officer once peevishly inquired of him. Norman's answer is not recorded.'

Between May and the end of June, 1st and 2nd Parachute Brigades trained hard on battalion and brigade exercises and parachuting. They completed 8,913 jumps, including one unsuccessful attempt to drop a donkey. The accident rate was low. Despite the hard ground, only two men were killed and 100 seriously injured. At this time the technique of dropping with rifle or light machine-gun attached to each paratrooper was pioneered by 2 Para. This was a great improvement on jumping armed with just a sten or pistol and having to find a container, possibly in the dark, before arming oneself with something more effective. As well as field training, some attended language training at Sousse. One wag remembers:

> We thought we'd learn phrases essential to the winning of the war such as 'Hand over those binos Fritz, for you the war is over' or, 'Let's have that splendid watch, that example of Teutonic genius, as you won't need to tell the time where you're going' or, 'Tell us the joke about the thousand-year Reich' and 'Your German uniform is required for our RSM, he's going into the POW cage with you,' But of course nothing useful like that; we picked up such gems as 'the grass is green', 'the brother is small' or 'Good morning mein Herr Gefreiter, if you will sit with the postillion in the pencil box of my aunt, I will purchase a beer from the hausfrau who has been struck by lightning!'

In June 1943 the commanding officers of battalions in the Division were given the outline of their part in the

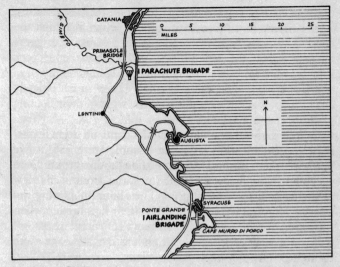

South east Sicily.

forthcoming assault on Sicily. The Division was ordered
to carry out three successive airborne assaults ahead of
13 British Corps, the leading formation of Montgomery's
British 8th Army. There were not enough aircraft for the
whole Division to drop on the same day, so the first assault
would be on the night before the sea-borne landings and
the others on two following nights. The three objectives
were: 1st Air-Landing Brigade – Ponte Grande, a road
bridge south of Syracuse, and the port of Syracuse itself;
2nd Parachute Brigade – a road bridge south of Augusta
and the port of Augusta; 1st Parachute Brigade – the
Primasole Bridge over the River Simeto. All three were
on the route up the east coast of Sicily towards 8th Army's
planned objectives of Catania and Messina.

The first away in 144 gliders on the night of 9 July
1943 was 1st Air-Landing Brigade under the command of
Brigadier Hicks. Because of the risk of enemy flak, the

tug aircraft, which were needed for subsequent operations, were ordered to release their gliders before reaching the coast. Many did so far too early; some because of trigger-happy sailors in the Allied Fleet. As the official report puts it so laconically: 'Seventy-eight gliders landed in the sea.' 'All is not well, Bill,' said Brigadier Hicks to his Brigade Major as they scrambled out onto the wing of their floating glider and swam ashore.

Of the sixty-one gliders that did land on terra firma, scattered over a wide area, the majority were within five miles of the Landing Zone. Although the ground was rocky and studded with small trees and stone walls, few of the passengers were injured. The glider pilots were not so lucky. Several were killed or had their legs broken when the noses of their gliders hit stone walls or large rocks. Of the 490 casualties in the Air-Landing Brigade, 252 were drowned. Of the 288 glider pilots, 101 were killed, wounded or missing. Nevertheless, by 11 pm the Ponte Grande was captured intact by Lieutenant Withers and his platoon of 2nd Battalion South Staffords. By morning a total of eighty air-landed soldiers had made the bridge. After holding it against an enemy battalion until 3.30 pm, by which time they had exhausted their ammunition, the few survivors were overrun. There was no sight or sound of 13 Corps, who, advancing from the beach-head, should have arrived at 10 am or earlier. The leading battalion of 13 Corps recaptured the bridge intact at 4.30 that afternoon.

The other soldiers of the Air-Landing Brigade who landed in the wrong place or had swum ashore had not been idle. Their determined and aggressive actions had created considerable mayhem over a wide area. That said, it was a disastrous affair and augured ill for future glider operations. In particular, this and the parachute operations in Sicily were to have a profound effect on USAAF thinking on night airborne operations, and their experiences in

Normandy served to confirm their view that large-scale airborne operations were possible only in daylight. As will become apparent, this preference for day operations on the part of the USAAF was one of the major ingredients in the disaster at Arnhem.

At 5.05 pm the following evening 2nd Parachute Brigade were standing by their aircraft at the airborne base in North Africa, waiting for the confirmatory order to take off for the parachute operation at Augusta. It was to be the Brigade's first taste of action, and everybody was tense and excited. Then, to their bitter disappointment, after a twenty-four-hour postponement the operation was cancelled; the road bridge and the port were already in British hands. It was fortunate that the drop did not take place; the DZs, selected from maps and air photographs, abounded with rocks and gullies. Casualties would have been heavy.

It was now the turn of 1st Parachute Brigade. A few days before, intelligence was received that the air defences in the Primasole Bridge area had been thickened up considerably. Beaufighters based at Malta attacked flak batteries and searchlights in the neighbourhood of the DZs by night, but no steps were taken to provide close air support for the Brigade from first light. The need to support lightly equipped airborne troops, who lacked artillery, with fighter-ground attack aircraft does not seem to have occurred to the planners. If it did, nothing was done. The first Parachute Brigade had a good, simple plan; 1 Para was to capture the Primasole Bridge while 2 Para blocked the approaches from the south and 3 Para did the same from the north. Eight anti-tank guns would be landed in gliders close to the bridge, once it was secured. There were four DZs: two for 1 Para, one each side of and close to the bridge; and one each for the other two battalions, about 1,000 yards from their objectives. The brigade was told that 13 Corps would link up with them as soon as possible on the morning after the drop. This was critical because there were German and Italian units in the vicinity plus some armour.

After a twenty-four-hour delay the brigade took off from North Africa starting at 7.01 pm on 13 July. Frost, commanding 2 Para, was very happy with the task and the DZ he had been given. There were plenty of landmarks to help the pilots find their way to the right place, and the three features he was to secure overlooked the road he was to block and should be easy to locate and defend. He gave them the nick-names Johnny 1, Johnny 2 and Johnny 3. He had an additional reason to feel confident: half his headquarters and most of A Company were being carried by one of the best USAAF squadrons whose commander had guaranteed that he would get them to the right place.

Frost and his stick landed, as predicted by the squadron commander, close to the correct DZ, as did most of Major Lonsdale's A Company. But very few others did. The first problem was anti-aircraft fire, again from trigger-happy Allied naval forces. Because of poor navigation the Dakotas strayed into the danger zone over the invasion fleet and were fired on. After taking evasive action some were so disorientated that they lost their bearings; a few turned back at this stage. Having arrived near the DZ, the Dakotas were fired on by enemy flak. Again they took evasive action and again some were so disorientated they missed the DZ by miles. For the soldiers in aircraft taking evasive action it was a nightmare. As the aircraft weaved, banked and bounced, heavily-laden men were hurled on the floor and against the sides of the aircraft, injuring some badly. Others were tangled in their static lanes, making it impossible to jump and blocking the exit for men behind them in the stick. The dark bellies of the aircraft were lit only by the streams of tracer flashing up past the windows and door, and the glow of the red 'ready' and green 'go' lights. The roar of the engines and the slipstream past the open door made conversation impossible, except by yelling in the person's ear. Less than twenty per cent of the brigade were dropped according to plan, and nearly thirty per cent were taken willy-nilly back to North Africa. Of the total of 1,856 all ranks who left the launching airfield, only 295 were available for the battle. 'Ground operations could not go according to plan' is the bleak comment in the official report.

Frost waited at his DZ until his party was about 100-strong and it was apparent that no more of his battalion would be arriving. By now it was well past the time to move off. He had pulled a ligament in his knee on landing and it was becoming extremely painful. There was no sign of Dover, his Adjutant, or of his second-in-command. He led off towards the objective, stopping only to wish Brigadier Lathbury a happy birthday. At the foot of his objective Frost met Lieutenant Frank. He and three sticks had dropped near the correct DZ, but had failed to contact the main body of the battalion. Using their initiative, under Frank's command they attacked and took Johnny 1 by themselves, capturing 130 Italians – an example of how highly-trained, well briefed and motivated men will carry on despite chaos and losses to fulfil their mission. Men of this calibre turn confusion and darkness to their advantage, while defenders of lesser ability are often paralysed into inactivity. Johnny 2, it transpired, was held by some German Paratroopers who unknown to anybody had dropped on 2 Para's DZ not long before Frost.

1 Para dropped at 10.30 pm, ten minutes late. By 2.15 the next morning Captain Rann and fifty men, all he could scrape together, had captured the Primasole Bridge, taken two half-tracks and fifty Italian prisoners. The USAAF captain of Pearson's aircraft reassured him before take-off that they would get to the right place. 'No problem.' Pearson was also glad to see that, unlike the majority of Dakotas, there was a qualified navigator in the cockpit.

They were flying over the sea quite low and Pearson was reading when flak from friendly ships below starting streaking up past the windows:

> The Dakota seemed to climb like a Spitfire. After a while I noticed that we were flying parallel to the coast, which was rather strange. I took off my parachute, which drew some odd looks from the rest of the stick! But it was the only way I could get to the cockpit past the long-range fuel tanks at the forward end of the fuselage. These were not self-sealing – not a happy thought! In the cockpit I found the pilot and the navigator holding their heads in their hands and saying: 'We're not going into that!'. 'That' was flak, and on the ground, what looked like the flames of burning Dakotas.
>
> I pulled out my pistol and told them to get on with it. They pointed out that if I killed them, there would be no one to fly the aircraft. I told them that in my stick was an ex-RAF pilot, dismissed for some misdemeanour, now a private soldier. When I asked him if he could fly the Dakota, he replied that he could, but not land it. My response was to say; 'you won't have to, we're all jumping out!' The American saw the point and turned towards Sicily, and I returned, put on my parachute and hooked up. We must have been flying well over jumping speed and diving. I was jumping number ten, and my parachute seemed to open just before I hit the ground. Everyone in front of me in the stick was OK, but numbers eleven to twenty were all killed or very badly injured. I landed right on the DZ.

By 4 am there were about 120 all ranks of 1 Para at the Bridge, the demolition fuses had been cut, and the charges thrown into the river. About two hours later three six-pounder anti-tank guns had arrived in gliders and a captured Italian anti-tank gun had been pressed into service. One medium machine gun, two three-inch mortars and three hand-held anti-tank weapons (PIAT) completed the support for the battalion. No radios had arrived.

Coxen, now commanding R Company, was in the leading Dakota of the 1 Para aircraft stream. He was jumping number three behind two men who carried the beacons for the gliders bringing in the anti-tank guns. He put them ahead of him in the stick because they had the heaviest loads. Coxen was unhooked and standing by the door. It was a moonlit night and as the aircraft crossed the coast he recognized the scimitar-shaped hook of the Simeto River east of the Primasole Bridge. Coxen went back and hooked up. The Dakota banked away and flew out to sea again. He unhooked, went forward to the cockpit and asked what was up. The pilot replied that they were four minutes early. Coxen told him to get back in at once.

He returned and hooked up, having told number one in the stick to tell him when they crossed the coast. They waited. Nothing! Then both the red and green light went on together. The Dakota banked sharply to port and numbers one and two were shot out of the door. The rest were thrown to the floor in a heap. As the Dakota banked and weaved the rest of the stick got out before the crew chief stopped the last man. Coxen was tipped out, head first on his knees. The drop was very low and Coxen's batman broke both his legs. Unknown to the paratroopers, they were dropped seventeen miles south of the DZ.

Coxen marched north-east hoping to hit the bridge but struck the coast. Here he and his party had a battle with a coastal battery, taking seventy Italian prisoners. He did not want them and ordered them to remain on the coast. But they followed him like dogs. Not wishing to be caught in daylight in the open coastal plain, he worked west back into the hills and struck north, eventually finding himself that night in the 2nd Battalion's position south of the bridge. On the way he had a small fracas with some German tanks. Coxen had actually been dropped on the same DZ as some German parachutists. When he went to open what he thought was one of his containers he found it belonged to the Germans.

The drop of 3 Para had been the worst of all. By 4 am the battalion strength totalled about two platoons, all with 1 Para at the bridge. It was impossible with these numbers to establish the blocking position to the north of the bridge. Brigadier Lathbury, with his Brigade Major and part of his headquarters, had dropped among enemy positions. Having extricated himself from this he had been wounded by a grenade while going forward to see if the bridge was held. He established his headquarters on the south bank of the river. They had only one working radio but were unable to contact 13 Corps who were unaware that the bridge had been captured, but was being held by the equivalent of three companies instead of three battalions. Quick relief was now even more important than before, but as yet there was no way of telling 13 Corps.

Soon after first light, Lonsdale took his platoon commanders forward to see what was on Johnny 2. The reconnaissance did not last long; they were fired on by Germans from the area of Johnny 2. The next four hours were extremely frustrating for 2 Para. Without mortars or artillery they had nothing with which to reply to the German machine guns and mortars. Lonsdale could see the enemy forming up for their attacks in the area of the small wood, but could only watch impotently. Fortunately each attack came the same way, and when within range was beaten off by small arms fire. There was nothing to stop them trying an out-flanking move, but they never did. Eventually the long grass on Johnny 1 caught fire and the flames forced the British paratroopers back into a tight perimeter, while the smoke covered the movements of the Germans. It was impossible to dig in in the rocky ground, and casualties in the battalion began to mount. By 9 am the battalion was in some difficulty as their light weapons were having no effect on the enemy. At this point, having been trying since day-break, Captain Hodge, the Naval Gunfire Forward Observation Officer with the battalion, finally managed to establish contact with a British cruiser offshore. Almost immediately the six-inch shells from the cruiser started pounding the enemy who were giving 2 Para such trouble, and by 10 am had stopped them moving forward, although they kept up sporadic fire until the afternoon. The depleted battalion now had two officers and forty other ranks killed, and about the same number wounded. During this battle the Brigade Major, after trying all morning, suddenly managed to get a message through to 4th Armoured Brigade, the leading brigade of 13 Corps, that the bridge was held. Contact was immediately lost, never to be re-established. Meanwhile 2 Para had taken 100 Italian prisoners and Lieutenant Panter, the mortar officer whose mortars had not arrived, had discovered an Italian howitzer battery. Panter and his mortarmen brought the guns into action. Unfortunately they started attracting counter-battery fire, so Frost ordered them to stop. The battalion had been out of touch with Brigade Headquarters except for a visit by the wounded Lathbury earlier in the afternoon.

At 1.10 pm, preceded by a shelling and an airstrike, the German paratroops attacked the forty men of 3 Para just north of the bridge. By 2 pm they had held two attacks at company strength by Germans and Italians. An hour later the enemy put in a battalion attack supported by guns firing at the bridge over open sights. At 5 pm both 1 and 3 Para had been ordered to withdraw back on to the south bank. But sufficient fire was brought to bear on the enemy to prevent them from reaching the bridge. The enemy started an outflanking movement crossing the river to the east of the bridge. Ammunition was running out, the positions held by the British were becoming very exposed in the burning reeds and cornfields, there was no sign of the relief force, and Lathbury was out of touch with 2 Para. At 7.35 pm, judging that the position had become untenable and unaware that the leading tanks of the 4th Armoured Brigade were only one and a half miles away, Lathbury ordered a withdrawal in small parties to 2 Para's position. Pearson demurred. Last light was not far away and he told Lathbury that the Germans were not night fighters. In his opinion, as darkness fell the attacks would die down. However, Lathbury was adamant and repeated the order. Pearson, his batman, and his provost sergeant did not cross the river immediately. He scouted the river bank until he found an unmarked ford, crossed, and mentally filed away its position for future reference. At about 7.45 pm Lonsdale saw some tanks approaching: 'I thought I'd better say my prayers. Fortunately they were 44th RTR and the fellow who stuck his head out of the turret of the leading tank was in the First XV at Sandhurst with me.' This troop of Sherman tanks of 4th Armoured Brigade motored into 2 Para's perimeter followed at midnight by more tanks and a company of the 9th Battalion Durham Light Infantry (DLI) The Durhams had marched about twenty miles that day in the dust and heat of a Sicilian mid-summer and were very tired.

As 2 Para saw the parties of men moving back they attracted their attention by waving and shouting. Major Lonsdale was particularly effective in persuading some men from the other two battalions to withdraw no further. Soon they had so many men in their position that they had to invite their Italian prisoners to leave for the night, but told them to be back in the morning!

'We went back and I got hit in the back of the neck,' related Corporal Stanion, who was at the northern end of the bridge.

I was knocked out for some time. When I came to I saw a couple of German machine-gunners in the ditch where our troops should have been. A shell burst in front of me and under cover of this I ran back to the bridge. The battalion had gone. Some Italians I met with tried to explain that they had gone over to the other side. I could not cross the bridge because it was under fire, so I went into the reeds and there ran into some Jerries and was captured. I sat there for an hour or two while they argued amongst themselves as to who was to take me back. Then apparently our chaps started firing into the reeds. Two Jerries got hit in the head straight away. The others ran back and I crawled along through the reeds, which were smouldering in parts. I got down to a point where they went into the water, into which I slipped and dog-paddled over to the other side, where I lay. I was in full view of both sides and feared that if I tried to identify myself I would be shot. I lay there waiting for darkness to come.

The only Germans to cross the bridge that night were a company of parachute engineers.

Pearson joined Frost during the night. Early the next morning Frost and Pearson had a grandstand view of a frontal assault on the bridge by 9 DLI which was bloodily repulsed by the Germans and the parachute engineers withdrew. At this point Lathbury, in considerable pain from his wounds, arrived and met the commander of 4th Armoured Brigade, who announced his intention of putting in another frontal assault on the bridge. Pearson was present:

I said: 'I suppose you want to see another battalion written off?'

The commander of the 4th Armoured Brigade said: 'How would you do it?'

'I can do it with the minimum of casualties. I want 2,000 yards of white tape. I will take the battalion commander and two company commanders with me.'

That night I tied one end of the tape to a tree and walked forward, having sent the provost sergeant and my batman ahead to the ford we had used the evening before. As we approached the river bank a fellow in the DLI fired his weapon by mistake and killed another man. I felt like killing him!

At the ford I told my batman to cross with torch and flash if it was clear.

'Who, me sir?' he said.

'Yes, you, and if it is clear go on to the bridge.'

He did and there was no one there. I suggested to the commanding officer of the DLI that he should get his first two companies forward to the edge of some scrub beyond the bridge before first light, and get his reserve company up as quickly as possible. He failed to do this, and althought the battalion took the bridge they were hammered the next morning.

The DLI fought with great gallantry, and were bitterly contested by the German paratroopers. Eventually the Geordie soldiers of the DLI cleared the north bank and the way over the Simeto was open.

Later that morning 1st Parachute Brigade was withdrawn to Syracuse and eventually back to Sousse. Afterwards, Frost was to say of the Primasole operation that, following on from the Air-Landing Brigade's débâcle, it was yet another humiliating disaster for airborne forces. The Airborne Division had hoped to play the same star part in Sicily and Italy as 1st Parachute Brigade had in Tunisia. Now they were all back in North Africa, having suffered heavy losses and in most cases failed to get to their objectives. In his view the American and British Airborne Divisions should have been landed on the

Catanian plain, if necessary in three lifts for lack of aircraft to get everybody in on one day. There were excellent beaches debouching onto the Catanian plain, and such a plan might have shortened the Sicilian campaign. The airborne weapon had again been used unimaginatively. There was a marked lack of professionalism in the planning for the division's operations in Sicily and later in Italy in headquarters 1st Airborne Division from Hopkinson downwards. Frost, who temporarily commanded 1st Parachute Brigade in Lathbury's absence in hospital, ran a post-mortem of the Sicily operation for the benefit of the USAAF to show them exactly how wide they had dropped their sticks. They were glad to come and learn from their mistakes. Headquarters 1st Airborne Division showed no interest. Out of a total of 116 aircraft carrying 1st Parachute Brigade, only thirty dropped their sticks on the correct DZs. A further nine dropped within half a mile of the DZs, and forty-eight over half a mile from the DZs.

That said, the 1st Parachute Brigade had captured their objective in spite of all that had occurred and had held it for longer than had been ordered. Even after they had been forced to abandon the bridge, by removing the charges, and continuing to dominate the approaches from the south, they were able to ensure that the bridge was eventually recaptured in working order. It was no fault of the 1st Parachute Brigade that most of them were dropped in the wrong place or not dropped at all. Among the many valuable lessons learned was the importance of having parachuting surgeons well forward. 1st Parachute Brigade's Main Dressing Station treated 109 casualties during the twenty-four hours or so of the battle, and thirty-five surgical operations were performed in 21 operating hours by two surgeons. The ability to use captured enemy weapons also proved useful. These and many other points, including the need for pathfinders to drop ahead of the main force to mark the DZs, were to be put to good use in three great airborne operations that followed.

Two key lessons were not learned. First, the difficulty of forecasting how long it would take for an advancing armoured force to link up with airborne troops landed ahead. This failure to allow for delays caused by what Clausewitz calls the 'friction of war' was to have tragic results in 1st Airborne Division's next, and last, operation. Second, the value of close air support for airborne troops, and hence the need for the division to have its own teams with communications to call for and control fighter ground-attack aircraft. The Germans did it better. In Sicily, according to Frost, they put OPs in behind the Allied lines with radios to call in ground-attack aircraft. But the Luftwaffe was in essence a tactical airforce, whose raison d'être was support of the ground forces. The RAF and the USAAF, with some notable exceptions, burdened with the now discredited theories of Trenchard and Mitchell, were slower to understand that in land operations they were a supporting arm.

While the division was resting and re-training in North Africa, a steady stream of men who had been dropped wide of the DZs reported in. One of the most remarkable was Captain Dover, Frost's Adjutant. He and his stick were dropped on the upper slopes of Mount Etna, twenty-five miles from the DZ. During his descent he had noticed a bright glow below him but thought it was a fire on the DZ. He had a very heavy landing among the jagged lava rocks and was unconscious for a time. When the morning mist cleared he realized that the glow he had seen was the crater of Etna. Eventually he found only four members of his stick. 'Some probably had not survived their landing – the crater was not far away. None of us had had previous experience of jumping onto a volcano!'

He decided that as they had probably missed the battle, the best way of getting back to their friends was to wait for their own side to advance to them. However, rather than do nothing they would do their best to harry the enemy. They patrolled to find food, at first without success, although they did find water. After five days, two of the party decided to attempt to regain the British lines. They were never seen again. Dover and Corporal Wilson, a signaller from Brigade Headquarters, then embarked upon a series of adventures. They killed a German sentry and took his weapon, ammunition and grenades. Following this they cut as many of the telephone wires along the main road as they could. Later they raided a German swill bin for food, deciding that it was likely to be cleaner than a British one! On the way back they found an apple tree which was to provide their only source of food for the next twenty-three days. A few days later they ambushed a German half-track by throwing a grenade into the cab. The half-track blocked the road for the following column of vehicles. Dover and Wilson then had the satisfaction of seeing two Spitfires on a random sweep finish off the remainder. On another day they killed a despatch rider by stretching a wire across the road. Although the Germans stepped up their patrols, they never succeeded in catching the intrepid pair.

Eventually, unable to stand the unrelieved diet of apples any longer – 'our extremities felt red hot' – they stole two eggs and a loaf of bread from a farm. When they returned the next night the Sicilian farmer was waiting for them. He took them in and hid them for five days until on 5 August, hearing sounds of battle quite close, they decided to chance it and set off to find their own side. When they did so they were fired at by a patrol of the Durham Light Infantry. Dover threw his red beret into the air, whereupon the leading scout shouted: 'Are you paras?' 'No you stupid bastards – we're the babes in the wood!' yelled back Wilson. This did the trick. Within four days they were back with their units. Dover was awarded the Military

Cross and Wilson the Military Medal. Frost wrote to
Dover's father: 'His performance is an epic and he set an
example which few men of any nation could equal. He
has just shown everybody here that there should be no
such word as "defeat".'

Sicily was the last airborne operation carried out by 1st
Airborne Division in the Mediterranean. Although the
division was held back ready for airborne operations, none
was forthcoming. 4th Parachute Brigade was ordered to
prepare an operation in support of the landings at Salerno,
but this was given to a regiment of the 82nd US Airborne
Division. There were also plans for what Brigadier Hackett
called 'more puddle-hopping operations' close to the
Straits of Messina. He produced an imaginative plan to
drop his brigade on a number of DZs in northern Italy
with the task of blocking several choke points on the
German reinforcement routes south; these were never put
into effect. General Alexander, the Commander-in-Chief,
needed a force of lightly-equipped troops who could be
transported in warships to seize the port of Taranto in
south-east Italy and advance north providing protection
on the right flank of 8th Army, debouching from their
beachheads at Messina. The division sailed from Bizerta
in ships of the 1st Cruiser Squadron, and on 9 September
took the port unopposed. Headquarters 4th Parachute
Brigade and 10 Para travelled in the cruiser *HMS Penelope*.
Jeeps and anti-tank guns littered the deck. On the way in
to Taranto they passed the Italian battle fleet sailing to
surrender at Malta. Just in case, the cruiser squadron was
ordered to train their guns on the Italians. The gunnery
officer of *Penelope*, realizing that his guns could not train
outboard because of the jeeps and other impedimenta,
rushed down from the bridge in a panic and ordered the
soldiers to throw their vehicles and guns overboard. They
ignored him. The only casualties occurred when the mine-
layer *HMS Abdiel* blew up on a mine and 130 all ranks of

6 Para were drowned, including the commanding officer; an inauspicious introduction to action for the battalion and the rest of 2nd Parachute Brigade.

Because the Germans were retreating and there was still some doubt about which side the more fanatical Italians supported, the situation was fluid and it was often difficult to establish the position of the front line. Thus the advance by 1st Airborne Division consisted of what the official account calls 'nine days of interesting though not very heavy fighting'. There were moments when it must have seemed a very lighthearted affair compared with what had gone before in North Africa and Sicily. Such was the attack on the town of Mottola carried out by 156 Para. Some drove up in jeeps and bicycles while C Company arrived in requisitioned civilian buses. The leading bus flew the flag given to the company by the Emir of Transjordan. 156 Para were on their way to seize the airfield at Gioia del Colle so that the RAF could fly in fighters. The Germans blocked the main axis about a mile south of the airfield. The battalion fixed them on the axis and swung round with a neat flanking attack, supported by their highly efficient mortar platoon, taking a considerable number of prisoners. Although Frost says that 4th Parachute Brigade, of which 156 Para were a part, saw 'quite stiff fighting' and he is not one to hand out compliments gratuitously, another officer saw it differently and wrote that the advance from Taranto 'amounted to little more than the chance to learn what it was like to be shot at. In the whole Brigade, less than a hundred men had been killed or wounded.' To the reader in the 1990s these remarks may sound callous compared with, for example, the fuss made about the loss of *RFA Sir Galahad* in the Falklands campaign. But in the context of a major war the fighting was not heavy and the casualties very light.

When the division finished their advance to the area of Foggia, they assisted in the escape of Allied prisoners who were trying to reach friendly lines from camps in Italy. After the Italian surrender many prisoners were trying to evade German attempts to recapture them. Teams were formed from the division. Captain Timothy of 2 Para was told:

> Select about a section of men from the battalion to do a job; no officers. I had to report to a hotel in Bari to get my orders. In addition to the chaps from the battalion I had an American Italian who had never jumped before and a member of the battalion intelligence section who spoke German and Italian. We were equipped with escape maps and money. After the Armistice it appeared that it was up to the senior British officer at each camp to decide what should be done. Some encouraged the prisoners to escape, others ordered them to remain. There were thousands of Allied prisoners swanning about. Our job would be to contact the prisoners and direct them to beach RVs, manned by the SAS, from where they would be picked up by the Navy.
>
> My party dropped from an Albermarle at dusk thirty miles north of the DZ. I was last out and got stuck in some trees. After extracting myself and burying my chute, I found myself surrounded by Italians. I established our position by asking where I was. I spent the rest of the night looking for my stick, and fell into a river twice. Finally I moved south to the correct area on my own. For two weeks I operated on my own, visiting farms to see if they were sheltering POWs. The next problem was to convince them that I was genuine. In many cases their morale was low. Some of them had been taken in the early fighting in the Western Desert and did not believe that such a thing as a British paratrooper existed. They were extremely wary of me, and when as a test they

asked me when the Crystal Palace had been burnt down and I replied: 'During the war' they were even more suspicious, and I was escorted out of the village.

After this I was lucky in meeting Sergeant Smith who had been in the 2nd Battalion with me in North Africa, and captured. We joined forces and got a big party of 400–500 together. After meeting the SAS and making contact with the Navy, in came the boats. Soon after the Navy started embarking the POW shooting broke out on the road behind the beach. I discovered that some POW had tried to break into a farm-house. The farmer fired his shotgun which alerted a German patrol who cruised up and down the road firing. Only about forty POW escaped, I left with them.

Sergeant Lawley, who had been captured after the Tragino raid, was in a camp whose Senior British Officer forbade the POW to escape.

On 8 September Italy asked for peace and for four days after everyone was free to do what they liked. But we were ordered by the Senior British Officer that we were not to try to get back to our own troops. If we did so it was at the risk of a court martial. If it had not been for this order many more would have escaped, instead of being recaptured and taken to Germany. It was on Sunday 12 September in the afternoon that my pal Clements and I were sipping a glass of vino in the garden of a pro-British Italian when suddenly a Jerry recce plane swept over us flying very low and flew around inspecting the whole valley. Guessing that something was wrong we hastened back to camp, only to find everyone making a bee-line for the mountain at the back of the camp. Some German officers had been to the camp and demanded it be handed over. I took the men of the room I was in charge of up the mountain, where we spent a very unpleasant night. On looking down on the camp next morning everything seemed very peaceful, so as we had no food it was decided to take a chance and raid the Red Cross parcel store.

We got down there all right, and everyone collected as many parcels as he could carry. But we had only just started on our way back up the mountain when suddenly shots were dropping around us. A platoon of Jerries had just driven up to the camp. Still hugging two parcels, I pressed on and got out of range. On reaching Clements we made a meal, after which we held an O Group and it was decided that we would attempt to reach our own troops, whom we knew vaguely to be in the area of Foggia. We started off up the mountain, which was 10,000 feet [*sic*] high, and we had got up about 300 feet when we heard someone shouting behind. Looking round, we saw a Jerry officer on the very spot we had just left shouting 'Come back or I'll shoot.' This only made us dig our toes in all the harder, and up we went gasping for air and water until I thought my lungs would burst. It was dangerous to stop for a rest in that it was so hard to get moving again, but the determination to succeed urged us on. Our efforts got us to the top at last, where we found one of the state-sunk wells and managed to get from it some very green and slimy water, which tasted delicious to us, and then bathed our feet which were badly blistered and swollen. After some hours rest we started off again, and by using the maps and money sent us, and keeping well away from the roads, by climbing mountains 8,000–10,000 high, we eventually arrived at a small village named Morrone perched high on a mountain which gave us a commanding view of the whole surrounding country. The people of this village were very kind to us, supplying us with food and information about the enemy, whose headquarters were at Campobasso not far away. We were right behind their front line, which we assumed was impossible to get through.

We decided to lie up for a few days, but as Jerry used to visit the village every day it was unwise for us to stay in it. It was at this stage that we made contact with a very brave and good-hearted Italian, Giovanni Melfi, who at great risk to himself and family gave us food and shelter. On 13 October we witnessed the withdrawal of the enemy and we went through him to contact the Green Howards in the village of Casacalenda on the main road to Termoli. What a day!

On arrival in England we were sent home on a couple of months leave. Later, after finding much difficulty in getting back into Airborne because of my age [thirty-nine] I found myself at Larkhill with the 13th Battalion. My regrets at not being posted to the 1st Battalion were soon dispelled, as I found the 13th a jolly crowd, well-trained and well-disciplined, who were training assiduously for their D-day roles.

One of the casualties in the early part of the Italian campaign was the Divisional Commander, Major General Hopkinson. Down, the commander 2nd Parachute Brigade, took over the division, but not for long. Those who knew Down well are convinced that the plan for Arnhem would have been substantially different if he had been commanding the division at the time. Instead he was sent by Browning to raise 44th Indian Airborne Division in late 1943. But all this was in the future, and in November 1st Airborne Division was sent back to England to prepare for the forthcoming campaign in France and Germany. They left behind 2nd Parachute Brigade, consisting of 4, 5, and 6 Para under Brigadier Pritchard as General

Alexander's airborne force. 4 Para had lost their Commanding Officer, Dene, when he was captured going too far forward. Coxen from the 1st Battalion took over.

Learning the lessons of 1st Parachute Brigade in North Africa, where they suffered because of the lack of their own artillery, engineers, supply, transport, medical and so forth, it was decided that 2nd Parachute Brigade should be designated a brigade group with appropriate supporting units. No sooner had they become 2nd Independent Parachute Brigade than they were warned by General Montgomery that they might have to serve as infantry in the line north of the River Sangro. Sure enough, on 2 December the brigade was put under comand of 2nd New Zealand Division to protect their left flank while advancing towards Orsogna. The brigade was still very lightly equipped, but with the jeeps and trucks they had won from various sources and some logistic support they were better off then 1st Parachute Brigade had been in Tunisia. In rain and sleet the brigade advanced along a narrow mountain road in thick mud to occupy a position north of the River Sangro and hold a front twenty-five miles wide.

There was great optimism in the brigade that exciting times lay ahead, that the two armies, the US 5th on the west coast and the British 8th on the east coast, would soon link up north of Rome before a triumphant advance to the borders of France and Austria. However, the focus of attention was about to shift to the invasion of north-west Europe, and most of the Allied effort was directed towards that enterprise. The Allied strategy in Italy was to exert sufficient pressure on the Germans to prevent them withdrawing troops to reinforce their armies in France and Belgium during the Allied landings in Normandy and the subsequent campaign in north-west Europe. Neither the Allies nor the Germans had a preponderance of strength on either side of the long boot of Italy. The Allied problem was to build up sufficient force to mount an attack one one side, while keeping the Germans sufficiently occupied on the other side of the backbone to prevent them pulling troops across to meet the offensive. The Apennines formed the backbone of the country with valleys and rivers running off each side in a herringbone pattern. The country was ideal for defence and the Germans, being excellent soldiers, made good use of it. All three attempts by the New Zealand Division to penetrate the enemy positions overlooking the Sangro failed.

To release divisions from the line for attacks, the 2nd Independent Parachute Brigade was constantly put in to hold large areas. Their initiative and their aggressive patrolling exerted pressure on the Germans exactly as the Army Commander hoped. Having been told they would be in the line for about ten days, they stayed in this area under 2nd New Zealand Division and later the 8th Indian Division for nearly four months. In the atrocious winter and spring weather the brigade was employed as normal infantry. Throughout New Year's Eve and the early hours of New Year's Day 1944 a blizzard howled; by dawn the drifts were six foot deep. Supply jeeps could not get through for up to two days. One company of 5 Para was cut off and could only be supplied by man-packing loads after forty-eight hours hard slog. Movement that winter and spring, even on the rough tracks, was difficult as they were usually filled with slush and melting snow. In many cases the positions occupied by the rifle companies were overlooked by the enemy and movement by day was impossible. The enemy patrolled vigorously too, and because of the wide frontages held by the brigade were sometimes able to infiltrate. No attempt was made to hold every piece of ground to prevent this – a fruitless task. The tactic was to identify the incursion and move forces to intercept it. Shelling and mortaring took its toll, as did the frequent patrol clashes, sometimes involving up to a company at a time. The standard of patrolling in the

brigade became the envy of the 8th Army. On one occasion
Army Headquarters ordered all units to make a special
effort to capture prisoners on a particular night. Not to
be outdone, each parachute battalion took two prisoners,
representing a different enemy unit, and inflicted considerable casualties without loss. This drew a personal message
of congratulations from the new 8th Army Commander
General Leese.

As always there was laughter too. The Intelligence
Officer of 4 Para, whose asides in the battalion war diary
are a delight, included an entry for 9 February:

> Two booby traps of a new type were discovered in
> the cook-house at Rear Battalion headquarters today.
> In appearance they were not unlike flasks of olive oil.
> RE assistance was summoned, but before it could
> arrive the booby traps were carried off by a civilian
> who claimed they were flasks of olive oil. Details of
> mechanism etc. may be had on application to the
> second-in-command or Captain Marlow!

The brigade was also responsible for its own recruiting
and training of reinforcements, all of whom had to be
found from within the central Mediterranean theatre.
From November 1943 to May 1945 not one reinforcement
came to the brigade from the United Kingdom. In early
April the brigade relieved 1st Guards Brigade in part of
the infamous Cassino front. Here they held a sector which
included Cassino station. It was overlooked by the enemy
on the high ground. Major Hargreaves' B Company in 4
Para spent some time holding the railway station. The
nearest Germans were in the hotel across the square. It
was very like World War One with thick mud and the
enemy so close. Casualties were carried out and supplies
and ammunition brought forward by mule and on man-
pack along the railway line, but only at night. German
machine guns firing on fixed lines along the railway line

and pre-registered mortar and artillery fire made movement hazardous, even under the cover of darkness.

By day the British gunners fired an almost continuous programme of smoke shells, augmented by smoke canisters set off by Basuto pioneers, crouching in shell holes and provided with sufficient food and canisters to last four days. Intensive night patrolling harassed the Germans. General Down visited the brigade at Cassino and insisted on being taken forward to the railway station. When Pritchard demurred, he said: 'Don't worry about me, I'm only a platoon commander.' As Pritchard and Down were moving in one of the forward areas an artillery barrage came down. Pritchard's head was cut with shrapnel and his arms burned by phosphorus, and another member of the party was severely wounded, but Down was unscathed.

6 Para's first task at Cassino was to reconnoitre the far side of the Garigliano river before sending over fighting patrols. Their predecessors had clearly never been across and were unable to tell them the extent of the minefields. Following this they relieved the New Zealanders in the mountains. Supply was by nightly mule train but some positions could only be resupplied by man-packing. One night Lieutenant Pearson and Sergeant Jones of C Company were sent out with a party to find a path through a minefield between the battalion and the Germans. He took sappers and mine detectors, but an exploding mine wounded four of his party, damaging all the detectors. As Pearson started to lead the party home, crawling on all fours he knelt on a mine which blew off both his legs below the knees. He lost consciousness, came to shortly, and directed the party to collect the other wounded but not himself. Jones and the remainder refused to leave him and he was lifted out protesting. He was carried for hours on the back of a mule. Despite the terrible pain he encouraged the other wounded. He was awarded the MC and Jones the MM. The brigade spent nearly two months in

the Cassino area, being withdrawn at the end of May 1944. They were battlewise and tested, often holding an area normally allocated to a division. They had been in the line for six months and eight days, with only ten days (a day here and a day there) out of contact with the enemy. They had fought, doing all that was asked of them and more, without any prospect of a parachute operation.

At the end of May 1944 the Germans were withdrawing in a deliberate and methodical way to a line between Pisa and Rimini, the Gothic line. They were being followed up by 5th Army, who were approaching Rome and 8th Army, advancing along roads east of Rome. The enemy were attempting to delay the Allied advance by blowing up roads, bridges and defiles, using very large-scale demolitions to cause maximum damage. On 30 May General Leese decided that he would use a battalion from 2nd Independent Parachute Brigade Group to prevent the demolitions being laid by harrassing the Germans on their withdrawal route. He selected the Sora to Avezzano road which was the axis of advance for the 2nd New Zealand Division. Pritchard advised the army commander that using a battalion would be a waste of resources and that the job could be done just as well and at less cost by sixty men. So at 7 pm on 1 June Captain Fitzroy Smith, two other officers and fifty-seven men of 6 Para took off in three USAAF Dakotas, accompanied by eight more Dakotas to drop dummy paratroops, with an escort of fighters.

The drop at 8.30 pm in the area of Torricella was completely successful and by 9 pm the force had all collected at the RV. There was only one casualty, a medic with a broken rib. They established radio communications with 2nd New Zealand Division, the nearest Allied troops, and asked for the supply drop to go ahead as planned. As always, the Germans reacted swiftly and in strength. Within twenty minutes of the drop they were on the move and twenty-four hours later, the strongpoint that Fitzroy Smith had selected as a base was attacked, although not particularly successfully. Fitzroy Smith, having already sent off one group under Lieutenant Ashby, split the remainder between Lieutenant Evans and himself. This may have been a mistake, because each party was too small to defend itself and risked being defeated in detail. Nevertheless, for a week some parties attacked the Germans on the road with limited success but at considerable cost to themselves. The next problem was to tell the force to get back to Allied lines. Radio communications had broken down, but knowing the company second-in-command, Captain Awdry, had gone to the New Zealand Division as a liaison officer, which was known to all paratroopers, leaflets were dropped in the area with the message 'Proceed Awdry forthwith.' About one third of the force, including Fitzroy-Smith returned to the Allied lines.

The operation was carried out at very short notice, and did not cause much damage, but it did cause some alarm. The dummy parachutists spread over a wide area made the Germans think the force was much larger, and they deployed numbers of troops to search for non-existent soldiers. In retrospect the force was the wrong size, and Fitzroy-Smith put his finger on the problem in his report. He proposed that future operations of this type should either consist of a number of small parties of no more than four men (the size of a present day SAS or SBS patrol) to operate independently, or at least one, preferably two, battalions able to stand and fight, blocking key points on the enemy routes, forcing them to re-deploy substantial forces, rather in the manner of the second Chindit operation in Burma. The rest of the brigade had by now been withdrawn to the Salerno area, where they were carrying out airborne exercises in preparation for future operations, which, unknown to them at the time, were to involve a brigade parachute operation at last! Meanwhile, great events were taking place in Normandy involving the 6th Airborne Division in one of the most successful airborne operations in history.

CHAPTER 5

Normandy

'As you can see, gentlemen, this is a bloody fine DZ; it's a pity so few people used it.' Thus did Lieutenant Colonel Alastair Pearson DSO MC address Staff College students after the war, standing on the spot where he had landed in the early hours of 6 June 1944, leading 8 Para in 6th Airborne Division. Pearson after the Primasole Bridge battle was invalided home with malaria, and later transferred to Brigadier Hill's 3rd Parachute Brigade in 6th Airborne Division. Hill had won a DSO in North Africa and had handed over 1 Para to Pearson after being wounded. He spent seven weeks in hospital in Algiers. One day in swept a bevy of nurses and changed his top sheet. Matron bustled in to inspect him, closely followed by a French General who, taking the medal of La Légion d'honneur off his ADC's chest, pinned it on the jacket of Hill's pyjamas! As Hill got stronger he started slipping out of the french windows of his ground floor room for walks in the hospital gardens to get himself fit. When he deemed himself fit enough he deserted from the hospital and eventually reported to Brigadier Flavell 400 miles away. It became patently obvious that 1 Para would want to keep Pearson after all they had been through, so Flavell put Hill on an aircraft back to England. On arrival he was sent to hospital in Tidworth.

Brigadier Lathbury, looking for a commanding officer for the newly converted 9 Para, asked Hill if he would like the job. Hill's problem, having accepted, was getting passed fit to command with wounds in the neck, arms and chest. He was on friendly terms with Major Salmon, the commanding officer of the hospital. So while she was out of her office he left a note saying that General Browning required him back and asked that a medical certificate be forwarded on to him. When the truth was discovered there was an uproar which went right up to the War Office. They were under the impression that he was still in Algiers! A medical court of inquiry was held which gave him permission to carry on with his command but absolved the authorities from any responsibility for his condition, including any pension for wounds received so far. Sergeant Garrett, a platoon sergeant in B Company 9 Para, first met him after jumping from a Whitley with an 'odds and sods' stick made up of officers and soldiers from battalion headquarters. As they lay in the RV a tall figure with a long stick approached Garrett, whose face was covered in blood, having 'rung the bell' on jumping. Although Hill was still recovering from his wounds, he accompanied Garrett's party as they doubled back to Bulford. Garrett recalls: 'Someone in the stick was grumbling. Colonel Hill stopped us and said: "I want to speak to you. I am probably the unfittest man here and I'm not grumbling. Anyone who grumbles can leave now." '

'When Colonel Hill took over the battalion,' recalled Sergeant Woodcraft, a section commander, 'he took us all on a forced march. At the end he addressed us, saying: "Gentlemen, you are not fit, but don't let this worry you because from now on we are going to work a six and a half day week. You can have Saturday afternoons off!" On Sundays we went to church parade in full battle order. Afterwards it was straight on to a thirty-mile route march.'

When he took over the 3rd Parachute Brigade from Lathbury, he was in his own words 'one of the oldest men in my Brigade at the advanced age of thirty-two!' Tall and fit, he had a quiet air of total command, inspiring confidence and respect in everyone he met. His men called him 'Speedy'. Years later, on the Staff College battlefield tours in Normandy, although he left the Army as a Brigadier he was still being addressed as 'Sir' by men who had served under him but were now Generals!

Hill's 3rd Parachute Brigade eventually consisted of 8 and 9 Para and the 1st Canadian Parachute Battalion. 9 Para was originally commanded by Lieutenant Colonel Lindsay, one of the first paratroopers, but he disagreed with Hill over a security matter and Major Otway, Royal Ulster Rifles, the second-in-command took over. Lindsay had brought 9 Para to a high state of training before handing over to Otway, and later his competence in battle was amply proved commanding the 2nd Gordons. The medical officer of 9 Para remembers how soldiers and NCOs who knew Lindsay rejoiced when he did so well in the Reichswald battles and was awarded the DSO.

The other parachute brigade in the division, the 5th, was commanded by Brigadier Poett, Durham Light Infantry. He had been commanding a battalion in Wales when he was offered command of a parachute brigade. He had never considered parachuting before, but was delighted and accepted. 7 Para was transferred to the newly formed 5th Parachute Brigade to add a modicum of experience. As related earlier, they had been 10th Battalion The Somerset Light Infantry. 'Then one day,' recalled Major Taylor, 'we were marched to the camp cinema and told that we would become a parachute battalion, but only volunteers would be accepted. We were very much a West Country battalion and many of us had been together for years, going back to Territorial Army days before the war. Everyone was given several days to make up his mind, and 450 volunteered. After medical examinations 200 were selected. Eventually our Commanding Officer was Geoffrey Pine-Coffin and the Second-in-Command Eric Steele Baume, known to us all as "Timber Casket" and "Tin Arse".' The 12th and 13th Battalions, formerly the 10th Green

Howards and 2/4 South Lancashires, completed 5th Parachute Brigade. These battalions had similar experiences when they were asked to volunteer for parachuting. Two hundred officers and men from the 10th Green Howards started parachute training. Major Sim joined them from the Hallamshire Battalion, The York and Lancaster Regiment, as did many others from this battalion.

They trained hard, concentrating on night work, long marches across country followed by attack and consolidation before first light.

To provide the glider-borne troops in the division, the 6th Air-Landing Brigade was formed from 2nd Battalion the Oxfordshire and Buckinghamshire Light Infantry (52nd LI), 1st Royal Ulster Rifles, and 12th Devons. Their Brigade Commander was the Hon. Hugh Kindersley. Already holding a private pilot's licence, he qualified as a glider pilot and passed the parachute course. He had won an MC aged nineteen in the First World War in the Scots Guards. 'When he arrived to take command aged forty-four, we thought he was so old that he was lucky to be alive,' remembers Major Crookenden, his twenty-seven-year-old Brigade Major!

Major General Gale had taken over command of the division in May 1943 while it was still in its infancy. Gale was a soldier's general, much loved for his forthright language and down-to-earth advice such as 'Beware of red hair and re-entrants!' A gifted trainer of troops and resolute commander in battle, he inspired his division to train and fight with a will. 'Go to it,', he said, 'let that be your motto in all you do.' They did. Every man had to be capable of marching fifty miles in full battle order in twenty-four hours. On the first major exercise in August 1943, 9 Para marched from Bulford to Bath as a warm-up before the exercise. After an eight-day exercise without transport the battalion found itself at Blandford, hot and tired but delighted to see transport thoughtfully provided by divisional headquarters to take them back to Bulford. Lindsay dismissed the transport. The battalion marched the thirty miles back; an excellent lesson to all concerned in what military trainers now rather pompously call 'dislocation of expectation', an almost constant feature of battle. Marksmanship was no less important. The division might have to last for days without re-supply. Every shot had to count. They also trained with the Royal Air Force who would be responsible for dropping them into battle. On one occasion 9 Para was taking part in an exercise to practise the Dakota crews in long distance flying followed by a precision drop as a demonstration. First out of the leading aircraft was Hill, who landed right by the smoke marker in the centre of the DZ, more to his surprise than the thousands of spectators'.

When Gale was first briefed by Browning for the Normandy invasion, he learned to his bitter disappointment and dismay that because there were insufficient aircraft for the whole division, only one brigade on its own, was to seize the bridges over the Caen Canal and River Orne intact. He gave the job to Hill's 3rd Parachute Brigade, who asked for gliders for this *coup de main* operation. Then a week later, to his joy and relief, Gale was told that the whole of 38 and 46 Groups RAF would be made available. His division could go into battle together.

Montgomery, having increased the size of the bridge-head he intended seizing, wanted the airborne divisions, British and Americans, to shield his flanks while the sea-borne landings were taking place and during the tricky period while he was carving out enough elbow room beyond the beachhead for a break-out. He was worried that German armour on his left flank, in particular the 21st Panzer Division and the 12th SS (Hitler Jugend) Panzer Division, might win through to the beachhead and roll up his assault divisions. He selected the River Orne and the Caen Canal, which runs alongside about a third of a mile to the west, as the anti-armour obstacles on the eastern flank of his beachhead. About eight to ten miles to the east of the River Orne, and roughly parallel to it, flows the River Dives. Lying diagonally between the two river valleys is a ridge of wooded country, the southern end covered by a thick forest: the Bois de Bavent. At the northern end the woodland is interspersed by pasture, cultivation and orchards, dotted with small villages and several stud farms. Between the ridge and the Orne lie open rolling cultivated fields and villages. Montgomery decided that the 6th Airborne Division would stake-out the high ground to the east of the Orne to buttress the twin water obstacles on his eastern flank. They were still to seize the bridges over the Caen Canal and the River Orne intact. This would enable him to break out of the beachhead in this direction without having to begin with a river-crossing operation. To impose the maximum delay on enemy armour approaching from the east, 6th Airborne Division was to blow the bridges over the River Dives at Troarn, Bures, Robehomme and Varaville. A battery of guns in concrete casemates at Merville was to be destroyed half an hour before first light to prevent it firing on the beaches. 6th Airborne Division was reinforced by 1st Special Service Brigade (Commandos) under Brigadier the Lord Lovat, who would land over the beach and march to join them.

Gale was not given enough aircraft to lift his division in one wave; it would have to come in two successive lifts. He originally planned that his Air-Landing Brigade, landing by night, would seize the bridges, occupy the villages of Ranville, Le Bas de Ranville and Herouvillette southeast of the Orne bridge, and hold a small lodgement west of the Caen Canal bridge. Simultaneously, 3rd Parachute Brigade would deal with the Merville Battery, the Dives bridges and hold the Bois de Bavent ridge. Both brigades would then await the arrival of 5th Parachute Brigade in

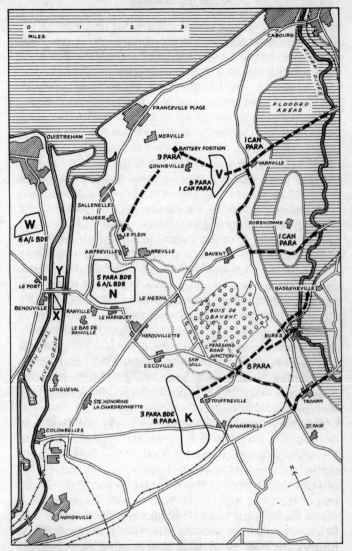

Normandy – Principal moves of Battalions 3 Para Brigade. First two days only. Moves of 5 Para Brigade not shown.

the second lift. Then, in mid-April 1944, air photographs showed that the Germans were erecting poles on every open space that could possible be used for glider landings. Gale decided that both parachute brigades would land first and the gliders would land by day, enabling the pilots to steer between the poles. The only exception was that the glider *coup de main* on the Orne and Caen Canal bridges would go ahead at night as planned. Gale, after reading reports of the German glider landings on the Eben Emael Canal in Belgium and on the Corinth Canal in Greece, was convinced that this method stood the best chance of success.

Brigadier Poett's 5th Parachute Brigade took the *coup de main* party, consisting of Major Howard and D Company of 52nd LI, under command. The pathfinders for Poett's brigade were to land at the same time as the *coup de main* force. This would allow them half an hour to put out the Eureka beacons on the DZ before the main body dropped fifty minutes after midnight. The DZ was only 1,500 yards or so from the bridges. Both parties needed surprise, so to avoid compromising each other the pathfinders and the *coup de main* force would land together. Just in case the *coup de main* failed, Poett prepared a contingency plan. 7 Para were to take twelve inflatable recce boats and thirty J Type dinghies. The twelve recce boats would descend in kit-bags on the legs of men in B Company, and twelve dinghies in kit-bags on the legs of men in C Company; the remaining eighteen dinghies would be jettisoned on cycle chutes (small parachutes for dropping folding bicycles). Equipped with these boats the battalion would be able to paddle across the river and the canal, to seize and hold Benouville and Le Port. Poett would be responsible for holding the lodgements astride the bridges and for clearing the landing zones north of Ranville to allow sixty-eight gliders to land two hours before first light on D-day, and 146 gliders to land on the evening of D-day. The first wave of gliders would bring in an anti-tank battery to assist Poett hold off German armour in the open country south of his positions, east of the Orne. Poett was clear in his own mind that his most difficult task would be to hold the bridgehead the first day. In the darkness and confusion the Germans would have difficulty identifying the strength and exact locations of the paratroopers. When they had recovered from their surprise they could be expected to react swiftly and violently. Gale's orders to Poett were unequivocal: 'The whole of your area must be held. Infantry positions will be fought to the last round and your anti-tank guns to the muzzle.' On being relieved by troops from the 3rd Infantry Division landing over beaches, and by Kindersley's Air-Landing Brigade on the evening of D-Day, his brigade would become the Divisional Reserve. Kindersley would expand the bridgehead to the south to include Longueval, St Honorine la Chardonerette and Escoville.

After the war Hill spoke about the tasks allotted to his 3rd Parachute Brigade:

My brigade's share of the divisional task was twofold. First of all we had to carry out works of destruction; the Merville Battery had to be eliminated, and five bridges destroyed. After we had done this we had to deny the enemy the high ground from exclusive of Breville in the north to the saw mill in the south. The interesting thing to me was the allocation of tasks to battalions. I found this nearly always easy. The reason is that battalions are temperamentally as different as chalk from cheese, they are really exactly like children. They have their strong points and their weak points. First of all the Canadian battalion; they were full of vitality, joie-de-vivre and élan. I knew very well that for the first 48 hours every chap would be trying to win a VC. I gave them the job of clearing

DZV, capturing an enemy command post, destroying the bridges at Varaville and Robhomme, aggressive patrolling, protecting the left flank of the 9th Battalion, and securing the Le Mesnil crossroads. Now who was to deal with the Merville Battery? There was only one battalion, and that was the 9th. The reason? They were an extremely finickety battalion, masters of detail and management techniques. They had a commanding officer who was a remarkably good trainer. Then I had to detach someone down to the south on their own to destroy the bridges at Troarn and Bures. The obvious battalion for that was the 8th. They were miners, they were rugged, and not very fussy. They were commanded by the redoubtable Alastair Pearson, who succeeded me in the 1st Battalion in North Africa when I was winged. His fame had spread before him, and when we captured prisoners here early on they knew Alastair was there and they were extremely afraid of him. Last but not least, one's field ambulance. I had had my life saved in North Africa by parachuting surgeons and was very conscious of the assets to be gained by having the field ambulance right up as near the battle area as you can possibly get it.

As D-day came closer the tempo of training increased. Troops with special tasks trained in areas similar to their targets or on mock-ups. 7 Para found themselves near Exeter, where the old by-pass crosses the River Exe and a canal at Countess Weir – a smaller version of the Caen Canal and Orne bridges, although the battalion was unaware of this at the time. Major Howard's company trained at Netheravon, and not long before D-day 'we did an exercise during which we pranged the bridges at Lechlade. The place was very like the part of Normandy we subsequently attacked.' As soon as he was briefed,

twenty-eight days before the operation, Pearson realized
that his battalion was going to have to fight in close wooded
country. They had no experience of this after being
stationed on Salisbury Plain. That afternoon he sent his
second-in-command to find a wood of about fifty acres
somewhere. No easy task because practically every wood
in southern England before D-day was full of ammunition
dumps. The second-in-command found a wood, and the
next morning the battalion started fourteen days intensive
wood-fighting training, mostly with live ammunition by
day and night.

Major Darling, the second-in-command of 12 Para,
arranged an exercise near the village of Wylye in Wiltshire.
Although the battalion did not know it, the River Wylye
represented the Caen Canal. Neither the commanding
officer nor the second-in-command jumped at these final
rehearsals to avoid key people being injured at the last
moment. Darling at thirty-four was quite old for a parachutist. In 1943 he was commanding the 11th Battalion
the Royal Fusiliers and became 'fed up with not going
anywhere and producing drafts for overseas. I had served
with James Hill in the Royal Fusiliers, and volunteered to
parachute. I was posted to the 1st Parachute Battalion as
second-in-command and after completing my parachute
training at Ringway took command of the battalion in April
1944. Frankly, I was horrified by 1 Para; they thought
they knew all the answers, which they did not, and their
discipline was not what I expected. The battalion did not
take to me either. Perhaps this is not surprising since I
had not heard a shot fired in action while the battalion
had plenty of battle experience, fighting in North Africa
and Sicily. So after a few weeks Gerald Lathbury removed
me. I switched with Dobie, the second-in-command of 12
Para. The CO, Lieutenant Colonel Johnson, had them
well in hand and they were a super battalion.'

Pearson was sent for by Gale and told he was wanted

back in his old battalion. Pearson asked to remain with
the 8th. It would not be fair to them to leave at this stage,
he argued. They had been in a bad way when he took
over. He had managed to train them to his ways without
undue interference by keeping them at Tilshead, away
from the rest of the brigade at Bulford. Finally, it would
be pandering to 1 Para. Gale was delighted. He wanted
Pearson in his division. He was not put out by Pearson's
outspoken comments. When Pearson had taken over the
8th he said to Gale that he did not wish to be 'buggered
about by senior officers'. On being asked what he meant
by 'senior officers' he retorted 'anybody senior to me!'

Because most of the battalion came from Birmingham,
Pearson decided to work an eleven day fortnight with
forty-eight hours leave every two weeks, which would allow
the soldiers time to go home. The return journey on the
specially chartered train full of happy soldiers was always
interesting, and usually ended late at night at Lavington,
four miles from Tilshead. Pearson never arranged transport, so that by the time everyone had carried their kit to
Tilshead they were once more in a condition to carry out
serious training!

The four guns of the Merville Battery (9 Para's objective) were in concrete emplacements twelve feet high, six
feet thick and five feet deep, with a thirteen foot thick
roof. It was thought that the casemates had doors of steel.
The battery was defended by one 20mm gun and machine
guns. Around it was: a barbed wire fence fifteen feet thick
and five feet high; a minefield forty yards wide except on
the north-east side; a cattle fence; and on the north-east
side an anti-tank ditch fifteen deep and ten feet wide.
More minefields had been laid to block approaches to the
battery, covered by machine guns. Between 180 and 200
men manned the defences. Otway's plan was intricate and
scripted like a complicated play, relying for success on all
the players arriving on cue with all the correct props;

timing was in one case to within thirty seconds! Otway's reason for planning in such detail was his concern that there would not be time for reconnaissance and further orders once the drop had been made, and because he was not confident in the RAF's ability to drop all his sticks in the right place. So each man had to be familiar with every facet of the plan and able to step in and play another's part.

The plan was approved personally by Hill, Gale and Browning. Three gliders were to crash-land on the battery, relying on the concrete constructions to tear off their wings, thus arresting the progress of the fuselages. Out of these would spring sixty men from A Company and eight Royal Engineers. Simultaneously the main body of the battalion, having marched from their DZ 2,200 yards away, would blow three gaps in the defences and charge in, joining the glider party in killing or capturing the defenders. The guns would then be destroyed by the half troop of engineers with explosive charges. Before the battalion left for the battery, five more gliders were to land on the DZ carrying jeeps, anti-tank guns and scaling ladders with which to cross the anti-tank ditch, and much miscellaneous equipment. Before the show started thirteen Lancasters and eighty-six Halifaxes were to drop 1,000-pound bombs on the Battery. It was thought by some that if the bombing was accurate it would leave nothing for the battalion to do. In ten minutes the battery would be hit by more bombs than were dropped on London on any night of the war, the troops were told. However, the plan was fraught with possibilities, not least the party in the gliders stood a good chance of being cut down by the fire from their comrades storming in through the defences as they landed. When the battalion had dealt with the battery they could not rest on their laurels. They had to capture the village of Le Plein and a German naval headquarters at Sallenelles.

A field near Inkpen in Berkshire was chosen for rehearsals. Although the land was under cultivation this training was so important that work began on constructing the mock-up two days after Otway asked for the use of the land, permission having been obtained from seven different Ministries in London. The battalion completed five days and four nights rehearsals, the last with live ammunition. The dress rehearsal went well – too well! The whole plan had been given to every man by Brigadier Hill, except for the time and place. To test the troops' security thirty attractive WAAFs in civilian clothes were employed to see if they could wheedle any information out of them. 'All concerned had an excellent time and the integrity of the troops was proved to be complete – at any rate as regards security!' says the official report. There was an atmosphere of great trust in the battalion, as in all other units in the division. Although they had not been briefed all ranks knew a great deal, but even before the dress-rehearsal they were still allowed to go on leave. There were never any absentees. The battalion came first.

After such preparation it is no wonder everyone in the division was so confident. A private soldier wrote to his parents from Normandy: 'nearly three weeks of really hard work by day and night, doing the same thing over and over again, meant that we could do the whole thing without thinking. Can one wonder that we knew and were confident that if everything went according to plan we could not fail.'

On 22 May the whole division moved to transit camps, usually near the airfield from which the battalions would be taking off. 12 Para was moved to a field near Keevil airfield in Wiltshire. Like everyone else they were wired in and no one was allowed in or out except on official business. There were no telephones. Here the troops were briefed in great detail. Few of the division had been in battle before, and the task facing them was daunting. They were to jump in the dark into enemy-held territory, to take on the German Army. Some, like 12 Para, were to jump from Stirlings from which they had never jumped before.

'New photos of the area came in daily, keeping us right up to date,' remembers Sim, then the second-in-command of C Company 12 Para. 'Three days before D Day we noticed two small circles near our DZ, and thinking they were AA gun emplacements a special plane was despatched to take another photograph and investigate. Within twenty-four hours we were informed that the marks were two cows tethered to a post!'

With briefings over, there was time for a little relaxation. The officers of 12 Para invited the RAF officers over from the airfield. 'Soon the party was in full swing,' remembered Sim. 'It led to a group of RAF officers holding a strategical position on top of the mess marquee, defying all and sundry with oaths and beer bottles. With cries of "Up the Airborne" we clambered up and waged battle with them. Khaki and sky-blue bodies rolled and tumbled until some bright fellow loosed the guy ropes and the marquee began to sway. A pole snapped and the mess collapsed.'

On 4 June D-Day was postponed twenty-four hours because of bad weather. For many people it added to the tension but for commanders it was a boon: 'It was simply marvellous for battalion commanders and people like myself because for the first time for days we were able to sit back with nothing to do,' recalled Hill.

Padre Jenkins of 12 Para, like padres in all battalions, held a short service outdoors on 5 June. He chose for his text 'Fear lay behind the door, Faith opened it and lo, there was nothing there,' Jenkins was revered by the battalion. On one occasion when parachuting in the Bulford area from Albemarle aircraft his parachute became entangled inside the aircraft while he hung outside. The pilot flew round and round over Bulford in view of most of the battalion. Eventually the crew pulled him back.

On the evening of 5 June the men of the two parachute brigades were driven to their take-off airfields. They sang and shouted lustily as the NAAFI girls and RAF groundcrews waved them farewell. Before leaving their camps they blacked their faces with camouflage cream. Many of 7 Para found that the cream cracked and peeled off so they used the soot from the bottom of the cookhouse kettles instead. The first to take off were the Albemarles carrying the pathfinders of 22nd Independent Parachute Company. Two sticks should have been dropped on each DZ, but in the event only one stick was dropped accurately on each. All the radar and visual beacons for DZ V (Canadians and 9 Para) were lost or damaged. One aircraft carrying a team for DZ K (Hill's headquarters and 8 Para) dropped them on DZ N (5th Parachute Brigade). Not realizing that they were on DZ N they set up their beacons and lights which gave out the signals for DZ K. One stick of Hill's headquarters and thirteen of Pearson's 8 Para landed on DZ N before the N pathfinders came panting up from where they had been dropped some distance away and put up the correct beacons.

Also travelling in one of the earlier waves in an Albemarle was Major Parry, who commanded A Company, 9 Para. Instead of commanding his company, to his chagrin, Parry had been detailed to command the advance party on the battalion DZ – 'an enormous number of troops totalling five: my batman, three sergeants and a corporal!' After guiding the battalion to the Forming Up Position (FUP) for the attack he was to be in reserve 'on the touch-line for the attack on the battery. I would thus be in good shape for the attack on Sallenelles which was to be my baby.'

Although Parry was aggrieved that he had been relegated to a minor role, Otway's reason was his wish to have an experienced officer by him in case all did not go according to plan. With a new second-in-command, Parry

was the only senior officer in the battalion on whom he
felt he could rely. Being taken to battle in an Albemarle
was Parry's second reason for feeling unhappy with his
lot. 'It was a twin-engined brute that had been designed
for Coastal Command. Rumour had it that the tail had a
habit of falling off and Coastal Command no longer liked
this aircraft. So it was allotted to Airborne Forces. To get
into this aircraft you had to crawl along on all fours,
weighed down with parachute and kit, under its belly;
climb a little ladder and again crawl on all fours along the
fuselage; turn around; put your back against the knees of
the person behind you; and there sit awaiting the order to
drop. This aircraft had one redeeming feature in that it
had a very large if uninviting coffin-shaped aperture, and
once you reached the edge of this, which you did by
shuffling along on your backside, there was no possibility
of not falling through it. We arrived bang on the dot at
midnight twenty. We didn't of course know where we
were. We assumed that we were in the right place.'

Hill had decreed that all the officers were to be
equipped with bird calls and troops would rally to the
appropriate call. After landing and trying to orientate himself, Parry sounded his 'ducks bakelite 1944 pattern'.
Nobody came. He then navigated himself towards the RV
which was 'believe it or not, a bushy-topped tree in an
orchard! Approaching it, I heard the drone of heavy aircraft, which were of course the Lancaster bombers due to
bomb the battery at midnight thirty. Unfortunately they
missed the target and a lot of bombs fell on the DZ where
I now was. I was scared out of my wits. I bit the dust and
there prepared to meet my end.'

Picking himself up after this unpleasant experience,
Parry set off towards the RV. Entering what he hoped was
the right orchard, he met his batman, Private Adsett, who
had arrived at the RV ahead of him. 'I congratulated him
and he said: "Well, what happened to you?" I replied: "I

had one or two little jobs to do on the DZ and here I am." That didn't impress him either! All this time I had been lugging the heavy kitbag with which I had jumped. It contained an Aldis lamp which I was to flash to mark the RV for the battalion, due to drop at midnight fifty. I knelt to unpack the bag, pulled out the lamp and my haversack. To my surprise there was another haversack. Adsett, who was leaning over me, said: "Thank you very much sir, that's mine!" I said to Private Adsett: "Now you go up that tree and I will hand you the lamp, and when I give you the word you can start flashing." He said: "Oh no, you're OC Party; you go up the tree, and I will hand you the lamp." So up the tree I shinned, and he handed me the lamp.'

The Dakotas started dropping on DZ V at fifty minutes past midnight on 6 June. The aircrews of the squadron dropping the 9th Battalion could not cope with the total lack of beacons on DZ V. The DZ was one minute's flying time from the coast; there was little time for pilots to orientate themselves before the run-in and the drop. All but the lead aircraft were buffeted by the slipstreams of the others. Before crossing the coast the soldiers were standing, hooked up, many men were thrown to the floor as the Dakotas bucked and lurched. By the time the heavily laden paratroopers had regained their feet the aircraft had overshot the DZ. Some pilots in aircraft that had not dropped all their stick came round again for another try, banking steeply in the turn and making it difficult for the soldiers to scramble up or keep their balance. After another tight turn the aircraft joined the stream, a hair-raising performance rather like joining the M4 in rush hour in the dark with everybody doing 100 mph without lights! The problem of locating the DZ, often after several passes, combined with a westerly wind, resulted in the drop being badly scattered over fifty square miles. 'Quite a big DZ,' was Parry's wry comment! Nearly two hours later only 150 all ranks out of a strength of about 700 had arrived at the RV. There were no anti-tank guns with which to blast open the steel doors, no engineers with their prepared charges, no jeeps, no mortars to fire illuminating bombs for the crash landing gliders. There were a few hand-held anti-tank weapons and lengths of Bangalore Torpedo and one Vickers medium machine-gun, but no mine detectors and other special stores such as white tape for marking lanes through the minefield. None of the five gliders had arrived. The naval gunfire observers, consisting of an Artillery officer and several RN ratings to direct the fire of the supporting cruiser *HMS Arethusa*, were missing. Otway remembers that for about five minutes his mind went blank as the enormity of the situation dawned on him. Then, with no thought other than his determination to carry out the task, he gave the order to implement the plan with his meagre resources. Lieutenant Jefferson had wrenched his arm on jumping as his static line caught underneath it. When he reported in at the RV, Otway, looking pale and tense, snapped: 'You're commanding C Company.' Jefferson, the junior platoon commander in the company, was somewhat surprised. He found his company, consisting of eight men, in a ditch. A few more trickled in in ones and twos, and eventually a more senior platoon commander, Lieutenant Parfitt. Otway decided to set off at 2.45 am and Parry led the battalion to the FUP.

They were met by a reconnaissance party under Major Smith, who told Otway that Captain Greenway and his taping party had managed to probe through the minefield on hands and knees, feeling for mines and tripwires with their hands in the absence of any mine detectors. They had no white tape and marked the lanes as best they could by scraping the earth with boots and entrenching tools. Otway decided to breach only two gaps in the wire, sending two assault groups through each. Upon arrival at the FUP Parry was appointed assault company commander in the absence of Major Dyer, the planned assault company commander. Parry, Lieutenant Jefferson, Company Sergeant Major Ross and Colour-Sergeant Long commanded the assault groups. Parry called in all the assault group commanders for a quick briefing. Although Jefferson had already been briefed to take Number 1 Casemate in the original plan, Parry gave himself this as an objective. Otway remained at a firm base about two hundred yards from the battery. At that moment two of the crash-landing gliders arrived over the battery. There were no illuminating mortar flares to assist them in locating their landing zone. One glider flew over the battery and disappeared. The second came in much lower than the first. The AA gun in the battery fired, hitting the glider's tail. It lifted and crashed in an orchard, 200 yards from where the assault parties waited for the Bangalores to blow, the signal for the attack. The Bangalore torpedoes blew the gaps in the wire, Parry sounded his whistle and the parties charged in. He recalled:

> It was every party for itself, we had no radios. Therefore there was no question of attempting to control the actual assault. I had my own little party of soldiers. I could hear mines going up left and right, and casualties were being suffered. It was a matter of luck whether one trod on a mine or not. Very slowly and laboriously we got through the minefield and the main wire obstacle. Cut and torn, we arrived on the other side. Fire was now increasing. I was struck in the leg by a bullet and went arse over apex into a bomb crater. I could do nothing for the moment. I saw my batman, who was just alongside me, looking at me as if to say 'bad luck mate' and off he went. My party went on and took the surrender of those of the enemy who were still on their feet. We had suffered fairly heavy casualties both from the minefield

and from fire. I used my whistle lanyard as a tourniquet round my leg and hobbled out of the bomb crater. I arrived at Number One Casemate and was faced with the problem of dealing with the gun. There were no sappers, and therefore no explosive charges. But there were no steel doors either. I could just see in this enormous casemate a very very wee little gun. We had expected nothing less than 150 mm guns and this was a little thing of about 75 mm. It seemed almost contemptible to have come all this way and to have been put to a certain amount of inconvenience to deal with these guns, and here was this little chap sitting here in this great emplacement looking rather stupid. However, it was a gun and obviously it could fire, and there were a lot of shells around it. Just at that moment while I sat in the entrance to the emplacement in a bit of a daze wondering what I could do about the gun, I was hit by a shell splinter in the wrist. I thought for a moment that I had lost my hand but it turned out to be only a nick. I then remembered that we all carried plastic explosive, detonators and fuse. So we made up a charge and set it off. To my inexperienced eye this seemed to have inflicted a minimum of damage. As OC assault party I was responsible to the Commanding Officer not only for this gun but for the remaining three. I understand that some attempt had been made to deal with the others and Lieutenant Slade, whom I met near Number 2 Casemate, reminded me that *HMS Arethusa* was due to fire on the battery unless we could send a message to the contrary. As there were no radios we could not contact *Arethusa* so we had to get out pretty quickly.

There had been hand-to-hand fighting both inside and outside the casemates. Some of the enemy disappeared into underground chambers in Numbers 1 and 3 Casemates. Although grenades were thrown down they exploded in the outer chambers and did not kill any of the crews who had taken refuge in the further chamber. The German machine-gun in the Tobruk stand of Number 1 Casemate did deadly work until its crew surrendered. Otway arrived as prisoners were being collected. Jefferson, lying with a wounded leg, saw him about to touch a stuffed dog. Thinking it might be booby-trapped he shouted at him not to be a bloody fool. Otway rounded on him for impertinence, and having detailed Lieutenant Halliburton to inspect 3 and 4 Casemates to ascertain if the guns had been silenced, moved off.

Parry again:

It was now daylight; looking around there were a lot of moaning wounded of both sides, and very few soldiers on their feet. The Signals Officer had inside his battledress jacket a clapped-out old pigeon. It was a bit of a gimmick. The ideas was that on success he would release this wretched pigeon and it would go off in a northern direction towards England. But this particular pigeon was reported flying east towards Berlin.

As increasingly heavy shellfire from other batteries rained down on to the Merville position, the sorely depleted battalion withdrew towards the rallying point which was a calvary about one kilometre away. They had lost sixty-five killed, wounded or missing. They had captured twenty-two prisoners; the remaining 200 of the garrison were dead, wounded or had disappeared below ground. A few latecomers joined them from where they had been dropped wide, bringing the battalion strength up to about 80. These included Lieutenant Pond and his men from the second glider, hit by the AA gun in the battery. One man carrying plastic explosive in the rear of the glider was burned to death when his load caught fire. The remainder survived. Pond and his men successfully prevented German patrols in Gonneville from attacking the battalion as it withdrew from the battery. The battalion now had to capture Le Plein which was strongly held by the enemy, but it was too hard a nut to crack with so few men. After taking and holding the Château d'Amfréville on the outskirts of Le Plein, Otway had to wait for the arrival of Number 3 Commando before clearing the rest of the village.

Parry, with OC B Company, the Adjutant, and Jefferson, together with four other ranks, was evacuated to the Brigade Field Ambulance at Le Mesnil by Gwinnett, the battalion padre. He commandeered a truck and ferried them from the stud farm where they had been left to fend for themselves when the battalion attacked Le Plein. For days and weeks afterwards men who had been dropped or landed wide, from the 9th Battalion and every other unit in the division, trickled in, in some cases from as far away as the other side of the River Dives. Almost all had stories of courage, initiative and endurance to tell, like the 3rd Parachute Brigade Roman Catholic padre, who on finding himself surrounded by the enemy laid about them with his shillelagh. As a cleric he did not carry a weapon. He was eventually pinned down and carted off into captivity, but not before he had knocked out several of his assailants. He was a troublesome prisoner and ended up in one of the camps reserved for the more recalcitrant types.

The next day, heavy shelling of Sword Beach was assumed to be from the Merville Battery back in action, so 6th Airborne Division were told to neutralize it. Gale passed the task to Lovat, commanding 1st Special Service (Commando) Brigade. Lovat, in his turn detailed off two troops of Number 3 Commando who were launched into unprepared attack. The commandos suffered heavy casualties, including Major Pooley commanding the assault.

They got right into the battery and on top of the casemates, hurling in grenades. But not having been issued with explosives they did not succeed in destroying the guns, as soon became apparent when the Germans, emerging from the lower chambers, wheeled out two guns to engage the commandos as they withdrew. As before, fire from neighbouring German batteries was brought down on the Merville position. The haste with which the assault had been laid on doomed it from the start. The guns, Czech 100 mm wheeled howitzers, remained at Merville until mid-August 1944.

The courage and determination of the officers and soldiers of 9 Para had not been in vain. It is now known that the battery's tasks included fire missions north of the Orne and Caen Canal bridges; far more threatening to the success of the D-Day operations than firing on the beaches which were covered by several larger batteries already. 9 Para neutralized the battery during the critical time that the other *coup de main* operation was in progress and Poett's men were consolidating around the bridgehead.

The first man of 5th Parachute Brigade to drop on DZ N was Poett, with a small tactical headquarters. He had decided that he must drop at the same time as the pathfinders and ahead of his brigade so that he could take control if the *coup de main* on the bridges failed. Despite all the rehearsals and preparation before D-Day, this was the first time he and his stick had ever jumped from an Albermarle. Like Michelin men in all their kit with weapons, life-jackets and parachutes, the aircraft was jammed tight. When Poett, who was jumping number one, tried to open the door in the floor, he found that he could not get his stick sufficiently forward to make enough room to pull up the door. Faced with the prospect of being carted ignominiously back to England while his brigade engaged the enemy without him he wrestled with the door, finally succeeding just before the green light:

I was out in the night air and almost immediately a big bump. I had arrived safely on the soil of France. I had no idea where I was. It was much too dark to see Ranville church or any of the landmarks on which we had been briefed. But I could see the exhaust of the aircraft disappearing and I knew it would be going over Ranville. I knew my direction therefore. All was black and still, not a shot had been fired.

Poett moved down the DZ in the direction of the flight of his aircraft and met another member of his stick. As he did so the silence was shattered. To his right explosions, firing and signal lights, the sounds and sights of battle. He now knew exactly where he was and set off at a brisk pace for his RV, the Orne River bridge. Soon fire was coming down on the DZ from the direction of Ranville. Almost the first of Poett's men killed was the officer carrying his radio set.

Poett arrived at the river bridge about half an hour after landing to find that the *coup de main* on the Orne and Caen Canal bridges had gone amazingly well. All the gliders had landed right by the bridges, except for one which was 400 yards out. This was described by a senior airman as the finest piece of airmanship so far in the war. After Major Howard's company had secured the bridges and discovered to their astonishment that they were not prepared for demolition, they dug in or occupied the German positions and waited for 7 Para to arrive from DZN a mile and a half away. Not long afterwards a German staff car came roaring up from the east, crossed one bridge, but crashed into a ditch near the second. In it was the German officer in charge of the defence of the bridges, some empty wine bottles, two dirty plates, and some rouge and face powder. Howard's men beat off an attack by three old French tanks manned by Germans. One tank caught fire, its ammunition exploding for over an hour; the men of 7 Para hastening from their DZ thought a major battle was in progress.

While Poett was being briefed by Lieutenant Sweeney at the Orne bridge he heard the roar of aircraft. It was the main body of his brigade dropping on the DZ he had just left. The German posts at Ranville were now fully alert, and the DZ came under machine gun and mortar fire. The darkness which made it difficult for the parachutists to find their RVs also hindered the Germans, who could only fire in the general direction of the DZ for lack of identified targets.

As Darling's Stirling started its take-off run at Keevil, it suddenly veered sharply to the right and came to a grinding halt off the runway, stuck fast. Darling's first reaction was that they would miss the drop. Then he remembered that he had organized spare aircraft and a truck for just this eventuality. Sure enough, within ten minutes he and his stick were in another Stirling and roaring down the runway. They emplaned in any order and spent a great deal of the flight sorting themselves out, encumbered with kit, in the lurching, vibrating gloom, unable to communicate with each other except by yelling at the tops of their voices.

Others got away without a hitch. Sim:

With a cheerful smile and a wave the RAF ground crew closed the door on us, leaving us in darkness – almost total darkness if it hadn't been for the six dim lights on the ceiling of the fuselage. My batman said something to me but I could not hear him for the din. We smiled and shouted to each other, trying to grin away that sickly feeling at the pit of the stomach. The adventure had started, and it was an adventure for us. None of us knew war. None of us could conjure up in our minds the horror and beastliness of battle. I fell asleep.

Darling's stick had a scattered drop at least three miles north-east of DZN in an orchard and among tall poplar trees. The fire-fight at the Caen Canal bridge helped him and many others to orientate themselves. He collected about six men from his stick and set off, avoiding the road. The close bocage country, which they had never encountered before, made movement in the dark slow and difficult. By luck they found themselves at the Breville cross-roads. There were telephone lines leading into a German position in the scrub. They could hear German voices, and Darling restrained one of his men from lobbing a grenade, saying that their job was to get to the battalion without delay. As they moved away, to their surprise they spotted a signpost. Britain had been stripped of its signposts in 1940 to make life difficult for German parachutists! It pointed the way to Le Bas de Ranville. By now it was nearly daylight, so they walked along the road and joined up with their battalion. On the way they passed the body of a signals officer of their division. Darling removed the code wallet from his pocket before walking on.

Sim's stick dropped on the correct DZ:

As we were approaching the coast, the despatcher asked me to help him open the double doors in the floor of the Stirling. As I was leaning out over the gaping hole, trying to hook up the door, I was very conscious that I was not hooked up and hoped that I wouldn't fall out! The battalion RV was a large stone quarry situated on the west side of the brigade DZ. I proceeded due west across the fields with the aid of my compass. On the way I collected men from my battalion. Groups of men from the 7th and 13th Battalions were encountered and duly despatched in what I thought was the direction of their battalion RVs. Soon afterwards the rallying calls of a bugle for the 7th and a hunting horn for the 13th added to the din of the aircraft flying overhead.

When Sim arrived at the RV, his CO told him that only a quarter of the battalion had arrived so far. The Adjutant, with an Aldis lamp to flash a red light to mark the RV, had not arrived. So Sim was sent to flash his torch through a red filter. After an hour only five more men had turned up. One was carrying the heavy base-plate for the three-inch mortar, and remarked that 'the f . . . ing barrel had better turn up!' The commanding officer of 12 Para decided not to wait any longer and ordered the battalion to move to its positions. When they arrived they found a large number of men already digging in. They had been dropped beyond the DZ and had decided to go straight for the objective.

Lieutenant Watson commanding 3 Platoon, of A Company, 13 Para, heard his batman say 'I'm right behind you' just before he left the aircraft:

The drop was a good one, except that my kitbag strapped to my leg would not come off, so I had to land with it still attached. I was extremely irritated at the prospect of breaking my leg after coming all this way. I landed at the north end of the DZ in an orchard. Everything was quiet and I thought I was miles away from Ranville, the battalion objective. But then I saw the distinctive tower of Ranville church to the south where it should have been. As I moved towards the RV, a wood north of the village, I heard, loud and shrill, the sound of hunting horns: the CO sounding 'L' for Lancashire and the company calls, 'A' for A Company etc. The DZ was a real bugger's muddle with people from all three battalions in our brigade, and some of the 8th who had been dropped on the wrong DZ. But our hunting horns seemed to cut through clearly, and were in my opinion better

than the bugles of 7 Para and the red light of the
12th. When I got to the RV, the company was about
forty strong. About half an hour later we were up to
sixty. But I was missing a section and my platoon
sergeant. My company commander decided to wait
no longer and we set off to clear DZ N of poles for
the first wave of gliders. The remainder of the battalion moved off and after a sharp fight captured
Ranville, the first village in France to be liberated.

Watson's platoon sergeant was Lawley, posted to 13
Para after escaping from Italy, on his first operational jump
since the Tragino raid:

When the green light came on, number one jumped
followed by the remainder up to number ten, a bren
gunner carrying a very heavy load. He fell across the
exit, preventing anyone else from jumping. The only
one who could help him to his feet was the RAF
despatcher. This took some considerable time, during
which the plane circled the DZ three times before I
could jump. The first thing I knew when I was airborne was that my rifle, kit and shovel had broken
away from me. I landed in a cornfield. I lay quite still
for a second, listening; in the distance I could hear
the noise of battle and guessed it must be the DZ. I
got rid of my chute, and with my fighting knife in
one hand and a grenade in the other, I made for the
DZ. I had gone some considerable distance when
suddenly I saw three bent figures. I got up close to
them, challenged, and heaved a sigh of relief to find
they were our chaps. Guided by the battalion call
blown by Lieutenant Colonel Luard on a hunting
horn, we were soon at the RV.

The noise of battle that Lawley heard was from the
Caen Canal bridge. So he must have dropped on the

eastern side of the DZ, and by marching, like the good
soldier that he was, to the sound of guns, crossed the DZ
and found the RV.

7 Para had a scattered drop, but forty per cent of the
battalion reached the bridges by 3 am. Captain Webber,
the second-in-command of A Company, was the second
officer to reach the RV:

> I landed in the right place on the DZ. Our CO
> had decided that everyone should keep their jumping
> jackets on after landing. Usually we discarded them.
> We all had a large green triangle painted on the back
> as a recognition sign; officers and sergeants had a
> circle painted around the triangle, a lovely aiming
> mark! From the RV it sounded as though a battle
> was still raging around the bridges. (In fact it was the
> exploding ammunition in the burning tank.) After
> some time I still appeared to be the senior officer
> there and was just considering whether or not to go
> and help at the bridges with the troops that had
> arrived when I heard the CO's voice in the darkness.
> I was delighted and relieved.

On the whole the drop of the brigade main body on
DZ N went well. In twenty-three minutes 123 aircraft
dropped 2,026 men and 702 containers over the DZ.
Many, like Sergeant Lawley, were blown by the westerly
wind to the eastern side, and the overloaded men were
slow getting out of the aircraft so that sticks were badly
spread, in particular those men of 7 Para with heavy
inflatable boats in their kitbags. The slower sticks were so
spread that some men dropped in Ranville, still held by
the Germans, and were killed, wounded or taken prisoner.
But it was a good effort by the aircrews. They were helped
by being able to see the Orne and the Canal and the
fireworks round the bridges where Howard's men were
fighting. Major Nigel Taylor of A Company, 7 Para, was

leading those of his company who had arrived at the RV towards the Orne bridge when he encountered Poett:

> 'Double, Nigel, double!' he shouted. So we broke into a double, crossed both bridges, and turned left towards the village of Benouville.
>
> I decided that I should try and get what information I could about what enemy there were in this village. I went into a small cottage, and you know what it is if you ask the way in the country, you always manage to get the village idiot. I didn't get the village idiot, but I did get the oldest inhabitants. They were naturally very frightened and took a lot of convincing that we were not Germans on an exercise. But they eventually realized who we were and then the trouble was getting out, they were so pleased to see us. They knew nothing. We pressed on, moving with sections staggered each side of the road. It was dead quiet by now. Suddenly a German motorbike appeared and came towards us. Every man in my leading platoon took a shot at him, and hit him. He swerved across the road and crashed, the engine still roaring, the bike on top of him. He was dead, but underneath him was my leading platoon commander, and he died about twenty minutes later. This was not good!

Taylor was not the only one to encounter the local inhabitants. Sim knocked on the door of a house which was opened by a woman. Behind her stood her husband and two children. Sim addressed her in bad French, but she stared at him blankly, and looked frightened. He tried again, with no response. On his third attempt:

> She suddenly, with tears in her eyes embraced and kissed me and said in perfect English:
>
> 'You are British soldiers, aren't you?'
>
> 'Yes,' I said, 'and I've been trying to tell you this

for some time. How is it that you speak English so well?'

'I was born and grew up in Manchester, and I married a French farmer before the war,' she replied.

She told me that my frightful schoolboy French and the back-chat I had with my Yorkshire soldiers convinced her that no German could possibly have acted the part. Apparently they had been testing the French by dressing up as British commandos.

A Company 13 Para, with 591 Company Royal Engineers, found that they only just had time to demolish sufficient poles and fill in anti-landing ditches to clear a path for the gliders expected at 3.30 am:

But despite heavy mortaring and machine gun fire the poles were removed and ditches filled by 3.0 am. The poles were fortunately not as large as expected. We had trained to move telegraph poles and the so-called Rommel's Asparagus proved much easier. With some funk trenches, dug to avoid being knocked down by a glider, we waited for them to arrive, bringing in General Gale and his staff together with some much needed anti-tank guns. At 3.15 they started to come in, but not all as expected from the north. They appeared from all directions. It was a nightmare and extremely frightening. I would rather be shelled! Some landed well, others crashed against each other; the sparks from the skids, the sound of splintering wood and the yells from the occupants was like a scene from hell! Some of our men were hit. It seemed a miracle to see the occupants get out and even drive away jeeps and anti-tank guns.

Poett was able to tell Gale the good news that his brigade had secured all its objectives by the early hours of D-Day when he met his general mounted on a horse in Ranville. Gale's glider had crushed its nose on landing, so his jeep could not be unloaded immediately. He set off on foot towards the place chosen for his headquarters. On the way he borrowed a horse which he found on the landing zone.

Throughout D-Day the German high command was in confusion. By 5.30 am Brigadier General Feuchtinger, commanding 21st Panzer Division, had sufficient intelligence to build up a clear picture of 6th Airborne Division's positions in Ranville and on the Bois de Bavent ridge. He asked his superiors at Army Group B for permission to attack. It was refused. He asked again at 7.30 am, and was allowed to send two Panzer grenadier battalions to attack Ranville. Finally, at 7.45 am, Speidel at Army Group B released the whole of 21st Panzer Division. This news took two hours to reach Feuchtinger, whose troops were approaching their start lines to attack Ranville, Le Bas de Ranville, and Herouvillette – 120 tanks and 3,000 infantry pitted against three weak parachute battalions, a glider infantry company, some gunners and sappers, six six-pounder and three seventeen-pounder anti-tank guns. Then Feuchtinger's orders were changed, to switch his main effort to the west of the Orne towards the beaches. Chaos followed, and although Feuchtinger with a few tanks got right through to the coast, he withdrew when 6th Air-Landing Brigade arrived, thinking they were landing among the rear elements of his division round Caen. The order and counter-order meant that the whole of 21st Panzer Division never carried out a co-ordinated attack against Ranville and Herouvillette, although several armoured attacks accompanied by infantry were mounted at up to regimental strength.

The battle in Benouville steadily warmed up, starting with probing patrols by the enemy. It was a confused, noisy day. Taylor remembered that the Germans 'put in attacks on us all day. They did not use a lot of men but they did use a lot of fire, and some tanks. They eventually cut us off from the rest of the battalion, and we lost communication with them because our radios had not arrived. We let the attacks come right in and then let them have it! Casualties mounted as the shell fire intensified. At about 9 am a piece of shrapnel entered the inside of my thigh, so high up that it was a very close-run thing! That made me a bit immobile for the rest of the day.' Taylor continued to command propped up by a window, encouraging his men, but eventually had to hand over to Webber. He was wounded in the chest about fifty minutes after Taylor, but being mobile was able to carry on commanding. Taylor:

> We could not cross the road which was swept by fire. A German tank that came right up the village street was seen off when we threw Gammon bombs at it. These were lumps of plastic explosive with detonators stuffed into them in a stockinette bag. By mid-afternoon we were down to twenty men. We should have been relieved at midday, but it was 9 pm before a battalion of the Warwicks of 3rd Infantry Division got through. I was patched up in our Regimental Aid Post in the cafe by the Caen Canal bridge. Sitting outside drinking champagne, I saw the best sight of the day, the evening lift of gliders coming in on the landing zones on both sides of the Orne and the Canal, a huge stream of aircraft and gliders and containers dropping. Soon after, all these fit, fresh chaps came pouring over the bridges. I thought 'we've done it.'

It was a far cry from the disaster of Sicily. Out of 258 gliders that left England, 248 reached the landing zones.

A Company had held out in Benouville for seventeen hours. All the officers were killed or wounded. Webber eventually relinquished command of the company at 10 pm, having been evacuated on Pine-Coffin's orders. He had been alerted by Taylor on his way back. He was found to have a shell splinter in his lung, and other superficial wounds. He had been a tireless and inspiring commander throughout the long day, taking a hand in the sniping and appearing wherever a crisis threatened. B and C Companies had an equally testing day at Le Port. They were not strong enough to hold the whole village and the enemy attacked from the west and north. The pressure on 7 Para at Le Port was partly relieved by Lovat's Commandos, approaching from the beaches at about midday and taking some of the German attackers in the rear. The battalion was short of men and without many of its heavier weapons, medium machine guns and mortars, which had been in the kitbags of soldiers dropped wide. The platoon under Lieutenant Thomas, responsible for holding the canal bridge, was typical. His half of the platoon had landed in the centre of the DZ; the other half, under Sergeant Amey in a different aircraft, was dropped twelve miles away.

The church tower at Le Port was used by German snipers throughout most of the day. No sooner was one silenced than the next started. Corporal Killeen blew the top off the tower with a PIAT bomb. Later Killeen was interviewed by a BBC commentator and took pains to point out that he had caused as little damage as possible and had been careful to remove his helmet on entering the church to see the effect! He found the bodies of twelve Germans in the tower.

The day started quietly for Sim in an outpost sited in a hedgerow forward of his company position, south east of Le Bas de Ranville. He had about twelve men, an anti-tank gun and a spotter for Naval Gunfire Support. At about 11 am enemy infantry appeared in front of him, followed by two self propelled (SP) guns:

They stopped seventy yards away and started to shell

the hedgerow. Point-blank targets for the six-pounder anti-tank gun, but nothing happened. Moments later, a soldier crawled up the ditch to me on his hands and knees and saluted! He said that he was sorry but the six-pounder wouldn't fire as the breach block had slipped and must have been damaged at the glider landing. What can one say? It was all very frightening as there was a lot of noise, crashes and explosions around. I noticed that the man on my right had been shot through the head with his rifle at the aim and his hand on the bolt. I noticed a soldier crawling towards me, moaning and groaning, but he slumped over before he reached me and lay still. I crawled along the ditch to contact Sergeant Milburne, shouting: 'Have you any smoke grenades and Gammon bombs?' He said he had and I suggested he might be able to get to the nearest SP gun under cover of smoke. There was no answer, and I think he may have been killed at that moment.

As often happens, all fire ceased and silence reigned. To my amazement the hatch of one of the SP guns opened and a German officer, splendidly arrayed in polished jack-boots, stiff cap and Sam Browne, leisurely climbed out and lit a cigarette. He was allowed two puffs and was shot. But I don't think we killed him as we did not find his body later. Peeping through the thick hedge, I saw a German soldier standing up in another section of our hedge. I drew my batman's attention to him and ordered him to shoot the German. He did. Again we were subjected to fire, but this time mortars were crashing around us. We could do little but keep our heads down. Silence again. The sergeant, holding the right-hand edge of our hedgerow, had crawled up to me and said he was the only man alive in his area and along the hedge and that he had run out of ammunition. I called for anyone alive to close on me, but gathered only the sergeant, my batman, who had a gaping hole in his cheek, and one other soldier.

Sim decided that without ammunition there was nothing more that could be done, and withdrew his small party back to his company position.

When A Company 13 Para rejoined the battalion after clearing the DZ for the gliders, they spent the rest of the day laying a minefield to the east of Ranville. By now Lawley had rejoined his platoon:

The platoon was only at half-strength because of casualties. In the process of laying the minefield the mines had to be brought from the gliders to the field, a considerable distance. So I went and got a wheelbarrow from a house nearby. It took us the best part of the morning to lay the minefield and all the time we were being sniped at, suffering one or two casualties. Eventually we discovered that the sniping was coming from the house from which I had borrowed the wheelbarrow! A hand grenade soon brought forth four badly knocked-about Germans.

Through the long hours of daylight on 6 June, the 5th Parachute Brigade resisted all attempts by the Germans to break through. The brunt of the fighting in the brigade area at this stage had been borne by 7 and 12 Para. Gale was particularly concerned that German attacks on 12 Para at Le Bas de Ranville south east of the bridges would succeed in penetrating the bridgehead. When Lovat, leading his commandos and preceded by his piper, arrived at the Canal bridge it was an emotional moment, with little time to savour it. Gale ordered Lovat to leave one commando near the bridges to reinforce 12 Para if need be. However the crisis passed, and the commando was released to continue to its objective.

Hill did not join his brigade until 4 o'clock on the afternoon of D-Day.

I dropped in the flooded valley of the River Dives. The water in the whole area was four feet deep. They had wired it before flooding it and there were many deep ditches. I was a highly sophisticated officer, so I thought, and had tea bags sewn into my battledress. It was maddening as Brigade Commander to spend four hours making cold tea. With the party of chaps I had collected, I struggled out onto the edge of the DZ at about 5.45 am. I contacted the Canadian battalion and found out what they were up to, and then set off again. By this time I had forty-two stragglers, all as wet as I was. Among the party were two naval gunfire forward observers and a parachuting Alsatian war dog, Glen. As we were walking along a track we were bombed by a squadron or so of our own aircraft. For the first time in war, although I had seen a good bit of it already, I really smelled and tasted death. The place smelt of cordite. I looked and there was a leg in the road and I thought: 'By God that's mine.' I knew I'd been hit. I then saw it had a brown boot on it. There was only one officer who got away with wearing American brown boots, the mortar officer of the 9th Battalion. I got to my feet. There was only one other who could get to his feet, my defence platoon commander. The rest were either dying or dead. What do you do? Do you look after the wounded or do you push on? It is obviously your job to push on. So we gave morphia to the chaps who were dying, took morphia off the dead and gave it to the living, and moved on. The memory I can't get out of my mind, and sometimes I wished I could, is that as the two of us pushed off all these other chaps, every one of whom died, gave us a cheer.

Whitley bomber with rear turret removed – jumper has stati-chute not rip-cord version.

A stick at Ringway in the early days. Captain Lindsay fourth from left.

(*Above*) Waiting to jump from a Dakota with leg bags.

(*Left*) Out through the hole in the balloon cage.

(*Opposite above*) Stick from 151 (later 156) Battalion before jumping from a Vickers Valencia in India. Fourth from left: Lea (Later CO II Para), third from right Waddy. Note pregnant appearance in shorts!

(*Opposite below*) Jock Company rehearsing for the Bruneval raid in assorted hats!

Witzig's Parachute Engineers.

Opening the Whitley hole.

Mini-bike being taken from its container.

Street fighting in Athens.

Waiting to drop from an Albemarle.

Montgomery with 8 Para before Normandy. Lieutenant Colonel Pearson on Montgomery's right.

Browning and Brereton.

The Pontoon Bridge, Arnhem.
The main bridge is off the
picture to the left.

British POW, Arnhem.

Montgomery meets officers from the 6th Airborne Division in the Ardennes in Spring 1945. Left to right: Major General Bols, Montgomery, Brigadier Flavell, Brigadier Hill, Brigadier Poett and Lieutenant Colonel Crookenden.

(Unknown to Hill at the time, Captain Robinson of 9 Para and six others had also survived. When they looked around after recovering from the bombing, most of the dead and dying were so terribly shattered or buried in bomb craters that they were unrecognizable. Not realizing that their Brigade Commander lay unconscious under the body of a dead man, Robinson set off to try and find the Canadians, get their wounds treated and join in the fighting.)

I then arrived at the 9th Battalion and was briefed about what had happened at the battery. The medical officer seized me and patched me up. The bloody fellow told me that I looked bad for morale. I told him that if he had been swimming for four hours, and had lost a slice off his left cheek (buttock) he wouldn't feel all that hot either. I decided to go and see the Divisional Commander to brief him on the 9th Battalion and find out what had happened elsewhere. So I borrowed a bicycle, a chap pushed me, and I went happily down the road into divisional headquarters. I saw General Richard Gale who was in extremely good form and he told me : 'Well, James, you will be delighted to know that your brigade has carried out all its initial tasks.' So of course that made me feel a million dollars.

We had a greatly revered doctor called 'Old Technicolour'. He was the ADMS (Colonel MacEwan, the senior doctor), the most decorated man in the division, having fought throughout the 1914–18 war and later on the side of the White Russians. He said I must have an immediate operation in the dressing station, to which I agreed provided that he would guarantee to take me to my brigade headquarters himself as soon as he had finished. He agreed. I remember just as I was passing out hearing a heavy concentration coming down in Ranville which was, I think, the first of the counter-attacks launched by 21st Panzer Division. On my recovering some three hours later, Old Technicolour was as good as his word. He put me in the back of his jeep and we set off. On leaving the village of Ranville, six Germans crossed the road. To my horror and disgust he told his driver to stop, drew out a revolver and with his driver pursued the Germans into the bush, obviously hoping to increase his decorations – with an extremely irate Brigade commander sitting, rather tender, in the back. After a few minutes he returned, looking rather shame-faced I'm glad to say, and drove me to my headquarters.

A sapper, Lieutenant Breeze, remembers him arriving: 'For some reason he was standing up in the jeep. As he passed my slit trench he looked down and said 'Square off the sides of that trench and clean your boots!'

At his brigade headquarters Hill found Pearson. He was wounded in his hand, but was otherwise in good form and was able to brief Hill on the activities of 8 Para, whose first tasks were to blow the road and rail bridges at Bures and the road bridge at Troarn. 8 Para planned to protect the sappers while they blew the bridges by providing a company at Bures while the rest of the battalion held Troarn. The battalion had the most scattered drop of any. Only four of the thirty-seven Dakotas carrying the battalion dropped their sticks in the right place. As related earlier, thirteen sticks, totalling 230 men, landed on DZ N instead of DZ K, including most of the engineers of 3rd Parachute Squadron and their explosives for blowing the bridges. Some sticks landed close to the edge of the DZ, while others landed miles away. The 8th had an even bigger DZ than the 9th, about 450 square miles!

Pearson relates:

We had been in a Dakota flown by rather ancient flight sergeants from the Royal Canadian Air Force. They said they were bush pilots, and the one point they made was that if they did not make a very accurate landfall on the coast of France there was no hope of finding the correct DZ with so many aircraft milling about; it would be suicide to circle and find it. As we approached the coast my Intelligence Officer, who was standing by the door, shouted that we were right on course. The red came on, followed by the green, out we went. I always jumped at number ten or eleven. Having damaged my knees in Sicily, a grateful government had issued me with a larger chute. So I had time for a quick look round on the way down. It was obvious that things were not going to plan. Instead of the sky being full of parachutes, all I could see was my stick. I landed right in the centre of the DZ. The first thing that happened was that one of my stick decided to put a round up the spout of his sten gun. At the same time he pulled the trigger and I got a bullet in the hand. The round stuck in my hand – so much for the penetrating power of the sten! I made my way cursing to the RV.

When Pearson arrived he found thirty men there. Two and a half hours after the drop he still had only eleven officers and 145 soldiers, including six sappers, one light machine gun, two PIATs, two jeeps, and four radios, out of a battalion group of over 600. There was no news of Major Roseveare and his sapper squadron attached to the battalion for the purpose of blowing the bridges. Instead of a balanced force, he had a collection of people from all arms. Of his own battalion the only formed bodies were two platoons. The senior sapper was a lance corporal who collected all the plastic explosive from each man and told Pearson that he had enough to 'damage' the Bures bridge.

Pearson sent the sappers and one platoon to Bures to inflict the maximum damage on the two bridges. They were to return on completion of their tasks to the road junction, which would be the centre of Peason's defensive position later in the day. The remainder of the battalion set up a firm base to the east of the road to Troarn and about one and a half miles from the village. Lance Corporal Stevenson and three men armed with the two PIATs were sent to the main road from Troarn to Le Mesnil with orders to let nothing on wheels or tracks past them. At 5.30 am Lieutenant Thompson reported to battalion headquarters. He had landed on DZN with most of the mortar and machine gun platoons and some of A Company. At the road junction, he had met Roseveare and twenty-one all ranks of the battalion. Roseveare ordered Thompson to hold the road junction as a firm base while he went to blow the Troarn bridge. Thompson complied, but going forward on a personal reconnaissance, found Stevenson's PIAT party who directed him to the battalion firm base.

At about 6.30 am there was the sound of a battle on the main road. Stevenson's party had engaged six half-tracks moving up towards Le Mesnil. All six had been hit and the crews retreated taking their wounded with them, leaving three dead. The enemy subsequently recovered four of the half tracks that night. The dead were identified as members of 21st Panzer Division. Pearson congratulated him on his efforts, although Stevenson was rather disappointed that so many of the enemy had escaped. Pearson told him that this was the best thing that could have happened, for by the time the survivors reached Troarn their report would be grossly exaggerated and the enemy would believe that the end of the ridge was held in great strength. He was right. It was the first and last time the enemy tried to move up that road. Stevenson had done as much as any man to win the battle of Normandy.

If he had not stopped the half-tracks they could have reached Breville and the enemy would have occupied the ridge in strength by 8 am, well before the rest of Hill's brigade arrived.

At about 7 am Pearson heard the sound of explosions from the direction of Bures and Troarn, followed some time later by a very loud bang from the direction of Troarn. Major Roseveare had sent most of his sappers under Lieutenant Juckes to blow the bridges at Bures, while he made a dash for the Troarn bridge. Commandeering a medical jeep, unloading the medical stores and cramming in his explosives and remaining men, he drove at full speed for Troarn. The jeep, without windscreen or hood, bristled with weapons, the eight passengers covering the front and sides and Sapper Peachey lying on the loaded trailer with a bren gun to cover the rear. On the outskirts of Troarn they ran into a barbed wire knife rest barrier across the road. It took them several minutes to cut free. Having shot a German cyclist, which alerted the garrison, they drove through Troarn under heavy cross-fire but made the bridge by the skin of their teeth. In the wild ride Peachey was thrown off, wounded and captured. Working with frantic speed, Roseveare and his party blew a fifteen-foot gap in the bridge before driving off up a track by the river. The track petered out, so ditching the jeep and trailer they marched towards brigade headquarters at Le Mesnil.

The task of Major Terrell and A Company was to blow the Bures bridges. Despite being dropped on the wrong DZ, he gathered up thirty men, all he could find, and made straight for Bures from DZV. On the way he met the platoon sent by Pearson and Juckes. After blowing the bridges, they all returned to the battalion at 11 am.

At noon Pearson, still not sure that Roseveare had blown a gap in the Troarn Bridge, sent Juckes and his sappers to blow it with Lieutenant Brown and 9 Platoon of B Company as a covering force. By good battle-craft Brown's platoon managed to overcome the 21st Panzer Division Reconnaissance Platoon who were holding Troarn, suffering only two wounded. Juckes set his charges and was able to widen the fifteen-foot gap in the stone bridge to seventy feet. After some difficulty Brown withdrew his men from the welcoming party organized by the ecstatic villagers. At 1.30 C Company commander arrived with four officers and fifty-one other ranks. He had landed on DZ N. Seeing the 8 Para green and white Verey lights marking the RV he had made straight for it through Herouvillette, still held by the enemy. His party suffered six casualties fighting their way through the village. Shortly afterwards, leaving a string of standing patrols to cover his front to warn of enemy movement, Pearson moved back to the road junction. His plan, which he put into effect, was to allocate areas of responsibility to each rifle company in which they were to operate a mobile defence covered by patrols. By 5 pm the battalion strength had risen to about 250 all ranks and all was well under control. Pearson visited brigade headquarters to find out what was going on and have the bullet removed from his hand, which 'was giving me hell'. At 5.40 pm a half-hearted attack on B Company by five armoured fighting vehicles was repulsed.

Pearson had decided that the only way to fight the battle at his end of the Bois de Bavent ridge was to give the enemy the impression that the area was held in strength. If the enemy did not mount a full blooded attack before last light he would not do so before the following morning. Pearson ordered his company commanders to keep the enemy awake all that night and on succeeding nights by a series of fighting patrols, particularly to the south in the Troarn–Sannerville area. He felt that if the Germans were harassed all night they would conclude that the battalion was much stronger than it actually was, and this might persuade them not to attack for several days. There was no attack on 7 June, and Pearson stepped up the patrolling for that night. As well as local patrols, the whole of Major Hewetson's company was sent to Troarn and a fighting patrol of an officer and fifteen men was ordered to cut the Troarn–Banneville road. At about 8 pm a sergeant from the 9th Battalion appeared at Pearson's headquarters. He reported that his Dakota had crashed in the vicinity of Basseneville on the other side of the Dives and there were badly injured officers and soldiers in a chateau about a quarter of a mile beyond the village. Pearson decided that as soon as it was dark he would lead a patrol to fetch them. He knew there was a crashed glider at the railway bridge at Bures, and with luck the inflatable dinghy all gliders carried would still be intact. He set off with three other officers, a platoon from A Company, the mortar and machine gun platoons, a total of four officers, sixty soldiers and two jeeps. The jeeps would not be able to cross the Dives and the patrol had to be prepared to carry the wounded as far as the west bank.

Sure enough the dinghy was there. They inflated it. The first man in had fixed his bayonet and managed to drive it through the bottom. Pearson was so angry he booted him straight into the river. He surfaced protesting and was pulled out by the RSM with a few choice words. Leaving this soldier to guard the jeeps, the remainder scrambled across the wreckage of the bridge and moved along the railway track to Basseneville. As they passed through the village Pearson had the feeling that the rear half of the patrol had somehow got detached – the noise of movement had decreased. He was right, but pressed on towards the chateau. Of the wounded, about three were capable of walking, five had compound fractures or bad head injuries. Although they had brought folding stretchers, most were with the missing half of the patrol. Pearson scouted the farmyard and found a hay cart with large iron wheels. After giving the more severely wounded a dose of morphia, they loaded them on the cart and set off. As

Pearson approached Basseneville he began to worry that they might be ambushed by the rest of his patrol. Ordering his men to sing 'Roll Out the Barrel', he led them through the village to be met by Corporal McGuigan who told him it was lucky they were singing because they were preparing to ambush a half-track! Eventually they got the wounded back over the river, arriving at battalion headquarters just before first light.

The companies reported that they had had a successful night's patrolling, particularly in Troarn which was strongly held by the Germans. Again the enemy made no attempt to attack the battalion that morning. Thanks to Pearson's imaginative tactics and vigorous patrolling by the soldiers, often accompanied by their remarkable commanding officer, and although the battalion was frequently shelled and mortared, the enemy made only one serious attempt to break through the battalion position, on 16 June.

Hill found that his headquarters was very depleted. His two principal staff officers were missing. Collingwood, his Brigade Major (chief of staff) found the crew of his aircraft so determined to drop his stick in the right place that they went round five times. Collingwood, jumping number one, was crouching in the Albemarle with a foot on each side of the hole. To jump, all he had to do was bring his feet together and drop through the hole. As the aircraft was heading north before turning for a sixth try a German AA shell exploded underneath. Collingwood fell and was jammed in the hole with one leg up, his body on the other side, and the other leg with his sixty pound kit-bag attached, dangling out, buffeted in the slipstream. His batman, jumping number two, facing the hole from aft, threatened to shoot anyone who tried to shove him out or cut him loose. Eventually he was dragged back into the aircraft, which returned to England. Collingwood immediately went to Brize Norton to find Crookenden, the Brig-

ade Major of the Air-Landing Brigade, and hitching a lift
in a glider to France, limped in to brigade headquarters
that evening. Pope, the DAA&QMG (chief logistician),
landed on the far side of the River Dives and refusing to
surrender when surrounded, died fighting.

Alongside Hill's headquarters was his Brigade Field
Ambulance which set up a Main Dressing Station (MDS)
within twelve hours of the drop. The Airborne Division
was fortunate in its doctors and medical staff. Major
Young, the second-in-command, had been a diplomat
before turning to medicine, spoke fluent French and
German, and was one of the few with extensive battle
experience with the 1st Parachute Brigade in North Africa.
The vast majority had never been in battle and thirty per
cent of the private soldiers were conscientious objectors,
some of them Quakers with university degrees. They carried no arms and were ineligible for non-commissioned
rank. However, many had higher education and nursing
orderly qualifications.

Young had landed alone in the middle of a field. He
skirted the fighting around Varaville, found the planned
MDS location in German hands, and made his way to Le
Mesnil, planned as the Advanced Dressing Station for 8
Para. He arrived at 8.30 am with the RASC transport
officer and twenty-seven others. He was soon joined by
the junior surgeon and another MO. He set up the MDS
at Le Mesnil. The senior surgeon had been captured, so
to begin with the junior surgeon, Captain Gray, and the
most senior and experienced sergeant were the only members of the surgical team operating. Later on D-Day the
anaesthetist, by a remarkable feat of fieldcraft, got to the
MDS from where he had been dropped in the flooded
Dives valley. His arrival made major surgery possible.
When the Adjutant of 9 Para was brought in with severe
abdominal wounds, he was operated on with a cut-throat
razor. By the end of that day, ten operations were perfor-

med, despite two-thirds of the Field Ambulance being missing, and seventy-five per cent of the medical equipment having been lost, mostly in the Dives valley.

The adventures of Lieutenant Marquis are typical of the experiences of many of the doctors and medical staff throughout the division. Marquis was the section MO for 8 Para, his job to assist in clearing casualties from the DZ and set up an advanced dressing station. When he landed he found himself near Dozulé, about ten miles north-east of and on the other side of the Dives from DZ K, where he should have been. Finding three other members of his stick, his first order was to keep on their life jackets; they would have a lot of swimming to do. He and a corporal had a pistol and twenty rounds each; the other two were conscientious objectors and were unarmed. They set off, avoiding roads and tracks, swimming and wading, dragging their kitbags. They roped together using toggle-ropes which every man carried. Without these, some or all might have drowned in the deep ditches and streams below the surface of the flood water. By dawn, soaked and exhausted, they had covered only four miles. Marquis decided that they must lie up during the day. The party sat on a log, their feet dangling in the water, and blacked their faces. Marquis, longing for a pipe, pulled out a camouflage scarf to cover his spectacles. He had reason to be thankful that his matches were soaked and that he had no lighter, for as the light increased, there, 100 yards away, was a German pillbox. Outside, a group of soldiers looked in their direction but did not see them, they were so well camouflaged. At last after about three hours the Germans disappeared. Marquis and his party withdrew to a little island of drier ground, where they spent the day.

The next night, realizing they must make better progress, they walked along the lanes aiming for Robehomme, hoping to find the Canadians still there. On the way they were challenged. It was a bren gunner and five more of the original stick. Pushing on they found themselves on the flank of a battle between a Canadian patrol and the Germans. Lance Corporal Halstead's kitbag containing paraffin for the sterilizing stove was hit and the paraffin poured out. After dragging it all that way, he nearly wept with rage and frustration! The Canadians gained ground in their little battle, which allowed Marquis's party to cross the river over a fallen tree. Entering Robehomme, they joined Lieutenant Johnston, the section MO of 9 Para, who had set up a dressing station for the Canadians and the Germans in the village school. Later that day a runner arrived from brigade headquarters telling them all to get out because the Canadians were to withdraw to the high ground to the west.

A horse and cart were commandeered and the two medical officers, with sixteen orderlies and the Canadian patrol, set off for the main position some three miles to the west. As they were approaching the British lines, having had a battle en route in which they knocked out an SP gun, the Canadian patrol commander became worried that they would not be recognized by their own side. He invited the two MOs to lead with a Red Cross flag on the cart. The nearer they got the more nervous the MOs became, and started singing Scots songs at the tops of their voices. They were welcomed unopposed into the British lines in the belief that they were an advance party of the seaborne forces, and arrived at Le Mesnil at 4 am on D-Day plus two. Major Young ordered the two MOs to bed. Marquis was worried that having existed on the special emergency rations he would not sleep. As he discovered, 'those who imagine that the special emergency ration of malted tablets and a tablet of benzedrine would stand a chance against the normal physiology of sleep still have a lot to learn about the human body'.

Although the problem of lost equipment was serious, the most acute shortage would have been plasma. Marquis had jumped with a kitbag full of plasma but had lost it in the flood waters of the Dives valley. His RASC driver, Lance-Corporal Young, whose jeep and trailer loaded with stores including plasma had been commandeered by Rose-veare, managed to persuade some German prisoners with bicycles to carry his loads of plasma to Le Mesnil. Without his enterprise, resuscitation would have soon come to a stop, and many more lives lost. There were many instances of initiative by drivers and RAMC orderlies, notably the latter's readiness and ability to take over from their missing medical officers. The MDS, situated by brigade head-quarters, was subject to stray sniping and spasmodic mortar fire. This intensified as the battle progressed until concentrated attacks on Le Mesnil kept all except those on essential duties in their slit trenches. On 19 June heavy shelling forced the MDS to move to a quieter place. Eight hundred and twenty-two casualties had been treated, and 112 successful operations performed in these thirteen days.

Many others, particularly from Hill's brigade, landed in the flooded valley of the Dives. Sergeant Garrett:

My Dakota had bundles of Bangalore Torpedoes, for blowing gaps in the wire round the Merville battery in containers hanging from the bomb racks. The drill was to let the first ten men in the stick jump, stop the stick, release the containers, then I and the rest of the stick would go. The green came on, the first half of the stick went. I flicked the switch to release the containers. As I despatched number thirteen the red light came on. I unhooked, went forward, and after considerable argument persuaded the Canadian pilot to go round again. They gave me the position in latitude and longitude which was no use to me! All I could see below me as I descended was water. I thought: 'Oh God, I'm going to drop in the sea.' I

landed in flooded fields, the water stretched in all
directions. No matter where I waded I kept falling
into ditches out of my depth. I thought I was going
to drown. I nearly wept with helplessness and exhaus-
tion. I wasn't a kid, I was twenty-six years old.
Eventually I found a fallen tree which enabled me to
cross one of the nightmare ditches and scramble onto
a raised track.

After several narrow scrapes Garrett got through to Le
Mesnil and was sent to join his battalion. Most of Garrett's
stick were never seen again, nor were the Bangalore Torpedoes needed by his battalion. His spirit and persistence
were typical of the hundreds of men of the division who
were dropped wide but got back to their units. It is sometimes tempting in these circumstances to withdraw grace-
fully from the contest on the grounds that it is all too
difficult.

To begin with, the main thrust of the German attacks
against the bridgehead were in the south of the divisional
perimeter in the area of the villages of Herouvillette, Longueval and St Honorine. 5th Parachute Brigade and 6th
Air-Landing Brigade were well sited in reverse slope positions. Eventually, with some forty anti-tank guns and on
one occasion assistance from the Shermans of the 13/18th
Hussars, they beat off the German tanks and self-propelled guns.

Darling was wounded on D-Day plus one. He remembers: 'I went forward to A Company commanded by Major
Ritchie. He was wounded just before I arrived. Eventually
he had to be evacuated so I decided to take over the
company because the company second-in-command was
still missing. I was standing by my signaller, telling the
CO over the radio what had happened, when a mortar
bomb landed at my feet. It killed the signaller and some

shrapnel broke my right arm. So I too was evacuated with Ritchie.'

The first serious attack on 13 Para was on 7 June. Three German SP guns tried to penetrate A Company's position and were destroyed. The following day, 52 LI and 13 Para repulsed an attack, knocking out six armoured vehicles and giving the Germans such a bloody nose that the follow-up wave, consisting of several more tanks, called off the attack. At 3.30 am on 10 June Captain Kerr, commanding B Company 13 Para, reported large numbers of enemy on the north side of the DZ in the woods south-east of Breville. A patrol from C Company confirmed this and added that the Germans were forming up to attack in the direction of the brigade position. Luard, the commanding officer of 13 Para, ordered his men to lie low and keep watch. At 9 am the Germans started to move, crossing the DZ and making for the River Orne and Caen Canal bridges. 7 Para engaged with mortars and machine guns. The enemy swung towards Ranville, using the wrecked gliders and the high corn as cover. Luard issued the classic order: 'Don't shoot till you see the whites of their eyes.' The battalion waited until the enemy was fifty yards away before they opened fire, causing considerable casualties and taking a large number of prisoners. C Company, on Luard's order, counter-attacked with the bayonet, driving the remnants east into some woods. 7 Para followed up with tank support and eliminated the survivors, who turned out to be all that remained of 500 soldiers of 858 Grenadier Regiment of 346 Division.

The Germans had been steadily intensifying their efforts from the direction of the village of Breville, which they still held. Striking westwards, they tried to pierce the left flank of the Allied lodgement and seize the bridges over the Caen Canal and River Orne. Breville was a thorn in the side of 1st Airborne Division, between Lovat's 1st Special Service (Commando) Brigade and Hill's 3rd Parachute Brigade. Hill, holding the vital ground, bore the brunt of most of these German attacks on his wooded ridge overlooking Ranville and the bridges.

9 Para held Hill's left flank in 'five of the toughest days fighting that I saw in five years of war.' (8–12 June 1944). The battalion had an appalling drop, had stormed the Merville Battery and had captured and held part of Le Plein for twelve to fourteen hours longer than anticipated. On 9 June forty-eight hours after dropping, they were dug-in ninety strong in the fields and woods astride the road leading from Le Mesnil to Bréville. Hill had wanted the battalion to hold both the Château St Côme and the woods but with only ninety men it could not be done. So Otway was told to try to deny the château to the enemy by patrolling. As the days passed more men came in to join the battalion, bringing up their strength but never to more than 270. At first light as the battalion stood-to the Germans attacked each side of the Bréville road. The men of B Company held their fire until the enemy were only fifty yards away, and opened up with rifles and brens. The mortars and machine guns joined in and the attack withered away. Among the dead was a German captain, in his pocket a letter to his wife forcasting how he would drive the English parachutists back over the Orne. In other papers captured that day was a copy of Hitler's order that no British parachutists or commando troops were to be taken prisoner.

Collingwood was not the only member of 3rd Parachute Brigade to hitch a lift. Most of Sergeant Woodcraft's company were in the gliders for the attack on the Merville Battery. He was a stick commander in a Dakota, jumping last man, his usual practice. He had an entrenching tool handle strapped to his leg. The handle went through the static lines of the nineteen men who had jumped before.

I went arse over head. I lay in the doorway and that

was it. It took the combined efforts of the despatcher and the navigator to get me on my feet. I asked the pilot to go round again, but he'd had enough and was on his way back to England. They put me on a glider! I was dead scared, I was sick as a pig, and I felt very naked without a parachute! But we landed safely and by nightfall were firmly established at the Le Mesnil crossroads. We stayed there for three days, engaged in the fighting in that area. Our number increased as the stragglers came in from all over the place. I then rejoined my platoon which was about fifteen strong. My platoon commander had been killed on D-Day. After digging in along the line of a ditch on the edge of a wood, I and my friend Sergeant Frith then found ourselves detailed to take a patrol forward of our battalion positions to the Château St Côme. Our task to find out if there were any enemy in the château or the grounds.

After moving in bounds up the drive we dashed into the building, and in the hall we saw the first indication that the Germans had been caught by surprise by the D-Day landings. The dining tables still had plates of half-eaten rhubarb and custard on them. We started up the staircase. Going round the first bend of the stairs very cautiously I was suddenly confronted by a very scruffy individual, green paint on his face, pointing a sten gun at me. When my helmet settled I realized I was gazing into a full-length mirror! When my backside returned to normal I went into the first room. This happened to be the officers' dormitory. All the beds were still made up and personal effects littered the place, including some rather nice Leica cameras. The next room I have always been intrigued by. There was a strong smell of perfume and there were two beds with women's underclothing on them; comforts for the troops I suppose! In the last room I entered there was a large roll-top desk. As I picked up a poker to force open the lid there was a burst of automatic fire right under the window.

Woodcraft realized that they were in danger of being overrun by a strong German patrol, and ordered an immediate withdrawal:

We burst through the french windows in a shower of glass and window frames, ran across the lawn into the wood and immediately found ourselves in a German transport park consisting of horse-drawn vehicles. We took up a position behind one of them, and as a small party of Germans came round the far end of the chateau and crossed our front we opened fire on them.

This was the first intimation that the Germans were moving back into the château in strength. The battle round this area and the village of Bréville was to continue for several days.

The battle swayed back and forth with repeated German attacks supported by SP guns, some ending in hand-to-hand fighting. On one of Otway's visits to his own regimental aid post he found 183 German and British wounded being treated by his doctor and orderlies. Dead horses and cows littered the fields as well as the bodies of dead Germans. The airborne soldiers made every effort to recover their own dead and give them a decent burial. The smell of dead animals and men, the flies, the mosquitoes from the flooded Dives valley, and the heat during the day added to the discomfort of the soldiers dug into the ditches and hedgerows, enduring artillery and mortar fire. Patrols went out every night, so very little sleep was had by anybody. Meanwhile men on sentry, at least one in each two-man slit trench, desperately tried to keep awake until the time came to wake the other man for his turn. After kicking and shaking him, sometimes having to drag him to his feet, the man going off duty would slump down, falling asleep before he hit the bottom of the trench.

After three days Gale told Hill to clear Bréville and gave him the 5th Battalion the Black Watch. To assist, 9 Para occupied the château to protect their flank. Sim, now the second-in-command of B Company 12 Para, saw a column of soldiers in close order led by their company commander coming across the fields near his position in Le Bas de Ranville 'as if they were on a route march in England. It was broad daylight, and although I remonstrated with the company commander he took no notice. It was the 5th Black Watch on their way to Bréville.' Previously Otway had suggested an alternative start line and axis to the Highland brigadier when he came up to plan the attack, to be curtly told to 'go elsewhere'. The Black Watch attacked without a proper reconnaissance. Unaccustomed to the close fighting among the Normandy hedgerows after their experiences in the desert with the 8th Army, they advanced uphill through open fields in daylight with their rifles at the high port as though they were at the battle of the Somme; with no attempt at skirmishing forward. The leading companies were slaughtered and the reserve companies were caught in the forming up position by a German mortar 'stonk'. Eventually the survivors dug in with 9 Para and took over the château.

The next day, 12 June at noon, the enemy shelling and mortaring began, rising to a crescendo at about 3 pm when the whole area became an inferno of bursting shells and bombs. In the middle of this B Company could be heard singing: 'Oh dear what a calamity, six old maids got stuck in the lavatory, they were there from Monday to Saturday, nobody knew they were there.' This was the prelude to a full-scale attack supported by tanks and SP guns against 9 Para and the remnants of the Black Watch. By 5 pm the

seemingly endless assaults had failed to evict the Black
Watch from the château, but had so battered some of their
soldiers that they began to fall back through 9 Para. Padre
Gwinnett nailed the battalion battle flag to a tree in battalion headquarters. German SP guns were firing at close
range into A and B Companies. The battalion mortars
were firing as fast as they could. Otway radioed to brigade
headquarters that the situation looked serious. As he did
so the enemy began to pull back. Hill, realizing that the
crisis of the battle was at hand, and although in pain
from his wound, personally led about thirty men which
constituted the reserve company of the Canadian Parachute Battalion through the woods in a counter-attack to
restore the situation. By this time Gale had decided that
the running sore of Bréville must be dealt with once and
for all. That night 9 Para lay listening to the storm of fire
as the village of Bréville blazed under the fire of a hundred
guns. The overs from the British tank guns whistled
through the 9th Battalion, and German soldiers escaping
from the cauldron of Bréville ran back into the battalion
positions. Otway heard nothing. He was unconscious,
having been blown several yards across the road by a shell.
He came round the next day to find the padre sitting
beside him looking rather worried. But he recovered sufficiently to lead the remnants of his battalion out to a
quieter position when relieved by the 52nd LI later that
day.

Gale reckoned that a quick attack just before nightfall
would catch the Germans unprepared after a hard day's
fighting when they had been doing the attacking. As 3rd
Parachute Brigade was too exhausted he decided to use
his reserve, 12 Para, D Company of 12th Devons, and a
squadron of the 13/18th Hussars, supported by four field
regiments and one medium regiment of artillery. Lieutenant Colonel Johnson of 12 Para was given orders at 5 pm
and told to attack at 10 pm from a start line held by

Number 6 Commando in the orchards east of Amfréville. Johnson had very little time to reconnoitre, plan and give orders for an attack against a village strongly held by infantry and self-propelled guns. He started the battalion moving and then went forward with his company commanders to look at the ground and give orders. D Company 12th Devons had even less time and further to go. At 7.30 pm the company commander, Bampfylde, rushed off to meet Johnson in Amfréville, having given orders to his second-in-command Warwick-Pengelly to bring the company forward as quickly as possible. To the layman, accustomed to war on the large or small screen, three hours may seem generous. An infantry soldier, every private, needs to know what is required of him in far more detail than for example the member of a gun crew, who on the whole carries out a series of drills by rote, or a sailor who goes where his ship goes willy-nilly. Apart from the distance to march to the start line, the briefing of each platoon and section's part in the battle, who like the musicians in an orchestra may each be doing different things to produce the overall result, takes time. The trick is only learned by training and practice, plenty of practice. Orders confined to the phrase 'Let's go' may work in war movies but in real life, at least in the British Army, they would be greeted by a host of questions, the first of which would be 'Where?'

12 Para had spent a very pleasant sunny day resting and in reserve in some quarries by the River Orne. Since D-Day they had been moved several times: to assist 1 RUR in an abortive attack on St Honorine; to the DZ area where they had met 5th Black Watch on their way to attack Bréville; up to Hauger and Le Plein to reinforce the commandos; and back to the quarries. They were down to about two officers and forty men in each of the rifle companies. Sim, now second-in-command of B Company, which after the last six days had only one other officer,

the company commander, Major Rogers, relates: 'A rumour went around that we were going to attack Bréville at dawn. It was almost 8 pm and we had just eaten an evening meal when orders came that we were to prepare for battle.'

Dumping their haversacks in the quarry, the battalion moved in single file to Amfréville, alternately doubling and walking across the north side of DZN.

> There to our surprise we all filed into the church. We sat in the pews speaking in hushed whispers and gawped at the brightly painted effigies of saints and the Virgin Mary and Child, and the elaborate gold cross on the altar. The minutes dragged by, then the platoon commanders were called for. Soon there was a scurry and a bustle by the big church door, quick orders were given, we filed out. Major Rogers joined us and just had time to give the plan of attack to me and the two sergeants before we moved.

Time was so short that platoon commanders had to brief their men as they pushed on up the narrow lane.

Johnson's plan was for all the companies to advance on the same axis. As the leading company took its objective the next would pass through its objective and so on in succession. He had finished giving orders at 9.40 pm. At 9.50 the artillery programme started. Sim:

> Suddenly there was a great whistling of shells overhead and the crump of explosions on Bréville. Then shells started to crash around us and we all flung ourselves to the ground on the sides of the road, covered our faces with our arms and prayed. After a time the shattering noise ended abruptly. We were on our feet and continued our advance to the start line. On our way we passed many dead and a stream of our men coming back towards us: bloody faces,

limp arms, staggering and weaving. Some collapsed
and remained still, some crawled on hands and knees.

Some of this fire was clearly from British guns dropping
short. Soon it took its toll, killing Johnson, Bamfylde and
all the members of their command groups and badly
wounding Brigadiers Lovat and Kindersley. The latter,
worried by the inauspicious start to the attack, had come
up to try and unscramble the mess. Despite this, C Company, the leading company of 12 Para, crossed the start
line at 10 pm sharp. As they did so they lost the only two
officers and the company sergeant major. Led by Sergeant
Warcup they reached their objective fifteen strong.

A Company were the next away, but the fire on the start
line killed or wounded the whole of number 2 Platoon and
the company commander. The company advanced under
the command of the CSM. As the company entered Bréville the CSM was killed. Eventually they took their objective, a château in the village, under the command of two
platoon sergeants. One of the remaining two platoons in
A Company was down to nine men.

The next company to cross the start line was D Company 12th Devons. They were late through no fault of
their own. As they forced their way up the narrow sunken
lane through the river of wounded, bloody paratroopers,
limping and crawling back from Bréville, they were hit by
a rain of shells which caused several casualties. Major
Warren, Support Company Commander 12th Devons, had
come forward to watch the battle but not take part in it,
and had been asked by Bamfylde to bring on D Company.
Warren said: 'Any conversation was carried out in a shout
because of the noise of the shelling. I was chivvying everybody on as best I could when shell and mortar fire came
down on us. It seemed to go on for a very long time, as
it always does.'

After going forward to find Bamfylde and discovering

him dead alongside Johnson 'the immediate reaction was even more fear, and that it might be a good thing to go back to my own battalion and tell my commanding officer that it hadn't really been a terribly good attack and I would get the hell out of it. But one didn't.' He eventually found about half a dozen men of the Devons. Neither he nor they knew the plan of attack. Approaching a commando sergeant dug in by the hedge, he said: ' "Good evening sergeant. Could you tell me the way to the objective?" Imagine yourself as the sergeant and a "spare" major comes up and asks the way to the objective! He made it quite clear that the objective was out there and the sooner I got on with it the better! More afraid of what the sergeant might do, I stepped out into a field towards the village.'

As Warren advanced across the field to the left of the road to Bréville he saw three Sherman tanks ahead of him 'and better still there were about fifteen men also advancing towards the village. I found that little lot was commanded by Corporal Edgar of the Devons. I said: "What are you doing?" He said: "Well, we're going forward sir!" which they were in a very gallant manner. He was being assisted by the troop of tanks. I established communication with the troop leader by climbing on his tank and beating on the turret with the butt of my pistol. We had a short conference, by which time I had made a sort of do-it-yourself instant plan. I would go through to where the road from Cabourg came into Bréville from the east and I would get astride it and dig in. This gave me a peg on which to hang my thoughts for the next hour or so. It was probably entirely useless, and was going to achieve nothing, but at least it was a plan which one could work to, and one could feel that one was beginning to do something which might be useful to someone, some time.'

Warren, who should not have been there at all and got involved in the battle by accident, reached his self-appointed objective in Bréville and dug in until the morning. He was awarded the DSO for his initiative and bravery. Warwick-Pengelly, who managed to find Bamfylde before he was killed, and receive some orders, took a party along the right of the road to the village. He was wounded twice and could go no further. The remnants of his party joined up with Warren in the morning.

B Company, 12 Para, the reserve company, crossed the start line last. As they went Colonel Parker, the Deputy Commander of the Air-Landing Brigade, joined them. He had been the Commanding Officer of the 12th, and hearing that they were involved in the attack came up to see them. He was present when Johnson was killed and decided to take command. He had been wounded in the hand but said he was not in any pain. The company reached their objective, an orchard north west of Bréville, without finding any opposition. The few Germans they found alive in the orchard were ordered to assist in improving the slit trenches to accommodate the company. Bréville was taken. But the trials and tribulations of the night were not yet over. Dusk was falling and the whole village was enveloped in smoke. The church was blazing and from inside for most of the night came the eerie sound of the organ, caused by hot air passing through the pipes. The soldiers started digging in and many had equipped themselves with German automatic weapons. Sim had just returned from going round the company to find that Rogers' trench was too small to take him as well. Without warning a torrent of shells fell on the village, causing more casualties among the exhausted and sorely depleted assault force. Sim dived for cover in a hollow. When the shelling stopped he found Rogers dead, leaning half out of his trench. It could have been the enemy's preparation for a counter-attack, but none came. It is more probable that it was part of the artillery programme for the attack being fired again in error by guns across the Orne. Captain Ward the artillery forward observer, a particularly well-known and popular officer, was killed by this shelling. Patrols went out during the night but found no Germans. All remained quiet except for the crackling of the fires and the wail of the church organ. A liaison officer came up during the night with a jeep-load of mines. Sim decided to wait until daylight before laying them. At dawn the Quartermaster of 12 Para gathered up a pile of haversacks from the dump in the quarry and brought up some containers of hot tea. The soldiers, grabbing anybody's haversack, took out a mug or mess-tin and eagerly gulped the hot sweet brew. Sim's batman told him: 'You've been hit!' His jacket sleeve was torn and bloodstained but he felt nothing. When he arrived at the regimental aid post the doctor sent him on his way to the field hospital and eventually to England.

Later that morning 1 RUR marched in, led by Crookenden, the Brigade Major of the Air-Landing Brigade. As the Irishmen passed a dead German whose torso was sticking out of a hedge, a number of them shook his hand with cries of 'the top of the morning to ye', and 'take that man's name, his helmet's not on straight'. They relieved 12 Para and 12th Devons, who between them had lost nine officers and 153 other ranks in the battle. 12 Para, a single company, fifty-five strong, marched away down the hill to the quarry they had left fourteen hours earlier.

The enemy never retook Bréville and the last chink in the perimeter was plugged. A few weeks later Crookenden was sitting in the Air-Landing Brigade command post. The telephone rang. It was the GSO 1 of the division telling him to take command of 9 Para and that he would have a difficult job because 'morale was low and they were only about 130 strong'.

Although I had done my jumps, I was the BM of the glider brigade and wore my Cheshire cap badge in my red beret. I was uncertain of my reception, although delighted to get command. On walking up through the orchards to join the battalion I found them all in terrific spirits. I was made extremely welcome by the senior remaining major, Allen Parry, and indeed by everyone, and in the rifle companies I found the senior NCOs competing vigorously for the next night patrol.

Although not fully recovered from his wound, Parry had persuaded the hospital staff at Swansea to discharge him. Dreading the prospect of returning to the Airborne Forces Depot at Hardwick, he reported to the headquarters of airborne corps at Moor Park.

I knocked on the door of a senior staff officer, dressed in full battle order including my steel helmet, which was all the kit I had, and said that I was ready to go back to war. I admitted to being wounded but nothing else. The staff officer was curious but did not probe too deeply. Eventually I found myself on a Dakota from Fairford en route to the only newly constructed airstrip in Normandy. A few days later I was going about my business in the battalion. General Gale visited and summoned me:

'You're absent,' he said.

'No sir, I'm not. I'm here,' I replied.

'Well, the War Office has reported you absent.'

'They must have made a mistake.'

'The War Office doesn't make mistakes.'

With that I returned to my slit trench to continue the war!

The 6th Airborne Division, with 1st and 4th Special Service (Commando) Brigades under command, held the left flank of the Allied beachhead until mid-August. On 17 August the division was given the task of protecting the left flank of the Canadian Army as it drove forward out of the Normandy bridgehead to the River Seine. The Airborne Division's final objective was the mouth of the Seine. To reach it they had to cross several other rivers, sometimes near the sea, where the water was deep and tidal. Gale drove his division hard, marching and attacking both by day and night.

Two battles, both fought by 5th Parachute Brigade, will give the flavour of this part of the campaign. 3rd Parachute Brigade and the Air-landing Brigade started the advance, with 5th Parachute Brigade held in reserve, ready to exploit forward when the other two brigades were held up. When 3 Parachute Brigade reached a large, deep tidal canal with sheer banks west of Putot-en-Auge, Gale decided that a co-ordinated operation by two brigades was required. Hill was told to seize a crossing place by night, over which Poett would exploit and take the high ground known as Hill 13, which dominated the approaches to Dozulé on the main axis to the Seine. Patrols from 3 Parachute Brigade reported that all the bridges had been blown. However 9 Para, commanded by Crookenden, managed to clamber across on the wreckage of the railway bridge. Crookenden's command set operator lost his balance and, clasping his commanding officer, dragged them both under.

13 Para, commanded by Luard, were ordered to march through the night and cross the canal following 9 Para. But when they arrived they found that the tide was still coming in and the water was far too deep. The steep banks made the exit particularly difficult. Poett was faced with a problem. The summer night was short and there appeared to be no way over the canal. To his relief he heard the Canadians had found an undamaged bridge not marked on the map. Hastily changing his plan, he ordered all his battalions to use this bridge. Once across, 12 Para would take Putot-en-Auge, 7 Para capture the railway station,

and 13 Para pass through and take Hill 13. They were well north of the bridge, and it was about 11 pm. Luard:

Then started a most hazardous march. We had to make the journey at great speed and the only chance of doing it in time was to move directly across the enemy front on a compass bearing. My second-in-command, Major Ford, and I, both experienced yachtsmen, led the battalion and on my orders the utmost silence was maintained. All went well, nothing was heard by the other side, and at about five minutes to midnight we reached the main road. I knew we would get shelled down the road directly the 7th Battalion made their attack. So I ordered the whole battalion to run as fast as they could in the ditch, which we did for about 200 yards until we could move away from the road towards our new RV. By the grace of God we got away with it and as the first shells fell the last man was off the road and safe.

We settled down to rest with our backs to a big bank which ran along the line of the river. Gradually dawn broke, and with it a mist. Slowly the mist cleared, and there was the German-occupied high ground immediately overlooking us. It was unpleasant, but unavoidable, and there was nothing else to do but stay there and hope for the best. The Germans, never fools, saw where we were and shelled us, but their bursts either hit the bank and did no harm, or the shrapnel was mostly away from us. As a result we suffered no casualties and in any case the shelling gradually slackened off, but did not completely stop. The brigade commander came along and told me we were to cross to the other side, pass through the 12th Battalion who were in the village, and attack the top of the hill.

Obviously speed was the only way to cross the open

space. We had a fool's chance, and a good one, to get away with it. In any case we had no real alternative because there was no cover. So off we went. The distance was about three quarters of a mile, of which the middle two hundred yards was the most hazardous. We were all very fit young men, and there is no doubt that everyone knew that the speed they made was likely to save their life. The whole battalion was across except for the last four men before the Germans realized the danger and opened fire. There were a couple of casualties, neither serious, and I lost my water bottle.

Major Tarrant and his company went straight up the hill, with A Company under Major Cramphorn supporting. I remember so well seeing them storming into the Germans using the bayonet, and then right on to the top of the hill. They were counter-attacked and a well-sited machine gun opened up, seriously wounding Major Tarrant and killing Lieutenant Bibby, who was leading his platoon, and many of their men. The leading platoons were almost all killed or wounded and the supporting platoon fell back to join us on the intermediate ridge. At that moment a fresh German battalion had arrived to reinforce the hill position, and they had done the damage. Had we been just a little earlier and been able to consolidate on the hill top, all would have been very different.

Poett stopped 13 Para exploiting forward, telling them to hold the intermediate ridge.

So we stayed where we were. I had a company commanders' meeting and in the middle of it so tired was I that I went to sleep as I was actually talking. They left me sleeping and left word that I was not to be disturbed. I woke up two hours later and the rest of the meeting was resumed with my apologies.

Gale was delighted with the progress made and ordered 3rd Parachute Brigade to continue with the advance. They had a tough battle for Dozulé, particularly for the railway station, which was taken by 9 Para. 5th Parachute Brigade passed through again and on the morning of 22 August the brigade advanced from Dozulé to secure Pont L'Evêque and open up the route to the Seine. 12 Para was told to by-pass the town, 13 Para was to secure a bridgehead over the canal and the river Touques. 7 Para were in reserve. The 12 Para attack was to have been after dark, but later in the morning it was thought that the Germans were pulling out from Pont L'Evêque and the high ground. Poett was told to force the crossing immediately at all costs.

12 Para were confronted by a very strong position overlooking the river and the surrounding country. A gallant Frenchman volunteered to go with the leading company and show them a ford, thought to exist through the river. The guide was unfortunately in a group caught by fire and only Captain Baker and eight men of A Company succeeded in crossing by wading and swimming; they were soon pinned down by fire. The remainder of A Company and the whole of B Company were held up in the open on their side of the river. Poett decided to stop any advance in that area until after dark. Baker's party remained until their ammunition was reduced to six rounds for his pistol. They withdrew to the river to wait for dark. Some of the men on the other side worked forward into the river and lay in shallow water under the bank, the only cover. As night fell they all withdrew. The casualties suffered by 12 Para were sixteen dead and forty-eight wounded.

13 Para had little difficulty in the western outskirts of the town. They had succeeded in crossing the canal and advancing up to the main bridge over the River Touques, where they met stiff opposition. A troop of tanks sent up to help the battalion could not ford the river, so were

unable to give support. Many of the houses were burning fiercely. An armoured bulldozer was put to work pushing the debris into the canal. At 6 pm the tanks clambered over this makeshift causeway and moved forward to help the 13th Battalion. The blaze was so intense that one tank caught fire, and that part of the town between the canal and the river became almost untenable. Poett told Luard to go firm until first light, or when the fires went out, before advancing to secure a bridgehead over the Touques. So far the brigade had suffered thirty-four killed and sixty-one wounded, but the enemy had suffered more; there were 127 new graves.

During the night the fires died down, though several houses were still burning. A patrol under Captain Skeet had succeeded in crossing the river and Poett ordered Luard to follow up with utmost speed. The only known means of crossing was by a steel girder eighty feet long and eighteen inches wide, or by swimming. One company was soon over, but made little progress. Luard pushed two companies across, and then attempted to outflank the enemy. In the street fighting every yard was bitterly contested; progress was slow and eventually ground to a halt. It was clear to Poett that further attempts to advance would result in unnecessary casualties for little gain, and he ordered Luard to withdraw. The withdrawal was skilfully conducted by Luard. The battalion found an alternative to the girder: a rope was stretched across, to which most men clung as they waded back. Not a single wounded man was left on the far bank, which speaks volumes for the morale, discipline and leadership in 13 Para. The battalion suffered twelve killed and thirty-three wounded.

At first light the next day, patrols from 7 Para found that the enemy had pulled out. Poett ordered the battalion to advance as fast as possible. The German tactics were typical of this phase: they held, gave the advancing troops a bloody nose, and then withdrew to the next position to repeat the performance.

At the end of nine days the division had reached Pont Audemer and the mouth of the River Risle. They had advanced forty-five miles against considerable enemy opposition in country well suited to fighting a delaying battle, which the enemy had further impaired by the use of demolitions. They hustled the enemy without respite and captured over 1,000 prisoners.

The division embarked for England in early September to rest and retrain for whatever lay ahead. Before D-Day they had been told that they could expect to be relieved after about a week. They had shown that well-briefed determined men, particularly under the cover of darkness and using their initiative, could achieve their tasks despite scattered drops, losses on landing and chaos. A few days after their arrival in the Bulford area, their 'elder brothers' of 1st Airborne Division were in action at Arnhem. Their performance was no less glorious, but the battle was a disaster because those who planned it seemed to have ignored all the lessons concerning the use of airborne troops learned at such cost over the past two years, yet demonstrated so successfully in Normandy just three months before.

CHAPTER 6

Operation Market – The Battle for Arnhem

'As far as I can tell, we have jumped into a grand military cock-up.' Staff Captain 1st Parachute Brigade to Major Dover commanding C Company 2nd Parachute Battalion.

Arnhem. Millions of words have been written, several radio and television programmes, and at least two films have been devoted to this battle. Any author attempting to describe the events of the fateful nine days and those leading up to them is faced with the problem of interesting the reader already surfeited with almost every scrap of information that has been gleaned so far, and aware of at least some of the reasons for the disaster, because disaster it was. Nevertheless, it would be an insult to the soldiers who took part, both living and dead, to give scant attention to a battle in which, as in another battle six months later and half the world away, 'uncommon valour was a common virtue'. It has all the ingredients of great drama: a glittering prize, high hopes, a distinguished cast, human failings, bravery and self-sacrifice.

The plan for Operation Market was to seize the crossings over the three broad canals and four great rivers that stood between 2nd British Army on the Meuse-Escaut Canal and its objective: Hitler's Reich. The prize: to end the war in 1944, saving thousands, if not millions, of lives thereby. The commander of 1st Allied Airborne Army, General Brereton, an American airman, was in overall command of the airborne operation, which was to be car-

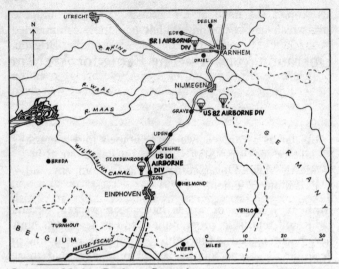

Operation Market Garden – September 1944.

ried out by Lieutenant General Browning's 1st Airborne
Corps consisting of the 82nd and 101st US and 1st British
Airborne Divisions. The canal crossings between Eind-
hoven and Veghel were allocated to the 101st, the
'Screaming Eagles', placed under 30 British Corps for the
operation. The giant bridges over the Maas and the Waal
and the Maas-Waal Canal bridge, were the objectives of
'Slim Jim' Gavin's all-American 82nd. At thirty-seven,
Gavin, an ex-ranker, was the youngest divisional commander in the US Army. Both US Airborne Divisions,
having been kept on in Normandy after the D-Day airborne operation, fighting as normal infantry, were battle-
wise and, with the exception of 1st Parachute Brigade, more
experienced than the majority in 1st Airborne Division.
Commanded by Major General Urquhart, this division
consisted of three brigades. Two were parachute brigades,
the 1st, commanded by Lathbury who had recovered from

his wound sustained at the Primasole bridge; and the 4th, which had seen some fighting in Italy, commanded by Hackett. The other brigade, 1st Air-Landing Brigade, was led by Hicks who had swum ashore in Sicily. The British were given the job of seizing the bridge over the Neder Rijn at Arnhem and holding it. Browning was given 52 (Lowland) Division, an airportable formation, to be landed in transport aircraft on Deelen airfield north of Arnhem once this had been secured. The mission for all three airborne divisions, said Brereton, was 'to grab the bridges with thunderclap surprise'.

In the van of 2nd Army, as it advanced northwards and linked up with the airborne divisions, would be 30 British Corps led by the much-loved and greatly admired Lieutenant General Horrocks. The dashing and charismatic 'Jorrocks' had under command two infantry divisions, 43rd Wessex and 50th Northumbrian, and the Guards Armoured Division. On his flanks would be two other corps. The codename for the ground advance was Garden, hence the name for the whole operation: Market Garden.

As Gallipoli for the Allies was the great might-have-been of the First World War, with its tantalizing glimpse of a road to quick victory, so was Arnhem in the Second. By a twist of fate Major General Urquhart had studied Gallipoli for his promotion exam before the war. Some of the lessons he learned were not wasted. So why did Arnhem, like Gallipoli a bold and imaginative idea, go wrong? There were a host of reasons, some well known to the layman, and others only to more avid military historians.

At least one of the reasons, intelligence both about the enemy and possessed by him, has become surrounded by myths and half-truths. Among these is the idea that the plan was betrayed to the Germans by a traitor in the Dutch resistance, and this led to the positioning of the German armoured formations which sealed the fate of 1st Airborne

Division. There is no evidence to substantiate this. On 14 September 1944, Model's Army Group B Staff prepared an appreciation of Allied Intentions, as if written by an allied staff officer, which included the following passage:

> 2nd British Army will assemble its units at the Maas-Scheldt and Albert Canals. On its right it will concentrate an attack force mainly composed of armoured units, and after forcing a Maas crossing will launch operations to breach the Rhenish-Westphalian industrial area (the Ruhr) with a main effort via Roermond. To cover the northern flank of this drive, the left wing of 2nd Army will close the Waal at Nijmegen and thus create the basic conditions necessary to cut off the German forces committed in the Dutch coastal areas. In conjunction with these operations, a large-scale airborne landing by 1st Allied Airborne Army north of the Lippe River in the area south of Munster is planned for an as yet indefinite date.

Model must have concurred for he sited his headquarters at Oosterbeek, well clear of the Allied thrust lines forecast by his staff.

The actions of the German commanders on the days leading up to Market and when they learned of the arrival of British airborne troops to the west of Arnhem are an indication that they were taken completely by surprise. For example, on the night of 16 September the guns of 9 SS Panzer Division were parked in a barracks at Hoenderloo. On 17 September Colonel Harzer, the acting divisional commander, held a parade of 9 SS Reconnaissance Battalion and was about to go into the mess for lunch with the officers when the Dakotas carrying the leading wave of 1 Airborne Division passed overhead.

Another myth, purveyed by Browning's detractors, is that he deliberately withheld from his subordinates the intelligence that 2nd SS Panzer Corps was refitting in the vicinity of Arnhem, preferring to believe, and passing to his subordinates, the information that the Germans had about a brigade group with a few tanks in the area. Browning was an austere man and gave the impression of arrogance and aloofness. To many Americans he appeared too dapper. Brereton did not trust him and neither did Gavin. Browning in his turn detested Brereton, who was disliked by many of his fellow-countrymen. But Browning's integrity was beyond question. During the planning for a previous operation, codename Linnet, which was never mounted, he had shocked the Americans by threatening to resign on the grounds that his troops were about to be thrown into the battle ill-prepared because there were not enough maps for junior commanders. This is not the action of a man whose ambition takes precedence over the lives of his soldiers.

The intelligence picture was further confused by another important factor. Some time before Arnhem the British SOE discerned that the Germans had penetrated the Dutch Resistance. Although the process of cleaning up the organization had been completed before Market Garden, there was still a residue of distrust at SOE headquarters and information from the Dutch Resistance tended to be treated with reservation.

The information on enemy strengths passed down to 1st Airborne Division was not wildly inaccurate. Although Obergruppenfuhrer (Lieutenant General) Bittrich's 2nd SS Panzer corps, consisting of 9th and 10th SS Panzer Divisions, was indeed refitting north-east of Arnhem, their strength after the mauling they had received since July 1944 was more or less as given to 1st Airborne Division: about a brigade group and a few tanks. They were not, as has been portrayed in some accounts, sitting in Arnhem or on the DZs. 9th SS Panzer Division around Zutphen, twenty-one miles from Arnhem, consisted of a Panzer grenadier regiment, an artillery battalion, two assault gun batteries, an armoured reconnaissance battalion, an armoured company equipped with Panther tanks, and elements of engineer and flak batteries. 10th SS Panzer Division, in the vicinity of Ruurlo, twenty-five miles from Arnhem, was weaker still, and consisted of part of a Panzer grenadier regiment (only partially motorized), two artillery battalions, one engineer battalion, one flak battalion, and one armoured reconnaissance battalion. Corps head-quarters was at Doetinchem, twenty-one miles from Arnhem. The two divisions were distributed in several villages over a wide area and not deployed tactically.

1 Airborne Division Intelligence Summary, dated 10 September 1944, includes the following passage:

> There is no doubt that the enemy has made a remark-able recovery, at any rate in the 21st Army Group area ... his stand at the Albert Canal has enabled 25,000 men from 15th Army to escape via the Dutch Islands. A captured document indicates that the degree of control exercised over the regrouping and collecting of the apparently scattered remnants of a beaten army was little short of remarkable. Further-more the fighting capacity of the new battle groups, formed from the remnants of the battered divisions, seems unimpaired. New divisions are being formed in Germany, and the degree of control being exer-cised by the Nazis is such that the Germans will fight to the bitter end.

This Intelligence Summary was repeated verbatim in all brigade intelligence summaries in the division.

1st Parachute Brigade Intelligence Summary of 13 Sep-tember 1944, includes the phrase: 'a reported concen-tration of 10,000 troops reforming south-west of Zwolle on 1 September may represent a battle-scarred Panzer division or two reforming.' Zwolle was a long way from Arnhem, but the tone of these intelligence summaries should have caused a few ears to prick up and set nostrils twitching.

The missing part of the information passed to 1st Airborne Division was who the enemy were. This was the nub of the problem faced by the British airborne: the quality of the German troops and their commanders. Field Marshal Model, the commander of Army Group B, had his headquarters in Oosterbeek, about two miles west of Arnhem. Efficient and ruthless, Hitler had called him the 'saviour of the Eastern Front'. General Bittrich was one of the most respected Waffen SS Generals in the German Army. South of Arnhem and facing 2nd British Army was General Student, the 'father' of German parachute forces, commanding 1st Parachute Army. 'Time and again, however empty of Germans and peaceful the scene appeared to be, if you touched them in an area important to them, their reaction was swift and violent,' said Hackett, referring to the astonishing ability of the majority of formations in the German army, right up to the end of the war, regardless of the punishment they had taken, to be quicker on the draw in a tactical sense than most of their opponents. SS Panzer divisions were the cream of the German Army: tough, hard-bitten, well-trained soldiers, led by resolute and shrewd commanders. Why did the British so grossly underestimate the German army after five years of fighting them?

From August to September 1944 the Allies had been advancing so rapidly that many people believed the war was almost over. Although by mid-September the German resistance was starting to stiffen, the effects were not yet evident, despite the intelligence pointers. The over-confidence engendered by the feeling that the war was all but won was compounded, in the case of 1st Airborne Division, by an air of cynicism and increasing boredom. While 6th Airborne Division had been fighting in Normandy, 1st Airborne had been held back in England as airborne reserve. Between 6 June and 12 September the division had been stood by for sixteen operations, all of them cancelled, on four occasions when the aircraft had been loaded, and once when some aircraft were actually in the air. Urquhart told Nigel Hamilton, Montgomery's biographer: 'By the time we went on Market Garden, we couldn't have cared less ... you have to visualize the euphoria which existed across the channel and in the airborne corps that the war was nearly over.'

'A feeling of total exasperation and despair was felt by many of us in 1st Parachute Brigade,' remembers Hibbert, the Brigade Major, one of the founder members of 2 Commando, who had been waiting since 1940 to do an operational jump. 'If we had been asked to drop into the middle of Berlin and wait for the Russians, we would have gone quite cheerfully.'

4th Parachute Brigade, who had never dropped into action as a brigade, and as related earlier had seen very little of the war so far, was most affected. The war could well be over before they got into it. ' "The Stillborn Division" we had started to call ourselves, to be kept for use in the victory parade, nice and tidy in our smart red berets,' wrote one company commander in his book *Men at Arnhem*. Even in 1st Parachute Brigade, one of the crack brigades in the British Army, Frost remembers that 'there was much unrest in one battalion, and another failed its test exercise.' A change of commanding officers was needed to put matters right. Battlewise though this brigade was, it had taken heavy casualties in North Africa and Sicily, and many of the reinforcements had yet to be blooded. Some observers were of the opinion that perhaps they were not quite as well trained as they thought they were. Throughout the division, fights with Americans or alongside Americans against the common enemy, the Military Police, were regular events. In 4th Parachute Brigade the VD rate, usually caused by carelessness – failure to carry out the correct 'drills' – rose rapidly, another indicator of indiscipline and lowering morale.

Hackett said:

> I prayed to get my brigade into action before things got really bad. The better people go off the quickest. Bad soldiers don't care if they never get into battle. Mine were the best. Several times we had written our last letters and been sealed up in the transit camps for twenty-four hours. You just can't keep on doing this.

Time was short. There were only seven days available to plan for Operation Market Garden, and the various headquarters involved were widely separated; some in Northern France and Belgium and some in England. For security reasons discussions could not be held on the telephone. The distances involved, and the limited time, meant that personal visits by commanders and staff officers to iron out problems were infrequent. Whereas the commander and staff of 6th Airborne Division had three months to plan and prepare for Normandy, Urquhart gave his orders thirty-six hours after receiving his mission from Browning. Neither 2nd British Army nor 30 Corps sent representatives to 1st Airborne Corps to discuss what was being agreed; a singular disinterest in such a critical operation. Yet 6th Airborne Division's report on the Normandy operation is specific on this point: 'In future operations it is most desirable that airborne planning marches in step with that of the formations with which they are cooperating. *In the case of hastily laid-on operations this is essential.*'

Both Browning and Urquhart were worried about key features of the plan. But there simply was not time to argue the case with the plethora of headquarters involved – 21st Army Group, 2nd Army and 1st Allied Air Army. As it was, Browning had already shot his bolt by threatening to resign once. If he handed in his cards a second time they would have been accepted and the operation would have gone ahead unchanged. There were several people in the wings happy to take his place, including the American Ridgeway, fretting at two American airborne divisions being placed under British command. In his book *Montgomery in Europe 1943–45* Richard Lamb quotes Brian Urquhart, no relation to General Urquhart but Browning's intelligence officer: 'Browning was uneasy about the plan for Arnhem. He was made the scapegoat for this disaster. The film of *A Bridge Too Far* is a travesty on this score, as on many others.'

Urquhart had fought in the western desert and commanded a brigade group with distinction in Sicily and Italy, winning a second DSO after bitter fighting at Rizo. He knew more about soldiering than most of the division, and had more experience of commanding large numbers of men in battle than many senior airborne commanders at the time, including Browning. But because he had no previous airborne experience, his arrival as Divisional Commander was not greeted with universal enthusiasm within his formation. Some felt his contention that Airborne was just another way of going to battle showed that he had failed to hoist in the key elements surrounding this new way of warfare, not least the total dependence on another service, the Air Force, to get the soldiers to the right place and keep them supplied and supported until a link-up with ground troops was made. There are still people who contend that Urquhart acquiesced too readily with the air plan for Arnhem simply because he lacked the airborne experience to give him the confidence to argue his case. It is possible that had Urquhart already commanded a large and successful airborne operation, like Gale, or had Down's forthright manner and experience of airborne matters, he would have had an authority that even Browning and Brereton might have found difficult to resist. But as a commander he is hard to fault, and he certainly had no self-doubt about his own competence. Major Powell, who fought at Arnhem, wrote: 'Urquhart will be remembered by all who served under him for his rock-like qualities, his cool and clear mind, and for the care he took of his men. He was an inspiring leader.' Hackett, who had plenty of battle experience, said about him: 'For my part I had seen no better battlefield commander in any previous campaign, and have seen none since.'

The American Divisional commanders planned to fly in all nine parachute battalions on the first day. Urquhart was given the least number of aircraft of the three divisions, and when he asked Browning for forty more his request was refused. Browning took thirty-six aircraft to fly in his Corps Headquarters on the first day. Had he not done so, and had Urquhart not taken in his artillery on day one, he would have been able to fly in most of his infantry on the first lift.

'It is in general better to take landing losses and land on the objective than have to fight after landing in order to reach the objective,' said Gavin. Lightly equipped airborne troops are neither hard-hitting, nor after landing, fast-moving in comparison with mechanized soldiers. The shock effect of an airborne operation is achieved by surprise, landing preferably by night on, or very close to, the objective. As had been amply demonstrated only three months before in Normandy, well-briefed determined men, despite scattered drops, could take advantage of the chaos and cover of the night to grab their objectives. Once there, and particularly in among buildings or close country, they could then hold them against much stronger opposition. However, by the time the senior airmen had had their say on Operation Market the soldiers of all divisions, and particularly 1st Airborne, had been shorn of two vital weapons: shock and the cover of darkness.

After their experiences in Sicily and Normandy, the

USAAF had an aversion to night airborne operations and insisted on conducting Market by day. Air Vice Marshall Hollinghurst commanding 38 Group RAF was happy to allow the RAF crews to fly to Arnhem twice on the first day, starting with a take-off in darkness, dropping and landing at dawn, followed by a late evening lift the same day. But Major General Williams USAAF, the coordinator of the airlift disagreed and his views prevailed. The reasons: the navigation problems without a moon, and the danger of German night fighters. However, the targets over the conspicuous rivers and canals should not have been hard to find, and diversions by bombers might have drawn off the night fighters. There is no doubt that, on past experience, a night operation would have resulted in the losses on landing being far higher than they were in daylight. But on balance it would have been better to have accepted these for the gain of smaller losses in the subsequent battle.

One of the *raisons d'être* of airborne troops is to be able to 'leap over' obstacles such as rivers and avoid long approach marches which give the enemy time to react. Yet at the Wilhelmina Canal at Zon, at Arnhem, and at Nijmegen, the air plan for the first day for all three airborne divisions resulted in landings on only one side of a major obstacle, in the latter two cases about eight miles away from the bridges. This decision was to have fatal results. A critical factor in 30 Corps' failure to link up with 1st Airborne was the delay caused at Nijmegen by having to bring forward canvas boats. American paratroopers, who had never seen these craft before, were then invited to paddle across an obstacle which they were trained at great expense to cross in aircraft. At Arnhem, one end of the bridge was never taken.

The reason for this decision was largely the fault of the air planners. Their worry was the flak around the objectives and in the surrounding area. Yet by this stage in the war the Allies had overwhelming air superiority and rocket-firing Typhoons or Tempests could have been used for flak suppression. It must be said that the airmen were not worried for their own safety, as subsequent events were to prove. However, in their concern for their passengers' safe arrival they insisted on DZs and LZs so far away from the objectives that in the case of 1st Airborne Division thousands of casualties were suffered after landing and the operation failed. No use was made of gliders to land close to the bridge at Arnhem despite the successful operation in Normandy. Again the airmen decided the ground was too rough south of the bridge, the only open space. Yet the Polish Parachute Brigade was supposed to land south of the bridge on day three and gliders had been included in a night *coup de main* role in a previous plan for taking the Arnhem bridge, Operation Comet. Moreover, the terrain was no rougher than the immediate vicinity of the Caen Canal bridge where Howard's men had landed successfully at night. Comet was to have been carried out by 1st Airborne Division and the Polish Parachute Brigade, their task to capture all the objectives that a few days later were assigned to a whole airborne corps. Glider *coup de main* parties were to land right by the Arnhem, Nijmegen and Graves bridges. These were to be followed up by the parachute brigades and the air-landing brigade on DZs/LZs close by. For example, 4th Parachute Brigade's objective was the half-mile long road bridge over the Maas at Grave. Like the other brigade commanders, Hackett chose a DZ only three-quarters of a mile north of the bridge, while four gliders carrying a company of 1st Air-Landing Brigade would land right by the southern end of the bridge. B Company of 156 Battalion, commanded by Major Waddy, would leave all their heavy equipment on the DZ and in light order double for the bridge, to meet up with the glider party. When orders were given for this operation, Major Powell turned to Waddy and said: 'That's either a wooden cross or a Victoria Cross for you!' The Comet plan was imaginative, incorporating many of the lessons learned over the years. It might have succeeded had it been implemented immediately while the Germans were still disorganized. The day it was cancelled Market was substituted, to take place a week later.

Market was a bold idea, but the plan for its execution was pedestrian. The airborne soldiers were to be committed to battle without any of the advantages of surprise, cover of darkness and shock to mitigate their disadvantages – lack of mobility, armour and fire-power. Having imposed these limitations on the plan, the airmen delivered the final blow. As far back as the airborne landings on Sicily, over a year before, it should have been apparent that close air support – aircraft using guns, bombs and rocket to fire on targets at the request of ground troops – would have been invaluable until friendly artillery was in range. Although the arrangements for this type of support were not as sophisticated as they are today, it could be done. However, the air planners decreed that no missions in support of ground troops were to be flown by the tactical airforces while escort fighters were in the air. In the event, the arrangements were so ham-fisted, and the liaison so loose, that the 1st Airborne Division in particular was denied the use of a weapon that the Germans, after their Normandy experience, dreaded. The enemy was able to bring reinforcements into Arnhem by road, in daylight, with impunity, a move which would have been fraught with risk in Normandy a few weeks earlier.

Browning must bear some of the blame for acquiescing to the air plan, including the lack of close air support. A commander in a joint operation cannot abdicate the responsibility for seeing that the transporting service, in this case the air force, delivers the soldiers to the place and in the manner that allows them to do their job. Browning was the 'father' of British airborne forces. He forged

the airborne weapon, nurtured it through the difficult days and insisted on high standards of performance at all levels. But on Operation Market he allowed himself to be persuaded to break many of the rules. Indeed, at Nijmegen he insisted that Gavin take the Groesbeek Heights before going for the Nijmegen bridges. The Groesbeek Heights were of no tactical significance whatsoever. It is difficult to avoid the suspicion that Browning wanted the heights secured as the site for his headquarters. Montgomery must also share the blame. His shrewd eye had spotted the flaws in the plan and he sent his acting chief of staff, in the absence of the persuasive de Guingand, to speak to Brereton. But Brereton, not being a soldier, did not understand the problem and was not flexible enough to change the plan. Monty was not usually one to suffer fools gladly. He did on this occasion.

Over-confidence, lack of a sense of urgency, and inflexibility plagued this operation from its inception. Practically no lessons learned in previous operations, other than purely procedural ones, were applied to Market. The German attack on Crete had been avidly studied by their airborne counterparts in Britain and America. The two factors that swung this battle in favour of the Germans, the use of ground attack aircraft in support and the introduction of reserves by air at a critical part in the battle, were ignored by the Market planners. The air plan for Market did not allow for any switching of follow-up formations to influence the battle as it was actually progressing, as opposed to how the planners thought it would go. So the 4th Parachute Brigade and the Polish Parachute Brigade, instead of being flown in to DZs where they could exert a decisive influence on the course of the battle, were flown in to a pre-arranged plan and timetable. Perhaps the planners forgot that the enemy thinks too. According to Hackett, 'some airborne planners cooked up the plan like a sort of airborne picnic, and then added the

Germans like pepper and salt to taste. You should start by taking the Germans into account.'

Bad weather has been given as one of the reasons for the failure of Market. But 38 Group RAF stated that the weather had not unduly hampered operations. The missing ingredient in the conception and conduct of the operation was the 'thunderclap' that Brereton had demanded. The Germans may have been surprised by the scale of the airborne operation at first, but there was no thunderclap. The senior airmen saw to that.

Urquhart's plan for the first day was to drop Lathbury's 1st Parachute Brigade on Dropping Zone X, and Hick's 1st Air-Landing Brigade, less two companies, on Landing Zone S, and land Divisional Headquarters, most of his artillery, 21 Reconnaissance Squadron and other units such as medical and sappers, on Landing Zone Z. The reconnaissance squadron would then dash for the Arnhem Road bridge in their jeeps equipped with Vickers K guns. 1st Parachute Brigade would follow on foot at best speed. Hicks would protect the landing zones and dropping zones until the arrival of Hackett's 4th Parachute Brigade and other units on day two. Thus the air-landing battalions, the best equipped and strongest in the division, were tied to protecting ground rather than going for the divisional objective – the bridge. On day three the Polish Parachute Brigade would drop south of the bridge on Dropping Zone K. If all went well by the end of day three, the division, consisting of four brigades of infantry, would be formed into a three-sided box on the north, east and west sides of the town, with the south resting on the river. There they would await the arrival of 30 British Corps advancing from the south.

When Deane-Drummond, by now the second-in-command of the Divisional Signal Regiment, heard the plan forty-eight hours before take-off, his reaction was that it only stood a chance if there was little opposition. Landing

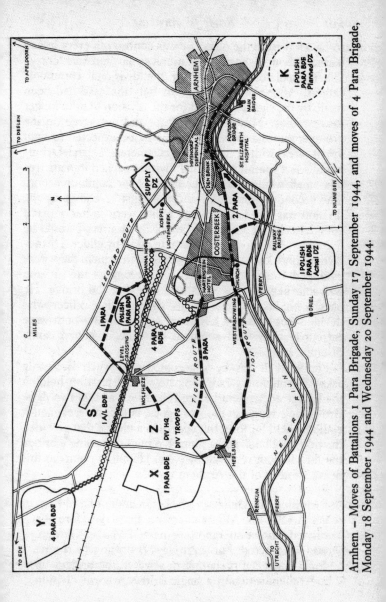

Arnhem – Moves of Battalions 1 Para Brigade, Sunday 17 September 1944, and moves of 4 Para Brigade, Monday 18 September 1944 and Wednesday 20 September 1944.

so far away from the objective was contrary to every lesson learned about airborne operations so far and was 'crazy'. His immediate worry was for the divisional communications. After the experience in Italy the case had been made by the signal regiment for the division to have longer range radios. The Airborne Corps did not agree on the grounds that the division would only be expected to fight in an area with a three-mile diameter. Deane-Drummond's tart comment is that a division packed into an area this small would hardly need radios for communication! The second argument advanced against re-equipping the division was that longer range radios were so heavy that a complete change in the loading plans of aircraft would be necessary, and most would have to go in by glider. Deane-Drummond knew that the radios with which they were equipped could not be relied on as long as the division was split between the DZs and LZs and the bridge. He passed on his concern to his commanding officer who decided not to worry Urquhart or his GSO1; both were extremely busy, and about to emplane in gliders some distance away.

For years it has been accepted that when Browning asked Montgomery how long he should plan on holding the bridge at Arnhem before relief, he was told two days. Browning's reply, so the story goes, is that he reckoned it could be held for four, but added, in a phrase that provided the title for a book and a film: 'We might be going a bridge too far.' Recent research by Nigel Hamilton points to this being another of the Arnhem myths:

> Browning saw Dempsey (the commander of 2nd British Army), not Montgomery on the day before the revised Comet operation, re-named Market Garden, was resurrected. For seven days Browning's airborne corps had been preparing to seize all the bridges up to Arnhem with only a single British airborne division

and a Polish parachute brigade (the Comet operation); to have protested that Arnhem was a 'bridge too far' when Dempsey offered him no less than three airborne divisions plus the Polish parachute brigade, was inherently unlikely.

Besides, it was a fatuous remark because if the Arnhem bridge was not included there was no point in going at all. Browning was not given to making ill-considered comments. In Urquhart's confirmatory notes to his verbal orders he gave enough passwords, a new one each day, for six days. In the event that was not to be enough.

SUNDAY

On Sunday 17 September 1944, 2 Para, with a 10 am take-off, had a leisurely start in comparison with the chaos they had experienced before their drop in Tunisia. Frost had no misgivings about the task given to his battalion; the guns and tanks of 2nd British Army would soon be supporting them. He arranged for his gun, cartridges and golf clubs to travel in his staff car which, with other transport, would follow by sea. Tea, sandwiches and the Sunday papers helped pass the time as the aircraft carrying the 1st Parachute Brigade formed up over England, flew over the North Sea and over Holland. There was some minor damage from flak; about one foot of the wing-tip of a Dakota alongside Deane-Drummond's aircraft was shot away. But the escorting fighters attacked most of the flak guns that revealed their positions by firing. The gliders started landing at 1 pm, preceded twenty minutes before by the pathfinders of 21st Independent Parachute Company. At 2 pm the 1st Parachute Brigade began to drop. There were only small parties of enemy on the DZ and LZs, and these offered no opposition. About ninety-five per cent of battalions were soon at their respective RVs. Wilson, commanding the pathfinders, released some pigeons to take the message that so far all was well back to England. They flew to the roof of a nearby barn and had to be dislodged by a shower of pebbles before they would take off on their mission.

As the streams of aircraft passed over Model's headquarters in Oosterbeek he was drinking a glass of white wine as an aperitif before lunch. He and his staff jumped into cars and drove at high speed into Arnhem. Having restored order in the garrison headquarters, whose commander had been killed in an air raid earlier in the day, he motored off to find Bittrich, the commander of 2 SS Panzer Corps. Many of Bittrich's units were due to leave for Germany that day and had entrained already. Some trains had left Arnhem station. Working with frantic speed Bittrich's staff reassembled the equipment of the two divisions. Most of the corps' radio equipment had been destroyed in the battles in France, and the passing of orders over the Dutch telephone system was made difficult by the civilian operators being as slow as they dared. When Model arrived at Bittrich's headquarters at about 3 pm he found to his intense satisfaction that 2nd SS Panzer Corps was on the move. A battle group of 9th SS Panzer was already on its way to the DZ and LZs with orders to destroy the enemy troops landing west of Oosterbeek. The rest of 9th SS Panzer Division, a division in name only, was moving to set up blocking positions west of Arnhem. Bittrich had also ordered 10 SS Panzer to drive south as fast as possible and to seize the Nijmegen bridge. Bittrich planned to prevent the British from reaching Arnhem and by holding the Nijmegen bridge, halt, or delay, the link-up forces, thus enabling him to destroy the British airborne soldiers with the help of reinforcements brought in from the rest of Army Group B. Bittrich had moved so fast that by the time the British troops were landing his men were almost in a position to defeat them.

Stationed between Oosterbeek and Wolfheze was Sturmbannfuhrer Kraft's SS Panzer Grenadier Depot and Reserve Battalion 16. In early September he had been ordered 'to prepare for and attack airborne landings, and to defend the bridges and ferries over the Rhine at Arnhem, and to prepare them ready for demolition.' When at 1.30 pm Kraft saw the landings in progress he had no doubts about what he should do. His battalion war diary records:

> We knew from experience that the only way to draw the teeth of an airborne landing with an inferior force is to drive right into it. From a tactical point of view, it would be wrong to play a purely defensive role and let the enemy gather his forces unmolested.

The action of this battalion with only twelve officers and 294 men was to cost the British dear.

Lathbury's plan for his brigade was for 2 Para to move along a road running into Arnhem along the north bank of the Neder Rijn (Lion Route). They were to seize the railway bridge, the pontoon bridge and the road bridge. 3 Para was also to make for the road bridge but take the main Heelsum – Arnhem road into the town (Tiger Route). 1 Para was ordered to provide a company as brigade reserve while the rest of the battalion took the most northerly route (Leopard Route), making for a piece of high ground overlooking the town. To push a brigade forward in three routes simultaneously on so wide a front was unconventional. But Lathbury hoped that by advancing on a broad front his brigade would find the weakest point in any defence. He would then switch the whole brigade onto that axis. About an hour and a half after the brigade landed, Lathbury ordered battalions to move.

Of the 358 gliders in the first lift, 319 landed, far more

than had been expected. Several were damaged, including at least one that had its wings peeled off. 'This is a frightening experience although not a particularly dangerous one,' wrote Colonel Warrack, the senior doctor in the division. But the thirty-nine missing gliders included some of the twenty-two allocated to the Divisional Reconnaissance Squadron containing their jeeps. Others were in crashed gliders and could not be unloaded for some time. However, contrary to some accounts, the squadron was not too far below strength. But the plan which employed the squadron as armoured reconnaissance, which they were not, accounted for the majority of the remaining jeeps and soldiers. The dash to capture the bridges by Major Gough's men ran into an ambush near Johannahoeve. As the battle progressed other jeep patrols were ambushed.

To begin with there were few signs of enemy, and at first it was hard to imagine there was a war in progress. The soldiers had come from peaceful England to peaceful Holland. The advance towards Arnhem was in many cases hampered by the holiday mood of the Dutch people who joyfully but courteously pressed food, fruit, flowers, jugs of water and even gin on the paratroopers. The soldiers caught the mood of this friendly, happy atmosphere and according to some accounts soon started showing excessive respect for property, politely knocking on doors to ask permission to move through gardens. The advance was very slow. Opinions among those who were present are divided on whether or not the advance was unnecessarily slow, and if it was, why? There was a feeling of inertia after landing safely. Many of the younger soldiers had not been under fire before, and inexperienced troops tend to pause when shot at the first time, or go to ground under mortar and artillery fire, instead of moving out of the area. Not all the soldiers were as battle-hungry as has sometimes been suggested, particularly the veterans. An operator from the brigade radio link to 2 Para, and travelling with the battalion:

> I remember having that Christ-here-we-go-again feeling. I suspect I wasn't the only one to feel that way. Those months in England had done little to improve the warlike proclivities of most of us. When we were in Africa and Italy, home and the end of the war were so remote that we had a different attitude, not exactly 'do or die' but at least more of a willingness to accept whatever the fates might bring. Now only a few short hours after leaving England, and not many more since we walked its streets and drank its beer, with war news indicating the end in sight, there was a general feeling that this was not the time to get killed or maimed. Some of our brigade already had three campaigns under our belts, and could already dimly perceive that civvy suit not too far down the road. There might be something touchingly tragic about dying for a lost cause. To that most of us would have added that it would be downright bloody foolishness to die for one already won.

It would have been better, according to Hibbert, if the battalions had started by forced marching, that is alternately walking and running, until they met opposition. The adrenalin was not flowing, the landing had been unopposed. Small pockets of resistance seemed to take ages to clear. But it is difficult for lightly equipped infantry to brush aside armour. The plan required an advance through a built-up area where even a handful of snipers can hold up many times their number; 1st Parachute Brigade was facing more than a few snipers. Oosterbeek and the suburbs of Arnhem consisted of woods and detached houses and gardens. Every garden had a stout chest-high wire fence round it. When the 'point' was held up by enemy fire, the following sections and platoons would try to outflank the enemy. Outflanking movements round the backs of houses were painfully slow as every fifteen or twenty yards the heavily-laden soldiers had to climb a fence. The slow dawdle of troops at the rear of a battalion which is fighting its way forward on a one-man front can be infuriating to a commander following up behind. Urquhart arrived at 1st Parachute Brigade headquarters enraged that the brigade was not moving faster, and went to find Lathbury who was with 3 Para to instil a greater sense of urgency into his brigade. His concern was heightened because he thought that few of the radio sets in the division were working, and he seemed unable to communicate with anybody other than by face-to-face conversation. His division was taking time to wind up. The trouble was, as Hackett said:

> Airborne units have little practice in fighting as formations. Once committed, moreover, they do not approach the battlefield in a series of moves such as help a divisional staff to grasp the articulation of the whole. They are dismantled before departure, packed in small pieces aboard aircraft, then sprayed out in the very area of the battle. Reassembly is far from easy.

As 2 Para moved through Oosterbeek, Major Dover, who had existed on the diet of apples in Sicily, took C Company away from the route followed by the rest of the battalion to capture the rail bridge. Frost had ordered Dover to cross the bridge, move along the south bank of the Neder Rijn and capture the southern end of the road bridge. As Lieutenant Barry, the leading platoon commander, was a third of the way over the bridge, covered by fire from the rest of the company, the southernmost span blew up in his face and collapsed into the river. Unless the pontoon bridge was still in place, 2 Para would have to take the southern end of the road bridge by crossing over it first. The decision not to drop or land on both sides of the river was now coming home to roost! Dover, whose orders in the event of being unable to cross the railway bridge were to advance into the town and capture the German headquarters, moved off under sniper fire. C Company never met up with the battalion again. As night was falling they caught about eighty Germans fallen-in on the road outside the St Elizabeth Hospital after debussing. C Company despatched most of them. They pressed on and soon became involved in a battle in the town. The advance of C Company into the town along two of the main roads may have persuaded Colonel Harzer, the commander of 9 SS Panzer, that this was the route being taken by all British troops. He was unaware that Frost had slid past along the lower road by the river and after dark had secured the northern end of the road bridge. The pontoon bridge had gone. There was only one way to the other side, a dash across the road bridge. At 7.30 pm, before 2 Para had secured the bridge, Hibbert spoke on the radio to Lathbury, who had gone to find 3 Para, and suggested that he switch them to follow behind 2 Para, who were making good progress. Lathbury did not agree with his Brigade Major's suggestion saying that 1 Para was in trouble at Wolfheze, and 3 Para were stuck and would remain where they were for the night. He ordered brigade headquarters to continue to advance to the bridge. At about the same time Hibbert was joined by Gough, who asked him to pass a message on the divisional radio net to direct all the Reconnaissance Squadron jeeps along 'Lion' (the southern route), yet another indication that this was the best route.

Meanwhile, 3 Para commanded by Lieutenant Colonel Fitch had set off down the Utrecht–Arnhem road soon after Frost had left on his route. About an hour later, having advanced little more than a mile, at a crossroads two miles west of Oosterbeek the leading platoon fired on a German staff car, killing the Major General commanding the Arnhem area, returning from a visit to Kraft's battalion. While the leading platoon sorted themselves out after this incident, the remainder of 3 Para concertinaed, bunching up around the cross-roads – always a likely pre-registered target – and were treated to a concentrated mortar bombardment. Instead of moving on immediately the battalion went to ground, but the bombs burst in the trees above them and soon several men were screaming in agony. A combination of inexperience among the new men and 'stickiness' among the older hands kept the battalion bogged down. The friction of war was clogging the system in the brigade. Eventually Lathbury came up and ordered Fitch to get his battalion moving. Urquhart had now joined Lathbury and they were following 3 Para when it was held up again, this time by self-propelled guns. Urquhart's unease increased. Darkness was approaching, he had no idea if the bridge was in British hands; the only part of the brigade with whom he was in contact was at least five miles from the objective. The price for allowing the air force to choose DZs eight miles away from the target bridge was now being paid; the currency his soldiers' lives.

While his battalion dealt with the SP guns, Fitch sent C Company round the southern flank of the block. Eventually the battalion was held up on the outskirts of Oosterbeek by Kraft's men, reinforced by the battle group from 9th SS Panzer. With the onset of night, 3 Para rested where they were for a few hours.

C Company under Major Lewis used side roads and the railway track to get right into Arnhem. On the way Private McKinnon, feeling hungry, entered a butcher's shop. The butcher, speaking English, offered him a glass of wine and some bread and cheese. The butcher's small daughter said to him in halting English: 'Many happy returns after your long stay away.' The company was within a few hundred yards of the road bridge when they encountered a German armoured car. They destroyed it with a Gammon bomb but found their way blocked by a Panzer Grenadier company. After a brief fire fight some of the company managed to slip past the Germans and make their way to the bridge.

On the northern route 1 Para, commanded by Lieutenant Colonel Dobie, were making good time when they ran into German tanks and half-tracks just north of Wolfheze. A chaotic battle ensued as the paratroopers fought against the mechanized unit that sought to block their way. At one stage the Germans got round behind the battalion. Everywhere they turned or moved they were swept by fire. Dead lay all around, wounded were crying for water. Groans and shrieks of pain filled the air. Time and time again they overran portions of the battalion and had to be driven out with the bayonet. R Company, leading the battalion, was cut off at about this time by German armour. The battalion clawed its way forward until Dobie realized that the high ground which was his objective was too strongly held for him to take with his battalion unaided. His signallers picked up a message from Frost at the bridge asking for reinforcement. On his own initiative Dobie decided to go to his assistance. The battalion waited until dawn before advancing.

During the night and early morning Frost was joined at the northern end of the bridge by most of brigade headquarters (but without Lathbury), Gough and a few of his Reconnaissance Squadron, some engineers under Lieutenant McKay, and a platoon of the Divisional Royal Army Service Corps with a captured truck loaded with ammunition from the DZ. They had slipped past the enemy along the same route used by Frost.

The news that the Germans might have left a gap in their blocking positions was apparently not known to Urquhart, although Lathbury knew. At 9.30 pm the pre-

vious evening Hibbert had again managed to get through
on the radio to Lathbury, still with 3 Para. Hibbert told
him that 2 Para were on the main bridge, which was intact.

The Reconnaissance Squadron's proper role, using the
mobility afforded by its jeeps, was to sneak forward cautiously on a broad front to gain information about enemy
dispositions and the best routes for outflanking them. They
could also be used for liaison and the passing of orders
and information, like mounted messengers in days gone
by; invaluable when for one reason or another radio communications are not working as well as they might – exactly
the situation in 1st Airborne Division. If the depleted
squadron had been used for its proper job instead of the
abortive attempt to seize the bridge by *coup de main* they
should have discovered this unguarded route to the bridge
even before Frost. Acquainted with this information,
Lathbury or Urquhart could have switched the rest of 1st
Parachute Brigade to follow 2 Para. Even after Frost had
got through, a switch would not have been impossible
if the Divisional Reconnaissance had been available as
'gallopers' to supplement the radio sets.

If, during the night 1 and 3 Para had immediately swung
south and followed Frost's route to the bridge, they might
have managed to join him before the Germans blocked
this last way in. It was a pity that Lathbury allowed them
both to stop for a while during this first night. It must
have been clear to him from the two radio conversations
he had had with Hibbert that the southern route offered
the best chance of getting his whole brigade to the bridge,
provided he seized the opportunity at once. As has been
previously noted, the Germans did not operate well at
night. They were to show this same tendency at Arnhem
and the British should have capitalized on this weakness.
General Crookenden, who commanded 9th Parachute
Battalion in 6th Airborne Division, once remarked that if
the British Army had a fault it was a lack of ruthlessness

on the part of commanders, among whom he included himself, when their men showed signs of flagging. They sometimes stopped when they should have pushed on, not appreciating that the enemy might be exhausted too. In the end casualties might have been averted.

At the end of the first day there was another way to reinforce Frost, using the inherent flexibility of airpower. 1st Airborne Division had some communication with the UK base and it was becoming clear that the advance from the DZs west of Arnhem was being blocked by the enemy. Sitting in England were two parachute brigades, the 4th and the Poles. South of Arnhem bridge was DZ K, already on the briefing maps and known to the aircrews. It was technically perfectly possible to use this DZ for the second lift. Doing so would have freed the Air-Landing Brigade from the task of protecting 4th Parachute Brigade's DZ west of Arnhem and allowed them to be used more productively. Probably the only man who could have pushed through the command decision to switch 4th Parachute Brigade's drop from DZ Y to DZ K was Browning. But instead of being alongside Brereton in England, able to re-jig the plan, Browning was sitting impotently within 82nd Airborne Division's perimeter on Groesbeek heights south of Nijmegen, out of touch with the other division in his corps.

'The terrible "ifs" accumulate,' as was once said about the Gallipoli campaign. A brigade, even if under-strength, might have held the bridge, particularly had the Germans been forced to counter-attack both ends of the bridge and face a threat by the remainder of the division from the west at the same time. 10,095 men, ninety-two guns, more than 500 jeeps, 400 trailers and 300 motorcycles were eventually delivered to the DZs and LZs west of Arnhem with far smaller landing losses than had been suffered in airborne operations before. But the distance from the objective, communications failure, poor reconnaissance, no second lift on the first day, and inflexibility resulted in only some 500 men reaching the 1st Airborne Division's objective, the bridge.

Frost's men made two attempts to cross the bridge and capture the southern end. But the enemy fire from a pillbox and armoured vehicle on the northern end was too fierce. The battle for the pillbox started a fire in a German ammunition dump. Just then four German trucks crossed from the southern end, and halting near the fires burst into flames. These spread to the bridge, burning the paint-work but not the bridge itself. The fires on the bridge lit up the whole scene and any attempt to cross would have failed. No boats or pontoons could be found to enable 2 Para to cross and outflank the German defenders.

MONDAY/TUESDAY

When Frost took stock of his battalion, he found that he had his own A Company, two platoons of B Company, and Headquarters Company. The other parties that had slipped through also included the remnants of 3 Para's C Company. Of his own C Company there was no sign. The battalion now had over 100 prisoners to feed and guard. But as Frost walked round his men in the small hours of 18 September he felt that there was reason to be satisfied with the situation. He held one end of the bridge. It was unlikely that the Germans could blow it because the fires would have destroyed the fuses on any charges that had been laid. Finally, 2nd British Army was due to reach him by mid-morning the following day.

Soon after dawn the German attacks on the bridge started. They continued throughout the day. The bat-talion's morale was high as they fought back with skill and vigour. At times Frost heard laughter among the din of battle. The signallers picked up some radio traffic from

the leading units of 30 Corps, which sounded so strong
that they must be near. The thought occurred to some of
the battalion that they might even greet the relief force
before the rest of the brigade arrived on the scene.

By the afternoon the situation was not looking so promising. Ammunition was running short so Frost ordered the
sniping to stop and firing only to be directed at attacking
enemy. This allowed the enemy to move about more easily
but also led him to think that the defenders had lost heart
and tricked him into some foolhardy moves for which he
was made to pay dearly. It then became clear that the
remainder of the brigade were further away than Frost
had supposed. There was now only one day's food left,
with no prospect of re-supply. The enemy had also
brought up heavier weapons with which to blast out the
tenacious paratroopers, 40 mm flak guns and a 150 mm
gun hurling 100-pound shells demolishing the walls of the
houses. There seemed no answer to this gun until one of
the battalion mortars dropped a bomb right on it, killing
or wounding the crew and putting the gun out of action:
a fluke. Gradually the quality of the soldiers they were up
against became apparent. The prisoners they took were
healthy, surly and contemptuous, well-trained SS Panzer
Grenadiers. They were not in the least cowed by being
taken prisoner. Indeed on at least one occasion a Panzer
Grenadier found an opportunity to turn on the water taps
in the building in which he was being held in an attempt
to waste the defenders' water supply, even though he
would suffer from thirst himself. But when Frost visited
his men after dark, morale was high. 30 Corps was due
the next day. 'Our most enjoyable battle.' they said. 'Let
us always fight from houses.' At 3 pm Hibbert, who had
heard nothing from Lathbury since the previous evening,
asked Frost to take command of 1st Parachute Brigade.

Early that same morning 3 Para had renewed the
advance. The intention was that they should switch to

Lion Route but half the battalion, including A Company, the mortars and medium machine guns, three out of four anti-tank guns, and Urquhart's and Lathbury's radio jeeps, were cut off by German infantry and armour while still on their original route. Lathbury, somewhat petulantly: 'The reason for this serious mistake was that the move had begun in pitch darkness and the CO had led the battalion very fast by a somewhat circuitous route. His battalion staff were very blameworthy that this occurred.' Again progress was terribly slow, to Urquhart's continued dismay, but neither he nor Lathbury were able to quicken the pace. Few of the men had any experience of fighting in built-up areas. Advancing in the open, along roads dominated by buildings was an unnerving experience. Every house could hold a sniper or a machine gun post. Again the advance was slowed further by the kindness and hospitality of the Dutch. Some troops were even seen chatting to an attractive blonde through the window of a house. On the outskirts of Arnhem the battalion was held up by formidable opposition, including tanks and self-propelled guns. The fighting became more and more confused as groups of tanks and infantry cut in behind and eventually surrounded them. At 3 pm remnants of the part of the battalion cut off earlier, consisting of twenty men under Lieutenant Burwash, got through, bringing with them a Bren gun carrier loaded with ammunition.

The chaos was increased when 1 Para on the northern route into Arnhem, changing direction to link up with Frost, found themselves involved in the same battle. Dobie found 3 Para's headquarters company, including the anti-tank guns and medium machine guns, and took them along with him. His own anti-tank guns were with the missing R Company. By mid-morning the German tanks dominated the streets. The leading company of 1 Para was soon down to twenty men with no more than five rounds of ammunition each. The rest of the battalion was half a mile back taking heavy losses from tanks and self-propelled guns. At 6.30 pm Frost sent a radio message ordering 1 and 3 Para each to send a flying column to the bridge under the cover of darkness. 1 Para received the message and Dobie, although almost without ammunition and down to about 100 men, decided to try the route along the river bank. Urquhart and his batman were hiding in a house to avoid capture, with a German self-propelled gun outside. Lathbury was lying, wounded through the spine, in a friendly Dutchman's house. Six days later the senior doctor of the division, Colonel Warrack, drove through the area of the battle: 'There must have been a hell of a battle all along the road as there were wrecked vehicles, bodies, smashed houses, tramwires, burnt-out jeeps and the road for over two miles looked as if it had been hit by a tornado.'

Waiting impatiently in England, unaware of their fellow parachute brigade's increasingly desperate situation, Hackett's 4th Parachute Brigade chafed at a four-hour delay in take-off. Was this to be yet another cancelled operation, they asked? Although the majority of this brigade had seen far less of the war than 1st Parachute Brigade, one of the exceptions was their commander who had already won a DSO and an MC fighting in the Western Desert, and was as experienced as either of the other two brigadiers in the division although at thirty-four he was the youngest. At last the order to load the aircraft was given, and the scene of the day before was repeated, the streams of aircraft flying in formation towards Holland.

There was the usual singing, puffing on cigarettes, the strained grins, the yawning and the sweaty palms. There was less airsickness than usual, and at least one officer has recorded his relief at being spared the unpleasantness of travelling with a planeload of vomiting soldiers. The trip was more eventful than the previous day. Ninety enemy fighters tried to penetrate the Allied fighter screen but failed. The flak was more effective, and one Dakota was hit and plunged to earth with a full load of paratroopers on board while their watching fellows wondered who the poor buggers were. Major Waddy, number one on his stick could see out of the door:

> The Dakotas were rocking and yawing in the turbulence caused by so many aircraft flying in close formation. Black puffs of bursting flak shells dotted the sky around us. We passed right over a flak gun, I could see the faces of the German gunners staring up. The American pilots did not flinch, pressing on straight and level. They were magnificent. A Dakota ablaze from wing-tip to wing-tip passed under our aircraft and crashed in flames. We were hit by some flak. The red light was on for about ten minutes. At last the green light came on. With a great yell of 'Go!' from the whole stick, we poured out.

Other aircraft were hit but most of the soldiers jumped. Major Lonsdale, by now the second-in-command of 11 Para, was hit in the hand by a burst that came through the floor of his Dakota as the red light came on. Everyone was thrown to the floor. As the stick was scrambling up, three others were found to be wounded: the signal officer, jumping number one, and one man each side of Lonsdale in the middle of the stick: 'The signal officer jumped but the men each side of me appeared to have lost interest in going; very stupid, because the best thing to do was to get out of the aircraft. They were a damn nuisance, because we had to unhook them so that I and the rest of the stick behind me and could get out.'

Two of 11 Para's aircraft were shot down. In Captain King's Dakota the crew chief was killed by the door. The aircraft started losing height; at about 200 feet King gave the order to jump without waiting for the green light. As he looked up, he saw both engines blazing. The last man jumped at about eighty feet; his parachute did not open. King's stick landed miles away from the DZ. Nevertheless, they with others that he collected reported to 4th Parachute Brigade headquarters at first light the next day.

The main body of 4 Para Brigade began their drop at 3 pm onto DZY, even further away from Arnhem than the first day's DZ. They found the DZ under fire from small parties of Germans. Some men were hit as they stood in the doors of the aircraft. Waddy's signaller had a round through his kitbag just as he left the door, destroying the radio it contained. Some of the brigade landed in woods just north of the DZ and were shot as they hung in the trees. 10 Para had the worst time at Ginkel, their RV at the north-east corner of the DZ. About two hours later the brigade, about 100 men short in each battalion, started moving towards Arnhem.

Thirty years later, Hackett wrote in a *Sunday Times* article:

It was perfectly clear that whatever surprise might be gained for the first lift, the rest of the British Division would run very early into bad trouble. After my own final briefing conference of 4 Parachute Brigade officers, when final touches were made to the meticulous plan for occupying Arnhem – our objective on arrival in the second lift – I kept back the battalion commanders and senior staff officers to tell them that they could really forget all that. Our heaviest fighting and worst casualties would not occur defending the perimeter of the town against eventual counter-attack, but in trying to get there from eight miles away against fully aroused German opposition.

When Hackett arrived he found that Hicks, the commander of the Air-Landing Brigade, had taken over command of the division in Urquhart's absence. Hicks, although older, was junior. But Urquhart had ordained

that Hicks was to take over if anything happened to him.
Through the gunner radio net which, as in many operations before and since, was the only net working well,
Hicks had learned about the critical situation at the bridge
and had despatched the two companies of the South Staffords that had landed on the first day into Arnhem to
assist the 1st Parachute Brigade. Like the battalions in 1st
Parachute Brigade, the South Staffords had made slow
progress, taking thirteen hours to cover three miles.

Hackett was met on the DZ by a staff officer from
divisional headquarters and told that Hicks had sent 11
Para to follow the South Staffords into Arnhem to help
1st Parachute Brigade. The GSO1 (chief of staff) Mackenzie had met Lea and told him to take his battalion into
Arnhem as soon as possible. Lea, who had dislocated his
shoulder on landing, did so without question. However,
Hackett was furious at having one of his battalions detailed
off without reference to him:

> I should just have been told to send a battalion as
> soon as possible, leaving the choice to me. At this
> stage the whole command set-up was in a state of
> some confusion. In the absence of the divisional com-
> mander they gave the impression of being right out
> of their depth and without much idea of how to take
> charge of such a fluid situation. Instead of sending a
> senior officer with a jeep and radios into town to
> pick up 11 Para, the Staffordshires, and whatever
> remnants he could find and then take them to the
> bridge, two fresh battalions were messed about
> because they were sent into Arnhem on a 'do what
> you can' basis.
>
> When I came in for orders, there were none. I
> asked a number of bread and butter questions about
> report lines, fire support and so forth, but no one
> had thought of these. In the end I was so aggrieved

that I reminded Pip Hicks that I was senior in the division, and would have to take command in order that I might issue myself some proper instructions. In the end I wrote out some orders to myself and signed them!

Hackett decided to advance into Arnhem north of the railway line, picking up the 7th Battalion the King's Own Scottish Borderers (KOSB), on the way; his first objective the high ground at Koepel. This was in line with the orders he had been given by Urquhart before the operation started. With the advantage of hindsight, this was the most critical day in the battle. Despite the missed opportunity of switching 4th Parachute Brigade to DZ K south of the Arnhem bridge, the battle was still not lost. There was another way to get a whole brigade south of the river: the Driel ferry was still operating and was used by the Dutch right up to Wednesday 20 September. A night crossing and approach march to the southern end of the Arnhem bridge by the whole of 4th Parachute Brigade, following the only real principle of war, surprise, might have turned the tables. Alternatively, and less ambitious, Hicks could have ordered the seizure of the high ground at Wester-bouwing overlooking the ferry and there formed a bridge-head to await 30 Corps with their heavy bridging equipment. Either would have been better than the head-butting tactic of feeding battalions into the meat-grinder on the outskirts of Arnhem.

It is easy to criticize Hicks and Hackett for not doing what appears so obviously to be the right answer. But Hicks knew he was only in temporary command. He had not seen Urquhart carted off on a stretcher or been told that he was dead. It would have been a bold and confident Brigadier who took upon his own shoulders the responsibility for a complete change of plan for the division. If 1st Airborne Division had possessed a deputy commander he might have felt confident enough to make such a radical change to the plan. However, Hicks, even as caretaker divisional commander, can be criticized for not making more effort to assess just what was going on before despatching a fresh full-strength brigade without clear orders for a dose of more of the same. This brigade, correctly used, might have won the battle.

The confusion in 1st Airborne Division was probably at its worst during this period in the battle. With Urquhart trapped in Arnhem, and Lathbury wounded, there was no one to command and coordinate the remnants of the four battalions fighting in the town. Urquhart has been criticized for going forward and leaving his Division leaderless at such a critical stage. When he was unable to get through to his subordinate commanders on the radio from his headquarters or his Rover jeep, he correctly went to find out what was going on. He had no other choice. There was absolutely no point in sitting in his headquarters in communication with no one. It was unfortunate that he was cut off and was unable to return to his headquarters to take up the reins of his command just when he was most needed. The battle to reach the Arnhem bridge has a First World War texture. Once battalions were committed, the lack of radio communications meant that from the outset the brigade and divisional commander had no influence on events, and as the battle developed even battalion commanders could control only those men in their immediate vicinity. It is hard to overstate the qualities of determination and courage shown by the commanders and soldiers in the four battalions when early on Tuesday morning, faced by what they must have realized was a forlorn hope, they pressed on into the jaws of destruction.

At 8 pm that Monday evening, Dobie, 1 Para, had met McCardie commanding the South Staffords, who had brought a resupply of ammunition. Also with him was Timothy's R Company. After disengaging from the enemy, they had caught up with the South Staffords and moved with them to rejoin their own battalion. Although Timothy had radio sets on his own battalion net and the South Staffords net, they never got through. The two commanding officers formed a plan to get to the bridge, the start time to be 9 pm. News then came through that the force at the bridge had been overwhelmed. The attack was cancelled. At 11 pm 1 Para's FOO picked up on his radio 2 Para's FOO at the bridge giving fire orders. Dobie sent a runner with the news back to divisional headquarters. At 1 am on Tuesday morning Dobie and McCardie received orders to withdraw to a bridgehead at Oosterbeek. At this moment Lea arrived. Lea had had to completely change the plan for his battalion and give fresh orders as a result of being given a new task in a different area, and this delayed the move of 11 Para into Arnhem. The trudge through the darkness, with the threat of bumping into the enemy at any moment, took half the night. At 2.30 am the previous order to them all was cancelled, and they were told to proceed to the bridge. Some of this order and counter-order may have originated some time shortly before Urquhart was cut off. Lieutenant Heaps, sent by divisional headquarters with a Dutch liaison officer to take ammunition to the Arnhem bridge, after a number of narrow escapes discovered Urquhart and Lathbury at about 3 pm, by chance. Urquhart told Heaps to return to divisional headquarters if at all possible and get reinforcements through to Frost. Heaps took until well after dark to return to divisional headquarters. He was sent forward again with the message that 1, 3, and 11 Para and the South Staffords were to make every effort to break through to Frost. Heaps eventually found Dobie, McCardie and Lea studying the map by the light of a candle.

Lacking a brigade commander, the commanding officers of 1 and 11 Para and the South Staffords had no option but to cook up a plan between them. 1 Para would advance

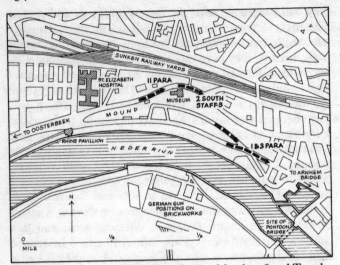

The final attempt to reach Arnhem Bridge, Monday 18 and Tuesday 19 September 1944.

along the lower river road, along which 3 Para was fighting at that moment, while the South Staffords pushed forward along a parallel but higher road. H Hour was fixed for 3.30 am. Between about 2.30 and dawn 3 Para had got as far as the site of the pontoon bridge where there was a basin cut into the bank, narrowing the frontage even more; here they were forced back. 11 Para was to follow 1 Para along the lower road. However, after realizing from 3 Para's experience that the lower road was too exposed to fire from across the river, Lea decided to follow the South Staffords along the upper road. After starting late, at 4 am, the South Staffords advanced about 400 yards in two hours when they were held up by heavy opposition around the Museum which stands on a small rise between the two roads. Lea tried to hook round to the left but failed.

At about 7 am Urquhart had managed to get back

to his headquarters, sited in the Hartenstein Hotel in Oosterbeek. He had finally escaped when the German self-propelled gun in front of the house in which he was hiding, had moved away during the night. Unknown to him, he had been about 100 yards from where the commanding officers of 1 and 11 Para and the South Staffords were making their plans for the advance on the bridge. When he got back to his headquarters he gripped the situation immediately, sending Colonel Barlow, the deputy commander of 1st Air-Landing Brigade, to take command of the four battalions fighting in the town. Barlow was never seen again. Years later his cigarette case was found near the St Elizabeth Hospital.

By about 10 am the second attempt along the lower road, 1 Para in the lead followed by 3 Para, was again stopped at the basin cut into the bank. All four battalions fought desperately to reach their comrades at the bridge, but were funnelled by the narrow corridor between the river and sunken railway yards 200 yards to the north. There was insufficient room to deploy properly and the soldiers fighting along the two roads were terribly exposed to fire from tanks and machine guns. German flak guns sited on the southern bank of the river added to the problem by shooting the battalions on the lower road, and those on the mound by the Museum, in the flank. That these battalions got as far as they did is a testimony to their courage and drive. Bleak sentences in Dobie's diary tell the story of the handful of parachute soldiers, their only armour their camouflage jackets, fighting desperately forward:

04.00 – Crossed start line – reached river bank. Dorrien-Smith, 3 Para, came up and said we would not get along bank – opposition too strong.

04.30 – Heavy firing, shelling, mortaring coming

down on us. Tanks and half tracks on high ground to left. Enemy infantry cleared with bayonets and grenades. Inflicted heavy casualties on enemy – remainder ran off or surrendered.

05.00 – Attacked by tanks. Gammon bombs used by R Company. Two infantry guns captured. German prisoners coming along with us. Opposition ahead intense.

06.00 – South Staffs seem to have retired. Shooting ceased some time ago. Our position becoming desperate as enemy on high ground and houses above us [ie to the north]. AA and machine gun fire from river direction, tanks firing at point-blank range.

> R Company – 6 [men left]
> S Company – 15
> T Company – 8
> Battalion Headquarters – 10

This my last check. No wireless touch with any companies. (Commanding officer forward at this stage, trying to find positions – became embroiled – had engagement – was wounded.) Orders given to make for houses on high ground.

06.30 – T Company cut off. Enemy grenading us from houses we were trying to get into. Managed to force an entry into one house, but only six men with me. Enemy now between us and S and T. Tanks outside our house. Enemy in rear also. Nothing more to be done. Four wounded in our party.

07.30 – SS enter house. Party taken.

Major Timothy commanding R Company 1 Para found

it like fighting through a 'narrow valley'. After leading a desperate bayonet charge which took them to the end of the valley, there were few men left. They took to the buildings as the tanks, and at least one flame-thrower tank, cruised the streets. Soon all their PIAT bombs were expended, and not long after the remnants of R Company were cut off and 'went into the bag'.

The Commanding Officer of 3 Para gave the order to withdraw to the area of the Museum as individuals as best they could. The second-in-command reached the Museum to find that only twenty men had made it. About 100 yards to the west he found a force of about 100 men from every unit in the brigade under Lieutenant Fraser, who had collected them up, having been cut off, and brought them forward to join his battalion. The second-in-command went back towards the bridge to find the commanding officer. He found the Intelligence Officer severely wounded, who told him that the commanding officer was dead. The second-in-command was cut off and did not return to the battalion until mid-afternoon two days later.

At about this stage Lea was summoned to the rear-link radio on the divisional net, which he had been given when he was detached from his own brigade the evening before. As soon as he started to talk on the set he lost contact with divisional headquarters. Later an officer from divisional headquarters got through to him with a marked map and fresh orders. 11 Para was to make a left flank attack to occupy the Heyenoord-Diependaal area, north of the railway. The origin of this order was Urquhart's intention that 4th Para Brigade occupy a north-south line between the railway and the river, halfway between Oosterbeek and Arnhem. In retrospect, this was impossible. Actually 4 Para Brigade were about four miles away as the crow flies and considerably more in marching distance. They would not get much closer.

The South Staffords secured Den Brink to protect Lea's flank. But as they were digging in they were violently attacked by infantry and tanks, who overran their position. The battalion regrouped to prepare for this attack. Lea was holding an O Group round his jeep when German tanks appeared at the end of the street and engaged. All weapons including anti-tank guns had been hooked up ready for the move and the companies had left their dug-in positions. In a few minutes all the anti-tank guns were destroyed and the men took cover in the houses. It was impossible to regain control of the battalion as individuals and sub-units were in the houses and the German tanks dominated the streets. None of the radios was working so there was no communication from house to house. Lea's walkie-talkie radio worked just once throughout the battle. Eventually most of 11 Para, fragmented into small parties holding out in houses, was forced into surrendering for lack of ammunition.

About mid-day the survivors of the four battalions drifted back towards Oosterbeek, their commanding officers dead or wounded. They were met by Lieutenant Colonel Thompson commanding the Light Regiment Royal Artillery. He organized them into a defensive position on the line of the railway just west of Den Brink to cover his gun positions in the vicinity of Oosterbeek church. They were put under command of Major Lonsdale, the second-in-command of 11 Para, who had discharged himself from the dressing station and gone towards Arnhem to find his battalion. He was the senior surviving officer of the four battalions. They fought off repeated assaults by German armour and infantry. Sergeant Baskeyfield, an anti-tank gunner of the South Staffords, won a posthumous VC when his own gun was knocked out. He took over another gun and fought single-handed until shot through the head.

Later that evening German flame-throwers set fire to

the woods where Lonsdale was holding the line; flames and clouds of smoke enveloped the soldiers, forcing them back. Lonsdale managed to get through to divisional headquarters on the radio 'the one and only time, and told them: "It's not the bullets that's chasing us out, it's the fire and smoke." I then asked permission to withdraw to the area of Oosterbeek church. Permission having been given, I said at 18.00 "I am going".'

Having withdrawn most of his force to a position near the Oosterbeek church, Lonsdale ordered the remnants of 3 Para, still fighting near the railway, to join him. They arrived thirty-six strong with only one officer, Captain Cleminson, and with the rest of Lonsdale force were assembled in the church for a briefing. All that remained of the 1, 3 and 11 Para, the South Staffords, with the addition of some glider pilots, was about 250 men.

Lonsdale addressed them from the pulpit, his bandaged hands gripping the edge, a field dressing wrapped round his head:

> You know as well as I do there are a lot of bloody Germans coming at us. Well, all we can do is to stay here and hang on in the hope that somebody catches us up. We must fight for our lives and stick together. We've fought the Germans before – in North Africa, Sicily, Italy. They weren't good enough for us then, and they're bloody well not good enough for us now. They're up against the finest soldiers in the world. An hour from now you will take up defensive positions north of the road outside. Make certain you dig in well and that your weapons and ammo are in good order. We are getting short of ammo, so when you shoot you shoot to kill. You will be known as Lonsdale Force, and my HQ will be in the church. Good luck to all of you.

They filed out of the church and dug in.

At the bridge that morning the first German attack was a rush by armoured cars, which was beaten off by anti-tank guns. The battery commander from the Light Regiment was still in communication with the guns at Oosterbeek and their fire broke up many of the attacks, which went on all day, as casualties among Frost's men steadily mounted. The water stopped running and medical supplies were sparse. The Germans sent a message with a captured sapper inviting Frost to surrender. The sapper told Frost that the Germans were concerned by their own losses. If only the ammunition lasted, Frost was confident that he could hold out. Later in the day tanks and self-propelled guns accompanied by infantry systematically moved along the streets into the battalion position. They fired into the buildings steadily destroying the upper floors; the defenders withdrew down the blood-stained stairs. The air was thick with brick and plaster dust and acrid with phosphorus smoke. The defenders were dazed by the shattering blast of the high explosive shells and the crash of falling masonry. If they wavered for an instant the German infantry would be on them. Finally the armour was driven off by PIATs and the crews of the anti-tank guns. As night fell the attacks on Frost's position tailed off. The night was turned into day by the burning buildings all around them. Casualties had been heavy. In the cellars it was difficult to avoid stepping on the wounded, they were packed so closely together.

The 4th Parachute Brigade had also been busy. After their drop the previous afternoon there was a two-hour delay before they were on the move. 156 Para led, using the track which ran in a south-easterly direction alongside the Utrecht–Arnhem railway. Progress was slow, and in three hours they covered only six miles. About an hour after dark the leading company ran into strong opposition along the Dreijenseweg, a road running north-south across the battalion's route and joining the two main roads into

Arnhem. Although the battalion did not know it, they had run into the 9th SS Panzer Division's forward outposts. The commanding officer, des Voeux, wisely withdrew to a position from which he could mount an attack in daylight. The members of 156 Para began to realize all was not well. By this time they, with the rest of 4th Parachute Brigade, should have been dug in on the high ground north of Arnhem waiting for the Germans to counter-attack. Instead they were only two-thirds of the way there.

The next morning Hackett ordered 156 Para to capture the high ground at Koepel east of the Dreijenseweg while 10 Para covered the left flank of 156. C Company, the leading company of 156, captured the battalion's first phase objective, but the second two companies, assaulting the Lichtenbeek feature on the far side of the Dreijenseweg, were cut to pieces by fire from armoured cars, self-propelled guns and infantry. Waddy:

My company supported C Company into their attack. From our position on the flank we could see SP guns among the houses. Having seen C Company on to their objective, I came round to take my orders from the CO. I was told to move through A Company, which had attacked round C Company's left flank; they seemed to be held up close to the Dreijenseweg although it is now known that Major Pott the company commander with a handful of men fought their way over and on to the Lichtenbeek feature, where after some hours they were all killed, captured or escaped. I came up through the woods astride a main ride, hoping to close up to the road. But by the time I reached the Dreijenseweg it was stiff with armour. Right in front of me was a twin-barrelled 20 mm flak gun. It was doing a great deal of damage, firing high explosive rounds. Both my forward platoons were badly shot up and there were heaps of A Company dead, dying and wounded lying all over the place.

Without thinking I went forward with a few soldiers and Support Company commander to try to knock out the gun. I got to within ten yards and had just told a man to throw a phosphorus grenade at it when he was shot through the head. There was a sniper in the trees above the gun. I fired at him with my pistol. I normally carried a Schmeisser which I captured in Italy, but my batman had it on this occasion. I fired five shots, missing with every one, and he shot me. I tried crawling away but he fired again hitting the ground very close to my hand. I lay doggo until a large Rhodesian soldier in my company, Private Diedricks, bravely came forward and carried me off.

10 Para had more success against lighter opposition. But here, as in Arnhem, lightly equipped airborne soldiers with little support and limited quantities of ammunition were invited to attack determined well-trained troops supported by armour. The results were the same, huge casualties and failure. Surprise was the airborne soldiers' main weapon; they were denied it by the air plan for this operation.

The survivors of this attack were then strafed by Messerschmitts. Next the paratroopers watched the supply drop by the RAF Dakotas onto DZ V, the correct supply zone but still in German hands. The German flak was heavy. One aircraft, a wing on fire, made a second run over the DZ. The watching soldiers could see the despatchers pushing the panniers through the door despite the flames spreading towards them. The aircraft crashed in flames, having dropped its load. The pilot, Flight Lieutenant Lord of 217 Squadron RAF, was awarded the VC posthumously. The supplies had been delivered, but almost all to the enemy. Although 1st Airborne had signalled a change in the supply drop zone to the UK base, the information was not passed to the airmen. Again and again the airmen were to fly and complete their missions with the utmost bravery despite the flak. Many of the senior airmen may have been timid and unadventurous, but the aircrews delivered the goods regardless of the odds.

Travelling in one of the aircraft was Darling. He was convalescing near Keevil airfield and had befriended some of the aircrew who had flown his battalion into Normandy three months before. One of them asked him if he would like to go on a supply drop. Telling no one, he climbed aboard a Stirling. Just before take-off:

> The air transport officer poked his head into the door of the Stirling and asked me to move to another aircraft; which I did. I stood behind the pilot, and as we approached Arnhem I began to wish I had not come on this jaunt. A burst of light AA fire came through the bottom of the fuselage of my aircraft and we lost an engine. My arm was still in plaster. I saw a Stirling go down in flames; I subsequently discovered it was the one I had originally boarded. When I got home my wife was absolutely horrified to hear my tale.

The devoted aircrews delivered a total of 1,431 tons of supplies to the Arnhem DZs in 601 sorties. Eighty-four aircraft were shot down and only 106 tons were collected. The rest fell into German hands.

Urquhart visited Hackett early that afternoon and they both realized that there was no question of advancing any further. Urquhart decided that 4th Parachute Brigade should be prepared to move south of the railway that separated them from the rest of the division, but not move until he ordered. This was passed to battalions, who in their turn gave warning orders to companies. Because of the steep embankment there seemed to be only two places that Hackett could get his jeeps and anti-tank guns across. One was already held by the enemy, the other was at Wolfheze, behind the brigade. At about 3 pm Hackett received a message that the 1st Air-Landing Brigade was under heavy attack in the area of Wolfheze. In the belief that if he did not secure the Wolfheze crossing at once he would lose all his jeeps, he ordered 10th Parachute Battalion to disengage from the enemy and seize the crossing. Where the information came from that the Wolfheze crossing was being threatened is not clear. The 1st Battalion the Border Regiment, holding positions along a line from Westerbouwing to Wolfheze, were not attacked until 7 pm that evening. They beat off the Germans without difficulty. Not until the following day, Wednesday, was the battalion attacked in strength. It is possible that an inaccurate report was received in divisional headquarters and passed to Hackett.

Things rapidly started going badly wrong. A withdrawal in contact with the enemy is difficult enough under the cover of darkness. It takes careful planning and skilful execution. In daylight, in full view of a thrusting enemy who has armour which gives him mobility, firepower and protection, all of which the airborne soldiers singularly lacked, it requires a carefully phased plan with a succession of layback positions. Sub-units cover each other back, preferably assisted by a healthy artillery programme to keep the enemy off the back of the withdrawing troops like a boxer giving ground, jabbing at his opponent, keeping him at bay, until a clean break has been achieved. Anything else leads to great loss of life and even greater confusion. However, Hackett was under the impression that he had no option but to withdraw at once or lose all the brigade's anti-tank guns; and it was becoming clear that they would be sorely needed.

As 10 Para withdrew the enemy followed. The battalion then discovered that the enemy held some of the rendezvous positions on their withdrawal route. The Germans continued to hound the brigade as it withdrew across the LZ on which the Poles' gliders should have landed that morning. At that moment the Polish gliders arrived. Gliders crashed, men were killed and wounded by mortar and machine gun fire. The Poles, discovering to their horror that what they thought was a secure LZ was nothing of the sort, shot at everybody in sight, including the KOSB who rushed forward to help them unload.

The KOSB had just seen off the enemy, inflicting many casualties and suffering few; their tails were up. Now they were being ordered to withdraw in daylight in full view of the enemy to keep the route open for the brigade jeeps. 'You just can't get up and rush away from the enemy in daylight like that,' one experienced soldier said, 'You just can't bloody well do it!' Within two hours the KOSB had lost two companies and nearly all their jeeps. 10 and 156 Para were also pursued hotly. In the 10th Captain Queripel, already hit in the face, carried a wounded NCO to cover before leading an assault on a German strongpoint consisting of two machine guns and a captured British anti-tank gun. Having killed the crew Queripel was forced to withdraw, so he and a party of men took up a covering position in a ditch. Queripel, now also wounded in both arms, with only a few grenades and small arms faced a rush of Panzer Grenadiers throwing stick grenades, which Queripel tossed back. Soon most of his party were dead and wounded. He ordered the survivors to get away while he covered them. He was last seen alone, still fighting. He won a posthumous VC.

In 156 Para, Major Powell, commanding C Company:

Orders for withdrawal in phases had already been given when suddenly we were told to get back as soon as possible. There was no panic, we did not run back, everyone was under control even though we were under heavy fire at the time; but we did not do it in phases. The column was split; one company and one platoon of mine did not cross the railway line.

The withdrawing battalions eventually scrambled over the railway embankment, which gave them respite from the pursuing armoured cars and self-propelled guns. A tunnel just wide enough to take a farm cart was discovered under the railway line through which the brigade's jeeps shot like rabbits to escape the attentions of the enemy. This enabled Hackett to abandon the plan to go back to the Wolfheze crossing. He re-organized his brigade south of the railway line. Each battalion was down to about a third of its strength. Hungry and exhausted by the events of the previous thirty-six hours, 10 and 156 Para dug in for the night. The KOSB were sent in to the divisional perimeter that was evolving between the river and the railway line. Hackett wanted to move into the perimeter that night, but unfortunately divisional headquarters did not approve.

WEDNESDAY/THURSDAY

At the bridge at 10 am on Wednesday 20 September one of the 1st Parachute Brigade radios which had been searching the frequencies for hours picked up the divisional forward net. Hibbert took the head-set and heard Hackett speaking to Urquhart. Hibbert asked Frost to come to the set to speak to Urquhart, who congratulated him and said that 30 Corps were expected soon. Frost briefed Urquhart on his situation, giving a tally of the damage his force had inflicted on the enemy so far. He added that he must have ammunition, rations, a surgical team and medical supplies immediately. Urquhart suggested that they should organize the local population to bring in food, ammunition and stores from some of the resupply containers which had gone astray the previous day. Frost replied that they were fighting in the middle of a devasted area, there were no civilians, and they were surrounded by a superior and somewhat aggressive enemy force, and it was by no means possible for civilians to wander backwards and forwards through the lines carrying containers full of supplies, of which in any case there were none in the vicinity! Urquhart told Frost that it was highly unlikely that the remainder of the division would be able to reach him.

The force was in pretty desperate straits. Many of the soldiers had moved into slit trenches in the gardens and road verges, abandoning the houses which had become death-traps under the point-blank fire from self-propelled guns and tanks. Most of the houses, with plenty of wood in their construction, caught fire easily. The attacks which had started at first light hardly ceased all day. At one point Frost received a message over the radio link with divisional headquarters to say that 30 Corps would be at the southern end of the bridge by 5 pm that day. As both Nijmegen bridges were still in German hands at that stage it was a misleading message, to put it mildly! Frost did not believe it. He could not hear, or see, any signs of fighting to the south.

Early in the afternoon Frost was wounded in both legs. Although he tried to carry on, he had to lie down. Gough took command of the force, consulting Frost when he could, and Major Tatham-Warter took over the battalion. McKay's sappers were down to ten men out of a strength of fifty. The school he was defending was no longer habitable and was collapsing. Blood was spattered everywhere, in pools on the floors, soaked into the smocks of the soldiers and in streaks down the stairs. He ordered a final charge, taking by surprise some fifty Germans standing near two tanks. McKay and his men stood in line, firing from the hip until ammunition ran out, and only four sappers remained standing. McKay ordered them to break out if they could. At 2.30 pm Urquhart spoke to Gough and said that his position was being attacked on both sides, and that far from coming to the aid of 2 Para he might have to call on them for assistance. Gough replied that he could hold out for another twenty-four hours but that there were no PIAT bombs left, and all types of ammunition were running low; morale was high.

Lieutenant Grayburn, wounded the first night when trying to cross the bridge, and wounded twice more later, refused to leave his platoon. Part of his citation for the posthumous VC reads:

> He was again wounded, this time in the back, but he refused to be evacuated. Finally an enemy tank approached so close to his position that it became untenable. He then stood up in full view of the tank and personally directed the withdrawal of his men to the main defensive perimeter to which he had been ordered. He was killed that night.

The Germans blasted holes in the walls of buildings held by the paratroopers and pumped in phosphorus smoke shells to set the structures alight. In the cellars of the building occupied by brigade headquarters, where over 200 wounded lay, the doctors told Frost that these men were in imminent danger of being burnt alive if they were not moved. A truce was arranged with the Germans. Under Hibbert's direction, about 130 fit men and walking wounded evacuated the building before the SS men moved in and helped carry the wounded up from the cellars. They were 'kind, chivalrous and even comforting,' according to Frost. 'They risked their own safety to get us out, but also used the lull to infiltrate into key positions.' As soon as the wounded had been removed, the battle started again. It could not last long now. Hibbert found that the building he had selected for his next position was burning, so he moved to another, and his men dug trenches round it. When he checked his ammunition state, he found that each sten or Bren had a magazine apiece, each rifleman had a few rounds, and there was no anti-tank ammunition. As his new position did not command the bridge, he gave orders to break up into small parties and infiltrate back to the division. Very few got through. Hibbert was captured hiding under a pile of coal in the coal-shed of one of the houses near the bridge. At dawn there were only 150 British paratroopers left. They had to be cleared house by house, room by room. From ground floor to attics the paratroopers made the Germans fight for every inch. When the ammunition ran out in one house, the Germans watched transfixed for a moment, while two paratroopers crawled towards them, one trying to draw their fire while the other clutched his fighting knife. Then they were shot. The last signal went out from the force, received only by German intercept. It ended with the words 'God save the King'. As the SS Panzer Grenadiers evacuated the remaining wounded, they offered them chocolate and brandy, congratulating them on the way they had fought the battle. The battalion did not surrender, it was overrun. It was 9 am on Thursday morning. For the first time since Sunday night the Germans could cross the bridge. The plan called for the complete division to hold it for forty-eight hours. It had been held for three days and four nights by a battalion strength force. Gavin called it 'the outstanding independent parachute battalion action of the war.'

North-west of the Airborne Division perimeter, Wednesday had seen the destruction of 4th Parachute Brigade. That morning morale in Hackett's depleted parachute battalions was high, despite the events of the preceding two days and the high casualties which left one of the battalions with only eight officers out of the normal thirty or so. The

brigade was ordered to make for the Utrecht road into
Oosterbeek to join the divisional perimeter that Urquhart
was setting up, having abandoned all further attempts to
relieve Frost. 'With the weak force I had left, I could no
more hope to reinforce Frost than reach Berlin,' recorded
Urquhart.

156 Para, with A Company consisting of twenty-five
men commanded by a Company Sergeant Major, led the
way. They turned into the Breedelaan, a ride through the
woodland, and ran straight into heavy fire from machine
guns and self-propelled guns. The brigade had collided
with strong German forces advancing towards Oosterbeek
from the west. Powell was told to put in a flanking attack
to open up a new axis. But enemy SP guns dominated this
route too. In this attempt Powell lost more men, and the
last of his officers, killed. Pulled back by his commanding
officer, he was ordered to follow what remained of the
battalion on yet another route. Hackett had ordered a
switch in direction, and had also told 10 Para to try outflanking to the left. But the Germans were in overwhelming strength. Soon des Voeux and his second-in-command
in 156 were dead, as were all but one of Hackett's staff
officers. During this time Lieutenant Colonel Heathcote-
Amory, who was on a 'swan' from headquarters 1st Airborne Corps, was lying wounded on a jeep trailer. A jeep
with a trailer-load of ammunition parked alongside caught
fire. Major Powell:

All of us watched, fascinated by the inevitability of it
all. Perhaps it would be better for the ammunition to
explode, then the officer would die quickly, not burn
slowly to death! Then out of the clump of trees on
the right a short spare figure was running across the
grass towards the burning vehicle. It was the Brigadier! He sprang into the driving seat of the jeep
attached to the trailer on which lay the wounded

officer. The engine roared into life, and with wheels spinning in a cloud of sand, the jeep and trailer roared across the clearing as he threw out the clutch and rammed the throttle to the floorboards.

Hackett eventually ordered Powell and his company, the only formed body left in the battalion, to turf the Germans out of a small hollow which would allow the remnants of his brigade to reorganize and draw breath. Led by Powell, C Company charged in, screaming wildly. The Germans ran away. Powell's sten jammed; he picked up a German rifle, as did several of his men in the course of the day's fighting. Hackett had also ordered 10 Para to 'pull the plug out!' They cut through the enemy with the bayonet and headed for the divisional perimeter. Urquhart saw them arrive;

> The men were exhausted, filthy, and bleeding; their discipline was immaculate. Their commander, Lieutenant-Colonel Ken Smyth, his right arm bandaged where a bullet had struck, reported breathlessly; 'We have been heavily taken on, sir. I have sixty men left.'

In the hollow, occupying a position about thirty yards across, Hackett, the survivors of 156 Para and his brigade headquarters fought off the encircling Germans for almost the rest of the day. The paratroopers made use of captured German weapons and ammunition to supplement their own dwindling supply. The German armour pulled back for some unexplained reason, and as the afternoon wore on the enemy infantry became less enthusiastic about attacking such a grimly determined foe. Hackett:

> The 20th was a difficult day for us, towards the end of which the men, though in admirable heart, were desperately short of water, food and ammunition. Many of them, myself included, were now using

German rifles. Much of the fighting was hand-to-hand. Signallers, orderlies and clerks (Staff Sergeant Pearson who was chief clerk at brigade HQ was one of the best fighting men there) and anyone else who happened to be present was hard at it. I remember using my rifle and bayonet all that afternoon like any infantry private (though no doubt less effectively) and having to lead a rush or two at close quarters, which is an unusual and stimulating experience for a Brigade Commander in modern times!

Staff officers fought too; like everyone in an airborne formation:

The behaviour of Major Dawson, Brigade Major, was beyond praise. He dropped with the advance group on D-Day (the day before 4 Parachute Brigade) and fought with those in operations to clear the DZ. He was a tower of strength during the period of confusion on the previous afternoon and he personally led counter-attacks and did much to get Brigade Headquarters away intact and keep the Boche away till dark. During the day he not only did his job as BM, but led several small attacks when immediate action was necessary. When wounded quite painfully in the right shoulder, he functioned as before and was killed eventually trying to rally Brigade Headquarters as it was being scattered by tanks.

Realizing that they would be overrun as their ammunition was running out, Hackett gathered his men together, and for the second time that day ordered what seemed to be impossible. But his men's trust in him was implicit. Leading a screaming mass of paratroopers, with blood-stained bayonets on their rifles, they cut through the Germans who gave way before them, and burst into the perimeter. 156 Para consisted of four officers and sixty soldiers.

It was a pity that the perimeter evolved where it did. About 1,000 yards wide and 2,000 yards deep, it was in the shape of an upside down sack, the mouth lying on the Neder Rijn, and the top just south of the Utrecht–Arnhem railway line. Oosterbeek church and the Light Regiment gun positions, were just inside the mouth of the sack, and Urquhart's headquarters in the Hartenstein Hotel were near the top. Perhaps it was the siting of the headquarters and the gun positions that influenced the location of the perimeter. In the stress of battle there is a tendency for temporary arrangements to become permanent. It was never intended that the Hartenstein should house the divisional headquarters. The staff set up shop there on the second day of the battle while they waited to move forward into Arnhem. It was actually the last place to choose for a headquarters or any other important military activity. It was large, standing in open grounds, easily approached by snipers, and very obvious. For some reason it was never damaged badly by artillery of mortar fire. Perhaps the enemy did not realize that it was being used as a headquarters.

If it had been possible, a better place for the perimeter would have been around the high ground at Westerbouwing, a few hundred yards to the west of Oosterbeek. From here the remnants of the division could dominate the surrounding country. But more important, they would have controlled the Driel car ferry, which would have enabled the relieving force to have reached them without using boats. Furthermore, Westerbouwing was opposite the spot where the network of side roads connected to the main Nijmegen-Arnhem road emerged on the southern bank of the river. Once it was clear that the Arnhem bridge would soon fall, the only way for the relieving force to reach the division was by those very side roads that connected with the Driel ferry. By Wednesday evening the Driel ferry had drifted away. The Germans established themselves on the Westerbouwing feature and had an excellent view over much of the British perimeter.

It is easy to be critical so many years later, sitting in an atmosphere very different from that which the division faced at the time. One brigade had ceased to exist, another was in the process of being destroyed, and the third was down to less than half strength. The whole plan was crumbling before Urquhart's eyes. That he kept so calm and inspired all with whom he came in contact is the sign of a remarkable man. 'The General, he never got rattled,' said a signaller. 'His calm and cheerfulness are really the sole cause of our optimism,' reported a Polish war correspondent.

On that Thursday there was visible proof that 30 Corps was not far away. Urquhart's chief gunner, Colonel Loder Symonds, was contacted on the artillery net. Having established identities, fire orders started to bring the big 5.5-inch shells from the medium regiments eleven miles south of the river crashing down within 100 yards of the British troops in the perimeter. The men cheered as the German attacks broke up under the weight of fire. The gunner net was used to pass most of the division's messages.

As well as shelling, sniping and pushing in armoured and infantry attacks almost continually, the Germans tried to lower the morale of the airborne soldiers by bringing forward loudspeakers to tell them they were cut off and invite them to surrender. On one occasion Major Wilson, commanding the Independent Parachute Company, got one of his German speakers to shout back that they were too frightened to come out and would the Germans come and get them. About fifty Germans came forward to collect their prisoners and were cut down by the fire from twelve Brens. Bittrich's tactics in this phase were to chip away at several points around the perimeter, his theory being that

British junior commanders lacked initiative, and as each bit was taken out nothing would be done about it by the strong points on either side. Also by keeping up the pressure he would deny the defenders rest or sleep. Throughout the day the Germans received a steady flow of reinforcements, including forty-five King Tiger tanks, another Panzer Grenadier battalion and another artillery regiment.

That evening the Polish Parachute Brigade arrived, dropping on a new DZ just to the East of Driel. The intention was to cross over the river using the Driel ferry to reinforce the division, at the same time holding a bridgehead on the southern bank to receive the leading troops of 30 Corps. The Poles arrived to a hot reception from the Germans, but Sosabowski the brigade commander quickly organized his battalions and was making for the ferry when he heard that the British had lost the Westerbouwing heights and the ferry was in German hands. The platoon of 1 Border, all that could be spared to hold this important piece of ground, had been driven off by tanks and infantry that very morning and attempts to retake the position were beaten off. Sosabowski's temper, always short-fused, was not improved by learning that the aircraft carrying one of his parachute battalions had turned back and that his glider units and anti-tank guns had landed on the other side of the river forty-eight hours before. Zwolanski, his liaison officer with Urquhart, swam the river to bring him a message that the division was organizing rafts to take the Poles over that night. Two hours before first light there was no sign of the rafts and Sosabowski pulled back from the river bank to prepare for the German attacks which he knew were imminent.

Although the Poles were unable for the moment to join the division in the perimeter, they indirectly brought some relief to Urquhart. Their arrival south of the river was seen by Bittich as a threat to the southern end of the Arnhem bridge. He moved a strong force of infantry and armour across the bridge to attack them. These units might have tipped the balance in the fighting at Oosterbeek.

Bittrich may have had a low opinion of the initiative of the British junior leaders and tailored his attacks accordingly. But perhaps he forgot an earlier remark, also attributed to him, to the effect that the British were amazing in defence. In Oosterbeek once again British infantry were showing what they did best, stubborn, bloody-minded defence. By the end of Thursday the perimeter had been squeezed a little but was holding. 10 Para was overrun and the remaining two officers were killed, including the commanding officer. The remnants, about fifty strong, were commanded by Captain Barron from the anti-tank battery and the artillery forward observer Lieutenant White. Hackett had lost his second Brigade Major – Major Madden, borrowed from divisional headquarters – killed a few hours after taking over. But there was hope that 30 Corps might arrive on the south bank at any moment and the shells from the guns of the corps artillery bursting among the Germans was most encouraging. Rocket attacks by Typhoons and Tempests on German gun and mortar positions would also have been invaluable. None was forthcoming. Close air support might have tipped the balance during the early days of the battle, enabling sufficient troops to get to the bridge and subsequently hold it. In the defensive phase of the battle, interdiction of the roads being used by the Germans might have slowed down the rate at which they could feed reinforcements into the attacks and denied them fire support and re-supply. The special communications for requesting air support and for talking to the pilots when they were overhead never worked, and were soon destroyed by enemy fire. The lack of liaison between 1st Allied Airborne Army and the 2nd Tactical Airforce was another reason for the meagre support received by 1st Airborne Division.

Despite the valiant defence, Urquhart knew that he could not hold out for much longer. On the evening of Thursday 21 September he sent a signal to Browning, part of which read: 'casualties heavy. Resources stretched to utmost. Relief within twenty-four hours vital.'

By now the three hotels which had been used as dressing stations by the British were in German hands. Despite this, the British doctors went on operating and the Germans still allowed British casualties to be taken through the lines. Colonel Warrack, the senior British medical officer, wishing to return to divisional headquarters through the fighting, recorded in his diary a discussion he had with another of his doctors about the problem of establishing his identity:

The form if challenged was to shout 'Arzt'. If the reply was 'hole' obviously it was safe to go through the English lines; if it was in German then presumably they knew it meant 'doctor' and again all was well! 1,200 seriously wounded congregated in some ten buildings in the medical area (the hotels Schoonoord, Taffelberg and Vreewyk) and RAPs (regimental aid posts). Practically no surgery possible. Meanwhile outside the battle continued with unabated fury.

Grim though this was, humour still shone through:

The unfortunate Corporal Hollingsworth (medical orderly) had taken a packet when the bombs burst in the ward and was the worse for wear, his main trouble being a grossly swollen testicle; he has been assured that function will be OK and is now happy. A soldier was found giving a girl the once-over in the cellar during the mortaring. It was difficult to know what to do with the soldier; presumably emotional releases are not punishable.

Waddy, lying wounded in the Taffelburg and subsequently wounded twice more, found Warrack a most inspiring man. He seemed to be everywhere, caring for the wounded, arguing with the Germans and apparently without fear.

A young woman schoolteacher in Oosterbeek, Riek van der Vlist, worked in the Hotel Schoonoord as a volunteer nurse. She recorded in her diary: 'Our first dead got a real grave.... now it is too dangerous to bury them.... now they have to be put in our garage.... the garage is full up now.... the others lie on the grass of the lawn.'

There were 700 wounded in the Schoonoord alone.

FRIDAY TO TUESDAY

For the next four days the bitter fighting continued. Casualties mounted, ammunition ran low, and rations and water were almost non-existent. Many men had only rain-water to drink, and survived for days without food. On Friday 22 September leading elements of the British 43rd Division linked up with the Poles at Driel. On two successive nights attempts were made to reinforce the airborne division by the Poles and the 4th Battalion the Dorsetshire Regiment, from 43rd Division. Only about 200 Poles got across; lacking sappers trained in watermanship to drive the boats, the arrangements for the crossing were inept. The Dorsets were swept downstream and most landed on a part of the north bank in German hands.

By Saturday, according to many the worst day in the perimeter, all hope of relief by 30 Corps had become a sick joke. Everyone had lost close friends and death seemed a certainty. Most of the British anti-tank guns within the perimeter had been knocked out. The German tanks could stand off, out of range of the PIATs and handthrown Gammon bombs, and reduce each house to rubble. The

defenders took to slit trenchs in gardens and hedgerows.
They stalked the tanks or waited until they approached
close enough for them to fire their PIATs. They tried to
shoot the infantry before the tanks appeared, lest their
positions were spotted and destroyed by their huge guns.
The most terrifying weapon, that made the bravest quail,
was the flame-thrower tank. At least half of the British
soldiers had equipped themselves with captured weapons.
When small sections of the perimeter were cut off they
continued fighting grimly and prevented the enemy from
getting past them in strength. It was for his actions during
this period of the battle that Major Cain of the South
Staffords was awarded the only non-posthumous VC of
the five awarded on this operation.

On Saturday 1st Airborne Division got their first close
air support attacks of the operation, followed by twenty-
two sorties on Sunday and eighty-one on Monday. The
effect these few fighter ground attacks had on the enemy
was proof of how their proper employment earlier could
have made such a difference, and even turned the battle.
Hackett was wounded for the second time on Saturday,
this time seriously in the stomach and the legs. At about
this time Warrack obtained Urquhart's permission to contact the Germans to seek a truce during which the British
wounded could be evacuated to hospitals in Arnhem.
Eventually Warrack was driven to the German headquarters in Arnhem. There, according to Bittrich:

> This request was granted immediately, although I
> had no authority to do so. The large number of
> wounded testified to the bitterness of the fighting.
> These wounded were taken care of in the hospital of
> 2nd SS Panzer Corps. Only later I obtained Field
> Marshal Model's approval of my unauthorized order
> to suspend hostilities.

Soon the evacuation of the wounded was under way.

Hackett was one of those evacuated to the St Elizabeth Hospital. He had removed his rank badges so that the Germans would not know they had a brigadier in their grasp. Because of lack of resources the surgeons were operating triage (dealing with casualties most likely to respond to surgery first, leaving those probably about to die and the lightly wounded to last). Hackett, a fluent German speaker, was lying on the floor. A German surgeon turned him over with his foot, and said: 'We won't bother with that one.' Eventually Hackett found himself on the examination table, a para surgeon bending over him saying: 'Hole of entry here. Where's the exit?'

The surgeon could find none and his face fell. Hackett was taken to the operating table, where a conversation took place over his head. 'Stomach wound or head wound, give them an injection and leave them,' was the opinion of the German doctor when he heard Captain Kessel proposing to operate to remove the shell splinter from Hackett's stomach. Kessel said he would operate all the same and the German said it would still be a waste of time but it was up to him. Captain Kessel, a Jewish South African surgeon in one of the British parachute field ambulances, operated on Hackett, saving his life.

As late as Sunday 24 September, 2nd Army told Urquhart that they still intended making a crossing. An entry in the 1st Airborne Division war diary records a report from 2nd Army which stated that 130 Infantry Brigade would assault the river that night with two battalions. Engineers would then build a class 40 bridge and 129 Infantry Brigade would follow across. Yet twenty-four hours later Urquhart received a note from Major General Thomas commanding 43rd Division telling him that 30 Corps would not be attempting a crossing of the river in strength, and that the Airborne Division would be withdrawn at a time to be agreed, codename Operation Berlin. Urquhart decided that Operation Berlin would be that night. Powell had described his feelings on hearing the news:

> The first emotion was grief. And then utter disappointment. The battalion (156) had been destroyed to no purpose. But the sorrow swelled to rage as I cursed the 2nd Army for their failure. But after a few minutes relief supplanted anger. Now there was at least a chance that we might escape.

His men's reactions were the same:

> As the words sank in, I could see the disappointment in their weary blood-shot eyes. They had seen their mates killed or maimed, the battalion had been wiped out. Yet they were not to be given the consolation of seeing the tanks and infantry of the 2nd Army driving northwards through the shattered streets. It had all been a pointless waste. The muttered chorus of protest rose to a spontaneous angry babble, full of bitterness about the troops in the south who had failed to relieve us. Above the rest, I heard Sergeant Weiner insisting that we were far from finished and could still hold the bastards off for days. Then they fell silent, and I sensed the conflict in their minds as relief supplanted anger.

The problem facing Urquhart was how to prevent the enemy from discovering that the British were withdrawing and follow up, cutting them to pieces as they moved out of their defensive positions and embarked in the boats. He wrote: 'At the back of my mind was Gallipoli. I called Charles Mackenzie over to help me with the evacuation plan. "You know how they did it at Gallipoli, Charles? Well, we've got to do it something like that." '

At 10pm on Monday 25 September, under the cover of a heavy bombardment from the corps artillery, the division started to withdraw. Glider pilots provided guides as the men stumbled towards the river through the pouring rain in darkness lit by the flashes of explosions. They clung to the unbuttoned tail of the airborne smock of the man in front. Men too badly wounded to walk volunteered to stay and fire machine guns and pass spurious messages on the radios to keep up the impression of normal activity as long as possible. The artillery programme was so effective that for some time the Germans thought that a major reinforcement of the perimeter was in progress.

Engineers with assault boats ferried the men across. Some boats were swept down river, some sank, in some the engines failed and men paddled with their rifle butts. By midnight the Germans realized what was happening and shelled the crossing; boats were hit, tipping the struggling men into the river. Some parties were split up. Lieutenant Blackwood, one of the three officers from 11 Para to get back across the Rhine, wrote in the battalion war diary: 'I can not say how the 11th Battalion fared, I was blind with blood and a field dressing, and I lost touch with my men in the darkness, crossing the river myself with 1st Battalion personnel.' By dawn the last rearguards reached the river. The Germans brought up machine guns and sprayed the water. Crossing by boat was now impossible. About a hundred men remained. Some tried to swim across. Most of those who swam naked made it, most of those who kept their clothes on drowned.

Over 300 wounded men were taken prisoner when the Germans advanced into the perimeter that Tuesday morning. Nearly 3,000 wounded were in German or Dutch hospitals in Arnhem. All the British chaplains and doctors stayed with the wounded. 2,398 men crossed the Neder Rijn, of whom 2,183 were members of the 1st Airborne Division which had flown into the operation over 10,000 strong. 1,400 were dead and over 6,000 were prisoners. Each parachute brigade could muster no more than the equivalent of a company, and the Air-Landing Brigade less than a battalion.

AFTERMATH

There were some epic escapes, too numerous to mention here, and two will have to suffice. Warrack decided to escape when there were less than 100 wounded in the Apeldoorn hospital. He hid himself in a cupboard and then made off. Deane-Drummond went forward into Arnhem and joined 1 Para in an attempt to sort out the communication problems on the second day of the battle. He was cut off with members of 1 Para, having taken command of one of the companies when the company commander was killed. He hid for three days by locking himself with three others in the lavatory of a house occupied by German soldiers, who on finding the door locked were too polite to force a way in! On the fourth night he and his party crept out of the house under the cover of noise from firing and swam the river. By the time he reached the other side he had become separated from the others and started walking along the bank towards the railway bridge, which he had chosen as the RV. At first light he fell into a trench full of Germans. To his fury he was a prisoner again.

He was taken to Velp and with other prisoners incarcerated in a large old house guarded by the SS. After a couple of days he hid in a wall cupboard. Imagining that 2nd Army would soon be over the Rhine, he thought he would have to remain hidden for only one or two days. The cupboard was so narrow he could only stand or kneel. He could not see out, but tiny chinks of light filtered in. He had a water bottle, a can of water, and a lump of bread about the size of a fist. On the second day a German interrogator placed his chair with its back to the cupboard and spent the next three days questioning British prisoners. The room was then used as a guardroom by the Germans, and as far as he could tell was never left empty. He urinated down a gap in the floor between some pipes which ran down through the cupboard to the basement. He had so little to eat that he had no need for a bowel movement. On the thirteenth day some tanks passed the house and everybody left the room to watch them go by in the fine autumn evening. The clatter of the tank tracks masked the sound of Deane-Drummond creeping out, opening a window, and dropping into some bushes. He eventually contacted the Dutch Underground. Six weeks later, with 130 others, including Lathbury and Hibbert, he crossed the Rhine in an escape operation laid on by the Dutch Resistance with the assistance of 2nd British Army.

The courage of the Dutch who assisted in these and most other escapes is beyond imagining. The penalty for the British soldier on being caught was to be carted off to a camp in Germany; for a Dutchman it was torture and death, not only of himself but his family as well. No wonder the airborne soldiers called them the bravest and most patriotic people we had liberated.

Although the Arnhem operation failed, this was not the fault of the officers and soldiers of 1st Airborne Division, nor the airmen who carried them to battle and tried to keep them supplied. It was almost doomed before it started by the air plan; subsequent events completed its destruction. Arnhem has become an albatross round the neck of the Parachute Regiment, a dreadful warning to anyone who suggests that there is a future for the bold use of parachute soldiers. 'We must never have another Arnhem.' It is time the albatross was removed.

Finally, let two soldiers who were there have the last word. Urquhart:

Even when one has taken into account every possible setback, large and small, which occurred during our nine days north of the Neder Rijn, the fact remains that we were alone for much longer than any airborne division is designed to stay. I think it possible that for once Horrocks's enthusiasm was not transmitted adequately to those who served under him, and it may be that some of his more junior officers and NCOs did not fully comprehend the problem and the importance of speed.

Frost:

30 Corps did not push as hard as they could have done. I spoke to an officer from the Guards Armoured Division (who later became a General) who told me they did not know that the airborne were in trouble at Arnhem. All the generals were 'off net' at the time; Monty, Dempsey, Browning and Horrocks.

CHAPTER 7

Operations in the Mediterranean

The Allied plan for the campaign in north-west Europe following the invasion in Normandy included a second major landing in the south of France by 7th US Army. After a seaborne assault between Hyeres and Théoule sur Mer the Americans would advance northwards up the Rhône valley and eventually link up with the right flank of the US armies advancing out of the Normandy lodgement area. The Germans were holding their reserves back from the Mediterranean coast, so little opposition to the seaborne landings was expected. However, it was important to land troops inland to block the routes that the German reserves might take to counter the seaborne assault, and hold them off until the Americans were firmly established ashore in strength. This task was tailor-made for airborne troops. So 2nd Independent Parachute Brigade, in Italy still waiting for their first brigade parachute operation, joined five American parachute battalions and one air-landing battalion to make up First Airborne Task Force under the command of Major General Frederick, United States Army, the only British troops to take part in the invasion of southern France.

The brigade was told to seize the area between La Motte and Le Muy, about ten miles north-west of St Raphael, and just north of where the autoroute between Aix-en-Provence and Cannes now runs. Le Muy sits astride the N7, then the only major east-west road in the area. Two other routes that the German reserves might use traversed the brigade's objective. Having landed, the brigade was to destroy all enemy in their area, and hold it for further airborne landings later the same day. High hills surrounded the DZs. They were small, rock-strewn and laced with stone walls, vines, poles and scrub, typical of southern Provence. But there was nothing better. Opposition on the DZs was expected to be light, but it was anticipated that the Germans, as always, would react quickly and in strength. The brigade was told to operate alone for forty-eight hours, after which the main force would arrive from the beaches. The brigade fully expected to remain in France after the initial landings and be used for further airborne operations or in a normal infantry role, as had been their lot for the previous seven months.

After the example of the very scattered drop in Sicily there was some apprehension in 2nd Parachute Brigade at trusting themselves to the navigational skills of the USAAF crews. However, at 3.23 am on 15 August 1944, the pathfinders of the 1st Independent Parachute Platoon landed accurately and unopposed on the main DZ and set up the beacon. They were the first Allied troops to land in southern France. This was a fine achievement by the American Dakota pilots who, because of the high ground, had to drop from between 1,500 and 2,000 feet through ground mist and cloud. The main parachute force also dropped from this unusual height and through cloud, an unpleasant experience. This time the drop was not so accurate and of the 126 Dakotas carrying the brigade, only seventy-three dropped their troops on the correct DZs. The remaining fifty-three aircraft delivered their paratroopers as far away as Agay, sixteen miles to the east, and Fayence, twelve miles north-east. This was still quite creditable, given the state of the art at the time – navigating on beacons, not all of them accurate, and dropping through cloud without seeing the ground at all. Furthermore, Major General Frederick had issued a hard-nosed order that no aircraft were to return with troops on board. The whole of the brigade headquarters arrived at the RV and 4, 5 and 6 Para reported in at forty, twenty-five, and sixty per cent strength respectively. Again a pretty good effort which made nonsense of the airmen's assertions about navigation difficulties at night which so fatally affected the landing plan at Arnhem.

Most of C Company commanded by Major Gourlay landed in the right place, thanks to the beacons placed by the pathfinders. Having captured their objective, Lieutenant Mortimer, a fluent German speaker, approached the next enemy position armed with a white handkerchief, demanding their surrender. They refused. He was too junior!

Major Hargreaves of 4 Para landed in the correct place, but in the top of a fir tree. His kitbag, still on its line and attached to him, was caught high above. He had considerable difficulty getting down. He could only descend the length of the line. Each time he was brought up short, and tugging, cursing, the kit-bag landed on his head! By the time he got to the bottom he was nearly unconscious. Taking two of his platoons – the third was dropped wide – he started climbing his objective, the hill overlooking Le Muy. Suddenly he was confronted by a number of Germans with their hands up. He had time to register how good their English was before realizing they were not Germans at all but US paratroopers! Hargreaves invited them to join him, putting them under command of one of his platoon sergeants, despite there being two officers with the party.

The battalions quickly secured their objectives, and by 10.15 am all initial brigade tasks were complete. In the late afternoon the brigade's gliders arrived with the artillery and the anti-tank guns. The American gliders suffered heavy damage on the LZ because of the rough ground and the vineyard poles, but the casualties were surprisingly light. 4 Para encountered the only fighting in the brigade area, accounting for sixteen Germans and taking twenty-nine prisoners and suffering seven dead and eight wounded themselves. The brigade headquarters was in radio communication with the Americans landing on the beaches from 6.15 that morning, and knew that all was going well. As the day passed, men who had been dropped wide started reporting in. The company commander of A Company in 4 Para caught a local bus. Covered in cabbages and shielded by the other passengers, he got through several German road blocks before rejoining the battalion. Hargreaves: 'The following day, American aircraft dropped copies of the US Forces newspaper which had headlines extolling the efforts of the Dakota pilots dropping the paratroopers right on target. The papers were put to good use!'

Many small parties had fought little battles on their way to join their units. Typical was the experience of D Company commander of 5 Para, dropped north of Fayence. Approaching Fayence with his small group, and finding it occupied by the enemy, he took up a defensive position in a neighbouring village. There they were joined by an officer from 517 Regimental Combat Team, US airborne, with sixty men, and together ambushed fifteen enemy vehicles and sixty to seventy men. After driving off the enemy and taking several prisoners, a farmhouse nearby was found to contain a colonel, the chief of staff of 1 Airborne Task Force and four other Americans who immediately put themselves under command of the major commanding D Company. The force moved south rejoining their units the next day. Coxen, the commanding officer of 4 Para, was among the late arrivals. He had been glad to see that he was in the lead aircraft of his flight, because in the USAAF only the lead aircraft had a qualified navigator. As they passed over the radio beacon located in a ship positioned seven miles offshore, the transponder and communications in Coxen's aircraft went unserviceable. Instead of continuing on a bearing for a set time from a known point, the pilot banked steeply out of the formation; the others followed. They were then treated to an aerobatic session by the leader, mirrored by the others. Eventually the leader, guessing his position, dropped his troops and the remainder followed. Coxen jumped number nine so he would be in the middle of the DZ. He landed in a tree and also had trouble with his kitbag. After extracting himself and gathering as many men as he could, he had a problem finding out where he was. Assuming he was more or less where he should have been, he crossed a river and came upon a farm in what seemed to be the right place. The farmer emerged with a yoke and two buckets and filled them with water from the well; Coxen, pistol in hand, followed him into the house – 'rather like Laurel and Hardy: de dum de dum, de dum de dum!' – to find a French family at breakfast. Eventually by showing them a map of the whole of the south of France he established his location, ten miles in a straight line north-west of the DZ and well off his large scale maps.

Coxen's party walked all day across the massif, taking care to avoid the Germans. There were some Americans with Coxen who kept telling him where they were. In the end, exasperated, he turned on them: 'Look, Buster, I don't know where we are. But we are certainly not where you think we are!' At nightfall, Coxen halted the party and told them he would go on by himself:

I am always happier walking alone at night. I could always whip in to the side of the road and hide. A couple of columns of trucks went by, but they did not see me. I went into a farm near Le Muy. Having checked my position with the inhabitants, I asked one of them to go back to where I had left my party and tell them I had gone on, and lead them to this farm.

I reached my battalion headquarters in the early hours of D plus one. The next morning we attacked Le Muy, capturing it. I and my batman Stanley, attached ourselves to Nigel Riley's platoon. I took off my rank badges and said to him: 'Take no notice of me, Nigel. You can consider Stanley and I as being part of one of your sections.' I was bloody hungry and thought if I got in first I would get someone to cook me something to eat. I captured the local brothel. It had been used as a first aid post and was full of dead Germans. I set the girls, who were still there, to work to cook me a chicken.

A major counter-attack did not materialize, but a number of brushes with the enemy took place in the first three days after the drop. The leading American division from the beachhead arrived at Le Muy early on the morning of 17 August, just over forty-eight hours after the brigade had dropped. The enemy, realizing that they could not contain let alone eliminate the beachhead, withdrew many miles inland. It was a model airborne operation, exactly what was required as an overture to drops against more serious opposition. The brigade was now well worked up, blooded after fighting in Italy, and with a brigade parachute operation under its belt ready for the sort of task in which its fellow parachute brigades had been or were about to be involved.

Ten days after landing in the south of France the brigade was ordered back to Italy and stood by for operations in Greece. It had become apparent to the Allied planners that as the Russians advanced through the Balkans the Germans occupying Greece would have to withdraw or be cut off. The British in particular wished to ensure that the political vacuum left behind by retreating Germans was filled by Greeks sympathetic to the Western Allies and not by communists who would draw Greece into the Soviet camp. The partisans fighting the occupying Germans were divided into royalist and communist groups. There had already been occasions when they had fought each other rather than the common enemy, and once the German threat was removed a civil war was highly likely. As soon as Russian forces were in neighbouring Yugoslavia and Bulgaria it would be easy for the communists to ask for assistance from their big brother, who would be all too pleased to provide it. Greece would then become a Soviet satellite. Churchill was determined to forestall his Russian ally. At first his plans were eyed with suspicion by many Americans.

2nd Independent Parachute Brigade was ordered to occupy Athens on the heels of the retreating Germans. The leading elements of the brigade were to land by parachute to secure an airfield and a port, into which the balance of the brigade would land by aircraft and ship. A follow-up force consisting of 23 Armoured Brigade, initially without their tanks, would arrive the day after the parachute brigade. In October the Germans started withdrawing from Athens. The DZ was Kalamaki airfield, to the east of Athens. At 6 pm on 11 October Coxen was briefing his officers. He was told to scrap the plan to drop on Kalamaki, take a force to Megara forty miles west of Athens, choose a DZ by observation from the air, and there drop his force. Megara could only be identified from a small scale map and one old photograph. There was insufficient time to take new air photographs.

At 2.11 pm on 12 October, after a preliminary run over the DZ, C Company of 4 Para, a sapper party, pathfinders and a radio team led by Coxen dropped on Megara airfield in a thirty-five mph wind. The result of dropping in a windspeed ten mph over the normal top limit for operational jumping was two killed and forty injured on landing. Coxen was dragged fifty to sixty yards before he could turn the knob and hit his harness-release box. The parachute whisked off, dragging his carbine and bergen rucksack with it. It snagged on the airfield perimeter fence, to be retrieved by Coxen's batman who had been dragged in the same direction. Private Cook of C Company: 'As usual my rifle, enclosed in its thick felt sleeve, was hanging below me as I dropped. When I went to pick it up I found the butt had broken off, but there were plenty of rifles lying about and I picked up one left by its injured owner.'

Luckily, apart from light shelling, there was no opposition and the company secured the airfield without delay. It was fortunate there were no enemy because bad weather postponed the rest of the brigade's arrival until 14 October. The wind was still strong, and several more casualties were suffered by men landing among rocks and trees. The Germans had blown the road to Athens so the brigade commandeered boats, including sailing caiques, and entered the city to a tumultuous welcome on 15 October. C Company 4 Para spent the first night in a four star hotel, previously occupied by the Germans. However, it soon became clear that the communists were making a bid for power. Noisy demonstrations in Athens by EAM and ELAS, the communist political and military wings, were a portent of things to come.

After a few days in Athens the brigade was busy in the wild mountainous country between Athens and the border with Albania and Yugoslavia. 4 Para formed Pompforce from B and C companies, detachments of the SBS and the RAF Regiment, to harry a German column as it withdrew through the Pindus Mountains on the western side of the Greek mainland. Pompforce succeeded in cutting ahead of the German rearguard on a number of occasions to inflict damage and casualties on the main body. They tried to avoid coming head-on against the strong armoured tail. However, on 26 October at Kozani there was nothing for it but to attack the rearguard. Kozani was occupied by the Germans while the town was overlooked by a hill about

1,500 feet high held by a German infantry unit. The side of the hill which faced the town was a long slope down to the main road below, with a narrow road winding up the slope to the top. On the reverse side of the hill there was a sheer drop to the valley with an almost perpendicular rock face. It was believed that the German defences were concentrated on the top of the hill, covering the approaches from the slope, as they did not consider an attack up the near vertical rock face possible.

Gourlay was ordered by Coxen to assault the position at night while B Company remained in reserve. At the briefing the commander of a local Greek partisan battalion offered to join in the assault. Gourlay thought it wise to decline, and suggested that they should operate in a supporting role. 'They looked, and were, an unsavoury lot.' Throughout the German occupation, despite propaganda to the contrary, the partisans had with a few exceptions been ineffective. They had spend most of their energy fighting and betraying each other, and German reprisals on the civilian population tended to discourage too much guerrilla activity. Their only action in support of C Company was reserved for after the battle, stripping the British dead of their uniforms and equipment under the cover of darkness. They were to use these uniforms against the British later. C Company succeeded in forcing the Germans off their position. Private Cook:

During the night we climbed the rock face, men helping each other from one foot-hold to another, and eventually assembled on the top. The enemy sentries had not been alerted, and the company formed up for the attack on the German positions somewhere in front in the darkness. As the company moved forward with Sergeant Wilmot's platoon in the centre, someone walked into a trip-wire which set off a green flare, warning the enemy. The company charged the German positions which they rapidly overran, the enemy having been taken completely by surprise. A number were killed, about twenty taken prisoner; the remainder took off into the darkness. During the assault Sergeant Wilmot, who was at the forefront of the attack leading his platoon, was badly wounded. Captain Teed, our company second-in-command, was also badly wounded and unfortunately later died of his wounds.

When it was daylight the Germans made repeated attacks on our positions, using light weapons and grenades. But they were unable to dislodge us and suffered heavy casualties. A mist came down, causing very poor visibility, and the Germans were able to get within a few yards of our positions, but again their casualties were heavy and they withdrew. When the enemy shelled our positions from the town using air-burst we suffered casualties, almost the whole of one section being killed. We hadn't been able to dig in because of the rocky ground. During the subsequent attack, one of our platoon commanders saw that the Germans were coming through our defences where men had been killed by the air-bursts. Regardless of his own safety, he walked towards the Germans firing his Tommy gun. He killed several of the enemy and forced the infiltrators back, but sadly was killed by sub-machine gun fire. We called him Corky because when inspecting us on parade he always examined our water-bottle corks for specks of rust on the little metal discs. Because of continual air-burst shelling our position became untenable, and we withdrew from the hill, leaving our dead but carrying the wounded who could not make the difficult climb down to the valley bottom.

Pompforce eventually closed up on the Albanian border.

A small party crossed into Albania, to be recalled by the headquarters in Cairo. Not far from the border Lieutenant Riley of B Company was sent to ambush a train. After the satisfaction of seeing it completely de-railed by his explosive charges, he sent a message over the radio to his company commander. To maintain security he used a code called Slidex, a system that was to plague the British Army well into the 1980s. He encoded a simple message, 'mission accomplished,' and a grid reference. Some minutes later, the reply came: 'Repeat message.' He did so. After an even longer pause he got an answer, not in code but in very plain words: 'Start swimming! Your position places you middle of Aegean sea. Congratulations on blowing up enemy submarine. Return immediately to base.'

6 Para in the meanwhile, based around Thebes, had been involved in internal security duties in Attica, while brigade headquarters with 5 Para and Number 9 Commando under command was sent to Salonika (Thessaloniki) in north east Greece. It was clear that the communists controlled the town, but at first they were co-operative. By the end of November the brigade was beginning to move back to Italy. Brigadier Pritchard was in Italy with advance parties, planning the next operation. 5 Para had already embarked and the other two battalions were about to move to their ships when Colonel Pearson, the deputy brigade commander, was summoned to the British corps headquarters and told that civil war had broken out in Athens; the brigade would remain and was to concentrate in Athens as soon as possible. Reports had been received of many thousands of well-armed ELAS troops marching down from the hills and converging on Athens with the intention of taking the city by force. Athens was held by two British battalions of 23 Armoured Brigade, the Greek Mountain Brigade, and some Greek National Guards. These last were to prove loyal and steadfast.

2nd Independent Parachute Brigade were ordered to hold positions in the centre of the city in the area of Omonia Square and Constitution Square, and then clear as much of the centre of Athens as possible as well as occupying the Acropolis and Likavittos, two heights dominating the whole of the city. By 7 December, after some fighting, all the initial objectives had been secured. At first the brigade found itself up against bands of armed political fanatics, fighting delaying actions until the regular ELAS forces arrived. Soon it became apparent that ELAS were converging in force on the centre of the city and the brigade was almost cut off from its re-supply base. Pritchard managed to rejoin his brigade before ELAS mounted a series of attacks, forcing the British to withdraw in some sectors, including the hospital at Psichiko, abandoning the staff and patients to the protection of the Red Cross. For the next few days the brigade held on, slowly clearing more elbow room and strengthening their positions by local attacks with tank support. By now the civilian population was in danger of starvation as food distribution was at a standstill. The brigade, in addition to its other worries, had the problem of opening soup kitchens which fed over 20,000 civilians daily.

On 18 December, 4th British Division landed, and the time had come to go over to the offensive. The first task was to open the main line of communications between Athens and the coast. On 22 December the second offensive started, with 5 Para supported by two squadrons of tanks and a troop of armoured cars clearing more of the city, taking nearly 400 prisoners and killing at least fifty ELAS. The turning point in the battle came at the New Year. On 4 January, 2 Para Brigade and 12th Infantry Brigade attacked together. Resistance was fierce and the leading battalion, 6 Para, had five officer casualties within thirty minutes. 5 Para were held up by fanatical opposition which was very difficult to clear because the supporting armour was held up by demolitions blocking the narrow streets. Fighting from house to house, the battalions battled their way forward. A bridge on the ELAS escape route was captured at about midday. Realizing that their main line of withdrawal was cut, they were forced to stand and fight while another way out was found. By that evening 170 ELAS dead, and seventy wounded were discovered; 520 were taken prisoner.

At first light the next day the advance continued, and it quickly became obvious that the fierceness of the previous day's fighting and the destruction of over a regiment of ELAS, had broken the spirit of the rebel movement in Athens and that a general withdrawal had taken place. The ELAS defence had not been in depth, and once the crust was broken it had collapsed. The brigade handed over its sector to two Greek national guard brigades on 16 January 1945. The British casualties for the period 3 December 1944 to 6 January 1945 were 237 killed and 2,101 wounded – not all 2nd Para Brigade, but as an indication of the severity of the fighting, 6 Para, out of a strength of about 520 all ranks, had 123 casualties. ELAS casualties are harder to calculate and will probably never be known. A British report dated 9 January, puts their losses in dead, wounded, and prisoners, as fifty per cent of their force committed. Some 25,000 ELAS were believed to have taken part in the battle. By the end 8,000 were taken prisoner and 4,000 were dead or wounded.

As in most civil wars, atrocities were committed by both sides, but the communists distinguished themselves by acts of barbarism against their fellow countrymen, whether partisans of the opposing party, or innocent uncommitted bystanders of all ages and both sexes. They were to continue to do so for several years to come in the civil war which lasted until 1949, backed by Yugoslavia, Albania and Bulgaria. The fighting throughout the Athens battle had been vicious, and as the partisans did not hesitate to disguise themselves as women or wear British uniforms, it was often difficult to tell friend from foe. There was frequently no front line, platoons and companies being cut off for hours and sometimes days. The medical officer of 4 Para, riding in a vehicle clearly marked with a red cross, was shot while on his way to tend the wounded. 4 Para found a well down which had been stuffed the bodies of 230 men, women and children murdered by the communists. One of the communist torturers was found in possession of a whip bound with brass wire. About a week after the battle C Company of 6 Para discovered the bodies of eighty civilians and S Company found fourteen, including the mutilated corpse of a British lance corporal. The royalists were not entirely blameless. Coxen stopped handing over his prisoners to those attached to his battalion when he discovered they were shot immediately. Among the savagery there was, as always, humour, such as the occasion information was received that the partisans were floating mines down the sewers under the building occupied by British political/military mission in Greece. Headquarters 2nd Para Brigade, who worked next door, were treated to the sight of staff officers from the mission vacating their quarters in unseemly haste, some scrambling out of windows and gingerly letting themselves down, only to find they were already on the ground floor! Inspection of the sewers revealed nothing other than the normal contents of sewers.

The soldiers disliked being the jam in the sandwich in this bloody and dirty civil war, but reserved most of their resentment for the left wing press and politicians in England. They criticized the paratroopers for killing communists, who were seen in left wing circles as allies, merely because they espoused the same political cause as the Russians. Eventually feelings ran so high among the soldiers that a Trades Union Congress delegation was sent to Greece to investigate the situation. After conducting interviews with soldiers who had volunteered to give evidence they reported back. This apparently did the trick because the critics were heard no more, at least not in public.

In February 1945 the brigade returned to Italy and spent the next three months in the frustrating situation familiar to so many airborne soldiers; planning and standing by for operations that never materialized. Between 6 March and 4 May they prepared for thirty-three airborne operations, all of which were cancelled. In the course of this planning the brigade staff looked at 90,000 air photographs and 36,000 maps. When the war ended in Italy the brigade was shipped to England, and from there, in October, to Palestine. The 2nd Independent Parachute Brigade had spent more time in contact with the enemy than any other British airborne formation.

CHAPTER 8

The Ardennes – A Christmas Trip

In early December 1944, 12 Para stationed in Bulford had a new commanding officer, Lieutenant Colonel Darling, who had last seen them six months before after being wounded the day after landing in Normandy:

After Breville they were a shadow of their former selves. There were few officers left and when they got back to England they had trouble settling down. I was horrified at what I saw. Almost the first day, at my orders, I saw about fifteen to twenty men drawn up to await my punishment for various misdemeanours. The adjutant said this was normal and in addition there were a lot of absentees. I lost my temper and addressed the whole battalion, including all the prisoners, whom I put in the front row. I told them that our job was to fight the Germans, not each other; all prisoners would be released, and the next lot of men who went absent without leave would be on the first boat to the Far East. This did the trick and really got them going. Then the Ardennes operation came along, which in my view remade the battalion.

The 6th Airborne Division was about to go, or was on Christmas leave, when a message arrived telling them to move in forty-eight hours. There were no absentees, and by a remarkable feat of administration they were moved to the continent by sea and air, starting on Christmas Eve. Nine days earlier, after the heaviest artillery barrage fired by the Germans in the whole campaign in north-west Europe in 1944–45, preceded by parties of parachut-ists and by saboteurs in civilian and Allied uniforms, three German armies had attacked five United States divisions on a front of fifty miles. The German aim was to drive a wedge between the British and American armies, cross the Meuse and seize Antwerp, the main logistic base for the northern group of Allied armies. Although the German generals considered the plan imposed by Hitler to be too ambitious, and proposed a more limited aim, he refused to take their advice and ordered them to press on. The German troops were of very high quality, and included the 1st SS Panzer and 12th SS Panzer Divisions and the 3rd Parachute Division. By 23 December the German armoured spearheads were driving for Dinant on the River Meuse, and a salient fifty miles wide at its base and forty-five miles deep had been punched in the allied line. The Americans who had born the brunt of this attack, fought with great courage and tenacity, particularly at St Vith and Bastogne. The dogged resistance by the Americans slowed down the German attacks; this caused hold-ups of enemy traffic on the congested roads and by Christmas Day the offensive was sealed off. The Allied task now was to pinch off the German salient as quickly as possible before the drive into Germany in three months time. The bulk of this task was to fall to the American First and Third Armies. The British contribution was a drive on the nose of the salient by 30 Corps between the two American armies. 6th Airborne Division was the right leading div-ision of 30 Corps.

The weather was bitterly cold as the soldiers of the division were driven in trucks through the frozen Belgian countryside. They moved into defensive positions west of Marche, relieving the US 84th Infantry Division. In night temperatures of twenty-eight degrees of frost, the soldiers slept in their slit trenches piled on top of each other.

Patrols were sent out each night in the snow, sometimes camouflaged in requisitioned sheets. On 3rd January the Allied attacks started. The 5th Parachute Brigade was to see the hardest fighting, 13 Para in particular at Bure, bitterly defended by troops of the Panzer Lehr Division.

13 Para had eaten their Christmas dinner at Namur on 30 December. On 2 January they were ordered to clear the village of Bure before advancing to Grupont where a bridge crossed the River Homme. They moved forward in transport on the morning of 3 January, and having marched about six kilometres formed up for the attack in a wood about 1,000 yards east of Bure. A Company, commanded by Major Watson who had been its second-in-command, was left forward assault company, with B Company on the right and C Company in reserve. At 1.20 pm enemy shell and mortar fire caught the battalion in the forming up position, causing heavy casualties. As the two leading companies advanced they came under fire from enemy SP guns sited about 1,000 yards on the battalion's left flank. B Company, because they were on more exposed ground than A Company, were worst hit, losing their company commander as they crossed the start line. B Company, moving round the village to the high ground beyond it, were met by intense fire from tanks, assault guns and infantry. A German counter-attack was held up by Lieutenant Lagerern hurling grenades until he was killed. All three platoon commanders and the company sergeant-major were killed or wounded; soon there were only twenty-one men on their feet.

Watson decided that the best answer was to go like hell for Bure. Any hanging about would result in further casualties. A Company charged in and started fighting forward from house to house. By 5 pm A Company had cleared half the village and C Company was put in to relieve them and allow them to move forward again. C Company did not have an easy time. Lawley, now the

Company Sergeant Major of C Company commanded by Major Clarke:

> We got through to the centre of the village. It was getting dusk now and it was then things began to happen. Everything became mixed up, something that can easily happen in street fighting. We had sent two platoons forward and had lost touch with them through their 38 (radio) sets breaking down. It was very difficult in the darkness to discern friend from foe. Sometimes we would be in one house and the enemy in the one next door. We were helped by a squadron of Sherman tanks, but they were of little use against the three Tiger tanks that Jerry had. We were suffering many casualties through heavy shell and machine gun fire, but the order was to hold our footing at all costs. All that night we tried to contact our two lost platoons but it was to no avail. There were many wounded and dead lying around, among whom moved our padre administering morphia and first aid at great danger to himself.

By early evening, being unable to advance further, the battalion had formed a tight defensive position in about half the village. All occupied buildings were formed into strong points and the CO, Luard, ordered aggressive patrolling for the night. Lawley:

> When night came, Major Clarke decided that we would move forward and if possible find out what had happened to our two lost platoons. After we had gone some distance Major Clarke decided that we would enter the house we then found ourselves behind and try to make contact on the wireless, but we soon found the windows and doors bolted. I saw a passage up the side of the house, so went along it with the idea of getting in at the front. I tried to open

it but found it locked, when suddenly I heard voices in a strange tongue which I knew to be German. I tip-toed back and told Major Clarke. We both went back up the passage and listened. They were Germans all right and quite a large number too. They had a tracked vehicle with them and were busy loading it with documents from the building opposite. We went back to the others to decide on a form of attack when suddenly we heard footsteps coming down the side of the house. We were only six in number so we had to think quick. We all stood still and waited until the footsteps came very close, then Major Clarke shone his torch in their direction and we all fired. Then the torch went out and I ran across the opening to the next house and gave covering fire while the others got across. We then went back to our previous position. All that night we were being heavily shelled. Our lost two platoons eventually got back to us.

The Germans mounted four counter-attacks during the night, broken up by A and C Companies. The next day the Panzer Lehr counter-attacked five times, but were beaten back each time by artillery, tank and infantry fire. There was at least one chivalrous incident, Lawley:

In the afternoon the battalion medical sergeant had decided to drive the ambulance up outside our company HQ and get the wounded back. It arrived and the first couple of cases were put on board when there was a sudden burst of machine gun fire. Then we heard the rumble of a tank and the next thing we saw was a Jagdtiger (88mm assault gun) outside our HQ with the 88 trained on us. The commander was standing up in the turret, telling our medic that he was breaking the rules of war by his action, ie that he should wait until the battle was over before trying to evacuate the wounded and that if he did it again they would shoot the ambulance up. The Tiger then withdrew. I thought it very sporting of him, especially as I was then practically looking down the barrel of the 88!

The 23rd Hussars, in support of 13 Para, lost sixteen tanks during the day. Towards evening a company of the 52nd LI, from the Air-Landing Brigade reinforced 13 Para and cleared the remainder of the village. Once again the Germans demonstrated their resilience and counter-attacked, forcing back the 52nd LI company. A Tiger tank spent the night cruising the village streets. The next morning 13 Para succeeded in pushing the bulk of the enemy out of the village, but they left behind snipers and the persistent Tiger tank which could not be dislodged, despite repeated PIAT attacks. It took a further nine hours finally to clear Bure of enemy, during which 13 Para beat off four German counter-attacks, supported by Tigers. The battalion was withdrawn at midnight of 5/6 January, having suffered 189 casualties of whom sixty-six were killed.

The enemy in front of 3rd Parachute Brigade withdrew without fighting. As 9 Para was probing forward they saw the village of Bandes below them. Running up the hill towards them came the priest in a very distressed state. He asked: 'Are you British, American or German? Can you promise that you are British? Please come with me, something terrible has happened.' He went on to say that the Germans had taken all the men in the village between the ages of eighteen and forty as a reprisal for a staff car being blown up in the village. They had been taken to the cellar of a bombed building. The Germans had told the villagers not to go to the buildings or do anything about it. Crookenden, the commanding officer, sent the medical officer to investigate and he found a pile of bodies. Each had been shot in the back of the neck. They were buried with full military honours by the men of 9 Para.

Soon after this incident the division spent about a month in Holland to hold positions on the line of the River Maas. There was much patrolling which served the purpose of keeping everybody in practice. Crookenden: 'Despite the cold, everybody was very healthy. Back in Bulford there used to be about thirty people sick at any one time with minor complaints. In the Ardennes and in Holland, living in the open in the snow we had no sick at all.'

In mid-February the division was taken back to England to prepare for the Rhine Crossing.

CHAPTER 9

Varsity – The Crossing of the Rhine

'If risks have to be taken it is best to take them early rather than late.' *General Sir Kenneth Darling* (in 1945 commanding 12th Parachute Battalion for the Rhine Crossing).

Before daylight on 24 March 1945 the 6th Airborne Division in 242 Dakotas and 440 gliders took off from their airfields in England and flew over France and Belgium to the River Rhine. No pathfinders preceded them because the amphibious assault across the river would have started by the time the aircraft approached the target in daylight, so the pilots should have no difficulty in recognizing the DZs and LZs. At 9.50 am, nine minutes early, 3rd Parachute Brigade commanded by Brigadier Hill started dropping. In nine minutes the complete brigade was on the DZ, right on their objective. By the time forty minutes had elapsed, the whole of 6th Airborne Division had landed on or very close to their objectives. Eighteen Dakotas were destroyed by flak or were missing; 115 had flak damage. Thirty-five gliders did not make the LZs, mainly because of technical failures. It had taken the bitter disaster of Arnhem to drive home the point that airborne troops must land on or near their objective and that divisions must be taken in in one lift.

6th Airborne Division with 17th US Airborne Division formed 8th US Airborne Corps. They were fortunate in having Major General Ridgeway United States Army for their Corps Commander. He was a large impressive-

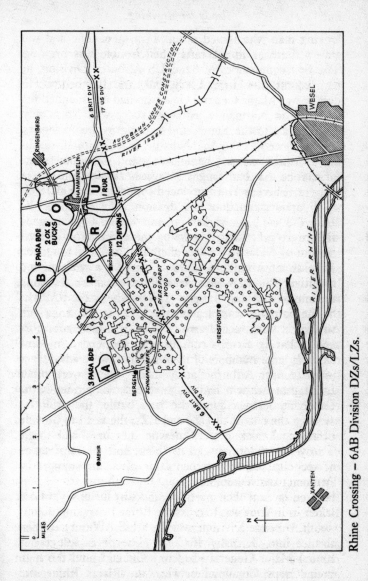

Rhine Crossing – 6AB Division DZs/LZs.

looking man who issued orders in a quiet tone and was
always there or thereabouts when trouble was brewing.
The first commander of 82nd US Airborne Division, he
had led the division in Sicily, Italy and Normandy. His
deputy was Major General Gale who had commanded 6th
Airborne in Normandy. After its success in Normandy,
the advance to the Seine, and fighting in the Ardennes,
6th Airborne was thoroughly battle tested, without reaching the stage of being battle-weary and sticky, like some
formations that had fought with little respite since 1941
or 1942. There were experienced commanders at all levels
in all units throughout the division. The machinery of
command had been worked up, and divisional and brigade
staffs were practised in grasping the articulation of their
formations. Since Normandy there had not been too much
sitting about waiting for action, a recipe for cynicism and
boredom. 'We were an extraordinarily mature division,'
remembers Captain Marquis, who had been the RMO of
the 9th Battalion since leaving the MDS in July 1944. 6th
Airborne's track record as a division, and their good fortune in having a corps commander experienced in commanding large numbers of men in battle, were advantages
denied to 1st Airborne at Arnhem. There were other
advantages: Arnhem had taught the senior airmen some
elementary lessons about the land battle, the priorities
affecting the choice of DZs and LZs, the need to provide
sufficient aircraft, even if drastic measures had to be
employed to find crews to fly them, and the importance
of tying up the arrangements for close air support by
Typhoons and Tempests.

Ridgeway had been given four tasks by Dempsey, whose
British 2nd Army was to cross the Rhine by an amphibious
assault, codename Plunder, in the area of Wesel and then
advance into Germany. First, by airborne assault, codename Varsity, Ridgeway had to seize and hold the high
ground north of Wesel between the Rivers Rhine and

Issel. Second, he had to defend the bridgehead against enemy counter-attacks. Third, he was to ensure that the enemy was not allowed to seal off the bridgehead before enough troops were concentrated there to permit the advance to continue. And fourth, he had to be prepared for offensive action to the east. Montgomery, reverting to his normal thoroughness after his untypically casual approach to planning for the Arnhem operation, insisted that the DZs and LZs should all be in range of friendly artillery firing from the west bank of the Rhine, and that the link-up with ground troops should be effected on the first day of the crossing. The artillery fireplan for the operation was impressive, starting with 280 guns firing for four hours the preceding day, 487 guns firing for one hour until thirty minutes before the landings, and culminating in thirty minutes worth from 544 guns for the final half hour. Ridgeway decided to take advantage of the Allies' overwhelming air supremacy to mount the operation in daylight, and insisted that the whole corps should land in one lift on top of their objectives. Artillery observers with efficient radios to call for fire support, and teams with radios to talk to ground attack aircraft were to land with the corps. As part of his careful preparation, and to ensure that his senior commanders were in his mind, Ridgeway held a planning exercise in England to which he invited commanders down to brigade level. Here he posed a series of problems to which all present had to give their solutions.

Ridgeway allocated the northern half of his objective to 6th Airborne Division and the southern half to 17th US Airborne. He had been given 6th Guards Tank Brigade who were to cross the river on the second day; and 1st Commando Brigade, after they had captured the town of Wesel, were to come under his command. The commanding officers and squadron leaders of the Guards Tank Brigade made a special journey to meet the officers of the two airborne divisions before the battle. Finally, Ridgeway

set up his corps tactical headquarters close to the headquarters of the corps conducting the amphibious crossing
of the river. From fire planning to liaison, every aspect of
the preparation for this operation bore Ridgeway's hall-
mark; he was a great commander.

The enemy in the area of the Airborne Corps objectives
consisted of 84th Infantry Division and 7th Parachute
Division; both very weak after the retreat to the Rhine,
numbering about 4,000 men and fifty guns. The local
reserve was thought to consist of 116 and 15 Panzer
Grenadier Divisions. Although badly battered after covering the withdrawal across the Rhine, it was likely that they
had received armoured reinforcements. More worrying
was the presence of 712 light and 114 heavy flak guns.

Major General Bols, who had taken over 6th Airborne
from Gale, decided that Hill's 3rd Parachute Brigade
should drop on DZ A to capture the Schnappenberg.
They were then to clear and hold the western edge of the
Diersfordt Wood and the road junction at Bergen. They
were to patrol out and be prepared to hold the area of the
railway line running through the north-east of the wood
and to link up with 5th Parachute Brigade. Poett's 5th
Parachute Brigade was to drop on DZ B and clear and
hold an area astride the main road running from their DZ
to Hamminkeln. They were to link up with 3rd Parachute
Brigade on the railway line. The Air-Landing Brigade was
to try out a new tactic. Instead of landing on one LZ as a
brigade, they were to land by company groups right on or
near their objectives within the battalion tactical areas of
responsibility. Two of the battalions had road or rail
bridges to seize, and taking a leaf out of the Normandy
experience, the gliders carrying men to capture these
would land right alongside them.

'For each Parachute Brigade,' recalls Darling, 'the
essence of the plan was rapid and decisive action before
the enemy could recover from the initial surprise. The

fact that the airborne landings were to take place after and not before the crossing of the Rhine itself was a surprise for the enemy. The arrival of 2,500 pugnacious soldiers in an area some 1,200 yards by 1,200 yards in a period of ten minutes would be a nasty shock.'

Early in the morning of 24 March, the parachute brigades assembled in their transit camps and moved to their airfields. Darling: 'The aircraft flew into our airfields almost like a fleet of Green Line coaches to transport us to Germany.'

Crookenden, CO of 9 Para, went to see the USAAF colonel commanding the troop carrier wing taking his battalion to the Rhine: 'The impression I got was of a unit with iron discipline. On a previous exercise they had dropped us in the wrong place. The whole wing, officers and enlisted aircrew, had their leave stopped for a month. The USAAF regarded dropping airborne soldiers as a "proud task" and not, as in some quarters in the RAF, a job for the "poor relations". The colonel welcomed me and said: "It's a real pleasure to fly with you. I guess you will be with me in the lead ship." When I told him I most certainly would not, but somewhere in the middle of the formation so that I arrived on the DZ in the centre of my battalion, he clearly thought I was a bit of a wimp.'

The Dakotas of US Troop Carrier Command were a welcome change from the RAF Albemarles and Stirlings which had carried so many of the division to Normandy. The US dropping technique was to fly in tight formations of nine aircraft wing-tip to wing-tip, each formation following close upon another. Navigation was by the pilot of the lead aircraft, and all started dropping together to achieve a concentrated, mass drop, a battalion of 700 parachutists almost simultaneously arriving on the DZ. Just before take-off Crookenden drove down the line of aircraft in his jeep and heard the sound of a shot: 'There was a group of people at the end of the line. A sergeant

had deliberately shot himself in the foot. He was a really
good chap. He had just received a letter from his wife
telling him that if he went again she would leave him. He
was put away for eighty-four days detention. It was very
sad.'

Take-off was at 7 am. The aircraft taxied down the
runway in threes and took off together. In eleven minutes
they had formed up in the air. It was a beautiful clear day,
and the British parachute soldiers had a magnificent view
as the formations of transport aircraft crossed the Channel
between Folkestone and Cap Gris Nez, linked up with the
7th US Airborne Division over Wavre just south of Brus-
sels, and passed beneath the glider stream. Crookenden,
looking out of the astradome in his Dakota, could see the
aircraft carrying the British stretching to the horizon fore
and aft, and a similarly sized river of aircraft carrying the
Americans, until the sky was filled with aircraft as far as
the eye could see in all directions. The whole airborne
corps flew in one great armada of more than 2,000 aircraft
protected by fighters. Many of the soldiers thought and
hoped that this must be the final battle of the war. Sim of
12 Para: 'Going into battle the second time round meant
that I had no illusions. I knew what it would be like. It
was not fun any more, it was not exciting. I thought about
what was coming.'

As they approached the Rhine they could see ahead of
them the battlefield covered by the haze and dust of the
bombardment. At 1,000 feet they passed over the gun
lines and administrative areas on the home side of the
river. There was not time to look at the troops on the
ground below or the craft on the river; the red light was
on and suddenly they were over enemy territory. The flak
started to come up and the aircraft bumped and shook.
Many soldiers remember the tinkling sound of shrapnel
hitting the aircraft and the way the American pilots resol-
utely flew straight and level despite the flak. Then they

were over the DZ, the green light flicked on and they were out. There were several instances of aircraft hit and on fire being flown on until the whole stick had jumped.

3 Parachute Brigade's drop went absolutely to plan and very accurately. The woods surrounding the DZ were held by enemy who caused casualties on the DZ and had to be winkled out after a stiff fight. Hill on landing:

> I remember thinking: 'Those woods are occupied by enemy who are switched-on people.' Anyone who was unlucky enough to get hung up on a tree was usually killed. I went to my intended brigade command post which was at the junction of a copse and the main wood. I knew the copse would be occupied, and had detailed people to take it. When I landed it was still occupied, so I grabbed a company commander in 8 Para and told him to deal with it. He did and was killed.

Hill, having occupied the copse, was treated to the sight of a glider coming straight at him. It pulled up at the last moment and landed in the trees above his head. It contained his jeep, batman and signals officer! The pilot's legs were broken. It took much ingenuity to extract the jeep from the glider roosting in the trees.

Jefferson, now the mortar platoon commander of 9 Para, had a good drop. As he raced towards two of his containers, he saw out of the corner of his eye the alarming sight of the earth being furrowed by a stream of machine gun bullets keeping pace with him. It stopped as he reached the containers, but speeded the unpacking of the contents! Reaching the RV, he met Lieutenant Pond and McGeever, the Company Sergeant Major of headquarters company. Over the past months the three of them had developed a ridiculous little daily ritual:

'What is a grocer's wedge?'

'It's what you stuff up a fly's arse to stop it shitting on the cheese!'

And they solemnly exchanged the grocer's wedge, a minute piece of glass, in return for a signature in the time-honoured Army fashion. Standing at the RV, under fire, they enacted this small ceremony beneath the startled gaze of a medical orderly in action for the first time.

By 1.45 pm the Schnappenberg feature was in the hands of 9 Para and the Canadians were firm on all their objectives. 8 Para, after clearing the DZ, was ordered to clear the woods west of Kopenhof farm. B company under Major Kippen found its company RV held by the remnant of a battalion of German parachutists, well dug-in and concealed. There was no question of organizing to attack since it was the RV. Each individual had to charge towards the positions and do the best he could to kill the enemy. Major Kippen succeeded in getting into an enemy trench but was killed, and casualties among the officers and soldiers were high. A glider crashed into battalion head-quarters, killing Lieutenant England the Intelligence Officer (who had been captured in Normandy but had escaped), wounding Lieutenant Colonel Hewetson the commanding officer and several other members of battalion headquarters. The occupants of the glider were dead and the Adjutant was the only officer at battalion headquarters fit to take command. Shortly after 3 pm the leading elements of 15th Scottish Division, having crossed the Rhine, were in contact with the 3rd Parachute Brigade. Soon the link-up was secure. By this time the brigade had taken about 700 prisoners. They had suffered 270 casualties, a number being killed or wounded while they hung in trees suspended by their parachute harness, including Lieutenant Colonel Nicklin, the commanding officer of the Canadian Parachute Battalion.

The drop of 5th Parachute Brigade was not as accurate as 3rd Brigade's, but still good, and certainly better than their experience on 6 June the year before. But the drifting smoke and haze caused by the previous bombardment and by the enemy's mortar and artillery fire on to the DZ made visibility so poor that many men had difficulty in finding their bearings. At the time it was thought that the Germans were deliberately using smoke to cover the DZs and LZs, but subsequent interrogation of the local commander revealed that this was not so. Poett, the brigade commander:

> We were dangling from our parachutes and trying, in the very short time available, to pick up landmarks which had seemed so very clear and simple on the sand models and photos, but looked so different as we came down rapidly amid the firing and the smoke and dust which had been left from the preliminary bombardment which had finished ten minutes before. Heavy as this bombardment had been, ten minutes was ample time for those enemy not knocked out to recover their balance sufficiently to be a considerable menace to the parachutist as he swung in the air or disentangled himself from his parachute and gained his bearings. We felt very naked.

12 Para was dropped slightly wide. The battalion RV was actually mopped up and secured by Poett's headquarters, following his dictum that the headquarters of a parachute brigade should be able to fight as infantry. 12 Para, like everyone else in the division, had loaded their aircraft according to where each man was required on the DZ, so that sub-units were all distributed throughout the battalion's Dakotas. This greatly speeded up the rallying of men under their own commanders. To achieve rapid reaction and to maintain the impetus of the surprise of a mass drop, Darling ordered that the first twenty men at a company RV were to band together under the command of the senior person present and to rush to seize their

objectives. It could only have been attempted by well-trained soldiers, and in the event worked well.

This was where the experience and training of the brigade paid off. Darling:

> We found that with the reduced visibility there was greater difficulty than had been anticipated in recognizing our rendezvous; in fact the majority of the battalion assembled at a wood similar in shape to the correct one under Major Bucher and only a few men, about eighty, found their way independently to the correct rendezvous. Major Bucher soon realized that the battalion was at the wrong place and proceeded to lead the battalion across the completely open DZ to its correct rendezvous. The men moved in one long stream, during which time they were under constant small arms fire and, worst of all, shelling from 88mm guns which somehow were very much alive on the DZ. As shells fell among the column some men dropped and were picked up by stretcher bearers, while the remainder moved as straight as a die for the objective. Although there was nothing to be gained by stopping on the DZ, it required considerable determination to keep moving in these circumstances.
>
> The battalion rendezvous was at once under fire at very close range from the same 88mm guns and was a very unhealthy spot. Here magnificent work was done by many individuals in sorting out the battalion and directing men to their company rendezvous, among them Major Bucher, who walked about in a most nonchalant manner in his beret, and Captain Metcalf, the Adjutant, who continued at his duties although a bit of shrapnel had removed most of his teeth.

Eventually the troublesome 88mm guns were taken at the point of the bayonet by Number 1 platoon under

Lieutenant Burkinshaw. Most of the farmhouses in the area were defended tenaciously by the enemy and had to be cleared building by building. About thirty American paratroopers who had been dropped wide assisted 12 Para in taking their objectives.

Two gliders had been allocated to each parachute battalion to carry anti-tank guns and jeeps with a resupply of ammunition. About thirty minutes after the drop they came in. 12 Para's gliders both landed skilfully close to the RV. As they touched down they were hit by shellfire and destroyed. Every man except one was killed or wounded. Within one and a half hours 12 Para's objectives were secured and the work of clearing the battlefield could begin. The battalion medical section had been collecting casualties before the battle was over. The medical officer Captain Wilson and Corporal Houghton were both decorated for their bravery in tending casualties under fire. As both the battalion jeeps had been destroyed in the gliders, there was a problem of evacuating wounded back to the dressing station until someone hit upon the idea of using farm carts with German prisoners in the shafts. Darling found a horse and rode around the battalion position.

CSM Lawley in 13 Para, number one in his stick, was carrying out his first daylight operational jump. He had taken part in the first British parachute operation of the war and was in the last such operation in Europe:

I took up my position at the door. There was much flak bursting around and while I was watching intently for the signal to go, a burst of flak exploded a short distance from me. But for the fact that my hands were gripping the outside of the door, I would most probably have been blown across the fuselage. The next second the green light came on and I was away. It seemed a very long time before I landed. I was soon out of my chute harness and made for some

buildings where I found a number of my company.
The second-in-command was wounded. I took his
hunting horn and blew the company call, mustering
most of them. While this was happening a truck-load
of Jerries drove round the corner of a wood not more
than 200 yards away. We soon took care of them.
Taking the company back to the RV we found our
company commander, Major Priday. Soon the whole
area was cleared of enemy, large numbers of prisoners being taken, some of whom we made dig our
slit-trenches. They thought they were digging their
own graves! There were some nasty sights, burnt-out
gliders complete with personnel, paratroopers shot as
they hung helpless in the trees. It was sad for me to
find the body of our young colour-sergeant, a great
friend of mine. He had landed in a wood and been
shot in the back.

Casualties in the battalion RVs mounted as shelling and
mortaring increased. Nevertheless, while 7 Para secured
the DZ, 12 and 13 Para set to with great speed to clear
the enemy from the farms and houses in the brigade area.
By 3.30 pm the whole objective was in 5th Parachute
Brigade's hands.

Many glider pilots became disorientated because of the
smoke obscuring their LZs and landed in the wrong place.
Enemy flak was heavy, and the guns were turned on to
the LZs in the ground role for some time after all gliders
were down. Navigation problems, flak, machine gun and
mortar fire caused heavy casualties among the gliders.
Some were destroyed in the air, some crashed on landing
and others burst into flames after skidding to a halt. The
petrol in the jerricans and in the fuel tanks in jeeps was a
frequent cause of disaster. Nevertheless, the *coup de main*
parties all landed on their objectives and enough of the
Air-Landing Brigade landed in the correct places for the

enemy to be rushed before surprise was lost. By 11 am
the bridges and the town of Hamminkeln had been captured. The remaining enemy in the brigade area were
suppressed by rocket-firing Typhoons called in by radio.
By nightfall the Air-Landing Brigade had lost about one
third of its strength.

That night Ridgeway visited Bols at his headquarters
and gave orders for the following two days. 6th Airborne
was to be prepared to advance eastwards at first light on
26 March. Ridgeway and Bols had good reason to be
satisfied with the day's events. All objectives had been
taken – and were being held. The artillery support was
particularly successful. The forward observers who had
jumped with the division were in radio contact with their
guns within fifteen to forty minutes. A bold concept, boldly
executed, had paid off. Airborne troops had been used
correctly. There had been losses on landing and in the
air, but these were a price worth paying to avoid the
slaughter that would have ensued had the troops been
landed well away from their objectives in an effort to get
them down with minimal casualties. On his way back from
visiting 6th Airborne, Ridgeway encountered a large party
of Germans. He had to shoot his way out, collecting a
small graze wound in the process.

The next day was spent repelling small parties of enemy
attempting to penetrate the divisional position. Considerable assistance was provided by a continuous 'cab rank' of
fighter ground attack aircraft over the area throughout
the day. They were summoned down from their loitering
positions to attack about twelve targets. The next morning
the advance started. The airborne soldiers had the welcome but unusual experience of being supported by tanks.
Crookenden:

The 6th Guards Tank Brigade were splendid. As
foot-guardsmen converted to the tank role they were

not troubled by the Royal Armoured Corps' hang-up about only using tanks en masse. In their turn the Tank Brigade, who had been in action since the landings in Normandy, said they had never seen infantry who stayed with them as did the soldiers of the 6th Airborne Division when bullets were flying. We found the best way to advance with a squadron of tanks was to have one troop (three tanks) leading. The following troops carried most of a rifle company mounted on their backs. Battalion headquarters followed with the two jeeps and trailers from my two gliders. The main body of the battalion walked, Occasionally we were allocated trucks. We had a motley collection of other transport. At one stage I had a captured Mercedes open tourer as a staff car. The mortar platoon requisitioned prams to supplement the airborne trolleys. I and my batman had a horse each.

The routes followed by the division ran south-west to north-east across the main north-south and east-west highways. Using forest tracks and side roads they moved faster than 8th Armoured Division on their left flank. When the leading troop came under fire the rear troops stopped, the paratroopers dismounted and outflanked the enemy to the left or right of the axis of advance. The enemy were using similar tactics to those encountered by the division during the advance to the Seine six months before.

Hill found that the best way of getting about in those pre-helicopter days was on the pillion of a motor-cycle driven by his batman. In this way he could weave his way up and down the brigade as it advanced along the narrow tracks and roads. On one occasion having just captured a German corps headquarters:

We were swooping on and there, standing by the side

of the road, was a magnificent German colonel with a wonderful pair of binoculars hanging round his neck. I was extremely hot on looting, so was amazed when my batman stopped the motor-cycle by this colonel, relieved him of his binoculars, and proceeded to hang them round his own neck before pressing on. I was speechless for a moment, then said: 'If you can get me a pair, you can keep them!'

When 6th Airborne reached the River Issel they left Ridgeway's command, coming under 8th British Corps for the advance through Germany to the Baltic. Again the division's operations were marked by swiftness, boldness and initiative. Many of the attacks and outflanking marches on German positions were done at night. By now some transport had joined them, though not enough to carry all the troops. The brigades were passed through each other, taking it in turns to lead. At times the fighting was heavy as the division cleared the towns and villages on the route to the River Elbe, crossing the River Ems, the Dortmund-Ems canal and the Rivers Weser, Leine and Aller on the way. On one occasion 3rd Parachute Brigade marched fifteen miles in twenty-four hours, fighting almost continuously for eighteen hours, having eliminated a Panzer Grenadier training battalion and capturing or destroying many vehicles and flak guns. Another time 5th Parachute Brigade marched fifty miles in seventy-two hours, carrying out two night operations; at the end of the second day's march, after a two-hour halt for a meal, the soldiers went into the attack with their usual dash and spirit. Advances averaging eighteen or nineteen miles in twenty-four hours, and fighting battles en route, were commonplace throughout the division. They reached the Weser, a distance of 150 miles, in eight days.

Approaching the River Weser at Minden, 3rd Parachute Brigade found itself advancing on a parallel road to two

German tanks and an ammunition carrier motoring in the same direction and in full view. Hill was riding on the back of the third British tank in the column. The British and German tanks exchanged fire. The ammunition carrier was destroyed, but the two German tanks turned off and got ahead of the brigade to block the way into Minden. At this point 8 Para were leading, and although they pressed on they found the bridge blown, taking with it 9 Para's captured Volkswagen loaded with the officers' mess gin! The driver survived. The brigade crossed the river by rafting and swimming.

The Weser was fast flowing and about 100 yards wide. But the Air-Landing Brigade had also managed to cross, and soon the bridgehead had expanded sufficiently for the engineers to build a bridge capable of taking a forty-ton tank. While this was being constructed, 5th Parachute Brigade beat off two counter-attacks. 5th Parachute Brigade took the lead, and by 11 April the division was across the River Leine. After a few days spent consolidating the bridgehead the advance continued. The division had passed a few miles south of Belsen. Some claimed they could smell it from miles off.

'I couldn't,' said Crookenden. 'But like all other commanding officers in the division I was ordered to send my doctor into the camp to help. I had two German Jews in my intelligence section whom I sent in armed with a camera to accompany the medics. They made up a collection of photographs. From then on whenever we stopped in a village I used to parade the inhabitants and show them these ghastly pictures. They denied all knowledge of what had been going on.

At Celle, on the Leine, we found no opposition. In the town hall there was a Nazi banner which my signaller tied to the back of my trailer and dragged through the town. We had no feelings of chivalry towards the Germans at this stage of the war. It was quite different from the mutual respect in the First World War that my father had told me about. In a curious way the Hitler order that parachutists and commandos taken prisoner were to be shot worked in our favour. The Germans we took expected us to reciprocate. This made some of them much more pliable when it came to giving information. Naturally we did not shoot them. Later on, over the Elbe, one of my patrols reported a lot of Germans in a wood. I sent in a prisoner to tell them that we were a parachute battalion and if they didn't surrender at once we would cut their throats. Only one resisted and he was shot.

The pace kept up by the advancing division did not slacken. In the area of Ülzen, 9 Para had stopped for the night after a twenty-seven mile march. Hill rode up on his motor-cycle and told Crookenden to take his battalion on an out-flanking move to cut in behind enemy holding a village further up the road. This involved fifteen miles across country on routes which had not been reconnoitred. By first light the battalion was astride the German withdrawal route and ambushed the enemy as they pulled out. By the morning of 23 April the Elbe was reached. An advance of 103 miles had been made in fourteen days and 19,000 prisoners had been captured.

The River Elbe was about 300 yards wide and no bridges had been captured. The ground on the far bank was steep and wooded, affording the enemy excellent observation over the flat, marshy home bank, which he completely dominated by fire. The original plan was a smaller version of the Rhine Crossing. 1st Commando Brigade was to cross in amphibious tracked vehicles, aptly named Buffaloes, while 5th Parachute Brigade dropped on Lauenberg airfield on the far side of the river. 15th Scottish Division, who had been the first to link up with 6th Airborne on the Rhine, would follow the Commandos and expand the bridgehead, assisted by the Airborne Division. Hill had summoned his commanding officers a few days earlier, and, Crookenden remembers, to their astonishment opened the briefing by saying:

'Gentlemen, before I give orders, I must apologize. I have let down the 3rd Parachute Brigade.' He paused and we all wondered what on earth was coming next. James Hill let down the brigade? Impossible! He then said: 'The Corps Commander has asked for a parachute brigade to drop over the Elbe. The Divisional Commander has chosen 5th Parachute Brigade.'

When the O Group was over James Hill was rather put out to find his battalion commanders holding hands, dancing around in the meadow outside the headquarters, singing 'Ring a ring of roses.' We were delighted not to be dropping again!

However, the Germans pulled out of their positions and the parachute drop was cancelled. The amphibious crossing went ahead unaided.

As soon as 6th Airborne was across the Elbe on 30 April, they came under command of 8th US Airborne Corps for the last few days of the war. Hill was holding his usual evening briefing when in walked Ridgeway, two grenades on his shoulder straps. After telling them: 'Be at ease, gentlemen,' he continued: 'You have to be at Wismar before the Russians to prevent them getting into Denmark.'

The brigade was given trucks and an armoured squadron of the Royal Scots Greys and told to get there in twelve hours. 5th Parachute Brigade had been ordered to lead the advance. But Hill, knowing the end of the war

Pre-drop tension.

Jumping from a Hastings in the late 1940s.

En route to Suez, 1956.

Captured bren-gun carrier at Port Said. Lieutenant Newall, machine-gun platoon commander, at the wheel.

Captain (now General) Howlett, air adjutant 3 Para, tries out requisitioned transport in Port Said, 1956.

One of the three Russian SU 100 tanks captured by 3 Para. Note the Egyptian crescent marking and Russian Simonov carbine carried by the soldier (*top left*).

Lieutenant Colonel Farrar-Hockley and Major Ward-Booth.

Radfan – difficult terrain!

2 Para main base in Borneo.

Dental treatment for villagers.

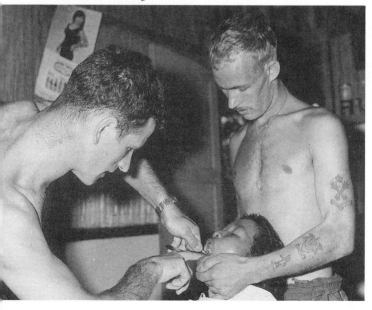

Letter from home – company base in Borneo.

Not Norway! Ireland – down on the border in Winter.

Lieutenant Colonels Hew Pike (3 Para) (*left*) and 'H' Jones (2 Para) standing on the flight deck of SS *Canberra* at Ascension Island *en route* to the landing on the Falkland Islands.

Sergeant McKay, VC, Mount Longdon, from the painting by Peter Archer, the property of the Officers of 3 Para.

Men of 2 Para waiting to move forward by helicopter for the battle
for Wireless Ridge.

was in sight, was determined to get to Wismar first. So he went flat out to reach a key road junction before the 5th Brigade, knowing that if he could cross first they would be unable to catch him. The division raced along the roads, meeting what seemed to be the whole populations of villages coming the other way, fleeing from the Russians.

The Canadian Battalion of the 3rd Parachute Brigade was first into Wismar. When Crookenden arrived he was ordered to send someone to contact the advancing Russians. He decided to go himself, taking two Russian-speaking sergeants from the Canadian Battalion. Flying a huge white flag made out of a sheet, he drove east out of town. The countryside looked dead and deserted. After a few miles they came upon the leading Russian tanks. Explaining who they were, Crookenden asked to see the senior officer. He was speaking to him through his interpreters when a column of tanks roared past them towards Wismar, covered with Russian infantry. Boarding his vehicle, and inviting the Russian to do likewise, Crookenden sped off down the road in pursuit of the tanks. After a hair-raising drive, pre-empting James Bond by at least ten years, he overtook them, half-in and half-out of the ditch, the Russian officer gripping his arm in a state of panic:

He was windy. Outside the town the Canadians had set up a road block with several seventeen-pounder anti-tank guns pointing down the road. The Russian was taken to General Bols, who intimated that this was as far as he was going without orders to the contrary. The Russian demurred, saying that his objective was Lubeck. After further fruitless argument Bols turned to the interpreter and said: 'Tell this bugger I have a complete airborne division and five regiments of guns. If he does not clear off I will open fire.' At this the Russian broke into a broad smile and became much more helpful.

Since 29 March the division had covered about 300 miles. Except for halts on the Rivers Leine and Elbe, operations had been continuous. They had been ordered to maintain the momentum of the advance at all costs, and this they had faithfully done. At the thanksgiving service in Wismar on 6 May 1945 it seemed to some of the division that the world had stopped and the future was a big blank.

CHAPTER 10

Peacekeeping – Java, Palestine and Egypt

Following the end of the war in Europe, 1st Airborne Division was sent to Norway to ensure that the Germans observed the terms of surrender, and 6th Airborne Division was warned for operations in the Far East. The initials BLA, British Liberation Army, of which 6th Airborne formed a part after the German surrender, were said by some wags in the division to mean Burma Looms Ahead. The division, having re-equipped, trained hard for the new theatre. They had seen in Normandy the example of veteran formations who, overconfident after successes in the desert, did not condescend to retrain for fresh circumstances resulting in bloodily repulsed attacks and occasionally, disgraceful scenes when complete sub-units ran away. The division sent advance parties to India, some being attached to battalions which had fought in the jungle to learn from their experience. 5th Parachute Brigade was the first to move to the Far East, arriving in Bombay in early August. Their first objective: Malaya in an amphibious landing. A few days after their arrival in India the Japanese surrendered after the atom bombs dropped on Hiroshima and Nagasaki. 'We were delighted,' recalls one commanding officer. His sentiments were shared by most airborne soldiers, who were in no doubt that operations in the Far East, including mainland Japan, the ultimate objective for the division, would be long and bloody, resulting in far more casualties, both military and civilian, than occurred at Nagasaki and Hiroshima; a fact ignored by those who, from the safety of their armchairs, deplore the use of the atomic weapon to force Japan to surrender.

The original plan for the 5th Parachute Brigade was to land over the Morib beaches on the west coast of Malaya and link up with 14th Army, advancing down the isthmus from Burma. The brigade would then be withdrawn to Rangoon in preparation for a parachute operation on Singapore. The first part of the operation, codenamed Zipper, went ahead, fortunately with no opposition! The brigade set sail in the P&O liner *Chitral* and, having transferred into landing craft offshore, were decanted into neck-deep mud. 'My batman's comment was "Zipper was not buttoned up",' remembers Darling, then still commanding 12 Para. After spending the night ashore the brigade re-embarked, wet and filthy, and were taken to Singapore. There they remained until December 1945.

In Singapore they found chaos. The Japanese had been locked up, leaving no one to keep law and order. The brigade trained a police force to assist them and eventually handed over their duties to a Malay Volunteer Force when they moved to Batavia (now Djakarta), the capital of Java, in early December 1945. Java, then part of the Dutch East Indies, was in a turmoil. The Japanese, having defeated the Dutch colonial forces with little difficulty and overrun the Dutch East Indies in 1942, removed the Dutch administrators to prison camps, to the intense satisfaction of many of the native Indonesians. In August 1945 the Japanese, ignoring the Dutch, surrendered to the Indonesians who, seizing the Japanese weapons, used them to pay off old scores, carry out armed robberies, terrorize the population throughout the country and kill each other, usually in the name of nationalism. They were united on one matter, that their erstwhile masters, the Dutch, would not again take up the reins. There were thousands of Allied prisoners of war and European internees throughout Java who would be at the mercy of Indonesian bandits.

The Dutch economy had been weakened by the war in Europe. They had few formed units anywhere, and none in the East Indies, and were in no position to regain control. In the meantime someone was needed to restore the rule of law, and the task fell to the British Army. Once this had been achieved the British could withdraw, and it would be up to the Dutch and the Indonesians to sort out who was to do the ruling. The 5th Parachute Brigade found Batavia a most unpleasant place, with the streets under sniper fire at night and riots by day. After restoring order they were moved to Semarang on the north Java coast between Batavia and Sourabaya.

The brigade arrived in Semarang at the conclusion of operations by 49th Indian Infantry Brigade to secure the town and evacuate the large number of Allied prisoners of war and British and Dutch women and children internees, many from remote camps in the surrounding countryside. Fighting had ensued while these operations were in progress. By the time the brigade arrived the area to be held consisted of the town and its immediate surroundings. As a result of the unsettled conditions, arson, looting and murder on a large scale were commonplace, and the inhabitants had lost all confidence in law and order. Business was at a complete standstill, markets were non-existent, people kept to their houses and hardly dared move about outside. There was no civil administration. The bandits, or freedom fighters depending on your point of view, had imposed a complete embargo on the import of footstuffs into the town and had cut off the water and electricity supply. So as well as keeping the peace Poett found himself the head of the military and civil government responsible for the administration of 250,000 people, his brigade augmented by a Japanese battalion. Darling wrote later:

It is necessary to explain how this somewhat Gilbertian situation arose. When the Japanese forces in Java surrendered. Major Kido, who commanded this battalion with a considerable number of other Japanese soldiers, was quartered in and around Semarang. In accordance with the orders of the Japanese high command, these soldiers handed over their weapons to the Indonesians, who put a large number of the Japanese in jail. One day the more extreme elements murdered a considerable number of Japanese in a most brutal manner. This aroused the wrath of Major Kido and his men. Although completely unarmed, they attacked with stones and bare hands various bands of armed Indonesians and little by little recovered their weapons. Having this rearmed themselves, Major Kido decided to re-establish control of the town in which looting and other crimes of violence were the order of the day. It so happened that the first of his operations started on the day on which the first British troops landed in the docks. Entirely unknown to each other, the two forces working from separate ends of the town met in the vicinity of the Secretariat building where a brief battle ensued. However, when both sides realized that their aims were similar, they joined forces. It was in this fashion that British forces found themselves fighting alongside their former enemies. There is no doubt that because of the shortage of British troops at that time in Semarang it would not have been possible to operate without these Japanese.

Poett decided that he must hold a feature called Gombel Hill which was vital for the defence of Semarang. It was also necessary to hold the airfield for logistic supply of his brigade, and to evacuate the sick and the prisoners of war and internees. He found that he had a twelve-mile perimeter to defend. When he came to allocate tasks to his battalions he was faced with the problem of what to do with Kido's battalion. On taking over the town he found them employed in guard duties, even providing the guard on the brigade commander's bungalow! The presence of a Japanese battalion in the town caused enormous resentment among those who had suffered at their hands during the occupation. But he could not meet all his commitments without them. He solved the problem by giving them responsibility for the defence of Gombel Hill. The vital ground for the defence of Semarang was therefore held by men who until recently had been implacable enemies!

The brigade found that the enemies consisted of various bands of cut-throats and bandits who lived by the rule of the gun. There was no evidence of any central control. They were armed with an array of weapons from swords and bamboo stakes to Dutch and Japanese rifles, British Bren guns, two or three 75mm and 105mm guns and some mortars. They wore a variety of uniforms, but always kept a suit of civilian clothes handy to change into when cornered. There appeared to be a few Japanese soldiers working with them. Although the bandits usually fled at the approach of troops, on occasions they would stand and fight, probably when the renegade Japanese took a hand in the proceedings.

In the town there were three main national groups; about 6,000 Dutch, 40,000 Chinese and the remainder Indonesians. Many of the Dutch had held responsible positions in the town before the Japanese invasion, but their confidence had been shaken by the events following the Japanese surrender. They distrusted and even hated the Indonesians. The Chinese having suffered at the hands of the Japanese were subsequently attacked by the Indonesians for co-operating with the British. The majority of the Indonesians wanted peace and quiet. Poett's first task was to restore confidence among the civil population. This was not made easier by a rumour which was current before their arrival that the whole of 5th Parachute Brigade, including himself, were convicts who had been released from long terms of imprisonment on the condition that they became parachutists! The arrival of the brigade was naturally watched with awe. However, a happier atmosphere was quickly created when the inhabitants found that they could walk about the streets without being robbed and murdered, their homes were safe from looters, and food, water and light were being provided. The brigade took over the policing, the organization of the medical services and the repairs to the roads, railways and the docks, which had been badly damaged by Allied bombing.

In mid-March 1946, a regimental group of the Royal Netherlands Army arrived to take over from the 5th Parachute Brigade. Darling, by now in command, was concerned that the hand-over should be as smooth as possible, and that the peaceful conditions that his men had worked so hard to secure would not be disrupted by the arrival of the Dutch, who were not regarded with universal enthusiasm by the majority of the population. Darling told the various communities in the town that the Dutch forces would be under his command and would implement his existing policy; they would be fully capable of keeping the extremist elements from entering town; and finally, there was no sense in having a disturbance just when Semarang was returning to normal. In the end all went well. There was about a two-month hand-over period which allowed the Dutch to settle in. Most of the soldiers in this regimental group were of high quality, having served in the Dutch resistance movement in Europe or with the Dutch forces operating with the British and American armies. The arrival of the Dutch allowed Darling to evacuate the Japanese. Major Kido gave him his sword as a token of his regard.

The last units of the brigade left Semarang in mid-May

1946. Several messages from the local communities show how the efforts of the parachute soldiers were appreciated:

> We shall miss you and your smiling smartness and tenacity to create law and order out of disorder.

> You are going away – let this be a parting word from your Chinese friends in Semarang: your sportsmanship and fairness in play and gentle consideration to all shall forever be enshrined in our hearts.

> At the time the parachutists came here – in January – conditions in town were awful and everything topsyturvey. It must be said that with their arrival and the things they did eg: the institution of the civil police etc law and order gradually were restored. Now there is no more English army here. There is only the Dutch army. We fervently hope that conditions we experienced during the English occupation might be continued by the Dutch army. (Translation of an article in the Indonesian newspaper, *City News*)

The brigade returned to Singapore and in July moved to Palestine. When the war in the Far East ended, considerable re-organization took place in airborne forces. Over a period of several months battalions were amalgamated, renamed or disbanded, and many of the familiar names and groupings went for ever. In essence it was as follows: The 1st Airborne Division was disbanded. In September 1945, 6th Airborne Division, consisting of the 2nd and 3rd Parachute Brigades, and 6th Air-Landing Brigade, was sent to Palestine. The place of the Canadian Battalion in 3rd Parachute Brigade was taken by 3 Para. Eventually, following the decision that the airborne division would be a parachute-only formation, with gliders reserved for heavy loads and *coup de main* operations, 6th Air-Landing Brigade became 31st Infantry Brigade and left 6th Airborne Division, its place in the division being taken by 1st Parachute Brigade, consisting of 1, 2 and 17 Para. In July 1946 the division was joined in Palestine by 5th Parachute Brigade, fresh from their adventures in Java. Before leaving the Far East 13 Para was disbanded. 7 Para replaced 17 Para in the 1st Brigade, and 12 Para was disbanded. In company with everyone else, Major Sim, who had been with the 12th since before Normandy and fought in nearly all their battles, was asked which battalion he wanted to join:

> I went to 3 Para. It was a very sad day. We in the 12th battalion paraded with all our kit. There were trucks lined up and the order was given: '12 Para to your vehicles, dismiss.' That was it!

13 Para had an even more unhappy ending. Unrest over the demob system and a new commanding officer in the place of the much-loved Luard, who had raised the battalion and commanded it in every battle, came to a head in Malaya after their return from Java. Disaffected elements, who had not served in the battalion for long, mutinied, resulting in the battalion being disbanded in the Far East.

Other reorganizations were not so abrupt. It was decided that each of the nine parachute battalions in the division was to be affiliated to existing groups of regiments, so for example 1 Para was sponsored by the Household Brigade, 5 Para by Scottish regiments, 7 Para by the Light Infantry, and so on. Soldiers from regiments in these 'tribal' groupings were allocated to the respective battalions on arriving from parachute training, or in some cases were transferred from another parachute battalion. So for example the 1st (Guards) Parachute Battalion took all its reinforcements from the Brigade of Guards, and most guardsmen serving with other parachute battalions were transferred. The battalion did have some men who were not guardsmen, among them Colour Sergeant Mitchell of the Argylls, a veteran parachutist who had served with 1 Para in Tunisia and Sicily before joining the SAS in 1943. He eventually saw the light and joined the Scots Guards! The battalion commanded by Lieutenant Colonel Nelson had, as one would expect, a character all of its own, and contained a number of highly decorated soldiers including Sergeant Keneally VC, Irish Guards, and RSM Cowley, Coldstream Guards, who had won his DCM with the Guards Armoured Division at Nijmegen.

The position in which the ex-5th Brigade soldiers found themselves in Palestine was less happy than the situation they had left in Java. The 6th Airborne Division had been sent to Palestine as Britain's strategic reserve in the Middle East. Palestine was selected as their base because the air training facilities and airfields were better than those in Egypt, Cyrenaica or other possible stations. But before long the division became involved in a two-and-a-half year campaign against Jewish terrorism. Very little parachute training was carried out, and even this dwindled as the internal security situation deteriorated. At the same time the RAF ran down their transport force, assisted by the Jews who destroyed twenty-nine aircraft on the airfields. In the end the RAF withdrew to Egypt.

The roots of the internal security situation in Palestine lay as far back as 1917 when the British government, aware of the need to make a gesture which would ensure the continued support of American Jews and their money for the war effort, very foolishly declared that they would look with sympathy on the concept of a national home for the Jews. Where this home was to be, and when it would come into existence, was left unsaid. At the end of the 1914–18 war, Palestine, which had been part of the Turkish Empire, was mandated to Britain to administer, by the League of Nations. The overwhelming majority of the population were Arabs. Up to 1939 the small but steady trickle of Jewish immigrants to Palestine was viewed with increasing unease by the Arab inhabitants. In 1939, in response to Arab pressure and violence, the British limited Jewish immigration to a maximum of 75,000 over five years, after which there would be no more without the consent of the Arabs; Palestine was, after all, their country. Following the Second World War the terrible experiences of the Jews at the hands of the Nazis, the huge numbers who were homeless, and the prospect of a fresh start in Palestine vastly increased the demand for immigration. Naturally there was worldwide sympathy for the Jews, and from America in particular, with its large Jewish population, considerable support, both moral and financial. American politicians ignored or flouted the wishes of American Jews at their political peril.

At the end of 1945 the Jewish Agency which dealt with Jewish affairs in Palestine decided to mount a campaign of violence and propaganda to persuade the British government to lift restrictions on immigration, and to gain worldwide support for Zionism, the concept of a national home for the Jews in Palestine. The fact that the country belonged to someone else, the Palestinian Arabs, did not concern them overmuch. As the 6th Airborne Division arrived in their camps south of Gaza, the Jewish newspapers were labelling them 'Gestapo.' Many Jews had fought in the division, the soldiers had seen at first hand the horrors of Nazi treatment of the Jews, the division's doctors had been sent into Belsen, many in the division had friends killed or maimed and had been wounded themselves fighting Nazism. Until they arrived in Palestine their sympathies lay with the Jews. They were astonished to be tagged as oppressors. Soon many of them were eyeing the Jews with distaste. 'I was impressed by the Jews, some behaved just like Nazis. They had clearly learned a number of tricks from the Germans,' sarcastically recalled a battalion medical officer who had been with the division in the advance to the Baltic. On the whole the soldiers came to sympathize with the Arabs.

There were four Jewish para-military organizations. The Hagana was the underground national army, raised mainly for defence, and usually moderate compared with the terrorist groups. Hagana was to become virtually a Jewish National Army in which the majority of able-bodied males and a large number of females were obliged to enlist and give part-time service. Within the main organization of the Hagana was the Palmach, consisting of regular full-time soldiers, well-trained and disciplined and led by good officers, of whom one was Moshe Dayan. These two were the 'official' Jewish forces, tasked by the Jewish Agency to carry out acts of sabotage. There were two other groups, who took their order solely from their own leaders: the Irgun Zvia Leumi (IZL) and the Stern Gang, or Fighters for the Freedom of Israel (FFI) as they preferred to call themselves. ' "Stern Gang" has been the name sponsored by the alien government of oppression in this country,' they said in a letter to the newspapers in April 1947 in a revealing example of 'terrorspeak' which others, such as the IRA, have not been slow to follow. The 'government of oppression' was of course the British, who, were doing their best to ensure that the Arab majority had some say in the future of their country. Both were extreme, the latter the more vicious of the two. The Jewish employed classic terrorist tactics, murder and sabotage which they hoped would result in over-reaction by the soldiers, thus alienating the population against the British Army, and propaganda campaign waged in Palestine and world-wide which, coupled with riots, sabotage and general disorder, would persuade the world at large and the British Government in particular that the country was ungovernable.

The first clash with 6th Airborne Division came in November 1945 when rioting broke out in Tel Aviv. The 3rd Brigade restored order. The brunt of the task was born by Hewetson's 8 Para. Great restraint was shown by the troops in the face of mobs several thousand strong, stoning and firing buildings. In April 1946 the Stern Gang murdered seven unarmed soldiers from 5 Para who were guarding the military car park. This served to destroy the trust and goodwill among the British soldiers that had existed until then. Which was of course exactly what the Stern Gang wanted. Intelligence was extremely poor, and the Palestine police had been penetrated by the Jews. It was impossible for the soldiers to take the initiative. They could merely hold the ring while first the British government and then the United Nations tried to find a settlement acceptable to Jews and Arabs. Looked at from the perspective of the late 1980s, it was a hopeless task. The Jews were determined to set up a Jewish state in someone else's country, and the Arabs were equally determined that they should not. The Jews were fortunate that they had to contend with the long-suffering and usually good humoured British soldiers. Ironically, the Israelis are facing a similar situation at the time of writing and are getting few marks from the world press for the standards of training of their troops and their restraint: the biter bit!

Despite the pace of internal security operations, there were, to begin with, a few parachute exercises. Exercise Gordon involved part of 3 and 8 Para dropping on Khartoum airfield. Because of the heat, the soldiers dropped in shirts and shorts. There was a high wind and strong down draught. In addition to one killed and three major injuries, seventy-four men were cut and scraped out of a jumping strength of 108! Major Dover landed in some telephone wires. While hanging, unable to release himself, a Sudanese seized the opportunity to make off with his boots, dangling so temptingly within reach!

Operations in Palestine followed the pattern of most internal security operations. The terrorists, or freedom fighters, carried out acts of sabotage on roads, railway lines, police headquarters and other important targets such as the King David Hotel, which housed the Secretariat of the Government of Palestine and Headquarters British Troops Palestine and Transjordan. There were a number of cases of kidnapping British officers and soldiers, on two occasions ending in the flogging or execution of the victims. The bodies of the latter, not members of 6 Airborne Division, were found hanging and booby trapped. The IZL posted notices justifying their barbarity which included the phrase: 'It is an ordinary legal action of the court of the underground which has sentenced and will sentence the criminals who belong to the Nazi-British Army of occupation!'

The division patrolled, searched villages for arms, and provided guards on vulnerable points. The situation was complicated by incursions across the frontiers with Lebanon and Syria by parties of armed Arabs. Controlling this area through 1947 and 1948 was the responsibility of 6th Airborne Division with the Transjordan Frontier Force under command. The TJFF soldiers were all Arabs, with British and Arab officers. They were commanded by Colonel Hackett, who had let 4th Parachute Brigade at Arnhem. In October 1947 the Arab countries surrounding Palestine announced the formation of an Arab League Army which would invade to safeguard the Arab inhabitants. The Palestine Arabs were heartened at the news of this force massing on the borders, which they imagined would soon be coming to their rescue. It was actually a propaganda stunt for the benefit of the United Nations who were considering the solution to the Palestine problem. The Jews, however, took the threatened invasion seriously and mobilized the Hagana. They also demanded the withdrawal of the TJFF, which they considered an Arab force. An incursion by a column of Syrian armoured cars, which was captured by the TJFF, gave them a chance to show their impartiality.

The period after the UN vote partitioning Palestine into Arab and Jewish states saw an increase in violence. The Jews, who were trying to show that they were capable of running their own country, had nothing to gain by violence. The trouble was started by the Arabs, stung into action by the result of the UN vote and the ostentatious manner in which the Jews celebrated the news. The inter-communal fighting was bloody and the British in the middle, as so often happens, became the main object of attention of the two contestants. The IZL reduced its attacks on the British Troops, but to the Stern Gang the British were still the main enemy, although this did not distract them from attacks on Arab villages, killing men, women and children indiscriminately. A typical incident of this period occurred when the IZL threw two bombs from a passing car at a group of Arabs waiting for a bus outside the oil refinery at Haifa, killing six and wounding forty. The Arabs, who outnumbered the Jews in the refinery, proceeded to beat to death any Jews they could find. By the time 2nd/3rd Para arrived and restored control, forty-one Jews had been killed and forty-eight injured. Despite this massacre being the direct result of an IZL terror bomb, the Hagana carried out a reprisal in an Arab village, firing sub-machine guns and throwing grenades into houses. They killed fourteen Arabs, of whom ten were women and children, and wounded eleven.

Until the UN announcement of partition in November 1947, Haifa had been almost free of inter-communal strife. But from December 1947 to April 1948 the struggle between Arabs and Jews for control of the town intensified. The British were particularly concerned to keep the port open, not only for daily resupply, but because they intended using it for the final withdrawal of troops on 15 May 1948. 6th Airborne Division, who had responsibility for Haifa as well as the rest of northern Palestine, were being steadily reduced in strength; the TJFF was about to be withdrawn, 3 Parachute Brigade was being disbanded, and 2nd Parachute Brigade had already been withdrawn to England and thence to Germany.

The fighting between the Jews and Arabs started with sniping, escalating into small arms battles. Later mortars and heavy machine guns were used, and finally truck and car bombs. On one occasion six Jews dressed as airborne soldiers drove a truck loaded with 1,000 lbs of explosives into the Arab quarter, set the time fuse and drove off in a jeep. The truck exploded, killing four Arabs and wounding nineteen. Later a jeep with two officers and a driver from Headquarters 1 Parachute Brigade arrived at the scene to investigate. They were seized by furious Arabs and nearly lynched. They were saved at the last minute by some of the more moderate element and eventually managed to establish their identity as genuine British soldiers. The car and truck bomb, so successfully pioneered by the innovative Jewish terrorists, is the plague of such cities as Beirut to this day, on several occasions being used against the inventors.

Throughout this turmoil the British troops strove to retain their impartiality, firing only when fired upon. On 6 March 1948 the withdrawal of the remainder of 6th Airborne Division started. By 6 April only the GOC, a small tactical headquarters, some divisional troops and 1 (Guards) Para remained of the division in Palestine. To everyone's bitter disappointment, the rest of the division was disbanded shortly after arriving in England. 1 (Guards) Para was specially selected to remain in the Jerusalem area. The battalion formed an armoured car squadron from vehicles destined to be destroyed before the final British withdrawal; drivers, gunners, and commanders were provided by members of the battalion who had been in the Guards Armoured Division in World War Two. The battalion was responsible for the evacuation of the Jerusalem garrison, police and RAF contingents northwards to Haifa on 14 May 1948. The commanding officer, Lieutenant Colonel Nelson, was in charge of a 5-mile long, 250-vehicle convoy. They arrived safely in Haifa just before sunset, the final stage being piquetted by 42 Commando Royal Marines. Three days later the GOC and divisional troops left Palestine. During the two and a half years the division had suffered fifty-eight killed in action, and 236 wounded.

To keep alive the memory of the 1st and 6th Airborne Divisions, 2nd Parachute Brigade, the only existing airborne force in the British Army, was renamed 16th Independent Parachute Brigade Group. The battalions were renumbered, the 4th/6th becoming the 1st Battalion, 5th becoming the 2nd Battalion, and the 7th becoming the 3rd Battalion. All were now battalions of the Parachute Regiment, which was welcomed into the infantry by the Director of Infantry on 1 April 1949. 1 (Guards) Para sent 200 of its best men to form the 1st (Guards) Independent Parachute Company, with a pathfinder role for the brigade. Originally only footguardsmen were eligible for the company, but later the Life Guards and the Royal Horse Guards (The Blues) sent officers, NCOs and troopers. The company was organized into troops and sticks rather than platoons and sections.

16th Independent Parachute Brigade Group was soon back in the Middle East. After being sent to Cyprus as a reserve during the Gulf oil crisis of 1951, the brigade found itself in Egypt following the Egyptian army coup which toppled King Farouk in July 1952. The brigade spent two years in the canal zone, a strip of territory administered by the British which ran down the west bank of the canal from Port Said to Port Suez, with a bulge in the middle to include the huge British base at Tel el Kebir. Operations consisted of the usual cordon and search, ambushes and patrols that are the staple diet of internal security. Brigadier Darling commanded for the first part of the tour. He found the brigade's parachute training at a very low ebb, so much so that he considered the brigade unfit to carry out a parachute operation. He set to work to put matters right. He persuaded the RAF to re-train their aircrew for parachute operations and set up a parachute school at Kabrit, where the Middle East school had been in the Second World War. The tempo of parachute exercises soon increased under Darling's energetic direction. As there were a number of deaths through parachute malfunctions, he agitated for a reserve parachute to be worn, at least in training. These were not his only problems. The officers for the battalions of the Parachute Regiment were all found by secondment or loan from their infantry regiments. Darling was not satisfied with the quality of some of these officers. In a few cases commanding officers were not permitting their best officers to volunteer. On the other hand, the soldiers were now able to enlist direct from civil life. Thus the regiment owned its men, but not its officers, which was unsatisfactory. It was not until 1958 that a regular cadre of officers was allowed, commissioned direct from Sandhurst or transferred permanently from their regiments.

The brigade left the canal zone in mid-1954. Within two-and-a-half years they would be back in rather different circumstances.

CHAPTER 11

Near East Operations – Cyprus and Suez

In December 1955 the 3rd Battalion was confined to barracks in Aldershot as a punishment for fighting in Southsea with Teddy Boys, the name for yobbos at the time. The press came down to Aldershot and the next day a headline appeared in the *Sunday Pictorial*; 200 Army Wives Sleep Alone. The wives of the Parachute Brigade, particularly the 1 and 3 Para, were to see very little of their husbands in the year that followed.

In January 1956 King Hussein dismissed General Glubb, the British commander of his army. The British government decided that there might be a need to evacuate British nationals from Jordan. With hindsight their fears seem ridiculous, but nevertheless there was a need to move a force very quickly to Cyprus as a convenient staging post for such an operation. 1 and 3 Para went at twenty-four hours notice in one of the first major airlifts of the British Army by the RAF since the Second World War. The two battalions were transported in Hastings and Shackletons from Blackbushe airfield and despite one aircraft being struck by lightning over Bournemouth, the move went without a hitch. After a few days spent under canvas in a water-logged transit camp near the airport, both battalions built themselves a more comfortable tented camp nearby.

Captain Walsh, seconded to 3 Para from the 60th, The Kings Royal Rifle Corps, was second-in-command of A Company. To his bitter disappointment he was ordered by his commanding officer to stay behind to take the Staff College exam and look after the families. The prospect of missing a parachute operation added to his dismay. It was a bitterly cold winter. The paymaster, a veteran airborne soldier, ordered the chains and padlocks on the coal bunkers to be smashed and the small rear party under Walsh issued coal to the families. It still has to be accounted for! Walsh sat the exam, which happy to relate he passed, and joined his battalion in Cyprus as A Company commander. By March the British government deemed the crisis in Jordan to have died down. Field Marshal Harding, the Governor of Cyprus, seized the chance to use the two battalions in the increasingly difficult anti-terrorist campaign being waged by the British in the island. Within a few days the battalions were deployed on a major operation in the Troodos mountains.

The island of Cyprus had been ceded to Britain by Turkey at the treaty of Berlin in 1878 for use as a base. In 1914 Turkey allied herself with Germany and the British annexed the island. In 1915 the British offered it to the Greeks as an inducement to come into the war against the Turks. The Greeks refused. Cyprus became a crown colony in 1925. The population was split, as now, into Greek and Turkish communities. Both retained religious and cultural links with Greece and Turkey. The Greek Cypriots outnumbered the Turkish Cypriots by four to one. From 1878 the Greek Cypriots had demanded union with Greece, Enosis. This was, and is, unacceptable to Turkey. The island is very close to Turkey's southern coastline, and the idea of such a strategically sensitive place in the hands of Turkey's most hated enemy, the Greeks, was anathema. Furthermore, Turkey had no wish to see the Turkish minority ruled by the Greeks. The Enosis movement gained momentum until in 1954 the Turks threatened to invade to protect the Turkish minority. The position was further complicated because both Turkey and Greece were members of NATO. The Alliance was in danger of being weakened by this quarrel, and if matters took a turn for the worse a three-sided war might break out involving Britain, Greece and Turkey on the sensitive southern flank of NATO. Seeing that Britain had no intention of precipitating such a situation by granting union with Greece, and with the tacit support of mainland Greece, the extremists on the island formed a terrorist organization calling itself EOKA. Its aim, similar to the Jewish terrorists, to attract world sympathy by provoking the British into acts which would be seen as repression of a downtrodden race seeking self-determination. Command of EOKA was given to a passed-over Greek Colonel called Grivas who had fought in the Greek army in the Second World War. The campaign started in autumn 1955.

Cyprus is a beautiful place, particularly in the two mountain ranges. In the centre of the island, Mount Olympus in the Troodos range rises to nearly 6,000 feet and has sufficient snow in winter for skiing. Pine forests cover the sides of the steep scree-covered mountains. Moufflon, the large, wild mountain sheep, can sometimes be seen on the higher and more inaccessible slopes. Except for the odd forester or shepherd the forests are deserted. To the west of Mount Olympus the Paphos Forest covers the hills as they descend in rolling waves to the sea at the birthplace of Aphrodite. In the centre of the Paphos Forest, Kykkho Monastery dominated one of the few north-south roads. The Greek orthodox church, steeped in intrigue for centuries, was deeply implicated in support of EOKA. The Kyrenia range in the north along the panhandle, is lower but more dramatic. The sharp peaks give a Disney castle effect, rising almost straight out of the sea in places. The central plain between the two ranges is dry and dusty, dotted with low hills, cultivation, lemon and carob trees. Vineyards cover the lower southern slopes of the Troodos mountains and the Paphos hills to the west. The mountain roads are narrow and unsurfaced. Hairpin bends, cliffs and steep slopes on each side make them an ideal place for ambush. The villages cling to the sides of the mountains, and in the main valleys. A driver approaching can sometimes be seen for half an hour or more, as he winds his way interminably towards his destination, seeming never to get closer. Only towards the end of the campaign were there any helicopters, and travelling in a vehicle was usually an invitation to be ambushed. Patrols stayed out for days and nights at a time. Ambushes would be set at night by likely forest tracks. Villages would be cordoned off by men marching all night over the mountains and arriving before day-break. Boots wore out in a few days on the razor sharp scree. Hot in summer, bitterly cold in winter, soldiering in the Troodos mountains was tough and demanding.

In their early operations the parachute battalions were deployed in areas of the Paphos Forest where few British had penetrated for years, if ever. Operations were challenging and exacting. Good soldiering paid off, and three terrorists were captured. As the weather became warmer the parachute battalions operated in the towns on the plains, mainly in Nicosia, the capital. In the narrow streets, particularly the infamous Ledra Street, grenade attacks and shootings were daily occurrences. The EOKA gunmen in the towns and in the country usually chose easy targets, preferring unarmed servicemen off duty or their fellow-countrymen suspected of opposing EOKA. They shot a sergeant in the back while he was shopping with his four-year-old son. They murdered village headmen and unarmed village constables. By a policy of terror they ensured that only the bravest would give information against them.

On the whole the parachute battalions preferred the forests and the mountains. In June they were back in the Paphos Forest for Operation Lucky Alphonse, an ill-fated name. It was thought that Grivas was holed up in a valley deep in the forest. A large area was cordoned off, which took several battalions. Men in the cordon must be in sight of each other, or at least cover the ground between each other by observation and fire. It was not good enough to have a ring of men with each man on his own. If a group of terrorists attempting to break out attacked a lone soldier they might overcome him, particularly at night. Cordon operations had to be capable of being sustained for days and even weeks. Often complete sections were allocated positions in the cordon. Observation posts and ambush positions would be forward of the section position, to which men returned to sleep and eat. Well-trained troops often changed their positions after dark, in case they had been under observation by the terrorists during the day and the position had been compromised. To be effective the cordon had to be set up quietly and completely surround the chosen area as quickly as possible. If the quarry suspected what was happening he would slip away. Long approach marches, often at night, were usually necessary. Accurate map reading was difficult, and the steep scree made quiet movement almost impossible. Once the cordon was in place, patrolling within it started. Navigation had to be good so that a patrol did not wander into another's patch and be shot for their pains. At night it was better to stay and listen and watch for movement, so the patrols would set ambushes within the cordon. Cordon operations in the forest were expensive in troops, and if they were to be successful demanded a very high standard of soldiering. Needless to say the parachute battalions and others such as the commandos were in their element. Some were not so good, and the larger the operation, the more chance there was of dozy sentries, chattering and cooking in section posts, and patrols 'bimbling' through the forest in a dream!

The operation started well. A hide was found and it looked as though there might be a chance of getting Grivas

or at least some of the leading EOKA players. After that
things went from bad to worse. A patrol of C Company 3
Para got very close to a group of terrorists when the clink
of boot on scree alerted them and the group fled. Shots
were fired, but shooting with a bolt-operated number 4
rifle at a jinking target among trees is not easy. There
were no hits. Examination of the hide showed that the
patrol had almost netted Grivas and his party. However,
there were no reports from the cordon to indicate that he
had got clear, and it was assumed that he was still somewhere inside. A few days later disaster struck. A huge fire
swept through the tinder-dry forest. It was thought that
Grivas had started it in order to give himself an opportunity
to escape. However, it was much more likely to have been
started by 45 Commando's mortars firing high explosive
bombs as part of the overall plan to flush the terrorists
into the cordon. Walsh was visiting the area in his Land
Rover:

> We came round the bend in the road and saw that
> the road was blocked by fire. Suddenly the spur
> behind us was engulfed in flames and the fire started
> roaring towards us. We tried to run out of it by
> running downhill through the flames. My driver, Pri-
> vate Hawker, and Captain Beagley were burnt to
> death. I was lucky. I tripped and fell into a small
> ditch and the fire went over the top of me, scorching
> my back. The most casualties were suffered by the
> cordon troops found by the Gordon Highlanders.
> The total dead was twenty-one officers and soldiers.

In July Headquarters 16 Parachute Brigade and 2 Para
arrived in Cyprus and were soon involved in anti-terrorist
operations. Although many did not know it at the time,
the presence of the whole brigade in the island was connected with a totally different problem. On 26 July 1956,
after threatening to do so for several weeks, President

Nasser of Egypt nationalized the Suez Canal. The British
and French decided that they would take military action
to restore the canal to international control, which in effect
meant British and French control. The Americans sat on
the fence, more concerned with the Presidential election
at the end of the year in which Eisenhower was running
for a second term. It was clear from the outset that a
parachute operation was on the cards, and the nearest
airfields from which it could be mounted were on Cyprus.
As a preliminary move, before nationalization took place,
Britain's parachute force was concentrated on the island
where it would be handy if required. However, there was
one immediate snag. Neither 1 nor 3 Para had done any
parachute training for eleven months. Walsh:

In early August 1956 the battalion was fairly isolated
from the events of the world. We did hear that there
was a problem over the Suez Canal and that the
Prime Minister of Australia was trying to organize a
Suez Canal Users' Association. We were recalled
from an operation to return quickly to camp because
we were going to be flown home to carry out parachute training. I was then with my company on a ridge
overlooking the village of Kambos. We of course were
delighted. We hadn't had any leave and hadn't been
home for eight months. From leaving Kambos to
flying off in civil aircraft was not much more than
forty-eight hours. The commanding officer, Paul
Crook, was told that his men had to carry out three
training jumps and one battalion exercise jump in ten
days. He turned to the battalion who had worked
hard and had no leave and said: 'We will get the
three jumps over, but the last one will have to be at
the end because the RAF have got to practice. In the
meantime I will trust you, and you can all go on leave,
but I don't want one man to fail to turn up.' Every

man came back. The last jump was at Imber, and lined up by the DZ was a fleet of double decker buses to take us back to Aldershot. Most people managed to fit in another forty-eight hours leave. With such a virile bunch of men who had not seen their wives for a long time, nine months to the date of our return for parachute training the resources of the maternity wing of the Louise Margaret Wing of the Military Hospital in Aldershot were overwhelmed with 'yet another Red Beret.'

When the two battalions returned to Cyprus it seemed that the Suez crisis had quietened down. The only indication to the contrary was the presence of a large number of French logistic troops, including parachute packers, on Timbou airfield. When asked where the paras were, they shrugged their shoulders and said: 'We are already fighting a war in Algeria.' Within a few days the whole Parachute Brigade was involved in Operation Sparrowhawk in the Kyrenia mountains. Not only was this a change of scene, but the operations were becoming better organized and planned. There seemed to be more intelligence, fewer troops were used, and altogether the style of operating was more subtle. The brigade netted six men and the largest haul of arms in one operation since the campaign began.

Although most of the parachute soldiers did not know it, the Suez crisis, far from dying down, was still on the boil. Apart from the normal difficulties encountered in planning a large joint combined operation, there were other problems, including the parlous state of the equipment in the British armed services, thanks, as ever, to political neglect. Many, such as the lack of amphibious shipping, need not concern us. There were some that directly affected the parachute soldiers. First and most important, the objective. Not until mid-September was it

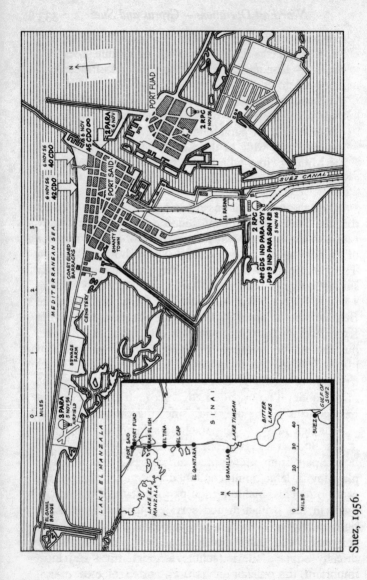

Suez, 1956.

decided that the landings would take place at Port Said. Until then Alexandria had been the initial objective, followed by an advance to Cairo and on to Suez after defeating the Egyptian army. However Mr Eden, the British Prime Minister, rightly decided that a major battle in a large port followed by the occupation of Cairo would not be acceptable to world opinion. The Port Said option, for a number of reasons, not least logistics, was very much a second best to Alexandria in every way. Once ashore at Port Said, the British and French would have to deploy down a causeway twenty-eight miles long and less than 300 yards wide in places, with a salt marsh on one side and the Suez Canal on the other. Two roads (The Treaty Road and The Canal Road), one railway and the Sweetwater Canal shared the space on the causeway. One road only was considered fit for tanks. Only after negotiating this section could troops deploy off the road onto the desert for the last seventy-one miles to the southern end of the canal. Port Said was also seventy miles from an adequate airfield, Abu Sueir. General Stockwell, who had been appointed to command the joint British/French land forces, said: 'Port Said is like a bottle with a very long neck, and we will have to extract the cork and squeeze the neck before enjoying the rich juices of the bottle.'

The key to his problem lay at hand, but he did not use it. The plan was pedestrian. First the French and British air forces would spend six days destroying the Egyptian air force on its airfields, a very necessary prelude to any operation of the kind being contemplated. But in the French view rather a long time was being set aside for this part of the operation. However, some senior British airmen justified it by voicing the opinion that the air attack would break the Egyptian will to resist further. Shades of Bomber Harris and Trenchard! On the seventh day, an amphibious assault would be followed half an hour later by a parachute assault. All this was fair enough. The place selected, everybody landing at Port Said, was not. Brigadier Butler, the commander of 16 Parachute Brigade, protested strongly and argued that a proper use of the parachute forces should be made by dropping his brigade at Ismailia, about halfway down the canal, the French paras under General Massu at Port Tewfik at the far end, and landing the Royal Marine Commando Brigade and French amphibious forces at Port Said, all simultaneously. Thus all three main points on the canal would be seized at one blow. Perhaps memories of Arnhem were at the backs of the senior planners' minds when they discarded this bold suggestion.

The British had other worries. The only aircraft in British service with a tail-gate which would allow heavy loads such as vehicles and guns to be dropped out of the back was the Beverley. Because of serviceability problems it could not be used. The other two aircraft available for parachuting were the Hastings and the Valetta. Both had one side door. The four-engined Hastings was a 1939 design. The twin-engined Valetta was a poor man's Dakota. Unlike that great workhorse, it was so badly designed that it had a main spar across the fuselage which gave the appearance of a low wall about eighteen inches high and eighteen inches wide about halfway down the aircraft. The last half of the stick had to scramble over this obstacle. This may not seem much until it is remembered that most soldiers fully kitted out with ammunition, weapon, kitbag and parachute were carrying a load in excess of their own weight. In the lemming-like rush of a stick to the door, while trying to keep their balance in an aircraft swaying in turbulence, this obstacle was an unwelcome challenge.

The only way of getting a vehicle to the DZ without gliders, which had long gone, was to mount it onto a platform and sling it under a Hastings. After dropping it would float down under a cluster of parachutes. Unfortunately the British had just replaced the jeep which could be dropped in this way with the Champ, which could not. Rumour had it that Ordnance Corps Officers armed with bundles of cash went round the Middle East buying back jeeps that had just been disposed of from the farmers and local business men. This was not all. The 1940 sten gun and the bolt action rifle were still in service. 106mm recoilless anti-tank guns had to be borrowed from NATO stocks because the ammunition for the new anti-tank gun had not yet been cleared for service in hot climates. A universal theme in the British reports following this operation is astonishment that the Egyptian army was better equipped. What the British lacked in equipment, they made up for in the quality of the men who were to carry out the assault. The paratroopers and commandos were fit, well-trained, well-led and thoroughly worked-up as teams after operations in the demanding terrain of Cyprus. With the élan and enthusiasm of their kind, they did not allow the problems to bear down too heavily.

As well as operations, 3 Para carried out some battalion exercises on the plain between the Troodos and Kyrenia mountain ranges. These exercises always included the same 'actions required on landing.' Every time Walsh was given a task involving moving to an objective to protect the west of an imaginary DZ. Other companies were given objectives to the east. The whole battalion practised storming pillboxes. On 28 October Walsh was again in the Kambos area on Operation Foxhunter in company with the whole brigade when they were all withdrawn to the camps outside Nicosia. On 29 October the commanding officer of 3 Para was ordered to plan for a parachute operation, but was not told where or when. The other two battalions, to their chagrin, were told that they would follow up by sea. 3 Para's camp was sealed. No one was allowed in or out. This caused problems for one officer, who shall be nameless, who was having a very successful affair with the wife of a RAF officer who was away bombing Egypt. He did find a secret way out!

On 2 November Crook was briefed on his task, but again not told when it would be, or how many aircraft he would have; the number changed daily. Intelligence was scant and he was told little about where the enemy was and in what strength. Crook briefed his company commanders in the only permanent building in the camp. Walsh saw that his company was to take the western end of El Gamil airfield. It was dominated by a prominent pillbox. They had good air photographs, and the promise of naval gun-fire support, close air support from the Fleet Air Arm, the French Navy Air Arm and RAF Hunters from Cyprus, although the latter would be overhead for only twelve minutes. The battalion second-in-command, Brevet Lieutenant Colonel Beckett, very wisely recommended to Crook that the battalion carry out a practice emplacement and fit parachutes, after which they could relax and leave the final mustering until as late as possible.

The plan was for 3 Para to drop on El Gamil on 6 November 1956, half an hour after amphibious landings by 40 and 42 Royal Marines Commandos over beaches directly north of Port Said and by French troops on beaches north of Port Fuad on the other side of the canal. At the same time a battalion of the French 2nd Colonial Parachute Regiment (2RPC) would drop at Raswa, south of Port Said, to seize two bridges, a pontoon bridge and a girder bridge. It was necessary to capture at least one intact if the tanks and other vehicles led by 2 Para were to drive south as soon as possible after landing. With the French paras would be Number 1 stick from 1st Guards Independent Parachute Company, commanded by Captain de Klee of the Scots Guards, and a sapper party under Captain Owen from 9 Parachute Squadron Royal Engineers. Captain de Klee was told to select eight guardsmen from his stick. He chose Sergeant Longstaff, Coldstream

Guards; Lance Sergeant White and Lance Corporal Williams, Welsh Guards; Lance Corporal Kent and Guardsmen Melville and Fletcher, Scots Guards; Guardsman Murphy, Irish Guards; and Trooper McNab, Life Guards. De Klee was given this brief by the commanding officer of 2 Para:

> Patrol down the Canal and Treaty roads, to the eight kilometre point to see if they were mined, blocked or defended in any way. 2 Para and the company (the remainder of 1 Guards Independent Parachute Company) were to be in the van of the advance down the canal and we were to meet them as they came through, with this information. Three sappers were to come with us as technical experts; the other three under Graham Owen were to clear the bridges of mines or charges. I think the thought of jumping from a strange aircraft with strange parachutes and aircraft drill, none of which we had seen, was very much more on our minds than anything else. Would they say 'Allez' or 'Go'? I had a brief look at the air photographs, from which I learned nothing, and the battalion Intelligence Officer told me that there were believed to be anti-tank guns on the east bank of the canal and section posts every fifty yards down the Treaty Road. At brigade headquarters I saw the Brigadier who gave me words of encouragement. The brigade Intelligence Officer also gave encouragement by providing information that the sentry posts were 500 yards apart. I secretary wondered if I went higher still (to a higher headquarters) whether they would become 5,000 yards apart! In fact none existed at all, but the thought of a section attack every quarter of a mile for four miles was not encouraging.

With the possibility of having to fight their way down

the canal on their own, de Klee's men took as much as they could in the way of weapons and equipment:

> Between the nine of us we took two LMGs with twelve magazines each; three sten guns with six magazines each; and four rifles, each with 100 rounds. In addition we took a two-inch mortar with eighteen high explosive bombs, twelve number 36 grenades, two Energa projectors and eight Energa grenades (for use against armour), a Verey pistol and cartridges, three pairs of binoculars, and a compass. Each man had his battle order, a pick or shovel, two full water bottles, forty-eight hours rations, ground sheet, light-weight blanket, jersey and spare socks, washing and cleaning kit, mess-tins, shell and field dressings. We took no wireless. We jumped with an average of just over 90 lbs and marched carrying about 70 lbs.

The tough and battle-hardened French paras, the 1st and 2nd RPC, and 1st Foreign Legion Parachute Regiment (1REP) had now arrived in Cyprus. De Klee met those he was to work with. 'No one in the regiment I met, 2RPC, had done less than 160 jumps; five or six of these were operational.'

On 29 October the Israelis had started their advance across the Sinai Desert. This attack was made in the full knowledge of the British and French governments. It had been planned for weeks. But for public consumption both governments expressed surprise and dismay and demanded that the Israelis and Egyptians disengage immediately or an Anglo/French task force, which was conveniently ready and handily poised in Cyprus and Malta, would be interposed between the belligerents. The Israeli advance went rather faster than planned, and it soon became apparent that there was every chance they would close up to the canal before the amphibious part of the Anglo/French force was within range of Port Said. In which case the Egyptians might surrender, removing at a stroke the need for a landing to interpose a force between them and the Israelis in the name of peace. Furthermore, relieved of the necessity to face the Israelis, the Egyptians might reinforce Port Said. In that event, and if the British and French landing went ahead, it might run up against more than three battalions, a few flak guns, the coast artillery, and four SU 100 assault guns. The French and British amphibious forces were at sea and there was no chance that they could land before 6 November. Action was required at once. A bold decision was taken to drop the British and French paras just after dawn on 5 November. They would be on their own for twenty-four hours and no friendly ships would be within gun range. Without artillery, their only support would be from the air, and the few mortars, machine guns and anti-tank guns they could take with them. Stockwell had not known about the collusion with the Israelis, so was taken by surprise at this turn of events. Had he been forewarned he might have agreed weeks before to Brigadier Butler's plan to seize all three key points at once. The politicians, Eden in particular, were to pay for their deviousness and lack of trust in their military commanders. Unfortunately so were the British people, and several soldiers.

Gamil airfield is situated on a narrow spit of land never more than 800 yards wide, west of Port Said. There were two runways and a control tower. Between the airfield and the town lay a sewage farm and a cemetery. Nearer to Port Said there were several blocks of high-rise flats, a coast guard barracks, an ophthalmic hospital and a shanty town. To the west of the airfield was a stone bridge. 3 Para's orders were to secure the airfield, capture and demolish the stone bridge to prevent reinforcement from that direction, and having cleared the area between the airfield and the town, link up with 42 RM Commando landing the following day. The drop was timed for 7.15 am local time. A total of twenty-six aircraft were available, a mix of Hastings and Valettas. In the first wave Crook could take 668 men, seven jeeps, four trailers, six 106 mm anti-tank guns, four medium machine guns (MMG), four three-inch mortars and 176 supply containers. A troop of sappers, two Air Contact Teams to speak to supporting aircraft, a section of the Parachute Field Ambulance and a field surgical team were included in this drop. A second wave was planned at midday bringing in fifty-six more men, ammunition, three jeeps, one trailer, thirty-six containers and forty-eight panniers.

The enemy, as 3 Para discovered, consisted of an Egyptian battalion group deployed between the ophthalmic hospital and El Gamil, sited to defend the beaches and oppose an airborne operation. About a company defended the airfield, with medium machine guns in two pill-boxes positioned to sweep the DZ, men in beach huts north of the DZ, and in the edge of the sewage farm. Another company occupied the cemetery with three medium machine guns, one six-pounder anti-tank gun and four 81mm mortars. Beyond the cemetery was another company, two 3.7-inch anti-aircraft guns and three Russian SU 100 SPs.

The approach to Gamil at first light posed a problem for the aircrew. If they came in from the east they would fly directly over the flak from Port Said. An approach from the west would be straight into the rising sun. It was decided to go for the latter, and some aircraft were fitted with visors to reduce glare. Because it was a daylight drop, pathfinders were dispensed with. A Canberra bomber would drop a flare five miles from the western end of the DZ to mark the run-in for the transport aircraft. A sea wall was chosen as the landmark for the release point for the drop. The Valettas would lead and the Hastings, with containers, jeeps and trailers, would follow. Crook decided that each aircraft would be loaded with sticks made up from men of all companies, the first men in each stick

from A Company to secure the control tower, silence a
pill-box west of the runway, destroy the stone bridge, and
secure the western end of the objective. Next in each stick,
C Company, battalion reserve; men from B Company
would drop last and push east after clearing the sewage
farm. The last time British paratroopers had jumped into
action was eleven years before, crossing the Rhine.

De Klee attended the regimental briefing by the commanding officer of 2RPC after supper in the mess tent,
the only tent:

> Huge bowls of meat and vegetables were brought in
> with some loaves of brown bread. Those present drew
> their knives, a heavy type of commando dagger, and
> set to. I had given the colonel a bottle of whisky, and
> that, with beer, brandy and red wine, all drunk in any
> order, ended our meal. Half an hour later the colonel
> held his O Group. It took just one hour in all, and
> was one of the briefest and clearest I have ever
> attended. We would jump at 400 feet. This would
> mean that we would be all out and down in less than
> four minutes and would be very concentrated. But
> this was necessary as the DZ was in the shape of a
> 'V' and only 150 yards long, bounded by the sea on
> the south-west, the roads and canals on the south-
> east, and the trees around the filtration plant in the
> north. A hundred yards beyond these lay the two
> bridges which were the French objectives.

Walsh remembers the evening of 4 November:

> The whole battalion attended an outdoor service
> taken by our padre, Horace McClelland, using the
> tailboard of a three-ton truck as an altar. As we
> were walking away the company commanders were
> summoned to receive the depressing news that the
> photo-recce at last light by a Canberra disclosed that

the Egyptians had put what appeared to be obstacles or mines both across the runway and in sand around the edges at Gamil. However, the photographs showed that the stone bridge which was to be demolished by Captain Brazier's parachute engineers had been destroyed by rocket attacks by the Fleet Air Arm. We loaded early next morning. The marshalling of the aircraft went well. We orbited over Akrotiri. We passed over the amphibious fleet, and someone remarked that they seemed a bloody long way away from Port Said. Standing in the door on the run-in, I was a bit worried because I could see only the Mediterranean, and wondered if the pilot had got it right! It was a terrible responsibility to leap out, taking my whole stick into the sea. Once I was out, I realized that the pilot was spot on. The spit was so narrow one could not see it from the door of the aircraft. I landed in a soft patch of sand, and from the crackling of small arms rounds knew at once it was not an exercise! The 'mines' on the DZ were empty forty-gallon oil drums placed by the Egyptians to stop aircraft landing.

Within ten minutes the battalion was down. To reduce weight, the battalion jumped without reserve parachutes. Even so, some men were so loaded they had to be helped to the door. In one Valetta the stick was badly held up crossing the main spar and the pilot went round again. Nine aircraft were damaged by fire, none was lost. The battalion's doctor, Lieutenant Cavanagh was the only man wounded on the way down by a shell splinter in the eye. He did not allow this to stop him from tending to the wounded until he was evacuated later in the day. Brigadier Butler and his Brigade Major jumped in the first wave but allowed Crook to fight the battle without interference.

Private Lamph of B Company was last man in his stick

in a Valetta. He got his strop round his leg crossing the main spar and the aircraft was over the sea heading for home when he jumped. As he came down well beyond the DZ he came under heavy small arms fire, and his kitbag was hit several times. Landing in the sea, he feigned death. As B Company began attacking he made his way towards the beach, recovered his rifle and was picked up by a patrol later in the day. Private Pugsley was the first to arrive at his platoon objective, the control tower. He landed in one of the only two ornamental palm trees by the tower and hung there muttering: 'Cor f . . . k me!' as Sergeant Legg and a platoon raced to secure the tower and the adjacent building. As Private Looker of B Company was still at about 200 feet, with his kitbag swinging beneath him, he saw that he was about to land in a slit trench. The Egyptian occupant obviously thought so too, scrambled out, and stood on the edge of the trench, pointing his rifle at Looker. The fates intervened and Looker's 80 lb kitbag swung into the Egyptian, knocking him into the trench. Looker landed on top of him and quickly despatched him. One soldier landed in a minefield and was killed.

Second Lieutenant Coates's platoon of A Company cleared the pillbox west of the airfield. Private Clements started the ball rolling by firing one round from his rocket launcher straight through the slit. The platoon destroyed a heavy machine gun, killed the crew, and took eight prisoners. By this time the remainder of A Company had secured the tower and buildings.

At the western end of the airfield, B Company under Major Stevens, who had been wounded in the hand on landing, destroyed a machine gun post in a pillbox and cleared the enemy in buildings on the beach and slit trenches at the end of the runway. The company then set about clearing the sewage farm. The thick reeds and swampy ground made it an unsavoury place. Beyond, on slightly higher ground and overlooking the sewage farm, the enemy entrenched in the cemetery brought down heavy machine gun and mortar fire on B Company, inflicting a number of casualties. Major Stevens was hit in the leg and was evacuated under protest, having refused to stop for the wound in his hand. Captain Beale took over the company. By now the Fleet Air Arm were in attendance overhead and a stream of rocket-firing aircraft attacked the enemy positions under the direction of the Air Contact Team. The strikes were very accurate, some as little as 400 yards in front of the paratroopers. B Company continued their advance and consolidated. From then on close air support was an important battle-winning factor. Over 400 sorties were flown that day. At least one was very close. Second Lieutenant Hogg was ordered to take his platoon through the sewage farm, make contact with the enemy and report back. The platoon advanced, but as it reached the open ground beyond the sewage farm it came under fire from the cemetery. Hogg withdrew as ordered, and had reached the rows of concrete troughs brimming with untreated filth when two French Mystères saw them below and attacked with canon shells. Hogg and his men dived into the troughs. As the aircraft pulled up, Hogg ordered his platoon to dash for the cover of the reeds from which they had set out half an hour or so before.

Crook ordered C Company to push through B Company and take the cemetery. They were commanded by a veteran soldier, Major Norman, who had fought against German paratroopers in Crete in 1941. The attack was preceded by air strikes by naval Sea Venoms and Sea Hawks, and supported by mortars and MMGs. The mortar platoon commander, Captain Morley, had been hit by shrapnel early in the battle. His place was taken by Sergeant Knight, who energetically managed to double up as platoon commander and mortar fire controller, spotting for his mortars. After some close-quarter fighting among the tombstones they cleared the area, killing over twenty enemy and capturing three Russian SU 100 assault guns, two 3.7 flak guns, four 81mm mortars, three MMGs, a Bren gun carrier and several rifles and light machine guns. Many soldiers threw away their 1940 vintage stens and picked up the excellent weapons they found on the objective. As the company was reorganizing on the objective they noticed that the apartment blocks beyond the cemetary were being used as observation posts by the Egyptians. Air strikes were immediately called for and the SU 100s in the vicinity of the apartments were abandoned by their crews. But machine guns in the buildings continued firing, holding up C Company's advance. Lieutenant Newall, the Machine Gun Platoon commander, well forward selecting positions for his guns, spotted the enemy machine gun positions and an abandoned Bren gun carrier between him and the apartments. Under fire, he raced forward to the carrier and with the help of Sergeant Davidson started up and drove straight at the Egyptian machine gun positions on the ground floor, silencing them both. On their return to their own positions they had a very narrow escape. A 106mm anti-tank gunner, seeing the carrier and knowing that the battalion did not possess one, fired his 0.5-inch spotting rifle, hitting the carrier. He was prevented from loosing-off the main armament by a quick-witted NCO!

About four hours after the airfield was captured, a French Dakota flew in with Colonel Fouquières, an officer on the staff of the French Admiral, to see if it would be possible to fly French reinforcements into Gamil. After deciding that it would not be possible to land a fully loaded aircraft the French pilot offered to take back the more seriously wounded. One was the medical officer, Lieutenant Cavanagh. who had been carrying on with his job for the past five hours despite his own wound. In a garage by the control tower Captain Kirby's field surgical team and Captains McElliott and Fearnby of the Parachute Field Ambulance treated the casualties. Soon afterwards helicopters started coming in from the fleet and took away further casualties. There was sporadic enemy gun and mortar fire on the DZ where Major Norton commanding Support Company and Warrant Officer Robinson, the Regimental Quartermaster Sergeant, had been organizing the ammunition re-supply, unpacking guns and getting jeeps and trailers off their platforms. But the airfield was usable, certainly for helicopters. Now was the time to fly in other troops to maintain the momentum by building up a force strong enough to start pushing down the canal as early as possible the next day. The natural choice was 45 RM Commando, already briefed for a helicopter operation. Regrettably, the opportunity was lost.

By the afternoon the battalion was running short of ammunition, particularly for the mortars, despite the second lift which brought a resupply. At this stage Brigadier Butler intervened for the first time and ordered Crook to pull back because the battalion was in danger of straying into the area of the bombardment which would precede the next day's amphibious assault. Mindful of the possibility of being counter-attacked, Crook decided to pull back C Company and go firm on the forward edge of the sewage farm. The second lift had not been without excitement. Corporal Brackpool of the battalion paymaster's staff was standing in the door of his Valetta when it banked sharply two miles short of the DZ. He fell out and landed on a sandbank surrounded by water. A patrol consisting of the officers' mess staff under the command of Sergeant Vokes was sent to get him before the Egyptians arrived. Brackpool, stripping to his underpants, swam for it against a strong current, eventually meeting Vokes's patrol who attacked an enemy post on the way, killing two of the occupants. Hogg's platoon spent an uncomfortable night in the reeds bitten by mosquitoes in company with everybody else, and caked with drying sewage.

That morning de Klee and his party had dropped at

Raswa from a Nordatlas, a twin door aircraft with a tailgate
and a vast improvement on the Valettas and Hastings that
were 3 Para's lot:

> There was no aircraft drill; we stood up, put on our
> helmets, hooked on our containers (kit bags), hooked
> ourselves up and shuffled towards the door. Red light
> on. Five minutes to go ... on went the klaxon, a
> second of buffeting and blackness and then the gentle
> swaying accompanied by the sigh of relief, slow twists
> and my helmet as usual jammed over my eyes. Twists
> cleared, container away and helmet pushed back ...
> the air was full of the sound of small arms fire. AA
> shells were bursting above us, the Nordatlas aircraft
> were weaving and jinking all over the sky to the north,
> and the Frenchmen drifting down around me were
> firing from their parachute harness.

Each French para dropped with a sub-machine gun
stuffed between his parachute harness and his chest. While
the British were hastily unpacking their kitbags to extract
their personal weapons, the French were able to fire back
at the opposition without delay. This was fortunate
because the Egyptians were engaging the paras as they
landed. The French dealt with the Egyptians and in no
time both bridges were in their hands. One had been
blown. After landing, de Klee set about collecting his men.

> The DZ was littered with parachutes and abandoned
> equipment, dead Egyptians and wounded French-
> men, spurts of sand and earth and all the accompany-
> ing noise. Murphy was hit but McNab was with him;
> Lance Corporal Kent and I went and carried him
> over. He had landed beside an Egyptian slit trench
> and had been shot in the stomach before he could
> defend himself. His assailant had promptly been
> killed by a French officer. I do not know if the Egypti-

ans had been expecting us or not, but about forty had been dug in on and around the DZ and were in the middle of their breakfast when we arrived.

After finding only one of their sappers, Coggen, wounded in the face, de Klee set off down the Treaty Road with what was left of his party.

The time was eight o'clock. By half past twelve we had gone ten kilometres down the Treaty Road, crossed the Sweetwater Canal by a wooden foot-bridge, and come back up the Canal Road. There had been no sign of life or opposition, except that both roads had been prepared for blowing at the six kilometre point, and there in the Treaty Road was a small hut containing 1200 lbs of dynamite and rolls of fuse. The occupants had evidently left in a hurry, leaving all their personal possessions and breakfast half-eaten. On return I sent McNab over to the French headquarters with a written message.

The way south was clear!

Owen and his sappers, slowed down by their heavy kit, had dropped very late and found themselves in the middle of a French attack on the pontoon bridge, so had little alternative but to join in.

That night Brigadier Butler and the French paratroop commander Colonel Joubert tried to arrange a ceasefire with El Moguy, the Egyptian commander of Port Said. In return for the surrender of the garrison, the air strikes and naval bombardment planned for the next day would be cancelled. At one point it seemed the El Moguy would aquiesce. But at the last moment he got through to Cairo on the one telephone line that Butler had been unable to cut and was ordered to continue the fight. To bolster him, Nasser told him that World War Three had started, the Russians were bombing Paris and London, and thousands of Soviet troops were on their way to Egypt. The Soviet consul in Port Said told El Moguy, that he should turn the town into another Stalingrad and hold out until the arrival of massive reinforcements of Russians, who would sweep the British and the French into the sea. He was so convincing that El Moguy was persuaded to order that crates of Russian AK47 assault rifles be opened and issued to anyone who volunteered to take part.

Just after first light on 6 November 3 Para was attacked by a Russian MIG. There were no MIGs flying, said the Intelligence Staff at Force HQ, when they were told. A little later this MIG, or another, returned and one solider was wounded. At 7 am the seaborne landings began. 3 Para lined up their MMGs to fire along the beaches in support of the commandos. As soon as they saw the commandos storming ashore, C Company moved back into the cemetery and cleared the flats beyond. After clearing the coastguard barracks and sealing off the shanty town, Crook reported that he had secured all his objectives, but decided to continue the advance to meet 42 RM Commando. Walsh's A Company was stood by to advance south down the canal. C Company pushed forward and immediately ran into heavy machine gun and mortar fire but managed to battle their way towards a building near the ophthalmic hospital. The latter was being used as a strong point by the Egyptians. The commander of 8 Platoon, Lieutenant Richardson, his platoon sergeant, Read, and two others were hit. The platoon withdrew, leaving Sergeant Read for dead. He regained consciousness and crawled 300 yards back to rejoin his company. Captain McElliott of the Field Ambulance drove up in a jeep under fire to rescue the wounded men. At this point the battalion came under fire from a police barracks in the shanty town. The police did not immediately run away when fire was returned, so Crook asked for an air strike but was refused. So he ordered a 106 to fire; the exploding shells set fire to the shanty town, burning it to the ground. The police withdrew. As the battalion had reached their limit of exploitation, Crook sent a signal saying 'what next?' There was no reply, and no sign of 42 Commando, so the battalion pressed on, halting at about midnight. Crook spent the night in the only salubrious looking house in the area, which turned out to the local brothel. There were no girls, just fleas and the whiff of scent! But the bed was comfortable. At dawn on 7 November, 3 Para linked up with 42 Commando.

Captain de Klee had also been busy. Early that morning he had met Brigadier Butler, told what he knew, and pestered him to let him go south again, but a little bit further this time. Butler agreed, but only as far as Ras-el-ish, fifteen kilometres away. By midday they had arrived. Throughout the day they collected a number of prisoners fleeing from Port Said, mainly in civilian clothes. The first two turned out to an Egyptian commando and an air force cadet; each was armed and their uniforms were hidden in the pillion seat of their motor-cycle. De Klee:

> By the tears, blubbering and supplications, they evidently thought that their last hour had come. They offered us money, riches and their services for life if they were spared. As it was, one became our cook and the other our grave-digger for the following twenty-four hours. If we had known then that most of the Egyptian army in Port Said discarded their uniforms and became civilian terrorists we might have behaved differently. Next came a car. On being signalled to slow down it stopped violently and went flat-out in reverse. Fletcher's Bren opened up and it went full-toss into the Sweetwater Canal and disappeared completely. A pause, bubbles, and eight heads appeared on the surface, screaming for mercy. They were pulled out. The bag this time consisted of one

soldier, who swore he had worked faithfully for the British for fourteen years; a member of the secret police armed with a loaded .38 revolver, but as two of the rounds in it were 9 mm, his authenticity was viewed with some suspicion; and six civilians. The policeman had been hit in the arm, and one civilian in the chest. We did what we could for them, and, keeping the former, put the latter in a wheelbarrow, now our only form of transport, and sent him with his five friends on towards Port Said.

Little happened for the next hour or so, but suddenly Sergeant Black, who was in our OP, sixty feet up in the Canal Station signal mast, cried out: 'Here comes the Egyptian army'. Mugs, razors and cleaning rags were dropped, Lance Corporal Williams and McNab shot out of the canal where they had been swimming, and we stood-to. Down the canal road, evenly spaced out in parties of two or three, were coming about forty people. In the heat haze, even through field-glasses it was impossible to make out who they were. Soon there was no doubt – they were refugees from the villages to our south, though why they were heading for Port Said, which from this distance appeared to be a blazing inferno, we were unable to understand. Three were soldiers, obviously deserters, as they had thrown away all their equipment except for belts, bayonets and water bottles, and were wearing galabirs over their uniforms. They joined our other prisoners. One couple, a man and a woman, had their six-year-old daughter with them, The child had a gaping hole in her cheek-bone and a deep gash above one eye. McNab gave her all his sweets, which she managed to eat, while I and an Egyptian soldier washed her face. We had used all our dressings so I indicated to her father that I needed his shirt to bandage his daughter. He shook

his head. More explanations. Even more violent prot-
estations and head shaking. I hardly had to look at
the guardsmen near me. I nodded; in a matter of
seconds I had sufficient blue cotton bandages to
finish my job. The little family left us, the father in
his singlet, the mother evidently grateful, and the
child with mouth, hands and pockets stuffed with
sweets. Except for these two, all the refugees were
ablebodied men. A taxi was halted and out got fourteen civilians. We kept the taxi and its owner and
sent the others on towards Port Said, telling them
the next troops they would meet would be paratroops
from the French Foreign Legion. They did not
appear very enthusiastic about continuing their journey and we later discovered that they stopped half a
mile further on and were still there when we left
the next day. The taxi had come from Cairo; they
confirmed earlier refugees' reports that El Qantara,
the Egyptian army headquarters, was completely
deserted and that they had seen no sign of military
life in Ismailia either. I sent Sergeant Black and
McNab back on the motor-bike with the news for
what it was worth.

A shout from the OP: 'Egyptian soldiers coming
up the railway line.' Two in front and one behind,
well spread out and all armed, it looked like a recce
patrol. We let the leaders come within thirty yards
before Lance Corporal Kent and I stepped out of
cover and challenged them. They turned and ran.
Our final capture was an Egyptian complete with steel
helmet, medal ribbons and brand new Russian rifle
and bayonet who somehow had escaped from Port
Said. He was caught slinking past the back of the
Canal Station by Sergeant White and Lance Corporal
Kent and was overpowered before he could do any
harm. He was an unpleasant character and made it

quite obvious he had no intention of staying with us if he could help it; however, he was given no chance and went with the others into the POW cage the next day.

At about half past four we heard the rumble of tanks and down both roads from Port Said came the leading troops of the 6th Royal Tanks. Though we tried to stop them they went straight past us without even a wave. Out of each steel hull protruded a steel helmet, looking neither right nor left. I got our motor bike and gave chase but it was a wasted effort, for however much I waved and shouted they would not stop, and all I achieved was to amuse some French paratroopers who were sitting on the back of the rear tanks. However, on getting back to the Canal Station we had the satisfaction of watching them fight a completely futile battle with an empty pill-box half a mile south of us. Shortly after the Company and 2 Para came through, and after they had heard a brief account of our doings, went on southwards, telling us to catch them up the next day. While this was going on, the Intelligence Officer cunningly pinched our highly-prized Russian rifle but it was quickly recovered when we joined them later.

All that morning 2 Para had been waiting offshore in their landing ships (LST) to get into battle. Shortly after midday the LST *Empire Parkeston* nosed towards the shore near the De Lesseps statue in the outer harbour. She had difficulty lowering her ramp. The first soldiers got ashore by scrambling down nets into lighters. Once ashore, the battalion set off at 4 pm towards Raswa led by the Guards Parachute Company in Champs and three-ton trucks. Number 3 stick had already got through the town to set up a road block about nine miles south of Port Said, waiting for the breakout to begin. Skilfully the Guards

Parachute Company skirted the fighting and cleared minor opposition before joining number 3 stick at their road block. B Company 2 Para then passed through to head the advance. The plan for the break-out consisted of an advance guard of 2 Para and a squadron of Centurions of 6th Royal Tank Regiment (6RTR) driving south at best speed, followed by General Massu in overall command with the main body, some in the road and some in craft on the Suez Canal. Waiting in Cyprus were the 3rd Battalion 2RPC, ready to drop since first light that day on Qantara, a third of the way down the canal, and the whole of 1RPC to drop on Ismailia once the advance got under way. The squadron of 6RTR crossed the bridges at Raswa, advanced to El Tina, about fifteen miles south of Port Said, and waited.

Through no fault of 2 Para, the advance had taken a very long time to wind up. Stockwell had reserved to himself the right to order the break-out, but hearing that the Egyptians wanted to surrender he had come ashore by boat at 9 am with his deputy the French General Beaufre. After nearly being shot when he was landed in the wrong place, he made his way to the headquarters of 3rd Commando Brigade. Here he borrowed a vehicle to drive to the Italian Consulate where he understood the surrender negotiations were to take place. The Egyptians did not turn up. Unfortunately he spent so much time on these fruitless surrender negotiations, out of touch with his two bridgade commanders, Butler of the Parachute Brigade, and Madoc of the Commando Brigade, that the momentum seeped away. There were a number of options to speed things up. 2 Para could have been lifted to El Tina using the helicopters that had brought 45 RM Commando ashore earlier. The Buffaloes in which the leading waves of 40 and 42 RM Commando had landed could have married up with 45 RM Commando landed on the already secure French DZ at Raswa instead of landing in Port

Said. The town could have been cleared by follow-up troops, including 1 Para who were sent back to Cyprus to prepare for a follow-up parachute operation. Time was getting short. Pressure was building up on the British and French governments for a ceasefire. Some of the troops ashore heard of the ceasefire by tuning spare radios on to the BBC. They were stupefied. All their efforts had been for nothing.

2 Para and the Guards Independent Company pushed on down the road at best speed, making good progress to El Tina. Here they found the squadron of 6RTR leaguered for the night. A swift altercation took place between Lieutenant Colonel Bredin and the 6 RTR squadron leader before the Centurions got moving. Bredin, knowing that the ceasefire was set for 2 am local time, wanted to make Qantara before he had to stop. But time ran out and he was ordered to stop at El Cap, where his battalion dug in to the evil-smelling mud on a two-platoon front on the causeway.

The next night Walsh's company were sent to El Tina, by the canal, to dig in as a long-stop to 2 Para. Walsh as befitted his rank requisitioned the only bedroom in the Canal Company house close by his defensive position. In it was a vast double bed. Walsh shared it with his second-in-command, Captain Kingston. One morning, before dawn, Butler, his Brigade Major, and a very attractive French woman correspondent from *Paris Match* walked in. Seeing by the light of a torch two British officers in bed, she exclaimed: 'How very strange!' 1 Para was landed and dug in to the west along the coast. A week later the parachute brigade returned to Cyprus. 3 Para, who according to Cairo Radio had been wiped out to the last man, had suffered four dead and thirty-six wounded. The achievement had been considerable. They had seized an airfield which could be used again after four hours and cleared the enemy between the airfield and the edge of town, capturing a wealth of small arms, three SU 100s, two 3.7 AA guns, four 81mm mortars, seven medium machine guns, two Bren gun carriers and seventeen prisoners of war. To this day the Suez operation is frequently tagged a military fiasco. It was nothing of the kind. It was a political fiasco. The servicemen did all that was asked of them, reacting swiftly to changes of plan resulting from dithering in political high places; committed to battle with obsolete equipment, the result of indifference and parsimony by ministers, Socialist and Conservative alike. Eden, having decided to topple Nasser against the advice of the Chiefs of Staff, did not have the will to see it through. Britain's standing in the world, and with the Arabs in particular, plummeted.

When 3 Para arrived back in Cyprus they found that the Provost Marshal had ordered that the whole brigade be searched for captured weapons. Crook was furious, refused to comply with the order and marched his men off.

In December, 1 and 3 Para were sent back to England. 2 Para took over from the Gordon Highlanders in the Troodos mountains. They had a successful tour, being rejoined by the other two battalions in June 1958. The brigade had been sent to Cyprus to stand by for operations in Jordan in support of King Hussein during the first of many crises in Lebanon and the Middle East, including Iraq, where the King and his family were assassinated. 2 and 3 Para were eventually sent to Jordan, leaving 1 Para to continue with operations in Cyprus. In October the crisis in the Middle East died down and 2 and 3 Para left for England. 1 Para eventually returned to England in March 1959.

CHAPTER 12

South Arabia

RADFAN

Most of the region north of the coast of south-west Arabia
is mountainous, up through the Yemen and the Hejez.
Only by striking north-east from Aden does the traveller
eventually reach the gravel plains leading to the true
desert, the Rub al Khali, the Empty Quarter. Sixty miles
north of Aden and thirty miles from the Yemen border lies
the Radfan, astride the road to Yemen in the mountains of
what was the Western Aden Protectorate. The unsurfaced
road follows the wadi bottom, climbing almost impercep-
tibly until it snakes up the pass onto the Dhala plateau at
6,000 feet. From antiquity this road was the trade route
from the Indian Ocean to the Yemen, Mecca and the
eastern Mediterranean. Pilgrims to Mecca were frequent
travellers. The grim black volcanic mountains stretch from
horizon to horizon. Clusters of stone-walled houses make
up the scattered villages, each house like a miniature fort
with no windows, and sited for defence. Small watchtowers
crown the tops of some of the ridges, covering the likely
approaches, to protect the cultivated areas against
marauders. Scrub and camel thorn are the only natural
vegetation. There is a surprising amount of cultivation in
the wadis, where water from the heavy rainstorms soaks
away into the ground to be brought to the surface by
digging wells. In places the sides of the mountains bear
evidence of terracing, a relic of more fruitful days when
according to legend the Queen of Sheba ruled. All the

mountain people throughout the Protectorate are fiercely independent. To carry a rifle is a sign of manhood. The tribesman, rifle held by the muzzle on his shoulder, cartridge belts and curved dagger at his waist, owed allegiance only to his tribal ruler, and then only when it suited him. Blood feuds, inter-tribal warfare and exacting tolls from passing travellers were a way of life. Courage and strength were admired; conciliation, a sign of weakness, was treated with contempt. The Quteibi, the self-styled 'Wolves of the Radfan,' were among the most truculent; brave, excellent shots, adept at fieldcraft, with an eye for ground.

The British, following their custom in the tribal areas of the North West Frontier province of India, had never attempted to administer the sheikhdoms, sultanates and emirates that made up the Aden Protectorates. Each ruler administered as much of his state as he could without interference by the British. Justice was rough. Even in the 1960s prisoners were kept in chains, and there were occasional executions by beheading or being thrown down from a high place. Foreign affairs were the province of the British government and political officers resided in each state to see that British interests were not threatened. The exception was Aden itself, which was a British colony. A busy free port, it bustled with life and commerce.

By the early 1960s most of the states and Aden colony, renamed Aden State, had been joined into the Federation of South Arabia with their own federal parliament, responsible for the internal affairs of the Federation. The tribal rulers had always been encouraged to keep a small armed force for internal policing, known at first as the Tribal Guards and then as the Federal National Guards (FNG). Overall peace was kept by tribesmen recruited into the Federal Regular Army (FRA), officered at first by the British but with an increasing number of Arab officers. To back up the FRA, British battalions were stationed in Aden and 45 Commando RM in Little Aden. In scenes reminiscent of the North West Frontier of India, soldiers, Arab and British, patrolled, piquetted and manned outposts at scattered points in the mountains. Live ammunition was always carried. The tribesmen were wont to take a shot at a passing convoy or patrol, sometimes just for the fun of it!

It was the British intention that the Federation of South Arabia should become independent. There was considerable opposition to the Federation from a number of quarters. Britain had lost a good deal of influence and prestige in the Arab world after her agreement to setting up the State of Israel. Her reputation fell even further after the Suez campaign. Not all Arabs, many of whom regarded Nasser as an upstart, deplored the invasion. Indeed, according to Sir Tom Hickinbotham who was governor of Aden at the time, the ruler of Beihan in the Protectorate exclaimed: 'Praise be to God, the old woman (Britannia) has woken up at last.' But following the abject back-down by the British politicians after her soldiers had performed so well, any Arab support, however tacit, withered away. Any steps she took in this part of the world were subject to criticism by Arabs worldwide. To the north the Yemen had always coveted the Protectorate, and saw no reason to renounce her claim just because of a change of name. In 1962 the Immam of Yemen was overthrown by General Sallal, an Egyptian-backed republican revolutionary. The many Yemeni and pro-Yemeni elements in Aden gave their enthusiastic support to Sallal's regime.

President Nasser of Egypt, the self-appointed leader of Arab aspirations worldwide, had plans for the Federation. He wished to prise it away from the British sphere of influence and install a puppet regime under his control, as he had done in the Yemen. The trade unionists and merchants in Aden State deeply distrusted and feared the tribesmen and their rulers, to whom they were joined in a shotgun marriage. In their eyes the rulers were undemocratic and the tribesmen savages. The rulers, for their part, eyed the trade unions, deeply penetrated by Yemenis and Nasserites, with distaste. The tribesmen viewed the fat merchants, bankers and soft town dwellers with contempt. In the background, supporting Nasser in the hope of rich pickings in the form of bases and influence once the British had been kicked out, waited the Russians. By the end of 1963 the stage was set for trouble. It was not long coming.

For several months the Quteibis, having been forbidden to exact tolls from travellers on the road to and from the Yemen, had been defying the Emir of Dhala, their ruler, by shooting at convoys and mining the Dhala Road. The civil war in the Yemen was in full swing. President Nasser of Egypt, who was still heavily involved seeing the chance to foment trouble in a British protectorate, gave the tribesmen his support in the form of weapons and training in the Yemen. The FRA was sent in and after a highly successful operation, including the building of a jeep road into the Wadi Taym, the heart of Quteibi country, were withdrawn. The Yemeni airforce carried out a number of incursions into the Federation and attacks by Quteibi tribesmen on the Dhala road increased. The federal government decided that further action was needed and called on British forces to assist under the terms of the agreement between the two governments.

A force was assembled, dubbed Radforce. It was the start of the hot season in South Arabia. As the sun gains height, stepping out from the relative cool of a stone building is like opening an oven door, the glare striking like a blow. Even some distance from habitation the smells of goats, donkeys and cattle pervade the shimmering air. At midday the temperature rises to between 110 and 120 degrees Fahrenheit in the sun. There is little shade and soldiers carried strips of hessian to provide shade by day and a rough blanket at night. With the onset of darkness the temperature drops, but start marching, and thirst sets in. Water was to be a constant problem because there were few local sources. The ration was two gallons per man per day for drinking, cooking and washing. Almost every gallon had to be carried by soldiers or flown in by the tiny helicopter force.

In April 1964 in Bahrain, 1,000 miles to the north east, 3 Para were the first parachute battalion to be accompanied by their wives on a posting to the Persian Gulf. Following the Iraqi threat to invade Kuwait in 1961, parachute battalions had carried out one year unaccompanied tours of duty in Bahrain, standing by for quick intervention should Iraq threaten a repeat performance. The first company of 3 Para to arrive in Bahrain was A Company, commanded again after an interval of eight years by Major Walsh. As he arrived he was warned for a parachute operation on the island of Zanzibar. It never materialized. The rest of the battalion arrived, settled in and started a vigorous training programme. At short notice Major Walters' B Company was despatched to Aden and warned for a parachute operation in the Radfan under the command of 45 RM Commando.

As part of the overall plan to cut the tribesmen off from their cultivated areas and their routes to the Yemen, 45 Commando was ordered to capture the high ground on the north side of the Dhanaba Basin on 30 April. This they proposed doing by a night approach march to seize two features, 'Rice Bowl' and 'Sand Fly.' B Company 3 Para would drop the same night on the Wadi Taym and seize 'Cap Badge.' Unfortunately the DZ marking party provided by 22 SAS was discovered the day before. The ten-man SAS patrol was cut off by about 100 tribesmen and had to fight its way out supported by fire from RAF Hunter jets. The patrol commander and one trooper were killed, left behind and subsequently beheaded. Later their heads were displayed on spikes in the Yemen.

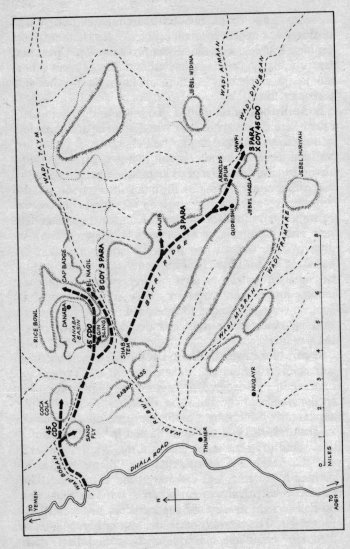

The Radfan

When the commander of Radforce realized that the DZ could not be marked he cancelled the drop and ordered B Company to come up to Thumier, the base for Radforce, by truck. At the same time he realized that 45 Commando, who had already set out, would be very exposed forward on 'Rice Bowl' without B Company on 'Cap Badge.' Eventually his orders on the radio, to halt on 'Sand Fly' and 'Coca Cola,' got through to the commandos as they marched through the night.

Three nights later the commandos, with B Company under command, again marched by night to secure two features on the eastern side of the basin, 'Cap Badge' and 'Gin Sling.' Two commando companies used a precipitous route led by one of the company commanders, a mountaineer. They reached their objectives without opposition after a stiff climb, outsmarting the tribesmen, who had spent the night in the village below. When the tribesmen climbed the ridge in daylight they received an unpleasant surprise and were swept off in a hail of fire. B Company had been sent on what was thought to be a longer but easier route through the Wadi Taym. The march took longer than expected. The going was harder than had been anticipated and on two occasions they had to lie-up while tribesmen went by. Daylight found the company on low ground dominated by the village of El Naqil, below 'Cap Badge.' The tribesmen, smarting from their reverse at the hands of the commandos on 'Cap Badge,' opened fire on the company from the houses and the lower slopes of the mountain.

Walters led one of his platoons to clear a small fort while the rest of the company assaulted the village. Having driven the tribesmen out, a group cut in behind the leading soldiers in an attempt to assault them from the rear. They ran into an ambush by the rear element of the company under the second-in-command, Captain Jewkes. All the tribesmen were killed. The company consolidated in the village. Snipers in the foothills above the village now engaged them, positioning themselves so that they were in dead ground to the commandos on 'Cap Badge.' The company called in Hunters to strafe the tribesmen, to good effect. Two Beavers dropped water and ammunition to the company. Captain Jewkes was killed assisting a wounded sergeant, one soldier was killed and six more wounded. The reserve company of 45 Commando was flown in to the top of 'Cap Badge,' and moved down to take the tribesmen in the rear. By mid-afternoon the enemy had made off. B Company climbed to the top of 'Cap Badge' after an eleven-hour march and a ten-hour battle. El Naqil was renamed Pegasus Village.

The next two weeks were spent reorganizing Radforce. Brigadier Blacker and Headquarters 39 Brigade were brought out to command with substantial reinforcements. Among them was Lieutenant Colonel Farrar-Hockley, the Commanding Officer of 3 Para, with two of his companies, Walsh's A Company and Major Ward-Booth's C Company. B Company was sent back to Bahrain for a well-deserved rest. Farrar-Hockley spoke to each company before they left Bahrain, telling them they must accustom themselves to the possibility of losing their lives on operations. This was not an exercise in Aldershot. To the majority of the battalion, facing the prospect of action for the first time, this wise advice added to the sense of anticipation; here was a chance for some real soldiering. One young officer, Second Lieutenant Pike, remembered the great feeling of confidence throughout the battalion. They were fit, well-trained, and well-led. Farrar-Hockley had won an MC commanding C Company 6 Para in the battle of Athens, and a DSO as the adjutant of 1st Battalion the Gloucestershire Regiment at the battle of the Imjin in Korea, and for his persistent escape attempts and resistance to torture for two years as a prisoner of the North Koreans and Chinese.

The next objective was the Wadi Dhubsan. The key to

the Wadi was the ten-mile-long Bakri Ridge which slopes up to a spur at a height of 5,000 feet. From the spur, the ridge drops almost sheer away for 3,000 feet to the Wadi Dhubsan. Patrols from 3 Para had discovered that the ridge was not strongly held, and there was a route up from Shab Tem. Farrar-Hockley was ordered to move up on the ridge as soon as possible. He was told that no medium-lift Belvedere helicopters would be available for supply for at least two days. His only helicopter support would be two Scouts. He decided that one of his two companies would act as porters for the other, carrying water, ammunition and food on manpack frames. At last light on 19 May, 3 Para set off. C Company led, with A Company portering.

Like all the officers, Walsh carried a load. He had a choice between boxes of ammunition or a jerrican of water. 'I made a mistake and picked a jerrican of water. The jerrican leaked. As the night wore on the water slopped out, and although the cold water was pleasant running down my back the partly-empty can swayed about, making it difficult to keep my balance on the rocky ground in the dark.' They advanced 10,000 yards without meeting opposition and halted for the day, sending out patrols.

The following night it was C Company's turn to porter with A Company taking up the advance, led by a fighting patrol formed by 1 Plátoon, commanded by Pike. The remainder of the company were to follow up behind this fighting patrol, whose task was to seize control of the Hajib feature. They were also ordered to capture a prisoner if possible, information on the enemy being almost non-existent. By this time Pike's clothes, like everybody's, were in tatters. When Farrar-Hockley finished briefing Pike he told him to take a needle and cotton to his khaki-flannel shirt and olive-green trousers.

After a long but incident-free advance along the wadi bed the patrol started their climb up the terraces and steep

slopes that led to the Hajib summit, 2,000 feet high. The
steps on the terraces were a long stretch for all but the
tallest. As they approached one of the stone towers that
guarded the feature they were engaged by very inaccurate
rifle fire from the general direction of the tower, most of
which lobbed harmlessly over their heads as if the tribesmen's rifles were being used like mortars. A running fight
developed as the platoon practised for real the fire and
movement so often exercised in the Jebels of Sharjah and
Dubai a few short weeks before. Pike takes up the story:

> Soon after the initial contact, artillery fire from J
> Battery's 105mm pack howitzers, which was on call
> to the patrol but had not actually been requested, was
> brought down on the area. So poor were the maps,
> however, that the shells landed behind the platoon,
> and uncomfortably close. The result was an urgent
> call on the radio to stop firing. All this was exciting
> and highly satisfying, but the aim of capturing a pris-
> oner was rather forgotten as the platoon moved for-
> ward from crestline to crestline. In the darkness,
> despite some further exchanges of fire, the tribesmen
> slipped away down the steep pathways and cliff-faces
> they knew so well. The objective was clear well before
> first light and Private Jack Watson, the platoon
> 'character', voted Hajib Feature a platoon battle
> honour, joining Rye and Aviemore, where we had
> also made our mark! We settled down to await the
> dawn, wrapped in our hessian strips against the chill
> of the night. My commanding officer's only comment
> when he met me on the feature the next morning
> was: 'Your navigation was commendable. However, I
> am much distressed that you have no prisoner!'

The following night the Anti-Tank Platoon, under
Company Sergeant Major Arnold, pushed through to the
spur at the end of the Bakri Ridge. On the way they

captured three tribesmen complete with their weapons, the first such prisoners in the campaign so far. The spur was named Arnold's Spur. Three days later the battalion advanced again, but was held up by heavy small arms fire from the village of Quedeishi on the highest point of the Bakri Ridge. There seemed to be about fifty tribesmen with a number of automatic weapons, well sited in strong positions. Farrar-Hockley sent C Company in to attack Quedeishi supported by J Battery and air strikes. Once C Company were firm on the objective, A Company advanced to the spur beyond the village and finished up poised above the Wadi Dhubsan. By 24 May, 3 Para were in control of all of the Bakri Ridge. It was a magnificent achievement. But there was more to be done and a great deal had been learned.

The soldiers had experienced the frustration and stress of being under fire without always being able to reply effectively. Manoeuvre without covering fire was dangerous. Locating the enemy was difficult enough, let alone bringing effective fire to bear on tribesmen in deep caves. Artillery was too imprecise, and not always successful. Fighter ground attack aircraft were more frightening and efficacious, but were not always available. To get moving again, the soldiers often had to rely on their own resources. The GPMG, in action for almost the first time, was a great success. Its rate of fire, considerably greater than the Bren, produced a stream of bullets that could claw their way through sangar walls, and greatly assisted in winning the fire fight. The 3.5-inch rocket launchers did not succeed in blasting a hole in the solidly-built watch towers. The soldiers re-learned the old infantry lessons, practised on exercises but only brought home under fire: when you stop, build a sangar – time-consuming, back-breaking, thirsty work – and the importance of battle discipline, silence on patrol at night, good weapon handling and fire orders. Thirst was a constant companion. One man went berserk with salt deficiency, was disarmed and evacuated. There were no individual ration packs available, twenty-four hours food per man. Ten-man packs unsuitable for marching infantry were distributed among the platoons, who tended to eat the contents at one sitting to save carrying the bulky tins. At least the margarine was useful. Lacking oil for their weapons, the yellow liquid served as a substitute. The men were brown, lean as racing snakes and ready for the next task.

The commander of 39 Brigade decided that as part of the next phase of operations 3 Para with X Company of 45 Commando under command would mount a raid into the Wadi Dhubsan on 26 May. This was regarded as an impregnable position by the tribesmen. The force would be very difficult to maintain in the wadi, so Farrar-Hockley was ordered to withdraw within twenty-four hours. The easiest and therefore the most obvious way in was by a long loop to the south-west using two other wadis. Instead, Farrar-Hockley decided to see if he could descend to the wadi by going straight down Arnold's Spur, a descent of over 3,000 feet, down what appeared to be an inaccessible escarpment. Two patrols discovered a steep track, which at one point ended in a thirty-foot cliff. Farrar-Hockley decided to use this route.

At last light on 25 May, C Company moved forward to piquet Jebel Haqla, which dominated the Wadi Dhubsan from the west. Two hours later, A Company and the remainder of the battalion started their scramble down the cliff face. They were heavily laden, with additional ammunition. Their task, to clear and secure the wadi as far forward as two towers guarding the approaches to the widening valley. The weather in these mountains was so unpredictable that air support might not be available. By first light, A Company had secured their objective. The plan was for X Company of 45 Commando to be lifted forward by helicopter to Walsh's position and then advance on foot. However, the weather conditions were not clear enough to allow the helicopter lift, and X Company were ordered to follow the same route as A Company. Nothing loath, they descended the escarpment and arrived at about 6.30 am, to be despatched towards their objective. The wadi appeared to be undefended. Meanwhile tribesmen could be seen hurrying back from their defences of the obvious route that 3 Para had not taken. At first X Company advanced without opposition. But as they moved beyond the cover of the C Company piquets on Jebel Haqla, they came under fire from La Adhab and the high ground above them which had not been piquetted. Altogether there were about fifty-sixty tribesmen with rifles and at least six automatic weapons. The company was pinned down in the open. At this point Farrar-Hockley and his Intelligence Officer, Lieutenant McLeod, flew forward in a Scout which had managed to get as far as battalion headquarters. Having been given the incorrect grid reference they overshot the leading troops of X Company and came under heavy fire. The helicopter juddered under the impact of the strike. McLeod was hit in the arm. The helicopter began to lose power but the pilot managed to keep it airborne long enough to land just forward of the leading commandos, who rushed out to cover the occupants as they hurriedly deplaned. Small arms fire continued to smack into the rocks and side of the wadi to where the second-in-command of X Company was being carried, badly wounded in the stomach.

Farrar-Hockley ordered A Company to move round on to high ground to the left of X Company, and C Company to push on beyond Jebel Haqla to get on to ground overlooking the enemy. Pike's platoon of A Company, attempting to make progress on the left of the wadi but well above the wadi floor, ran into fire from a very skilful and determined sniper on higher ground. He appeared to be moving round to a different fire position after each few shots, and most disconcertingly could not be located, let alone engaged by fire. As Pike paused on a rock, unwisely taking time to wipe his face with his khaki sweat rag, one round splashed the rock face by his right shoulder and another split the trunk of a thorn tree just in front of him. Captain Colley, the FOO with Walsh, brought down fire from two 5.5 medium guns of Imjin Battery, transferred to Thumier a few days earlier from the Far East, to assist the platoon forward. But this seemed to have little effect on the elusive tribesmen as the steep grain of the terrain made it impossible to see where most rounds landed, so successful adjustment to land the shells in the right place was very difficult. Hunters swooped in just above the wadi floor and blasted the enemy positions, the brass cannon-shell cases falling in streams from their wings, clattering and ringing among the rocks. A fine feat among the jagged peaks dominating the narrow wadi, this fire proved too much for the tribesmen, who withdrew. A and X Companies exploited forward. The casualties were one dead, a marine hit on the head by one of the empty cannon-shell cases from the Hunters, an indication of the closeness of their support, and seven wounded. Farrar-Hockley had been ordered to withdraw that night. However, before any withdrawal could take place the Scout had to be repaired and flown out, if possible. All night the REME fitters worked on the aircraft protected by two companies. At first light the pilot, Major Jackson, managed to get the Scout airborne, much to everyone's relief. Walsh remembers a faint cheer from paratroopers and marines echoing across the wadi as the helicopter lifted and flew away to safety. The prospect of staying in the wadi until the helicopter could be recovered, probably lifted out in pieces by a Belvedere, was not inviting.

3 Para withdrew back up Arnold's Spur on to the Bakri Ridge. From there they were flown by helicopter to Thumier. The battalion returned to Aden and subsequently

Bahrain. X Company remained on the Bakri Ridge until relieved by the FRA the following day. On 8 June, D Company 3 Para arrived in the Radfan and operated under the command of the Royal Scots. There were no major battles. So ended 3 Para's contribution to the campaign. Without the determination, initiative and resourcefulness of the battalion, particularly on the Bakri Ridge, the campaign would have taken a week longer to conclude. Farrar-Hockley was awarded a bar to his DSO. Some who took part find it hard to see why the battalion was ordered to descend into the Wadi Dhubsan. Nevertheless, having been ordered in they carried out the operation in style, as did X Company.

ADEN

Early in 1967, two Parachute Regiment officers dressed as private soldiers of the 3rd Battalion Royal Anglian Regiment accompanied a patrol from that battalion into the Arab town of Sheikh Othman in the state of Aden. The two officers observed the dominating position occupied by the old mission hospital on a bend in the road known as Grenade Corner, and the senior of the two, having come to the conclusion that to control the town soldiers must live in it permanently, took note of this building for future reference. Control Sheikh Othman they must, for it lay astride the road from Aden to Dhala; there were still operations in progress up country as well as a number of British political officers and their wives. As they clambered into the truck at the start of the patrol, the Royal Anglian company sergeant major did not lose the opportunity to give them a hard time, knowing perfectly well that they were Lieutenant Colonel Walsh and Major Starling, the commanding officer and second-in-command of 1 Para!

Their battalion took over the area on 25 May 1967.

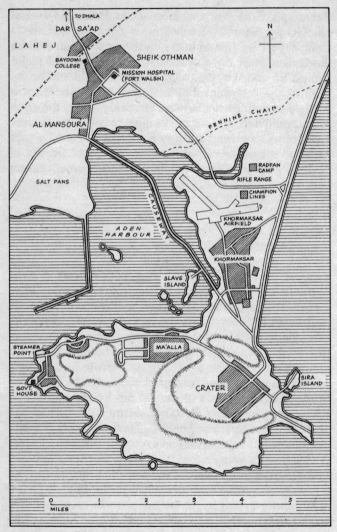

Aden, 1967.

The situation in Aden and South Arabia had changed considerably since Walsh led A Company 3 Para down the escarpment into the Wadi Dhubsan, exactly three years to the day before. The battles the battalion were to fight were different. Urban terrorists were the enemy, the battleground a squalid Arab town on the flat dusty plain north of the drowned volcano crater and stinking salt pans of Aden harbour. And the political scene had also changed. Until early 1966 the British government had always said that they intended maintaining base facilities in Aden and honouring defence treaties with states in the Federation, even after independence which they anticipated granting in 1968. During the year before the battalion arrived, the British government, Labour since late 1964, had pulled the rug out from under the Federal Government of what was now called South Arabia. In February 1966 the Defence White Paper announced: 'South Arabia is due to become independent by 1968, and we do not think it appropriate that we should maintain defence facilities after that happens. We therefore intend to withdraw our forces from the Aden base at that time.' Britain would also abrogate her defence treaties with the Federation. This came as a bombshell to the rulers. They had reluctantly agreed to the Federation in return for assurances that Britain would continue to defend the Federation after independence. They were now to be left to their fate, labelled British stooges, with 60–70,000 Egyptian troops in the Yemen. From this moment the people of South Arabia, townsmen and tribesmen alike, whether originally hostile or not, had no incentive to co-operate with the British in a smooth transfer of power. Nasser made it very clear what fate awaited anyone who collaborated with the British. To underline his point a number of so called traitors were executed. Nasser and the nationalists in South Arabia had been delighted and surprised by the British announcement. Nasser had been on the point of withdrawing from the Yemen, but now proclaimed that his troops would remain for five years.

The British government was given a practical lesson in the futility of negotiating from a position of weakness. The incidence of terrorism in Aden and guerrilla warfare in the mountains rose immediately. There were two nationalist organizations opposed to the Federation: the Front for the Liberation Of Southern Yemen (FLOSY) and the National Liberation Front (NLF). FLOSY's power base was in Aden itself, the trade unions and the Yemenis in Aden, and it was supported by Egypt. The NLF had broken away from FLOSY four months before 1 Para arrived and was supported mainly by the mountain tribes. Egypt withdrew support from the NLF soon after the break with FLOSY. Both organizations fought bitterly against each other to gain power in readiness for the day the British left. They also carried out attacks on British soldiers and civilians.

In July the Federation was given another example of the spinelessness of which Britain was capable in the swinging sixties. Two MIG fighters from the Yemen attacked a small town in the state of Beihan, injuring four tribesmen and damaging a number of houses. The Emir, with the full support of the Federal Government, demanded action by Britain under the terms of the defence treaty. To their consternation Britain refused and referred the matter to the United Nations. The outcome surprised no one, least of all the rulers of the Federation. The UN, having debated the matter for two weeks, including hearing a submission from the Yemeni delegate that the Beihanis had been seeing unidentified flying objects, asked the Secretary General to settle the dispute: in effect do nothing. The message to the rulers was clear. Britain was not to be trusted ever again.

In company with all other British units in Aden and the rest of South Arabia, 1 Para found themselves keeping the peace in a country that had been thoroughly stirred up by decisions emanating from Westminster, and within nine months would be abandoned by the government who were largely responsible for the mess. In the process the soldiers stood a good chance of being killed or wounded. Fortunately for the government, soldiers, British soldiers at any rate, do not contemplate dying for politicians of any party. They fight and die for each other; to see the job through; in order not to let down their comrades, their battalion, their regiment. It was in this spirit that 1 Para set about their task.

Walsh said goodbye to the commanding officer of 3 Royal Anglian at Khormaksar airport. As he drove back to Radfan Camp just north of the airfield perimeter he received a radio message to say that the general strike called by the Aden TUC the next day was going ahead. His battalion had been flown from England twenty-four hours before, straight into the heat and humidity of an Aden summer. By 10 am they had killed their first sniper as he stupidly changed his position. Fitness and training paid off as they patrolled and manned check-points and observation posts. The strike was fairly low-key compared with what followed. The first and greatest test came on 1 June with another general strike, called this time by the terrorist organizations.

Walsh recalls:

At 0200 hours I deployed D Company with, under command, a platoon of C Company, into the heart of Sheikh Othman. This force under the command of Major Brierley was to occupy eight observation posts including the main police station. These observation posts (OPs) provided good positions from which to dominate the main thoroughfares, the principal mosque, which was the centre of previous disturbances, and the main route to the north. By 05.00

hours all was ready for what proved to be the most
violent strike day ever experienced in Aden. The first
incident occurred when a patrol was grenaded outside
the main mosque. Fire was returned immediately
from one of our OPs in the Eastern Bank building,
killing two men running into the mosque and a third
who had taken refuge behind a plate glass window.
In the meantime the patrol captured a fourth member
of the grenade party before returning to the police
station. A good start.

This incident appeared to be the signal for battle
to be joined, because immediately all OPs were
engaged by accurate and sustained fire, in some cases
from as close as fifty yards across the roof-tops. This
fire fight went on continuously for nearly five hours,
and in the course of it one of our GPMG gunners
was killed by a sniper firing from close range, and
one man was wounded. Two troops of armoured cars
patrolled the streets and engaged targets indicated to
them by tracer fire from the OPs.

At 11.00 hours the main mosque began to broad-
cast what appeared to be instructions to the terrorists
to change positions, since a lull in the battle followed
for about twenty minutes. This was the moment
which changed the course of the battle because it
gave the company commander the chance to gain the
initiative. All OPs were ordered to fire short bursts
into all identified terrorist positions and into other
likely roof-top positions and this had a marked effect
on the terrorists, who were now forced to use positions up to 300 yards away from our own OPs. The
next round of the battle started at about 11.20 hours,
and by midday it was clear that one of the OPs was
untenable. Two patrols and armoured cars went to
cover its evacuation, which in spite of heavy fire was
achieved at the cost of only one man wounded in the

foot. The fire fight continued for the rest of the day, and it was then that the long training in battle shooting paid off. Most targets were necessarily of a fleeting nature, but the men of the company shot well – and many of the terrorist positions were silenced, one after the other, by accurate fire.

Just before last light the terrorists managed to lob a Russian grenade into an OP. It was a very relieved company commander who heard Corporal Tanner, commanding the OP, report laconically: 'We have just been grenaded, no casualties, just one or two headaches.' This grenade was accompanied by sustained fire from close range which was neutralized by the combined fire of the OPs and the armoured cars of C Squadron Queens Dragoon Guards, commanded by Major Morton, who gave us continuous and excellent support throughout the battle.

The shortage of ammunition became critical during the later stages of the afternoon, and in the police station GPMG belts had to be made up from individual bandoliers to keep the guns in action. My second-in-command quickly organized a resupply operation, which was bravely and successfully carried out by a party under the Intelligence Officer, and by 18.00 hours all positions and OPs had been replenished with ammunition and water. Firing died down a good deal after dark and by 21.00 hours all was quiet. I ordered Major Brierley, who had shown great skill and leadership throughout that long day, to withdraw under cover of darkness. They were relieved by C Company Headquarters, plus a platoon to occupy the police station. The withdrawal was carried out by an armoured troop carrier at 03.00 hours and a very tired but triumphant company group returned to Radfan Camp. The total terrorist casualties were eight killed and five captured, three of whom were wounded. These were of course the verified casualties. Many more had been inflicted but they were not recovered and could not therefore be classed as confirmed. There is no doubt, as the evidence later made clear, that the terrorist aim that day was to take over Sheikh Othman and to force us to abandon our positions in the town.

1 Para had lost one killed and four wounded during this action, on what came to be known in the battalion as the Glorious First of June. Few people, except those involved, appreciated what a general strike in Aden meant; open insurrection. Even so, the soldiers still had to remember that it was not war. They were not in Aden to kill as many Arabs as they could but to maintain law and order. The principle of minimum force always held good.

Early in June the Israelis, after destroying the Egyptian air force, defeated the Egyptians and their allies in the lightning Six Day War. It was to have severe repercussions in Aden. On 20 June the town of Crater on the Aden peninsula was lost to British control for two weeks. As early as 5 June, however, Walsh, hearing the news of Israel's invasion of Egypt, was determined that Sheikh Othman would not be lost. At an O Group called at ten minutes notice he gave orders to put into effect the plan he had been nurturing for some time: to occupy the town in strength, permanently, and move in his tactical headquarters so that he was on hand when trouble brewed. This would secure the main road to Dhala and to the north, dominate Sheikh Othman, and minimize the administrative traffic to and from Radfan Camp. Walsh also decided to cut down on the number of OPs which were costly in logistic effort and unwieldy to control. He ordered a company and his tactical headquarters into the unoccupied Church of Scotland mission hospital which he had spotted on his reconnaissance months earlier, and another

company onto the roof of the Bayoomi College, the latter
to replace the very exposed position occupied by Check-
point Golf on the road leading out of Sheikh Othman
to Dhala. Walsh again:

> Opinion had been sought as to the reaction if the
> mission hospital were occupied by security forces,
> but since the General Assembly of the Church of
> Scotland had ended its annual meeting a week before
> and extraordinary meetings are very rare, it was
> decided to brave a possible condemnatory resolution
> in June 1968 and press on!

C Company was already sitting in the transport ready
to go in to Sheikh Othman to man OPs and checkpoints.
In half an hour the orders were changed and they set out
to occupy the mission hospital. Early in the afternoon the
hospital came under fire from roof-top positions in the
town. All that night everybody in 1 Para in Radfan Camp
who was not on duty turned to and filled sandbags, which
were rushed up to the hospital in trucks. By dawn the last
sandbag, or so they thought, was in position and the mission hospital, occupied by a company and battalion headquarters and christened Fort Walsh, was ready for
anything.

On the morning of 20 June Walsh had worries in
addition to the task in Sheikh Othman when the battalion's
base in Radfan Camp came under fire from supposed
allies, the South Arabian Police in Champion Lines next
door. The seeds of trouble lay in a protest four days earlier
by a group of senior officers of the South Arabian Army
(SAA), as the combined FRA and FNG was now called.
The officers were suspended from duty. After some unrest
in the SAA, which was put down by the Arab officers, a
group of SAA apprentices rioted in sympathy with the four
suspended officers. Inter-tribal disturbances erupted and
an attack was made on the Officers' Mess and Guardroom

in the SAA lines. Shots were fired and some buildings were burned. Again Arab officers and NCOs restored order without any assistance from the British. However, the police in Champion Lines, hearing shooting and immediately assuming that the British were firing on their fellow-countrymen, mutinied, seized weapons and manned the perimeter wall of their camp. As they did so a British truck drove towards the camp carrying nineteen men of the Royal Corps of Transport returning from a morning on the nearby ranges. They were totally relaxed. Champion Lines was friendly territory. At about 100 yards the police opened fire on the truck, killing eight British soldiers and wounding eight others. The police then fired on two passing cars, killing two Adeni policemen and a British Public Works Department (PWD) civilian and wounding another PWD employee. The police then directed their fire onto Radfan Camp, killing 2/Lt Young, The Lancashire Regiment, whose 1st Battalion shared the camp with 1 Para.

The Federal government quickly asked for British troops to restore law and order. The stand-by company in Radfan Camp that day was C Company 1st Battalion Kings Own Border Regiment, under Walsh's command. He was placed in the difficult position of having to order men from another battalion to carry out the task. Major Miller, commanding C Company, with a troop of armoured cars, was told to secure the guardroom and armoury in Champion Lines but not to open fire unless absolutely necessary. News that British troops were firing on Arab forces might lead to attacks on British civilians. In the past mere rumour had been enough, and so it was to prove in the future. Very courageously, Miller drove with his company in open trucks straight into Champion Lines. They soon came under fire which killed the machine gunner in the leading truck and wounded eight men. They did not return the fire. Eventually they managed to restore order in the camp, but not before they had been subjected to more rifle and machine gun fire which wounded four men of a scratch force of 1 Para who had come to their assistance. At no time did the British force fire at the Arabs. It speaks volumes for the standard of training and discipline that young officers, NCOs and soldiers who had seen their comrades gunned down should refrain from replying in kind. The South Arabian forces were greatly impressed.

However, once again rumour that the British were firing on the Arab forces was to lead to another display of trigger-happy behaviour, this time by the armed police in Crater. Having mutinied, they eventually killed thirteen British officers and soldiers, wounding others in addition. Control of Crater passed to the mutineers and the terrorists. It had been a bad day for the British. They suffered twenty-two killed and thirty-one wounded by men who were supposed to be their comrades. The 1st Battalion the Argyll and Sutherland Highlanders re-occupied Crater on the night of 3 July, advancing with their pipes playing the regimental charge 'Monymusk.' They had been preceded some time earlier by Brigadier Dunbar conducting a personal reconnaissance in a Land Rover, a courageous act which attracted no comment in the press, unlike the highly publicized operation by the Argylls. Dunbar had served with 8 Para in Normandy and at the Rhine Crossing and was Butler's Brigade Major at Suez.

1 Para remained in Sheikh Othman for four months and were involved in nearly 800 incidents. Walsh:

A number of attempts, including rolling a Dambuster charge against the base of our OP in the police station tower, were made to dislodge us from our positions, and every 'happy hour' would bring its shower of mortar bombs, blindicides and grenades. To retain our initiative we constantly changed our tactics, patrol programmes and modus operandi.

The police station tower, which was a constant target, was eventually protected by a wire screen which, rather like a square mushroom, was lowered over the top by helicopter, brilliantly flown by the Army Air Corps. Luckily the local Arab gunmen were not out of bed that early in the morning! The wire detonated the fuses of the blindicides before they struck the walls, and deflected other missiles. The whole idea was Major Starling's, the battalion second-in-command. It must have saved many lives. On 6 September the battalion was treated to the sight of the NLF and FLOSY fighting each other in Sheikh Othman. The fighting continued until 11 September, reaching its climax on 10 September when 1,000 Yemenis arrived to take a hand on the side of FLOSY. Many innocent civilians died as well as terrorists. The SAA now decided to intervene and managed to get both sides to agree to a truce. In the aftermath of the fighting in Sheikh Othman, it was decided to bring forward the handover of the town to the SAA. This was accomplished on the night of 23/24 September. 1 Para retired to a defensive position on a line across the top of the Aden Peninsula known as the Pennine Chain. It was so positioned that Khormaksar, from which most of the troops would be withdrawn, was out of small arms range but not mortar range, from terrorists in the north. So seriously was the threat taken that Walsh had twelve mortar and ten artillery defensive fire tasks registered around his perimeter; in the event they were not fired.

On 6 November the SAA finally came off the fence and declared for the NLF, but not before a last bloody factional battle in Sheikh Othman. The final withdrawal, to be covered by 42 RM Commando, was set for 29 November. Forty-eight hours before, 1 Para handed over their positions to 42 Commando and, determined to leave with their tails high, marched in column of eights through the wire of Radfan Camp, cut for the purpose, straight across the sand, down the main runway of Khormaksar airfield, and emplaned for Bahrain. They were taking no chances for their weapons were not unloaded nor magazines emptied until their Hercules aircraft arrived in Bahrain, where they transferred across to RAF VC10s for the onward flight to England.

CHAPTER 13

Confrontation in Borneo

In early 1964, Number One (Guards) Independent Company, the Parachute Regiment, on monotonous and frustrating internal security duties in Cyprus, were ordered to train for special operations. The SAS urgently required another squadron in Borneo. The increasing strength of Indonesian incursions into East Malaysia, added to commitments in the Middle East, was over-stretching their resources. The Guards Parachute Company was selected to reinforce them. The success of SAS operations lay in surprise through stealth by patrols of four men. In addition to his soldiering skills, each member of a patrol was trained as a medic, a signaller, a demolition expert, or in the local language. The Guards Company was returned to the United Kingdom and split up to be trained in these skills. After two months they were flown to Malaya for a special jungle warfare course run by the SAS. A final ten-day exercise, operational go-ahead by the SAS, and the company was off to East Malaysia and the island of Borneo.

Kalimantan, part of the Republic of Indonesia, forms about three-quarters of the huge island of Borneo; the remainder consists of East Malaysia and the Sultanate of Brunei. Sukarno, President of Indonesia since independence from the Dutch in 1949, had long dreamt of bringing Malaya, Brunei, Singapore and the British Borneo colonies into a Greater Indonesia. His first attempt at doing so by force was in Brunei in December 1962. At this stage the Federation of Malaysia was merely a gleam in the eye of Tunku Abdul Rahman, the Prime Minister of

Malaya. He realized that only by joining together Malaya, Brunei and the British colonies of Sabah and Sarawak could he hope to resist Sukarno's expansionist schemes. From mid-1961, under the Tunku's guiding hand and with full support from the British, the concept of federation looked increasingly likely. However, the Sultan of Brunei was not convinced that joining the Federation was in his interest, and Sukarno seized the opportunity to make trouble. On 8 December 1962 pro-Sukarno dissidents calling themselves the North Kalimantan National Army rebelled against the Sultan, who asked for British assistance. By 16 December, after some minor skirmishes, most of Brunei was clear of dissidents, although it took until May 1963 to clear the last pockets of rebels. While mopping-up operations were in progress Sukarno announced a policy of confrontation towards Malaya 'because they represent themselves as accomplices of neo-colonialist and neo-imperialist forces pursuing a policy hostile towards Indonesia.' At the same time, groups of volunteers began to cross the border into Sabah and Sarawak, carrying out acts of sabotage and attempting to subvert the inhabitants. On 16 September 1963 the Federation of Malaysia came into existence, without Brunei but, until 1965, including Singapore. Sukarno immediately broke off diplomatic relations with Malaysia. The number of incursions by company-sized bands of Indonesian irregulars increased until in early 1964 the Indonesian army took control of operations.

In East Malaysia, the British, Malaysian and other Commonwealth forces faced a major problem. Borneo is in the centre of the Indonesian archipelago and there are several small Indonesian islands between the Commonwealth main base at Singapore and the main ports in East Malaysia. The terrain along the 900-mile-long border with Kalimantan, like all of Borneo, is one of the most inhospitable in the world. Except for patches of cultivation, and extensive mangrove swamps, the island consists of huge mountain ranges, deep valleys and rolling plateaus covered with dense tropical rain forest interspersed by large and frequently fast-flowing rivers. The latter sometimes provide a means of movement by boat, but just as often they are an obstacle to movement. Even if their course is more or less in the desired direction of travel, rapids and falls, except near the sea, can make all but the shortest boat journey a considerable undertaking. There were, in the mid-1960s, few roads outside the towns and larger villages, almost all on the coast. A few logging tracks penetrated a little way inland in areas where timber was being felled. In the steamy heat, trudging up and slithering down the sometimes near vertical hillsides, often through thick secondary growth, heavily-laden soldiers could take several hours to cover even a mile. Leeches and leptospirosis in the rivers and streams and scrub typhus ticks in the few drier areas added to the natural discomfort and dangers of the patrolling soldier, without taking into account what the enemy might do.

The troops were based in a series of jungle forts at intervals along the border and usually a few miles back. These were not intended to form a stop line to incursions but acted as a base from which troops patrolled and sortied to ambush and harry the Indonesians. A fort occupied by a company or platoon was usually sited on high ground. The defences included barbed wire and punjis, pointed bamboo stakes. Trenches and bunkers were dug, and most bases had at least one 3-inch mortar or a 105mm pack howitzer. The jungle forts were supplied by helicopter, or in the case of the bigger, more far-flung ones, by air-drop from Beverley and Argosy aircraft, or by Twin Pioneers which could cope with very short strips. Everything came in by air, from sand-bags to live chickens in crates. Somebody had the idea of saving parachutes and packing by throwing the chickens out to fly down under their own power, but as they could not be briefed on the correct LZ this method was discontinued! Life in the dank musty bunkers, sometimes infested with rats and snakes, was boring for the soldiers left behind to defend them while the remainder were out on patrol, and it was not long before they were looking forward to their turn to go out 'jungle bashing'. Except for their one week of rest and relaxation (R&R) in Singapore, and perhaps a few days in the battalion base, soldiers usually spent the whole of their six-month tour in these jungle forts or out on patrol. A typical routine would be eight to twelve days on patrol and four days defending the fort; one platoon would be in while the rest of the company was out. Time in the fort not on sentry duty would be spent cleaning up after the last patrol, washing and shaving off beards (shaving cream and soap give off a distinctive smell easily detected by sharp-nosed enemy soldiers). Jungle boots would rot after a few days on patrol and thorns tore the sweat-soaked jungle-greens. Rotting and torn clothing and equipment would be exchanged for new, and preparations made for the next sortie, including the endless search for means of cutting down weight. Toothbrushes were cut in half, rations sifted, repacked, and only the bare minimum taken. The more experienced the soldier, the fewer creature comforts he took.

Patrols sometimes walked direct from their jungle fort to their task, returning on foot. On other occasions they would be taken some of the way by helicopter. This saved time and energy but in some situations there was a risk that the clattering helicopter would reveal the patrol's location to a watching Indonesian. So, as a rule of thumb, patrols were usually landed at least one valley away from their objective. Unless they were landed into another base, a village or on one of the rare open patches such as a dry river bed, the only way of getting down through the jungle canopy was by roping down from the helicopter as it

hovered overhead. A pick-up by helicopter often necessi-
tated cutting sufficient space for it to descend. Explosives,
special hand saws and sometimes buzz-saws were lowered
through the 100 foot jungle canopy from a helicopter, and
soldiers became adept at the rapid clearance of helicopter
landing points for extraction of patrols and casualty evacuation. Patrolling was always punishing, mentally and physically. Contacts were usually fleeting and unexpected, and
often followed weeks, sometimes months, of slogging
through the jungle. Following a track could be fraught
with danger, leading straight into an ambush or onto a
mine. Movement off tracks might be as slow as 200 yards
an hour. Well before dark, the patrol would stop and move
away from its route in the hope of throwing any following
enemy off their trail. After posting sentries and erecting
poncho shelters, a cold meal would be eaten; the smell of
cooking would give away the patrol's position. A patrol
might have to be sent out to collect water, perversely often
quite hard to find in this rain-soaked forest. Basing up
close by water was an invitation to be attacked, and therefore avoided. Having collected water, it had to be filtered
through a Millbank bag and then sterilized with tablets
before drinking, a time-consuming process. Just before
dark came another ritual; the anointing of all exposed skin,
including the scalp under the thickest hair and under
rolled-down sleeves, with insect repellent, and taking the
daily dose of paludrine. The jungle nights were twelve
hours. Even the most exhausted men could not sleep for
that long. In most of Borneo, except close to the coast,
the nights were cold, and even in sleeping bags, they
shivered in their clammy, wet clothing. Preparing men to
fight in the jungle was a matter of inuring them to the
discomfort and training them to cope with the environment, so that operating in it became second nature. They
had to conquer the tendency to allow survival to assume
greater importance than finding and dealing with the

enemy. With the successful campaign in Malaya only four years past, there was a wealth of experience to draw on when facing the considerably more difficult terrain and circumstances of Borneo. The highly-motivated all-volunteer British and Gurkha soldiers rapidly became peerless jungle fighters. Operations in Borneo were well-planned, subtle and executed with finesse.

The Indonesians also established bases near the border, from which they sortied to raid the Commonwealth bases. Eventually the British government agreed to cross-border operations by British and Gurkha troops. They were usually carried out by a force of at least company strength and against Indonesian bases which had been located and well reconnoitred by either SAS or reconnaissance patrols from the battalion tasked with the attack. In this way the Indonesians could be forced to pull their bases back, making their incursions more difficult.

It was to this scene that the Guards Parachute Company came in June 1964. Their area was one of the wildest in Borneo, 300 miles of the border in the Third Division of Sarawak, their task physically and intellectually more demanding than that of most troops in the campaign. The sole means of communication overland was by river. Along the banks were the longhouses of Ibans, Kenyans, Ukits and Punans, all with their own customs and languages. The border was an arbitrary line drawn on a map. It was meant to divide the headwaters of the rivers that ran north to the South China Sea and those running south to Kalimantan. Broken ridges separating these watersheds rose in places to well over 10,000 feet, a fact that could not be deduced from the maps at the time, which were without contours in much of the border area. The company had the task of covering the huge tract of country with just sixteen patrols. Fortunately, although the enemy was stronger numerically, he had a total lack of air superiority and could not therefore use helicopters across the border. To mount an incursion he had to get his troops to the border on his side, frequently over great distances, then to the target and out again. He often did this by river. It was possible, therefore, to whittle down the options open to the Indonesians and allocate twelve patrols to the likely crossing places, leaving four patrols for 'hearts and minds' tasks in the longhouses, the secondary mission of the company.

The four-man patrols were inserted by helicopter into the border areas. For some, the next four and a half months meant a varied life travelling between the scattered longhouses where the medics and linguists practised their skills. For the majority, the whole period was broken only by the seven day R&R, with no company other than their own patrol. The daily routine: sweating all day through the rain forest, siting ambushes, blasting and cutting helicopter landing sites, mapping the unknown, and coping with the difficulties of radio contact at up to 250 miles.

Initially patrols were located according to the temperament of the patrol leader. For example, Ulu Aput boat station, a likely trouble spot, was given to Captain Brooke, Irish Guards. Punan Busang, the most primitive and interesting, went to Captain Cluff, Grenadier Guards, an officer whose unorthodox approach to military matters seemed to appeal more to his subordinates than his superiors. They all had to have confidence in the ability of the base staff to receive and read the weakest radio signal and react on it immediately; the support and expertise of 845 Naval Helicopter Squadron; and the safe arrival of fourteen days re-supply every fortnight.

By August 1964, Sukarno abandoned the pretence that the invasion parties were guerillas and freedom fighters; they were almost always well-trained regulars. Some Gurkha officers who had fought in Burma were of the opinion that they were in some respects equal in skill and determination, if not in fanaticism, to the Japanese. Not everybody agreed with this assessment. The company did so well in gaining the confidence of the SAS that in the last five weeks of the tour they were allowed three missions across the border into Kalimantan. The first two were named after the patrol commanders' girlfriends, the third, Annabels, the intended destination of at least some of the officers of the company on their return to England!

The undeclared war went on through 1964, but towards the end of that year Sukarno threatened to escalate by outright invasion of East and West Malaysia. He had a large army of 400,000 men, a Navy and an Air Force equipped with MIGs and other Russian aircraft. Reinforcements were required in Borneo. Among them were 2 Para, commanded by Lieutenant Colonel Eberhardie, and the Guards Para Company. 2 Para were recalled from Christmas leave and despatched to the Jungle Warfare School in Johore Bahru in West Malaysia. C Company were converted into a special patrol company to assist the SAS, the Guards Company and the Gurkha Para Company in long-range patrolling, particularly in cross-border operations. All these companies operated directly under command of the Director of Operations, so C Company was removed from Eberhardie's command for the period of the Borneo tour.

In March 1965, 2 Para arrived in Borneo and were flown by helicopter to their bases to relieve the 1st Battalion Argyll and Sutherland Highlanders. Eberhardie had thought long and hard about the task that lay ahead. His experience in Java as Darling's intelligence officer had given him an insight into the capabilities of the Javanese, reckoned by some to be Sukarno's best troops. Eberhardie did not rate them highly, but did not fall into the trap of underestimating them either. He believed, however, that the tactics being taught by the Jungle Warfare School, effective though they were against a guerrilla enemy such as the communist terrorists in Malaya between 1950 and

1958, were not always appropriate when faced by a well-equipped regular army operating from behind its own frontier. In his view the intelligence gathering methods used in the Malayan emergency and taught at the Jungle Warfare School were not appropriate in Borneo. Army-Police Special Branch co-operation had its place, but the movement of enemy sub-units who, unlike guerrillas, did not rely on the local population for logistic support, could only be plotted in the dense jungle by the eyes, ears and noses of patrolling soldiers. To cover the huge tactical area of operations needed large numbers of patrols. But because the Indonesians tended to sortie in company groups, the response by most units was to send out patrols of at least platoon strength. Platoons in the jungle made more noise than a small patrol but, more important, covered less ground and were, therefore, wasteful of resources.

Experience in Korea had also coloured his views, particularly on artillery and communications, and his battalion was already well trained in their use. He considered that more emphasis should be placed on the devastating effect of air-burst shells fired into the jungle from the 105mm guns in company bases, the flexibility conferred by helicopters, and the vastly improved radio communications which enabled helicopters and artillery to realize their potential. Eberhardie taught his battalion that patrols no longer had to rely on their own firepower; help and, if necessary, reinforcements were there for the asking provided the radio worked, and God help anyone who stood around wringing his hands if it did not. The message could be got through by moving to a better position, by relaying through another net; there was nearly always a way. Because the battalion was trained to operate in this way and the Indonesians were, in his experience, a third-rate enemy, he would ignore the current teaching and cover his tactical area of operations with small patrols. When the Indonesians and their intended routes were found, Eberhardie would concentrate his patrols into company-sized forces by using the helicopters and radio and, backed by artillery and mortar fire, destroy the enemy. To achieve the intensity he required, patrols were out for ten days at a time and spent the minimum time in base. To keep up the standards of battle shooting, early in the tour, a platoon at a time was brought back to battalion headquarters, where they underwent training with live ammunition down jungle battle lanes designed to Eberhardie's specification.

In formulating his tactics he exploited the special characteristics of the British parachute soldier: his intelligence, toughness, and capability for operations in small groups. To avoid the need for helicopter resupply, which could compromise the patrol's position, men were expected to exist for ten days on what they could carry. Large packs slowed progress through the jungle and made roping down from helicopters unacceptably tardy. So the battalion devised a belt-order on which everything was carried. The medical officer worked out that the soldiers could exist on about 900 calories per day for ten days; losing about one pound of body weight each day but putting it back in the base. There was much experimenting during training with what provided the best ration. Dried octopus was not a success; cheese was deemed the best. There was an added advantage to this policy; hungry soldiers and animals have a keen sense of smell. A hunting soldier, with his hand cupped in front of his nose, scanning the jungle like a radar dish, could smell an opened can of food in the hot enclosed air of the jungle at fifty paces, let alone the stench of ten sweating men lying in ambush ahead.

Because there were not enough Iban trackers to provide one with each patrol, Eberhardie decided that each section would have two men trained in the art. The battalion was fortunate that the Education Officer, Captain Woods, a

New Zealander, was an expert tracker and jungle scout and helped train the tracker teams. In every patrol the point man scanned with his eyes, number two with hands cupped to his ears, and number three was the sniffer.

Eberhardie banned alcohol throughout the battalion for the whole tour. Soldiers back in base, half-starved from the rigorous diet, would soon succumb to drink and he did not want them facing an attack with fuddled heads. This policy was seized on by one of the tabloids in Britain, who castigated him for denying the lads their beer. The lads were well aware of the reason, and supported their commanding officer wholeheartedly. However, the incident was used by the army headquarters in Singapore to try to reel in Eberhardie, who had aroused their ire by propounding heretical ideas about jungle soldiering. They ordered him to issue beer or relinquish command. The tabloid printed a snivelling article taking the credit for restoring beer to the troops. Curiously, or perhaps not so curiously, neither the Jungle Warfare School, who might have taken exception to his divergence of opinion on some key matters, nor many of his fellow battalion commanders shared the jaundiced views of Eberhardie's tactics held by the staff of the army headquarters. He had the full support of his brigade commander and, indeed others adopted many of his tactical ploys, either by coming to the same conclusion independently, or by imitation. This undermining of a commanding officer engaged on operations by the commander and staff in Singapore was a curious way to go about winning a campaign.

B Company was based at Plaman Mapu. The fort, on a pimple in a valley, located near a village, was not well sited for defence. It was 1,000 metres from the border ridge which overlooked the position. In daylight every movement was plain to watchers. Minimum activity was the rule and usually patrols went in and out only by night. Eberhardie wanted to resite this base, but the construction of a replacement would have tied up men and helicopters and taken considerable time. B Company did what they could to improve the defences thickening the panji stick belt, laying claymore mines, cutting fields of fire, and improving the bunkers. There were two 3-inch mortars in the base, and 105mm pack howitzers in an adjacent base at Gunong Gajak, had registered defensive fire tasks on and around Plaman Mapu. The base's defence sectors were divided like a circular pie cut in three slices. At night each sector manned its GPMG on a tripod while the remainder slept in dug-outs in the communication trenches. Everyone slept with boots on, weapon and belt-order at hand. They were allowed to take off their shirts, the only concession to the heat in the airless dug-outs. A mosquito net and repellent warded off the worst of the insects but did not discourage the rats.

It soon became apparent that Plaman Mapu was under close surveillance. Patrols and observers reported a chain of enemy OPs sited on top of the horizon ridge. Enemy patrols had also been sniffing around the base. Marks found on the ground where one patrol had halted were measured by the Intelligence Officer, Captain Conn, and assessed as being made by the bipod of a Russian RPG rocket launcher. Eberhardie sent Major Hodgson, his second-in-command, to work out how he would attack the base, and adjust the defensive fire tasks of the mortars in the base and guns in the adjacent base.

When the battalion left for Borneo they had been reinforced by a platoon of young soldiers, without completing training, straight from the depot. Eberhardie decided to send them to B company as a platoon rather than distributing them around the battalion. It was this platoon and company headquarters that were in residence early on the morning of 27 April. Their platoon commander, Lieutenant Barton, was away on the battalion jungle warfare course and they were temporarily under the command

of Captain Thompson of Support Company. In addition
to this platoon, Captain Fleming the company commander,
Captain Webb the FOO, CSM Williams, the company
colour sergeant, two cooks, the mortar crews and the radio
operators made up the garrison of thirty-four men.
Because of the indications of forthcoming trouble, everyone was on his toes. At 4.45 am, in pitch dark and a
tropical downpour, without any previous sightings of
enemy that night, the base was subjected to a bombardment by mortars and guns. Massed RPG rocket launchers
fired at the GPMG position nearest to the Indonesian
break-in position. Everybody stood-to. CSM Williams
rushed out, weapon in hand, belt-order on, bare to the
waist to ensure that the whole company were manning
their positions. As he ran towards the GPMG position he
met Private Kelly, who had taken two bullets along the
side of his scalp and was rushing about, disorientated,
pistol in hand, ready to repel the enemy. He stuck his
pistol in Williams's stomach, who knocked it aside, calmed
him down and took him to the company command post.
The company commander was speaking on the radio to
Eberhardie – as coolly as if he was taking part in an
interesting exercise.

As Williams emerged from the command post the first
of three assaults came in, heralded by the explosions of
Bangalore torpedoes, cutting lanes in the wire, panjis and
mines. The assault succeeded in taking part of the position, including one mortar. There was considerable confusion. Williams, who was the senior man above ground,
tried to bring order out of chaos while Captain Webb
called for supporting fire from Gunong Gajak. Williams
realized he must eject the Indonesians from the base while
they paused. He shouted to Thompson to bring over a
section and follow him. At that moment two mortar bombs
landed in the middle of the section, wounding several,
including Thompson. No sooner had Williams shouted to

the cook corporal to put up a 2-inch mortar illumination flare than his position was promptly hit by an enemy mortar. Williams next shouted across to Corporal Baughan, the acting platoon sergeant of the recruit platoon, to take the remaining section and attack one flank of the enemy. He ran across to the GPMG on the other flank, hit in the opening bombardment. He clipped two belts of ammunition onto the half belt already on the gun, pulled it off the tripod, and thinking 'this is it, this is the end of the story anyway, so I'll give them a little bit of rapid fire,' stood firing from the hip to give Baughan covering fire for his assault. As soon as he opened up the enemy retaliated and several came straight up the hill at him. He continued firing and the assault withered away, the nearest enemy falling dead two yards in front of him. Supported by Private Murtagh firing another GPMG, Baughan's section and Williams' linked up and cleared the position.

Williams went round the base repositioning men to ensure the whole perimeter was covered and resupplying the soldiers with ammunition. Having briefed the company commander and learned that Eberhardie was planning a helicopter lift at first light to cut off the Indonesians from the border, he was helping a wounded man down to the command post when the second assault started, preceded by supporting fire and Bangalore torpedoes. By this time the defenders had identified the axis of the attacks and the 105 howitzers in Gunong Gajak did sterling work. Sergeant McDonald manned the remaining mortar, firing it straight up into the air so that bombs fell only thirty metres away. Williams brought in another GPMG to fire on the killing ground. A combination of devastating fire from the two GPMGs and well-controlled rifle fire from the section under Baughan repulsed the second attack. After another quick dash round by Williams to re-supply ammunition and encourage the soldiers, a third attack materialized. It was not pushed home with the vigour of the preceding two. By now it was 5.45 am and there was a hint of dawn in the offing. It seemed that the enemy had had enough. It is a measure of the Indonesians' determination and training that they were able to find and fight their way up a small hill in total darkness and continuous pouring rain. Williams took out a patrol to clear round the perimeter. He killed the one Indonesian he found, thinking he was about to ambush the patrol. This man, and the Indonesian who had dropped two yards in front of him, were the only two they found. The latter had been wounded before the assault, for they found he had applied a first field dressing to his leg, but had bravely pressed on to be cut down by Williams. The only sign of the enemy was a wide trail heading towards the border, broken undergrowth, blood, discarded equipment and dressings. The blood trail was to persist, despite rain, for three days.

Williams returned to the base and seeing that the cook, although wounded, was making tea, ordered him to put half a gallon of rum into the brew. When the doctor arrived he took one look at Williams and ordered him to a casevac helicopter. He was hit by splinters on the side of his head, blinding him in one eye. He had bullet grazes down his skull, was deaf in one ear, and had shrapnel wounds caused by metal flying off his GPMG when hit by at least three bullets. He never regained the sight of the injured eye or the hearing in the damaged ear. He was awarded the DCM for his bravery and leadership that night.

Three platoons were sent by helicopter to rope down on likely withdrawal routes to cut off the Indonesian escape, or at least harass them as they withdrew, and two companies of Gurkhas were flown into the base to follow up the withdrawal and flush the enemy into the ambushes. But the Indonesians escaped. It is possible that the cut-offs were roped down too far behind the enemy, who found a way round them, and the flushing out took too long to mount. Maintaining contact in the jungle is as difficult as making it in the first place. It was early in the battalion's tour, and the first time Eberhardie's concept had been put into practice. A follow-up across the border would have been unwise without a detailed reconnaissance. Later it was learned that an Indonesian company was lying in wait across the border to ambush the follow-up. B Company lost two men killed and seven wounded. By examination of the area, piecing together intelligence, and reports of sightings by villagers, it was clear the Indonesians had mounted the operation with a regular para-commando battalion. One company had provided a firm base and counter-follow-up position on the Indonesian side of the border, one company had been the firm base for the actual assault which had been carried out by two companies, supported by eighteen Yugoslav rocket launchers, eight 50mm mortars and ten machine guns. The Indonesians were armed with excellent AK 47 assault rifles which fire in bursts, giving a heavy weight of fire. At first 2 Para were puzzled that they found so few bodies, particularly as the mortar and gun defensive fires had hit the enemy smack in the middle of the forming-up position, excellent forecasting by Hodgson. Intelligence was received that the para-command battalion had suffered about 300 casualties. The mystery was solved when Conn met an Indonesian para-commando officer on a course in England years later. He had taken part in the battle, and confirmed that half the battalion had become casualties, mainly from gun and mortar fire on the forming-up position. When they withdrew, the dead and seriously injured were tossed into the river which ran through the forming-up position towards the border. There had been some publicity about the arrival of 2 Para in Borneo, and the Indonesians had set about giving the battalion a bloody nose early on in the tour before they got into their stride; it backfired on them badly.

The Indonesians continued to show an interest in the Plaman Mapu area, and intelligence indicated a second, bigger attack in the offing. When it came, it was against a two-company base in the centre of the battalion's tactical area of operations (TAOR) commanded by Major Barnes. Again the guns and mortars took a heavy toll of the enemy. The helicopter reaction force made contact and harassed the Indonesians all the way to the border. Eberhardie and his battery commander controlled the guns and co-ordinated the operation from a helicopter. Although further contacts followed, the bases were never attacked again.

There were numerous patrol actions, but the last large helicopter assault was sparked off by patrol contacts, commanded by Corporals Tindale and Miller operating in the centre of the TAOR. They came upon a large Indonesian force, and several enemy were seen to fall in the ensuing fire fight. Eberhardie again took control of the helicopter operation, which followed much the same course as previously; a long chase to the border, punishing gun and mortar fire, and good work by the cut-offs. Corporal Tindale was awarded the MM.

On another occasion, following an ambush, information was received that seventy Indonesians had entered the village of Mujat. The villagers said that the enemy had not been after food or information. An ambush was assumed and Lieutenant Coxen led his platoon in, taking a small party of enemy by surprise and opening fire. One man was seen to fall, but the Indonesians got to him first and dragged him away. It was just too good to be true. Clearly the little party in the village was a come-on for a big ambush on the track outside. A follow-up team including an Iban tracker was flown in by helicopter. The tracker team followed the blood trail. The track divided into three; Sergeant Murray, following one with his team and two platoons, was led straight into an enemy ambush. But because he had wisely been following slightly off the track he found himself on the flank of the ambush. The enemy opened fire but caused only one casualty. The two platoons charged in and the enemy fled. The ambush had been manned by seventy men. The follow-up continued, and halted at night-fall. At moon-rise they took a chance and continued, the Iban tracker feeling for track marks with his hand until they came so close they could smell the enemy. The party stopped to wait for first light. Lying still in the dripping jungle, waiting for dawn which never seems to come, thirsty, hungry and apprehensive, requires training and discipline of the highest order. But when they picked up the trail again, the enemy had left. The trackers indicated that over 200 Indonesians had crossed the border.

A platoon ambushed an enemy party of fifty or so. As the enemy approached the ambush the platoon radio operator must have missed the 'enemy approaching' hand signal for he continued sending Morse. This could have alerted the enemy leading scout because he suddenly turned and loosed off a burst with his Armalite. The ambushers fired, killing about ten of the enemy. They fought back, and as the platoon were outnumbered they began a fighting withdrawal, the Indonesians on their tails. The platoon called for gunfire from base, but were out of radio contact. They managed to send a short message to a helicopter as it passed overhead, giving the enemy position and asking for artillery fire. Eventually the shells started falling and the platoon broke clear. This was 2 Para's last major contact in Borneo. Fighting the battle as it actually was, and not the one that existed in the minds of commanders and staffs 600 miles away, they had vindicated their commanding officer's tactics. By the standards that experienced soldiers set – high number of casualties inflicted on the enemy, the ratio of own to enemy casual-

ties, a low sick rate and virtually no disciplinary offences
– they were among the leaders throughout the campaign.

Meanwhile the Guards Parachute Company had also
been busy on a second tour. This time they were engaged
mainly on cross-border operations and watching likely
Indonesian incursion routes. Across the border the four-
man patrols sometimes operated in mutual support of each
other. On one occasion Sergeant McGill's patrol was
watching a dry river bed when eleven Indonesians came
round the corner. He and his supporting patrols killed
them all. Almost immediately his position was mortared,
so he put his exfiltration procedures into action. Eventually
everybody was lifted out with the exception of one young
Coldstreamer, Guardsman Shepherd, aged eighteen, who
was missing. He had become detached in the move to the
pick-up point and got lost. When McGill's party got back
to base that same day the company commander was
tempted to send a search party by helicopter to look for
Shepherd while it was still light. However, he was still
across the border. In the jungle it would be like looking for
a needle in a hay-stack and, moreover, highly dangerous
because the Indonesians in the area were by now fully
alerted. The company commander decided to trust to
Shepherd's training and discipline. The young guardsman
had a Sabre beacon with which he could transmit a distress
call on the rescue frequency; he had been trained that in
these circumstances he should go to the emergency RV
and wait. The company commander's faith in his man was
not misplaced. The next morning a helicopter sent towards
the RV picked up the signal and he was pulled out.

The Borneo campaign ended in August 1966 after
Sukarno had been implicated in dealings with the Indonesian Communist Party, resulting in his being stripped of
power, remaining President in name only while General
Suharto ruled the country. Malaysian independence and

freedom were assured, thanks in the main to the efforts of British and Gurkha soldiers.

The experiment of using the Guards Parachute Company in an SAS role was so successful, that within twelve months a troop from the company under Captain Fugelsang, Grenadier Guards, and Sergeant Mitchell became the founders of G (Guards) Squadron 22 SAS, whose first commander was Major de Klee, Scots Guards. Unfortunately financial pressure on the defence budget and the consequent cuts in manpower resulted in the disbandment of the Guards Parachute Company in 1975. In their twenty-seven years of existence they had served in over twenty different countries, including the Cyprus, Suez, Borneo and Northern Ireland campaigns, always with distinction and that special style which many other units secretly envy.

CHAPTER 14

Unfinished Business – Northern Ireland

'I don't understand youse Brits.'
'It's yourselves you don't understand, love!'
conversation between Belfast woman and soldier
who had just saved her child from a burning house.

There is no doubt that the Catholic minority in Northern
Ireland between 1922 and the early 1970s were subject to
discrimination. This had followed 800 years of what Winston Churchill called 'the long sorrowful story of English
intervention in Ireland'. In 1169 Richard de Clare, Earl
of Pembroke, a French-speaking Anglo-Norman baron
leading an army largely of Welshmen, invaded Ireland.
Before this, the Pope had granted the overlordship of
Ireland to the English King by a Papal Bull of 1155. The
Pope, Adrian IV, was not entirely disinterested, being an
Englishman, the only one ever to attain the papacy. There
is not room in this book to tell the full story of the present
twenty-year-long unfinished campaign and the important
part played in it by the Parachute Regiment, let alone the
preceding 800 years. Such an intractable problem cannot
be explained in a few paragraphs, and is not the author's
intention to try. However, the catalyst for the present series
of troubles was discrimination against the Catholics in a
number of areas, including jobs, housing and local government. The voting system was arranged to give the Prot-
estants a permanent majority, regardless of the distribution
of population by religion. For example, in 1967 in Londonderry the Catholic voters numbered 14,429 and other

voters 8,781. But the Protestant Unionists had twelve seats on the council, the non-unionists, eight. The bigotry on both sides of the religious divide, kept simmering by the educational system, is difficult to understand unless one is an Irishman. Sick jokes abound. A Protestant minister decided to give the job of repairing his church to one of two builders who gave the correct answer to a simple religious question. The first, a Protestant, quickly said: '5,000' in answer to the question: 'How many people did Christ feed with the loaves and fishes?' The minister turned to the Catholic and said: 'Name them!'

The discrimination against the Catholics led in 1968 to the formation of the Northern Ireland Civil Rights Association (NICRA). In January 1969 Protestant yobbos and followers of the Reverend Ian Paisley beat up several members of a NICRA march. In the following months serious rioting broke out, first in Londonderry and then in Belfast. Protestant mobs invaded the Catholic slums and set fire to houses. When, in August 1969, the British Army was called in they were greeted as saviours by the majority of Catholics. The exception was the almost de-funct Irish Republican Army (IRA) who, regarding them-selves as the protectors of the Catholics, had been so conspicuous by their absence during the riots that for a while the initials IRA were mockingly said by the Catholics to stand for 'I Ran Away'. Smarting at the taunts, they determined to use the opportunity provided by the con-tinuing rioting to reassert their position. Disagreement about tactics led to the breakaway Provisional IRA being formed, the dominant group to this day. The official IRA, after a brief attempt at violence, reverted to their policy of gaining their ends by political means. Despite feuding between the two wings, sometimes resulting in death or maiming, the goal which both publicly profess is the same: a united Ireland. It is a goal which is unlikely to be achieved while the majority in the North wish it otherwise.

Indeed, the political wing of the Provisional IRA, Sinn Fein, has consistently failed to gain power by democratic means. Meanwhile the slaughter goes on, mainly by the Provisionals, a small group of murderers killing for enjoyment, status and self-glorification. Using their armed muscle to intimidate competitors, they run an intricate network of rackets – clubs, taxis, smuggling and drugs – to finance their operations and line the pockets of the 'godfathers.' The last thing they want is an end to the violence, an end to their power and a return to the dole queue whence most of them came. Calling themselves an army, a stain on the name 'soldier'; choosing the easy target, unarmed soldiers on leave, bandsmen in a park, Christmas shoppers in London, they are totally cynical about causing civilian casualties despite giving warnings with sickening hypocrisy. More than any other single group of people, they are responsible for ensuring that Ireland will remain divided. Using the classic terror tactics of intimidation, shootings and bombings, always hoping that the security forces can be provoked into over-reaction, they work to undermine the morale of successive British governments of both political parties and to shock the British public into putting pressure on the politicians to wash their hands of the problem.

The first shots fired by Provo gunmen were at British soldiers engaged in keeping the Protestant and Catholic mobs from tearing each other to pieces. Soon this escalated into grenade throwing, and by 1971 into a full-blown terrorist campaign. The three battalions of the regiment have served a total of twenty-two tours in Northern Ireland, totalling nine years and eleven months. It would take a book to do justice to the achievements of the battalions and three incidents will have to suffice, one from each battalion.

On 25 May 1971, Sergeant Willets of 3 Para was in the police station in Springfield Road, west Belfast. A terrorist bomb in a suitcase was brought in and dropped in the station. When he realized what the suitcase contained, Willets immediately sent another NCO to the floor above to clear the upstairs rooms. He opened the door of the room containing the bomb and ushered a man, a woman, two children and some policemen outside, standing so as to shield them while they made their escape. Before he could follow, the bomb exploded, mortally wounding Willets. He was posthumously awarded the George Cross. As his body was carried to an ambulance the crowd outside the police station jeered and spat on the stretcher.

On Sunday 30 January 1972, a protest march in the Bogside and Creggan areas of Londonderry included about 150 yobbos whose aim was clearly to provoke a confrontation with the troops keeping order in the streets through which the march was to pass. As the march reached a security forces barrier the yobbos steadily escalated the violence, throwing bricks and eventually using tear-gas (CS) grenades against the soldiers. The brigade commander ordered 1 Para to arrest some of the yobbo element. At 5.55 pm a shot was fired at a group of paras: a moment later two paras shot dead a man in the act of lighting a nail bomb. Almost immediately after this incident the battalion entered the vicinity of Rossville Flats, attempting to cut off the yobbos. The soldiers were dismounting from their armoured trucks when they came under fire, then a burst of sub-machine gun fire from Rossville Flats sprayed the ground at their feet. More fire came from Rossville Street and nail bombs were thrown at the paras. At that moment three apparently armed men ran across the front of the flats and were shot. A gun battle followed. When it ended a total of thirteen male civilians were dead. This incident, which has been known as 'Bloody Sunday' ever since, was seized on by the Provos as a propaganda coup and exploited to the full. They alleged that the paras had indiscriminately fired on unarmed civilians and accused the Army of engineering the whole incident to bring about a battle with the IRA. The march had been banned, yet the organizers went ahead with it knowing, and hoping for propaganda purposes, that trouble would ensue. When, predictably, the situation got out of hand the Provos deliberately, cold-bloodedly and without any thought for their own people, women and children, opened fire on 1 Para, using the crowd as cover, a tactic they had used many times before. If the fire had been returned indiscriminately, as the Provisionals allege, at least one woman or child in the crowd of 3,000 would have been hit. It must have been a great disappointment to the Provisionals that all those shot were males between eighteen and twenty-six years old. It must also be said that the British public relations apparatus was not sufficiently quick off the mark, or subtle enough, to counter the Provisionals' propaganda.

On 29 August 1979, soldiers from 2 Para were travelling in a four-ton truck along a road on the north shore of Carlingford Lough close to the village of Warrenpoint. The Lough at this point is so narrow that the south side, in Eire, is only about 200 yards away. As the truck passed Narrow Water Castle, a medieval tower by the side of the road, terrorists across the Lough detonated an explosive device under the vehicle by radio control, killing a company commander and fifteen soldiers from 2 Para and two soldiers from the Queen's Own Highlanders. Lieutenant Colonel Blair, the Commanding Officer of the Queen's Own Highlanders, in whose operational area the explosion had occurred, flew by helicopter at once to the scene. As he ran towards the road, passing the masonary gateposts at the entrance to what had been a park, the terrorists initiated another device concealed in one of the gate posts. His body was vaporized by the explosion. When the Prime Minister, on a visit to Northern Ireland, asked about the incident, Blair's brigade commander held up one of Blair's cloth rank badges. It was all that could be found of his body.

History repeats itself. Three years before, a foot patrol of commando gunners under command of 40 Commando Royal Marines noticed wires leading up out of the water from across the Lough in almost the same place. Investigation revealed oil drums of explosives concealed under the road. The commanding officer of 40 Commando used the area of the gateposts for his Incident Control Post (ICP). The ever-watchful Provisional IRA took note; next time there were no wires to give the game away, and the convenient ICP was mined.

The campaign goes on, for another 800 years?

CHAPTER 15

South Atlantic – Falklands 1982

Before first light on 23 May 1982, 2 Para stood-to in their soaking trenches on the peat bog of Sussex Mountain overlooking San Carlos Water in the Falkland Islands. They had been ashore for forty-eight hours, their feet were wet, their clothes were damp, and it was bitterly cold in the southern hemisphere winter darkness. They were bored and wondered when they would get some action. They had seen plenty two days before. The Mirages and Skyhawks of the Argentine Air Force had spent most of 21 May attacking the ships in San Carlos Water and Falkland Sound. 2 Para, along with the rest of 3rd Commando Brigade, had ringside seats for the San Carlos Air Show. The battalion had watched with admiration as the Argentine pilots flew over their heads, or along the valley below and behind them, jinking as they sank lower and lower, hugging the contours of the yellow grass slopes before streaking across the water at masthead height, cannon firing, bomb away, pull up slightly, twisting and turning desperately, disappearing beyond the far headland. Sometimes they would not make it. A fireball, black smoke and ringing cheers from the watching soldiers and marines; a missile had found its mark. They had seen *HMS Ardent* sunk and a number of other ships hit. The battalion fired their machine guns at the enemy aircraft as they swooped overhead and had the satisfaction of seeing bits fly off at least four of them. The day before had been quiet; for some reason, probably the weather, the Argentine Air Force had not appeared. C Company of 2 Para were out in front with OPs overlooking the approach to the Darwin Isthmus and Darwin, twelve miles south and out of sight of the battalion position. Although most of the soldiers did not know it, the commanding officer, Lieutenant Colonel Jones, had been told by the brigade commander, Brigadier Thompson, to be prepared to mount a raid, date to be decided, the place Goose Green.

Seven weeks before, 2 Para and their sister battalion, 3 Para, now sitting in their trenches ten miles away across San Carlos Water, had been in England. 2 Para had been on leave before a tour in Belize. Their advanced baggage was already at sea, all the platoon commanders on a jungle warfare course in Belize, and everybody scattered far and wide. 3 Para were Spearhead Battalion, at short notice to go anywhere in the world, although the Falkland Islands did not figure in the list of possibilities. When the Argentines invaded the Falklands on 2 April 1982 there were no contingency plans to reinforce or retake the islands. The British were taken completely by surprise. Although there had been a number of indicators during the preceding weeks, they were almost completely ignored. With the exception of a flutter or two a few days before the invasion, which resulted in part of one RM Commando being stood by to go out to the Falklands, nothing was done, or almost nothing. The Commando was stood-down amid speculation about how they were to have got to the islands in time to pre-empt an invasion. In early 1982 the only way would have been by air, courtesy of Argentina. But at the same time the Commander-in-Chief Fleet, Admiral Fieldhouse, ordered naval units at Gibraltar to prepare for possible operations. Why the Navy did not see fit to tell 3rd Commando Brigade is anybody's guess; those extra two days would have been useful. Perhaps they forgot! However, early on the morning of 2 April, when there was no doubt that Argentina meant business, 3rd Commando Brigade was told to embark and sail south with all despatch. It soon became obvious that the enemy was likely to be present in such strength that the three RM Commandos in 3rd Commando Brigade would not be enough for the job. To the intense pleasure of the brigade commander, 3 Para, being Spearhead, were selected. The task ahead was daunting, and it would be good to have such stout comrades in the difficult days ahead. Besides, Lieutenant Colonel Pike, the commanding officer of 3 Para, was known to the brigade commander from days at the Army Staff College when Pike had been a student and Thompson was on the directing staff. Pike, a Wykehamist with a laid-back manner which concealed determination, considerable intelligence and spirit, was a welcome addition to a remarkable team of commanding officers.

3 Para embarked in the liner *SS Canberra* with 40 and 42 RM Commandos and a number of other sub-units from the brigade on 9 April, by which time the rest of the brigade, including the brigade commander, were already at sea heading for Ascension Island. Here they all gathered, the amphibious ships, the requisitioned civilian ships, the carriers, the oilers and stores ships and the escorts. A council of war was held in *HMS Hermes*, the flagship of Rear Admiral Woodward, commanding the Carrier Battle Group. Chairing the meeting was the Task Force Commander Admiral Fieldhouse, who had flown out from his headquarters in Northwood, England, from where he was to have overall command of the war in the Falklands 8,000 miles away. The meeting took nearly all day, and its details need not concern the reader, except that Thompson was asked if he needed more troops. He replied that as it appeared that the Argentines had about 10,000 men on the islands, and his brigade totalled about 4,500, it might be a good idea to have at least equal numbers. He was offered 2 Para, which he accepted with alacrity, hardly believing his luck. On being asked how many battalions or commandos he could command, he replied that five

was about the maximum that could be properly controlled
and administered by a single brigade headquarters: 2 Para
would bring the brigade up to that number. It then became
evident that there was a likelihood of a further brigade
and a divisional headquarters being sent south.

In England the commanding officer of 2 Para, had been
working hard to get his battalion sent to the Falklands if
further reinforcements were required. Because the battalion was not on the list to go, let alone Spearhead, Jones's
request to recall his men by posting notices at railway
stations and announcements on local radio was refused.
He reverted to the Airborne grapevine, and everybody
poured in. He ordered the platoon commanders back from
Belize without reference to anyone. The battalion was
under-strength. Any parachute officer or soldier who
asked to come, even over the telephone, was immediately
accepted. Several left their postings without permission.
While Jones pulled every string to get the battalion south,
he and Major Keeble, the second-in-command, did much
thinking and preparation for the battle which they hoped
lay ahead. The battalion was reorganized into three rifle
companies, a command company which included an
enlarged patrol platoon, fire support company, and logistics company. A second tactical headquarters was formed
to stand in should Jones and part of his tactical headquarters become casualties. Major Miller was borrowed
from the Airborne Forces Depot as the second operations
officer. Keeble managed to obtain an extra thirty-four
GPMGs, bringing the total up to sixty-eight! He also
acquired a few American M 79 grenade launchers which
project a 40mm grenade up to about 150 metres. Realizing
that the existing RAMC attitude and procedures for the
management of casualties was inadequate, and that steps
must be taken to produce a system which would sustain
morale and, in particular, prevent wounded men going
into shock for as long as possible, Keeble and Captain

Hughes, the battalion doctor, drew 1,000 bags of isotonic fluid and giving sets from the Cambridge Military Hospital in Aldershot. These would be distributed around rifle companies. Hughes trained the battalion to administer the drip intravenously or rectally; the latter easier for the layman in the bitter cold and the chaos of battle than finding a vein. The surgical teams of the Parachute Clearing Troop were also training intensively.

The wheels turned and on 19 April, to Thompson's delight, Jones and Miller of 2 Para, having flown to Ascension, appeared in his cabin in the headquarters ship *HMS Fearless* bearing the news that the battalion was embarking in *MV Norland* on 26 April and sailing south. Jones was known to Thompson from Northern Ireland days, a man who led from the front, brave, impatient, hot-tempered, sensitive, thoroughly professional and intolerant of fools or those he perceived as such – usually anybody who thwarted him! With a quick-fire delivery and boundless energy and enthusiasm, he was a formidable commanding officer.

As the ships steamed south, or paused at Ascension to restow their hurriedly packed loads, the soldiers and marines trained hard. There are difficulties training on board a ship. Space is usually at a premium and the environment does not lend itself to such activities as camouflage and concealment, firing the larger weapons and map reading! However, there was much that could be done and Thompson had insisted, among other things, that everybody was to keep himself fit and carry out first aid training. 3 Para was lucky; four times round the promenade deck in *Canberra* was a mile. In company with the commandos, the battalion pounded round the deck in boots and full battle order every day. 2 Para had much less space but were not defeated by the difficulties and trained as enthusiastically as everybody else. The first aid training was to prove particularly important in the days ahead.

At Ascension each battalion or commando except 2 Para, whose ship had time for only a twelve-hour stop, landed for one day of training, a march in full equipment, and firing all personal and battalion weapons. The logisticians had done well, flying out quantities of training ammunition to Ascension. 3 Para managed to expend thirty-seven and a half years' worth of the peacetime training allocation of anti-tank high explosive shells in one day! Several night loading rehearsals were carried out to practise heavily laden men embarking in landing craft in the dark and swell from doors in the side of merchant ships, or down scrambling nets; and also to give the brigade staff an idea of how much time to allow for transferring to landing craft in similar conditions off the beach.

By 13 May, when Thompson gave his orders to his brigade for the landings at San Carlos, it was clear that the Argentines had about 11,000 troops on the Falkland Islands. They had a reinforced brigade round Stanley consisting of five infantry regiments (each battalion size), including a marine unit, a comprehensive air defence system, supporting arms and logistic units. The artillery supporting this brigade was estimated at about a battalion and a half of 105 pack howitzers. They were thought to have some 155mm guns, and this supposition was proved correct when the British were shelled by 155s. Until the Argentine surrender it was not known how many, or what type. Three excellent French-towed 155s with a range of 24,000 metres were captured. At the settlements of Darwin and Goose Green there was an under-strength infantry regiment, air-force personnel to man the airstrip, artillery, air defence guns, and administrative units. Until well into the campaign there was speculation about the exact positioning of the Argentine main heliborne reserve. It turned out to have been located to the west of Stanley, and was committed before the main battle for Stanley began. On West Falkland there was a brigade of two infantry regiments (battalions) with artillery and air defence guns. Most of the thirty-four airstrips on the Falkland Islands were assessed as being capable of operating Pucaras, Aermacchis and other light aircraft; some could accept C-130s, and all of them helicopters. What airstrips were being used, and for what, was never clear right up to the end of the campaign. One set of clear air-photographs would have helped answer this and a host of other questions about the enemy; but there were none, and never were.

What was clear was that the 11,000 or so Argentine troops on the islands outnumbered the two parachute battalions, three RM commandos, and supporting troops of 3rd Commando Brigade by more than two to one. The force around Stanley alone was of about equal strength to the Commando Brigade but had more guns. At the start of the campaign they had more helicopters, air superiority, and the bonus of T34C Mentors, Pucaras, Aermacchi M339s, and Augusta A109A Attack Helicopters positioned in the islands. The enemy had been in position for about seven weeks, only 350 miles from home. The British had declared a maritime and air blockade, but during the day Argentine fighters were able to penetrate to the islands and carry out attacks; at night the air blockade was totally ineffective. The Argentines flew C-130s into the Falklands right up to the night before they surrendered. From the outset there was considerable nonsense talked in the press in Britain about the state of the Argentine Army in the Falklands. It was echoed by some of the British military, including a few senior naval officers with the Task Force. This attitude is epitomized by the remark made by a senior officer to Thompson before the brigade sailed, to the effect that the Argentines would run away when the British appeared on the scene!

Most of the ill-informed comment centred on the 'ill-equipped, half-starved, badly administered, poorly trained

Argentine Conscripts.' There is no doubt that they were second-rate troops in a totally different class from many described in this book. They were badly trained and not particularly well led. Even their special forces were poor. However, the British noted that the enemy was well equipped, in some cases better than themselves. The Argentine rations were excellent and plentiful, as many British soldiers and marines were to discover when they were forced to live on them in captured positions, for lack of helicopters to provide their own. The Argentine soldiers stayed and fought it out in many of the battles, and on occasions with great skill and persistence. Often the young conscripts pulled the triggers of their machine guns and automatic rifles until the assaulting troops got to the lip of the trench or rock-walled sangar. Their snipers, equipped with excellent night sights, a generation more modern than the British, were particularly effective in the night battles. Properly led, and with a co-ordinated joint command structure, the outcome could have been very different.

On 19 May, 3 Para was transferred by landing craft to *HMS Intrepid* for the assault. Their task on D-Day, 21 May, was to land in the second wave of landing craft at Green Beach One, secure Port San Carlos Settlement, the high ground to the north at Settlement Rocks, and Windy Gap. 2 Para, originally also in the second wave, were brought forward to land in the first wave alongside 40 Commando at Blue Beach Two, and to be the first ashore. Their objective was Sussex Mountain, overlooking the southern end of San Carlos Water and blocking the approach from Darwin and Goose Green, where the nearest sizeable body of enemy were located. The beach colours were chosen to match battalion and commando lanyards. H-hour, when the landing craft would drop their bow ramps on Blue Beach Two, was timed for 2.30 am local time. Through no fault of their own, 2 Para were late. The amphibious group had anchored one hour later than planned because of navigational difficulties caused by mist at the north entrance to Falkland Sound. *Intrepid*'s landing craft had to go over to *Norland* to pick up 2 Para, loading through a door in the ship's side. The battalion had not had the opportunity to take part in the many night loading rehearsals done at Ascension by 3 Para and the commandos. To compound the problem, a 2 Para soldier fell between a craft and the ship's side, crushing his pelvis. The battalion filled four of the large landing craft utility (LCU), a rifle company to each of three craft and battalion HQ and Support Company in the fourth. Ashore on Sussex Mountain the Naval Gunfire Support Forward Observer (NGSFO) attached to the battalion, Captain McCracken, who had landed several days before, waited for 2 Para to arrive. His OP looked out over the ground leading up onto Sussex Mountain from the direction of Darwin, where the enemy reserve was thought to be. If they started moving or were a threat while 2 Para was still on its way up, McCracken would call down fire from a frigate on the gunline in Falkland Sound.

2 Para's craft touched bottom about five metres off-shore. The ramps dropped, The order was given by the Royal Marines bowman: 'Troops out.' Nothing happened. The battalion had never carried out an amphibious landing and were not programmed to respond. A second 'Troops out,' equally unsuccessful, was followed by a bellow of 'Go!' from some senior NCO. That meant something at last! The battalion waded ashore. Their feet would remain wet until after the capture of Goose Green and Darwin nine days later. The salt-soaked boots drew in moisture like a sponge. After a pause to shake out, the battalion began its five-mile march to its objective on Sussex Mountain. Four hours had been allocated for the move. It took twice that, by men heavily laden with rucksacks, and particularly the air defence gunners attached to 2 Para. They

were not as fit as their Royal Marine air defence counterparts, and loaded down with cumbersome Blowpipes and
missiles had great difficulty in keeping up with the battalion. The time it took for heavily laden infantry to cover
the soggy peat was never properly appreciated by some in
the various headquarters in England. Their chinagraph
pencils marched effortlessly between places fifty miles
apart represented by a few inches on their small-scale
maps, dubbed by those down south 'children's atlases of
the world.'

3 Para loaded into their craft from *Intrepid*. They had
never rehearsed in this ship because it had always been
intended that they would load into craft from *Canberra*
until, at the last moment, the headquarters at Northwood
had ordered that troops were to be spread around the
amphibious ships. The long snake of sweaty, heavily-laden,
softly-cursing men on their way to the landing craft loading
positions, stumbled down ladders, forced their way along
the narrow passageways, tripped over obstructions, and
bumped into each other in the dim red light or total
blackness. 3 Para's LCUs juddered to a stop on a sand-
bar short of the beach; Pike ordered the smaller LCVPs
alongside to ferry his men off. The battalion encountered
the only enemy soldiers seen by anyone on D-Day. About
forty Argentine soldiers had woken from their slumbers
in the houses and settlement buildings to find 3 Para
landing a mile or so away and wisely decided to withdraw.
Driving the fleeing Argentines before them, the battalion
captured Settlement Rocks and Windy Gap by about 11.30
am.

The terrain in which the troops found themselves was
in many ways familiar. To the parachute soldiers and
commandos, brought up in the Brecons and Dartmoor, it
was almost like coming home. But there were differences.
Although the islands lie on the same latitude south of the
equator, as Britain lies north, the great southern ocean,

with no equivalent to the Gulf Stream to warm the sea, and the proximity of the vast frozen continent of Antarctica, Cape Horn, and the Andes, makes the climate significantly different. Icebergs regularly come within 200 miles of the islands. Snow, rain, fog and brilliant sunshine follow each with bewildering rapidity at all times of the year, even in summer; the only constant is the wind. The average windspeed throughout the year in Britain is 4 mph, in the Falklands it is 15 mph. Not for nothing did the sailormen of old call these latitudes the 'filthy fifties.' The climate was not as harsh as Italy in winter, but it was unpleasant enough. Most of East Falkland, where the fighting took place, is peat bog. Except for a few stunted growths in the settlements, there are no trees at all. In daylight and good weather, movement on the open hillsides, devoid of cover, can be seen for miles in the clear, unpolluted air. By Italian and Greek standards the mountains are hardly worthy of the name. But bog, tussocks, and stone runs make the terrain difficult to move over. Stone runs can be hundreds of yards wide, and several miles long. Doctor Wilson, stopping in the Falklands on his return from Scott's first Antarctic expedition, describes them in his diary:

> They look just like rivers of big boulders of grey lichen-covered rock, all higgledy-pig, etc. But when the bigger boulders are removed for building, as they are in places, you find they are resting on a basis of smaller and far more uniform stones, which are clean and without any vegetation on them, and down among these you can hear water trickling. The upper layer boulders vary from as much as you can lift alone, to the size of a large wagon.

Only specialist tracked vehicles, helicopters and men on their feet had any hope of getting anywhere in this terrain. Moving across stone runs by day was painfully slow. At night the stones clinked and men slipped on the greasy wet lichen.

The air attacks on the beachhead and anchorage started again on 23 May with increased ferocity, sinking *Antelope* and damaging more ships. On 24 May, during another day of air attacks, the plans for the raid on Goose Green and Darwin firmed up. An approach by sea down Brenton Loch, which Jones favoured, was ruled out. The difficulties of navigating LCUs down the loch by night made the idea far too risky. Furthermore, nobody knew what forces, if any, held the western side of the loch. An OP had reported, wrongly as it turned out, seeing an armoured tracked amphibian swimming across and climbing out on the western bank. A helicopter approach was also impracticable. There were simply not enough helicopters. The only answer was a night approach on foot from Sussex Mountain, past Camilla Creek and on to the northern end of the isthmus. Jones's plan was that D Company would secure the area of Camilla Creek House that night, so that three 105mm light guns and some ammunition could be flown in before dawn. Any attempts to fly guns forward by day would be a give-away to the enemy. Only three guns and around 200 rounds of ammunition for each gun could be lifted during the hours of darkness by the four helicopters equipped with night flying equipment. The remainder of the battalion would move down the following night and carry out the raid, supported by the guns at Camilla Creek House and gunfire from a ship. D Company, commanded by Major Neame, set off at last light.

However, the first helicopter task that night was to fly reconnaissance elements of D Squadron 22 SAS to Mount Kent, overlooking the key ground around Stanley. No sooner was this completed than the weather over the whole of East Falkland closed in and the visibility became so bad that the next helicopter sorties, to fly across Camilla Creek, became impossible. Without artillery a raid would be extremely hazardous. To Jones's annoyance Thompson cancelled it; it was either that night or not at all. The main objective was Stanley, so establishing a strong force consisting of the whole of 42 Commando and an SAS squadron on the vital ground of Mount Kent and the nearby features was the most important task. By the morning of 25 May, the weather had been so bad at night that only the insertion of the SAS reconnaissance party had been achieved.

On 25 May the Argentines sank *Atlantic Conveyor*. She had been carrying four Chinook helicopters, each capable of lifting about ten tons, and a number of old Wessex helicopters. She was due to unload her helicopters at San Carlos that very night. All except one Chinook, on a sortie when the Exocet missile struck, went to the bottom. This was to lead to 3 Para and 45 Commando walking to Port Stanley, and made Thompson even more determined not to have his eye taken off the ball by Goose Green. However, back in England, other ideas were afoot. A direct order to remount the Goose Green operation and hold the place was issued. The intelligence assessments on the enemy strengths varied, from three companies supported by two 105mm howitzers and some anti-aircraft guns, to the estimation by the SAS squadron which had attacked Darwin on D-Day, that the whole area was held by about a company. There is no doubt that at this stage Thompson should have taken his own tactical headquarters, 2 Para and a commando, probably 40 Commando who were the nearest, and mounted a two-battalion attack. He should also have taken at least one of the two troops of Scorpion and Scimitar light tanks (CVRT). This force, particularly with light armour, would have taken the position in half the time and with far lower casualties than was the case. In the event, 2 Para were left to carry out this daunting task virtually on their own.

As night was falling on 26 May, Jones led his battalion,

south off Sussex Mountain down towards Camilla Creek
House. Soon after first light the next day 3 Para set off
in two columns towards Teal Inlet Settlement, while 45
Commando made for Douglas Settlement. Originally Pike
had been told to follow 45 Commando to Douglas. But
he came up with a better route after speaking to locals
and marched south of Bombilla Hill and then due east,
avoiding the dogleg to Douglas. By this time 2 Para was
installed in the three small buildings of Camilla Creek
House. Jones had decided to lie up in and around the
buildings to provide concealment from the enemy air
reconnaissance. At 9.30 am a pair of Harriers attacked
Goose Green. Squadron Leader Iveson gallantly made
three passes and was shot down on the third. He ejected,
managed to hide, and was picked up by a light helicopter
after the battle. Two patrols from C Company reported
that there were enemy positions on Darwin Hill, south-
west of Darwin, south of Boca House, and on ring contour
50 on the north-western part of the isthmus. The patrols
were spotted and forced to withdraw under fire. At about
midday someone in the battalion tuned in to the BBC
World Service and heard the news that 2 Para were
advancing on Darwin while 3 Para and 45 Commando
were moving on Teal Inlet Settlement and Douglas. Jones
was furious and ordered the battalion to dig in to face the
attack that must surely follow this gross breach of security,
which can only have been sanctioned by someone in
England in the Ministry of Defence, or possibly a talkative
and thoughtless government minister. At the time 2 Para
believed this to be a deliberate leak to reinforce the political imperative underpinning the Goose Green operation.
Whether or not this was so, there were to be more of these
indiscretions.

However, no attack came and despite the alertness of
the enemy at Darwin, who had forced the withdrawal of
the C Company patrols, the Argentines mounted a highly

unprofessional vehicle patrol in a blue civilian Land Rover, up the track to Camilla Creek House. They were jumped by the Forward Air Control (FAC) party returning from controlling the Harrier strike, who allowed the vehicle to close their position and captured all three occupants before they could radio back to base. Interrogation by Captain Bell, a Spanish speaking commando officer sent to accompany the battalion, revealed that the officer in the party was the commander of the Argentine reconnaissance platoon and that the garrison was fully alert.

Towards the end of the afternoon Jones gave orders to his assembled company commanders. The mission, to capture the settlements of Darwin and Goose Green. The concept of operations: a six-phase, night and day, silent then noisy attack, aimed at defeating the enemy in the hours of darkness and taking the settlements in daylight when the civilians could be more easily identified. The plan in outline was: phase one – C Company, clear the route of possible minefields and secure the start line astride the track between Burntside Pond and Camilla Creek; phase two – A Company clear Burntside House while B Company cleared ring contour 50; phase three – A Company clear Coronation Point; phase four – B Company clear Boca House while C Company seize and clear the airstrip; phase five – A Company clear Darwin while B and D Companies clear and hold Goose Green; phase six – C Company seize and clear Bodie Creek Bridge. Fire support consisted of three guns of 8 (Alma) Commando Battery, Royal Artillery, two of the battalion's own 81mm mortars, the bombs carried down by riflemen, and the 4.5-inch gun of *HMS Arrow*. From first light two Scout and two Gazelle helicopters would be on task with the battalion. Of the two Blowpipe detachments put under command, one, a Royal Marine detachment, was to move with the battalion. Being fit they would be able to keep up; the other would remain to protect the gun position. Also with

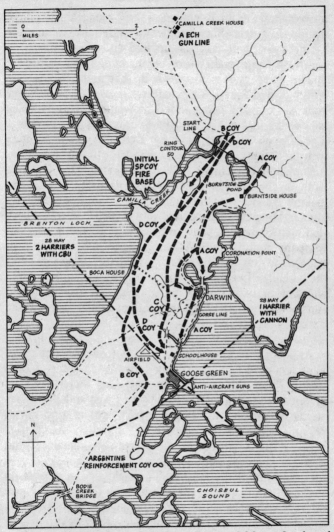

2 Para's battle for Darwin and Goose Green, 28 May 1982. Actual moves of companies.

the battalion was the Reconnaissance Troop from 59 Commando Engineer Squadron commanded by Lieutenant Livingstone; their task was to find and clear minefields and booby traps and destroy enemy equipment.

The three guns were flown in that night by the Sea Kings of 846 Naval Air Squadron, plus 320 rounds per gun. A Company commanded by Major Farrar-Hockley (son of the former CO of 3 Para) crossed the start line at 2.30 am on 28 May, and by 2.50 am was in contact with the enemy, who speedily withdrew. It began to rain. Accompanied by enemy artillery and mortar fire, B Company, on the battalion's right, began its attack at 3.10 am, making contact with the enemy thirty minutes later, and after fighting through aggressively in well-controlled section attacks the company secured Ring Contour 50. The company commander, Major Crosland, having fought in the Dhofar war, was by far the most battle-experienced in the battalion. D Company under Major Neame, in reserve and moving up between A and B Companies, also engaged some Argentines, killing a few; the remainder fled into the darkness. At 3.14 am, in the middle of this opening phase, *Arrow* developed a fault in her turret and stopped firing.

At about 4.00 am, before B and D Company objectives were secure, A Company pushed forward to occupy Coronation Point. Enemy artillery fire was increasing, the planned timings were already slipping past and *Arrow* was supposed to leave the Fire Support Area at 4.30 am to regain the safety of the air defence umbrella at San Carlos before daylight. But, repairing her gun, she remained until 5.20 am. To the right of A Company the night sky was lit up by Argentine illuminants. They felt very vulnerable on the bare landscape but pressed on with their 3,000 metre advance. Encouraged by the initial successes and reports of light casualties to other companies, their next objective was reached without opposition except for the ever-present harassing fire from the enemy mortars and artillery.

At first light, about 6.30 am, Jones ordered A Company to advance to assault Darwin. Farrar-Hockley left one platoon on Coronation Point to give covering fire: the remaining two platoons and company headquarters were ordered to follow the track round the west side of the inlet. There was a feeling of great confidence and the expectation of breakfast in Darwin, the company's final objective. As the two platoons and company headquarters reached the open ground a stream of fire from heavy and medium machine guns was unleashed from Darwin Hill, a distance of 400 to 500 metres. The platoons pushed on and reached a re-entrant which enabled them to avoid direct fire, but not the increasing rain of artillery and mortar fire. A Company's main headquarters was, however, caught in the open and unable to move. The rapidly increasing light enabled the enemy to bring down very effective fire.

The first attempts by A Company to clear Darwin Hill were unsuccessful and casualties began to mount. Dead and wounded were stripped of their ammunition, which was redistributed. Soldiers armed with Sterling submachine guns threw them away and picked up SLRs from their wounded comrades, or, better still, Argentine FALs which fired in bursts. The battalion mortars ran out of ammunition, and fighter ground-attack Harriers could not take off from the carriers because of mist at sea. However, the cloud base over East Falkland was high enough to allow the Argentine Pucara ground-attack aircraft to attack the battalion and the gun position. Several times as A Company tried to close with the enemy, the guns of 8 Battery had to stop firing just at the critical moment for fear of hitting their own men. About 800 metres away to A Company's right, B Company was caught by direct fire and artillery on the open, forward slopes, overlooking Boca House. The momentum of the battalion's attack ground to a halt. Casualties increased and ammunition stocks dwindled.

By about 9.30 am it was clear that A Company was completely bogged down and would not achieve the objective without some drastic action. Moments like this in battle are the test of a commanding officer. Anybody who knew Jones could have forecast what would happen next. He stepped in and took personal command of the company attack. Shouting 'Follow me!' he led Sergeant Norman and some of his tactical headquarters party round in an attempt to outflank enemy slit trenches. As he sprinted forward towards one trench he was fired at from another that had been overlooked. The bullets cut up the peat behind him as he charged, firing his sub-machine gun. Norman shouted: 'Watch your back!' but Jones either did not hear or ignored him. He fell mortally wounded at the lip of the trench. He was awarded the VC posthumously. The position was now critical; A Company could make no headway. B Company was pinned down north of Boca House, Jones was dying. Meanwhile D Company was calmly cooking breakfast in dead ground to the rear of B Company. Neame had offered to assist, but Jones had told him to stay where he was. With D Company was Support Company with their Milans and GPMGs sent by Major Keeble, the battalion second-in-command, on his own initiative some time before.

When Jones fell, Keeble was with battalion main headquarters. Jones's orders, in accordance with normal practice, required Major Rice, the battery commander, to assume command until Keeble with a duplicate tactical headquarters could move forward to take over. But Rice was caught up in the confusion on Darwin Hill, out of touch with the situation in the rest of the battalion, and in no position to take command. Keeble therefore ordered Crosland to take over until he could reach him. Keeble, having decided to reinforce his right flank and continue the attack in that area, ordered Support Company to move right up behind B Company with the brigade liaison officer, Major Gullan, also of 2 Para, who was in direct radio contact with Thompson.

The battle for Darwin Hill continued as Keeble moved forward and the battalion came under attack from Pucaras. At this moment a pair of Royal Marine Scout helicopters shuttling ammunition forward and flying casualties back were summoned to casevac the dying commanding officer. They were bounced by Pucaras, which shot down and killed Lieutenant Nunn, the pilot of one of the Scouts. His air gunner, Sergeant Belcher, having survived cannon and machine gun hits, severing one leg and shattering the other, survived the impact of the crash and lived. The Pucaras both turned on Captain Niblett's Scout, but by brilliant flying he evaded them. When the Pucaras attacked the gun position at Camilla Creek House they were driven off by GPMGs and Blowpipes – not the first or last time the troops saw off or shot down these menacing aircraft.

As Keeble was moving across to take charge Crosland managed to get his company off the forward slopes or into dead ground. He decided to use Milans from Support Company, now waiting behind him, to engage Boca House and the surrounding bunkers. The wire-guided missiles slammed into weapon pits and windows of the house. Neame, with great initiative and excellent eye for the ground, crawled with his company along the shoreline, below the minute cliff. Supported by GPMGs on the ridge-line and by artillery fire, he rolled up the enemy from a flank. They surrendered in large numbers.

By now A Company had taken Darwin Hill, supported by all the GPMGs available, using their 66mm LAWs to blast slit trenches. 'The Toms just put down their heads and went for it,' remembered Miller, the operations officer. By 11.10 am the battles for Darwin Hill and Boca House were over. So far the battalion had lost three officers and nine other ranks killed, and several wounded. Keeble ordered A Company to hold Darwin Hill while C Company, commanded by Major Jenner, and one platoon of A Company moved through to Goose Green. D Company was ordered to seize the airstrip while B Company moved to the west of D to capture the ground south of the settlement – in all a three-pronged attack, with A Company providing the necessary foot on the ground with the Fire Support Company. As the companies began to move they came under fire from a combination of artillery, mortars, machine-guns and anti-aircraft guns firing in the ground role. This fire caused several casualties among C Company as they pressed forward towards the schoolhouse on the outskirts of the settlement, while D Company were deflected from their route by a minefield and squeezed in towards the Settlement, away from the airfield. Lieutenant Barry thought he saw some white flags in the vicinity of the schoolhouse and received permission from Neame to arrange a ceasefire. Neame ordered his own company to stop firing. Barry and two NCOs went forward. The offer of a ceasefire was refused. Barry and his party turned to go. At this moment a machine gun from another company fired at the schoolhouse. The Argentines fired at Barry, killing him and his party. His platoon sergeant with the rest of the platoon overran the position, killing most of the enemy, although some of the occupants escaped, including the officer who had fired at Barry in the mistaken impression that the offer of a ceasefire was a ruse.

As C and D Companies reorganized, still under artillery fire, two Skyhawks attacked D Company, followed shortly by two Pucaras dropping napalm. Both napalm canisters missed. One of the Pucaras was shot down by combined small arms fire from B and D Companies. The other was shot down by a Blowpipe. This aircraft crashed close by, drenching several men with fuel which fortunately did not ignite. One man, lying face down, had his back pouches whipped off by part of the wing which scythed through them. Keeble could see the anti-aircraft guns on the Goose Green peninsula firing at him and his men on the ridge line, keeping them all pinned down. There seemed no end to this battle, and no answer to the fire coming from well out of range of anything he could fire back except artillery, which was almost out of ammunition. The decision hung in the balance. At long last, as the winter afternoon light began to fade, three Harriers arrived, having been prevented by bad weather from taking part in the battle all day. The battalion's FAC, Squadron Leader Penman, had long since fallen out with an injured foot. Captain Arnold, the NGSFO, was also a trained FAC. He brought the first two Harriers across the airfield and they dropped cluster bomb units (CBU), destroying or silencing the anti-aircraft guns on the point of the Goose Green peninsula. He brought in the third Harrier from the north-east to attack with cannon. This silenced the fire from the rest of the Settlement, including the Argentine artillery. The violent blast of the cluster bombs, forty-seven to a cluster, rippling like a giant Chinese firecracker across the peninsula, broke the will of the Argentine defenders and tipped the scales in 2 Para's favour. Civilians released from the Settlement the next day reported that the enemy soldiers had sobbed and screamed in terror. As the light faded 2 Para started to go firm in the positions ordered by Keeble. When an enemy Chinook and six Hueys were reported disembarking troops about two miles south of Goose Green, Keeble ordered B Company to set up a blocking position south of the airstrip and brought down artillery fire on the enemy. They were, it later turned out, the Argentine reserve.

Darwin was captured and Goose Green surrounded. J Company, from 42 Commando, was ordered to move down the following day to reinforce the battalion. The night passed slowly for 2 Para, lying out in the bitter cold, reaction after battle setting in as the adrenalin ebbed and the uncertainty about the morrow weighed in. The engineer section wandered into a minefield, taking cover for the night in holes which they took for shell holes but later found had been made by mines detonated by wandering cows. The morning light showed the trip-wires and the sappers tip-toed out of the minefield, thanking their lucky stars.

During the night Keeble made plans to assault the Settlement if the Argentines did not surrender in the morning. There was a complication; a patrol from the battalion made contact with the inhabitants of Darwin, who told them that 112 civilians were being held captive in the village hall in Goose Green. Keeble's plan was to offer the Argentines the chance to surrender, or be destroyed by artillery and air support. He drew up an ultimatum in Spanish with the help of Bell and sent it in with two Argentine prisoners at first light. At 9.40 am, after protracted negotiations conducted with great tact and skill by Keeble, the Argentines agreed to surrender. The battle had cost twenty British dead and forty-seven wounded, of which the battalion had lost eighteen dead and thirty-five wounded. They had taken 1,100 prisoners, and the captured equipment included four 105mm pack howitzers, two 35mm and six 20mm anti-aircraft guns, six 120mm mortars and two Pucara aircraft. It was perhaps the most remarkable individual action fought by a British battalion since the Second World War.

This battle was to have a profound effect on the conduct of the rest of the campaign. It signalled to the Argentines the determination of the British to succeed. It opened up the southern route to Stanley, and because the Argentines were convinced right to the end that the main attack would come from the south, it served to confirm their assessment, distracting them from what was actually the major thrust by 3rd Commando Brigade from the north and east. The fighting over the bare, open slopes in daylight had been costly. From then on, the brigade would if possible fight at night. The confusion of battle in the darkness would be offset by the greater skill of the British soldiers and marines, the better leadership, and the intimate and flexible fire support made possible by their magnificent gunners. Finally, and an unforeseen bonus, the Argentine heliborne reserve had been drawn away from the vital area of Mount Kent and taken prisoner with the rest of the Goose Green garrison. They were not, therefore, able to intervene during the highly risky three days when a light force of part of 42 RM Commando and an SAS Squadron with minimum support was pushed forty miles forward on to Mount Kent.

While 2 Para had been fighting at Goose Green, 3 Para were marching across to Teal Inlet. Having left Port San Carlos in two columns at 11 am on 27 May, they arrived in the valley of the Arroy Pedro River, about five miles short of Teal, at 11 am on 28 May. This was a remarkable effort for men carrying about sixty to seventy pounds. The weather was reasonable but the ground was very boggy, and in places quite steep, with lumps and tufts of grass which even in daylight made the risk of a sprained ankle an ever present possibility, and any sort of marching rhythm impossible. At night it was far worse. In the final hours of darkness the battalion could hear the sounds of the battle at Darwin. At the Arroy Pedro the two columns made their rendezvous and lay up during the remaining hours of daylight to avoid air attack. They were joined by their mortar platoon, which had been lifted across country in two tractors and trailers driven by farmers from Port San Carlos. The platoon brought news of 2 Para's casualties. As soon as darkness fell the battalion moved towards Teal Inlet settlement. B Company, under Major Argue, was deployed to the south-east of the settlement to cut off any escaping enemy. By 11 pm on 28 May the settlement was in 3 Para's hands. The first soldier to knock on the door of the settlement manager's house was greeted by Mr Barton in Spanish, but he quickly and thankfully changed to English when he recognized the new arrivals. The battalion dug-in for the rest of that night. The next morning brought further news of 2 Para, the surrender of the Argentine garrison at Goose Green, and the tally of prisoners.

The right flank of the move by 3 Para and 45 RM Commando was covered by the Brigade Reconnaissance Troop, formed by the Royal Marines Mountain and Arctic Warfare Cadre. They held certain key features on the chain of high ground along the whole route from San Carlos to Smoko Mountain. On 31 May a force of nineteen men of the Reconnaissance Troop under Captain Boswell eliminated a seventeen-man Argentine special forces patrol at Top Malo House. Two other Argentine OPs on neighbouring features, watching the fate of their comrades, decided to throw in the sponge and surrendered to 45 Commando and 3 Para. At a stroke, the Argentine eyes and ears on the right flank had been removed. By this time 3 Para were on the move again, securing Estancia House on the night of 31 May/1 June and collecting some prisoners on the way, stragglers from San Carlos and Teal Inlet. A Company under Major Collett moved up on the dominating ground of Mount Estancia, followed in the early morning of 1 June by battalion tactical headquarters, while B Company secured Mount Vernet. From some of these positions, Stanley could be seen in the brief lulls between the driving rain, fog and snow showers; as the weather turned increasingly foul, slowing down the rate of build-up of the rest of the brigade. It did not prevent 45 Commando from marching in a couple of days later, having been held back to protect Teal until the brigade defence troop and logistic units could take over. On 3 June 79 Commando Light Battery Royal Artillery was flown forward. Meanwhile, these forward positions, so crucial to the Argentine defence of Stanley, had been held by 42 Commando, 3 Para and one battery; for lack of helicopter lift, without minefields, wire or any other defence stores. Thompson kept his fingers crossed that the Argentines would not mount an attack in strength, particularly when he heard that Mr John Nott had announced in the House of Commons that the British were building up on Mount Kent as a prelude to an attack on Port Stanley. As a crucial part of the brigade plan had always been to conceal the strength and direction of the main thrust, this latest indiscretion was crass.

2 Para were by now also well forward. Major General Moore had arrived in the Falklands on 30 May, bringing with him Brigadier Wilson's 5th Infantry Brigade and taking over as overall land force commander. Moore told Wilson to move his brigade along the southern route to Stanley via Goose Green, and 2 Para were put under his command. Keeble:

Brigadier Wilson appeared in my headquarters carrying the biggest map I have ever seen, covered in large chinagraph arrows. He outlined a plan to march the brigade forty miles from Darwin to Fitzroy, leapfrogging battalions, guns, and mortars. He seemed determined to catch up 3rd Commando Brigade. Although the terrain was better here, and there was a track traversable by unloaded Land Rovers, it would soon have been reduced to a morass by large numbers of heavily-loaded vehicles towing trailers and guns. I suggested that we try something more subtle. We had discovered that the civilian telephone line from Swan Inlet House, about ten miles to the east as the crow flies, might still be working to Fitzroy. My plan was to send Crosland and a large patrol from B Company in five missile-armed Scout helicopters to Swan Inlet House and see if the enemy were in Fitzroy.

Wilson ridiculed the idea and departed. While he was away Keeble and Crosland, with Captain Greenhalgh, prepared a plan based on what they had told Wilson. Two days later he was back and said: 'Do it.' A stone through the window of the unoccupied Swan Inlet House, and Crosland was on the telephone, discovering to his amazement that there were no Argentines in Fitzroy or Bluff Cove settlements. That evening, 2 June, the only British Chinook helicopter was busy moving Wilson's headquarters to Goose Green. Keeble asked for it to move his battalion to Fitzroy; Wilson agreed. When the pilot was briefed on the task he replied that as darkness was approaching he was limited to two more sorties that day. He would, therefore, get only half the force to Fitzroy before nightfall. Keeble suggested doubling the load. The crew chief interrupted, reminding them that the peacetime load was forty men, at which a company sergeant major yanked him off the tailgate of the helicopter, intercom wire trailing, saying: 'That's one less!' Eventually the pilot, not the jibbing type, agreed to eighty men being crammed in, standing like commuters in the tube in the rush hour! There were no seats. In this manner A Company and a mortar detachment were lifted in, followed by B Company and a battalion headquarters, escorted by the Scout helicopters. The next day the remainder of the battalion moved up, and A, C and D Companies with battalion headquarters took up a position on a feature overlooking Bluff Cove while B Company held Fitzroy. The speed of these moves took Moore's headquarters by surprise because he was now bound to re-allocate resources to Wilson's brigade, which had a battalion out on a very long limb. Neither divisional headquarters nor Wilson passed the news to 3rd Commando Brigade. There was very

nearly a disaster when the commando brigade reconnaissance troop OP on Smoko Mountain, unaware that there
were any British Chinooks in the Falklands, reported
'enemy Chinook landing troops at Fitzroy.' The Argentines still had a Chinook helicopter and it was logical that
they should reinforce Fitzroy by air since the track from
Stanley to Fitzroy was now dominated by 42 Commando
on Mount Challenger. Two batteries were ordered to
engage. But as a precaution the Brigade Major of 3rd
Commando Brigade checked with divisional headquarters
first, and calamity was averted.

Keeble, recommended by Thompson for command and
an immediate award of the DSO, was not next in line for
command in the Regimental list, and was joined at Fitzroy
by the new commanding officer, Lieutenant Colonel
Chaundler. He had been taken from his desk in the MOD,
parachuted into the sea alongside the Carrier Battle
Group, and helicoptered forward – the only parachute
operation in the campaign! The battalion made good use
of the sheep-shearing sheds to rest some of the soldiers.
There were several trench foot cases, who recuperated in
time to rejoin their companies for the final battles. The
battalion was joined by 2nd Battalion Scots Guards on 6
June, who had an appalling seven-hour night journey in
LCUs, nearly being fired on by Royal Navy ships en route.
2 Para handed Bluff Cove settlement over to the Scots
Guards and concentrated on Fitzroy. Although an overland attack on these two settlements was highly improbable
because all the routes were dominated by 3rd Commando
Brigade, both Port Fitzroy and Bluff Cove were in full
view of the Argentines on Mount Harriett, obvious to
anyone after a few seconds examination of the map. There
was no reason to suppose that Harriett was unoccupied;
42 Commando's patrols and their OPs had built up a
comprehensive picture of the enemy on that feature, and
all this had been passed back. Despite this, first light on

9 June revealed to an astonished 2 Para, two logistic landing ships, *Sir Galahad* and *Sir Tristram*, sitting ducks in
the middle of Port Fitzroy. The reasons for their presence
in broad daylight in full view of the enemy are too lengthy
to relate here, but were the end result of back-seat driving
by Task Force Headquarters in its bunker in Northwood,
8,000 miles away. 2 Para were witnesses to the scene,
which so obsessed the media in Britain and which they
wrongly situated in Bluff Cove. The Argentine Air Force,
less active since the end of May, bombed the two LSLs
and caused a large number of casualties, mainly to the 1st
Battalion Welsh Guards. The newly arrived 5th Infantry
Brigade had not seen what the Argentine Air Force could
do; no member of 3rd Commando Brigade, green or red
bereted, having watched and been on the receiving end of
six days of furious air attack would have willingly spent
one second longer than he had to on any ship anywhere
near the Falklands in daylight!

3 Para, in company with 42 and 45 Commandos, spent
until 10 June in aggressive and intensive patrolling.
Thompson warned Pike that Mount Longdon was likely
to be his objective in the forthcoming attack. Pike moved
A and B Companies forward to establish a patrol base
nearer his objective, to reduce the time spent getting there
and back. The patrols were highly successful and penetrated the Argentine positions a number of times, bringing
back a wealth of information and causing a number of
casualties without loss to themselves. A and B Companies
were shelled regularly, and also attacked by Pucaras several
times. They beat off the air attacks, mostly with GPMG
fire. On one occasion a brigade staff officer on Mount
Kent was treated to the sight of a Pucara sheering off in
alarm when a 3 Para soldier fired his Carl Gustav ('Charlie
G') 84mm recoilless anti-armour weapon at the attacking
aircraft. The point was made that disciplined, well-concealed, dug-in soldiers are a very hard target for attacking

aircraft unless they use weapons such as napalm or cluster bombs. Battalion headquarters was bombed on a couple of occasions, as were other units, by Argentine Canberra high-level bombers at night, probably on co-ordinates worked out by radio intercept. Whatever the method, it was highly alarming; the aircraft were too high to see and in any case it was dark. The first Pike knew of the attack, as he lay in his damp sleeping bag under a poncho, was a series of earth-shaking explosions as a stick of 400 kg bombs exploded close by. Fortunately, as on many other occasions the soft peat absorbed most of the blast and splinters.

2 Para came back under command of 3rd Commando Brigade in time for the battles for Stanley. For the first night they were to be in reserve, moving down the centre-line behind 3 Para and 45 Commando. 3 Para were to set the ball rolling on the left flank of 3rd Commando Brigade's attack on Mount Longdon, Harriett, and Two Sisters, on the night of 11 June. The battalion had been given an H-hour of 8.01 pm, because at this time of the year it was dark by 4 pm; this would allow the approach to the objective to be made in darkness, with moon up soon after 8 pm, giving some light for fighting through the objective. By allowing three-quarters of the night, the objectives should be secure by dawn. In this way the assaulting troops would not be exposed to the fire of the Argentine 50-inch heavy machine guns in the coverless terrain in daylight. Furthermore it avoided the traditional dawn assault which the Argentines might expect. Pike's plan for his battalion was, like all good plans, simple. The three rifle companies and battalion tactical headquarters, led by guides from D Company (in 3 Para, Patrol company), would approach the objective in darkness, taking about three hours. The long, narrow summit of Mount Longdon, covered with rocks, allowed enough room for only one company to fight along it at one time. Pike decided that he had no option

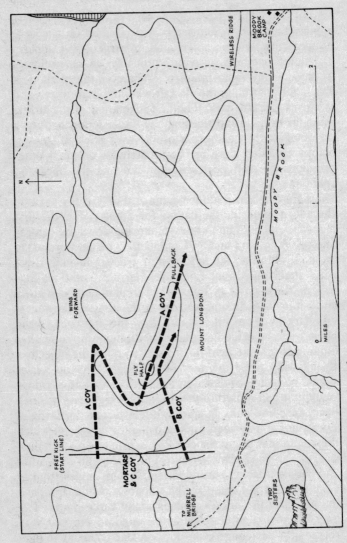

2 Para's battle for Mount Longdon.

but to attack Longdon end-on, from the west. Outflanking movements were not wise because of extensive minefields to the south of the mountain and known enemy positions on Wireless Ridge to the east. The ground around Mount Longdon was open in every direction for at least 1,000 metres, so an approach, even by night, would be hazardous. Pike selected the stream running north to Furze Bush Pass as his Start Line, a good choice because it lay at ninety degrees to his axis of attack, and was easily recognizable, even on the darkest night. He gave it the nickname Free Kick. The western summit of Longdon was nicknamed Fly Half; the eastern summit, Full Back, and the spur running north from the main feature, Wing Forward. It is hard for the layman to imagine how much information commanders at all levels in an infantry battle at night have to carry in their heads. The commanding officer orchestrating the whole is not sitting in a warm well-lit operations room, surrounded by staff, powerful radios and radar displays showing the positions of friend and foe; or even in a relatively warm armoured command vehicle. He is walking, crouching, running, lying, probably in pouring rain, under fire, trying to update his mental picture of the battle by conversations on a man-pack radio and going to see for himself if he can. The flashing of torches to read maps or look up codes can be unwise. Nicknames would enable the battalion to refer to these features on the radio without the time-consuming and, in the dark in the middle of battle, almost impossible business of using code. The Argentines listening to the radio would eventually work out the nicknames for each position, but with luck it would take them most of the night to do so. The other battalions and commandos used this dodge.

B Company was to assault the Longdon summit ridge (Fly Half and Full Back) while A Company seized the spur running north (Wing Forward). C Company was to be reserve for this phase while fire support teams equipped with machine guns and Milans, under Major Dennison, would remain on the Start Line (Free Kick) until called forward. The mortar platoon was to move independently and set up a base-plate position behind the Start Line. The ammunition resupply and casualty evacuation teams, under the command of Major Patton, the second-in-command, were to move in oversnow tracked vehicles (Bandwagons) and requisitioned tractors. Once Longdon was secure, it was Pike's intention to exploit forward on to Wireless Ridge with both A and C Companies to meet Thompson's orders that assaulting units should press on if the opportunity occurred. Such exploitation by 3 Para would only be possible if Mount Tumbledown, which dominated Wireless Ridge, was also taken. This was 45 Commando's exploitation task, but could not be achieved that night.

Major Argue, commanding B Company, decided that 6 Platoon would clear the southern slopes of Longdon while his headquarters with 4 and 5 Platoons would clear the northern slopes. The move of B Company to the start line went well initially until the Fire Support Group, moving to their positions, cut across the B Company column. Part of 5 Platoon, and all of 6 Platoon, became separated from the company and did not meet up again for thirty minutes. There was a further delay caused by the time it took to ford the Murrell River. Argue therefore decided to make up for lost time by assaulting from further south than intended and well to the right of A Company. Despite all this, both companies crossed the start line at 8.15 pm, only fourteen minutes late, a good effort. As they advanced it was still very dark, but soon the moon rose, silhouetting the jagged rocks on Mount Longdon and illuminating the yellow grass. Argue ordered his platoons to move in closer to the rocks to gain as much cover as possible. As the platoons shook out into assault formation, the left forward section commander of 4 Platoon trod on an anti-personnel mine. This alerted the enemy, who fired at both A and B Companies. The battle was on, and lasted until just before daybreak. Ten hours of gutter fighting, often at close quarters with rifle and bayonet, grenade and 66mm LAW, with support from guns, naval gunfire, mortars and machine guns. It was a battle in which junior officers, NCOs and private soldiers fought with courage, tenacity and aggression. 6 Platoon occupied the western summit of Longdon without fighting, although they grenaded some enemy bunkers on the way up. But they missed one bunker containing at least seven enemy, who fired into their backs as they advanced through Fly Half, causing a number of casualties. As they lay pinned down by this fire they also found themselves under fire from enemy shooting at 5 Platoon, who had fought their way up on to the ridge from the other side and had now made contact with 6 Platoon. 4 Platoon, moving on the left of 5 Platoon, became intermingled with 5, and both moved over the top of the western summit on to more open ground sloping away to the east. They could see the eastern summit in the distance when both platoons came under fire from a strong defensive position, the nearest part of which apparently contained a 105mm anti-tank gun, at least two medium machine guns and one .50-inch heavy machine gun as well as a number of snipers with night sights. It was a classic reverse slop position, sited to catch attacking troops moving down off a crest line.

Lieutenant Bickerdike, commanding 4 Platoon, was hit in the thigh and his signaller in the mouth by the first burst of fire. The platoon sergeant, Sergeant McKay, immediately took command. The signaller continued to man his radio, until relieved later. McKay decided to take out the heavy machine gun which seemed to be the key to the position. The weapon was sited in a sangar and protected by several riflemen. McKay quickly gathered up three men of 4 Platoon, from Corporal Bailey's section,

and assaulted the sangar. They were met by a hail of
fire. Corporal Bailey and a private soldier were seriously
wounded, and Private Burt was killed. Despite these
losses, McKay continued to charge the enemy position
alone. On reaching it, he despatched the enemy with grenades, thereby relieving the pressure on 4 and 5 Platoons,
who were now able to redeploy. McKay was killed, his
body falling into the sangar. For this action he was awarded
a posthumous VC.

However, a second heavy machine gun continued to fire
on B Company headquarters and 5 Platoon. Argue, hearing that Bickerdike had been wounded and McKay was
missing, sent Sergeant Fuller forward from company headquarters to take command of 4 Platoon, now without its
platoon commander and platoon sergeant. Fuller gathered
4 Platoon and with fire support from Corporal McLaughlin's section of 5 Platoon attacked the heavy machine gun
position. Although they cleared several enemy positions
on the way, they could not reach the machine gun and
were halted after taking five casualties. McLaughlin's section also tried to reach the machine gun, but he too was
forced to withdraw. Argue decided to withdraw 5 Platoon
and the remnants of 4, regroup his company and, after
giving the enemy a good dose of artillery and machine gun
fire, conduct a left-flanking assault on the position. The
gunners as usual were reacting splendidly and bringing
fire down within fifty metres of where 4 and 5 Platoons
were lying, keeping the enemy neutralized while Weeks,
the Company Sergeant Major, organized the withdrawal
of the remnants of the two platoons. Bickerdike and his
signaller had not given up the fight, despite their wounds;
they were firing from where they lay, helping to cover the
withdrawal of 4 and 5 Platoons.

Pike was now with Argue. The mortars were bedded in
at the Start Line, and Dennison had brought the machine
guns forward to the western summit of Longdon. The 105

mm guns pounded the enemy, assisted by salvoes from
naval guns. Argue took the remnants of 4 and 5 Platoons,
formed into three sections, and retraced the route along
which they had just withdrawn before putting in a left
flank attack. As soon as the artillery fire lifted on to other
targets further east, and after going forward about thirty
metres, the composite platoon came under heavy fire.
Lieutenant Cox and Private Connery fought their way
forward with grenade, 66mm LAW, bullet and bayonet,
killing a number of enemy. The fire died away. For a
moment it seemed the enemy had folded at last; as company headquarters moved forward they came under fire
again. Clearly the enemy in this area were not finished
yet. Pike decided that B Company had sustained such
heavy losses that he would pass A Company through to
continue the battle.

  A Company, after crossing the start line, had heard the
anti-personnel mine exploding to their right and seen the
enemy shells falling on Mount Longdon. To begin with
the company was in dead ground as they advanced towards
Wing Forward, the spur jutting north from Mount Longdon, so the bullets from the fire fight on the mountain
went over their heads. As soon as they emerged on the
top of the ridge they came under fire from the same
enemy on the eastern end of Longdon that was causing B
Company so much trouble. The company went to ground
among convenient peat banks, which afforded some protection from direct fire but little cover from the increasingly accurate mortar and artillery fire being directed on
them and C Company in reserve. The company had to
stop firing back at the enemy, which they could see through
their night sights, because of the close proximity of B
Company to the enemy position. Pike, realizing that A
Company could not advance from where they were,
ordered them to pull back and move round the western
end of Mount Longdon, pass through B Company and

take the eastern end of the feature (Full Back). This they did, still under artillery and small arms fire. The company commander went forward to find Argue and be briefed. It became clear that an attempt to outflank the northern side of the feature would prove too costly, so A Company would fight along the ridge in an easterly direction.

As soon as the artillery directed by Lieutenant Lee, the forward observer, and the GPMGs under Captain Freer gave covering fire, 1 Platoon advanced, working its way through the enemy positions. Clearing systematically, to avoid leaving any enemy behind to shoot them in the back, A Company, sometimes crawling, sometimes rushing, bombed and bayonetted its way forward. The supporting fire then had to stop; it was becoming a hazard to the company. The enemy could be seen withdrawing from the ridge, an encouraging sight, while 1 and 2 Platoons started to clear the numerous positions with the bayonet. As soon as the eastern end of Longdon was secure, 3 Platoon pushed on to hold the long narrow slope leading down to Wireless Ridge, and the remainder of the company re-organized and began digging in. When daybreak came, the heavy morning mist hid the position from Tumbledown, so the enemy artillery fire was inaccurate. But it became increasingly accurate and heavy as the mist cleared and the day wore on. Clearly there would be no question of going forward on to Wireless Ridge yet. That would be 2 Para's task, in conjunction with an attack to take Mount Tumbledown. Pike remembers that morning:

The misty scene as dawn broke will perhaps be the most haunting memory of this long, cold fight. The débris of battle was scattered along the length of the mountain, encountered round every turn in the rocks, in every gully. Weapons, clothing, rations, blankets, boots, tents, ammunition, sleeping bags, blood-soaked medical dressings, web equipment, packs –

all abandoned, along with the 105mm RCLs, 120 mm mortars, and .50 Browning that had given us so much trouble during darkness. The enemy dead lay everywhere, victims of shell, bullet and bayonet. The sour odour of death lingered in the nostrils long after many of these corpses had been buried, for it was a slow job, and eventually the task was abandoned when their artillery and mortars started again. The enemy bunkers provided an Aladdin's cave of Camel cigarettes, bottles of brandy, huge cakes of solid cheese, and of course bully beef! Standing among the shell-holes and shambles of battle, watching the determined, triumphant, shocked, and saddened faces of those who had lost their friends on this mountain, the Iron Duke's comment was never more apt: 'There is nothing half so melancholy as a battle won – unless it be a battle lost.'

With Tumbledown still in Argentine hands, 3 Para had a very unpleasant thirty-six hours under constant fire from 155s, 105s and mortars. All the brigade's positions were under shellfire, but 3 Para had the worst of it. Having lost seventeen men killed during the battle to capture Longdon, a further six were killed by the constant shelling which was sustained for the next forty-eight hours. 45 Commando had reported their objective, Two Sisters, secure at 4.30 am, and the commanding officer announced his intention of pressing on to Tumbledown. Thompson ordered him to stay where he was. By the time 45 Commando had reorganized for the next attack, first light would be only two hours away. Covering the 5,000 metres from Two Sisters to Tumbledown via Goat Ridge, the best route, would take until sunrise, revealing the commando attacking over open ground against a well-prepared position. Quite how well prepared, the Scots Guards were to discover in two nights time. In any case, 42 Commando had not yet secured Goat Ridge, a prerequisite to 45 Commando advancing on Tumbledown. The 105 batteries were running low on ammunition, and ships providing naval gunfire support had to leave the gunline before dawn. In these circumstances a daylight attack on Tumbledown would result in very heavy casualties.

2 Para had a frustrating and tiring ten-mile march through the night. The battalion 'snake' stopped, started, expanded and contracted like a concertina. Progress was in jerks, the soldiers ran or walked fast to keep up, then found themselves waiting for what seemed like hours. They could see the battles on Longdon and Two Sisters, and hear the shells from the British batteries whooshing overhead. By now several soldiers had 'Galtieri's revenge', common throughout the commando brigade, caused by drinking the brackish water. Puritabs sterilized it, but it did not remove the sediment which inflamed the gut. Men having stopped to drop their trousers galloped after the column which having momentarily stopped, continued when the reason became all too apparent! Before dawn, the battalion was ordered to swing north, dig in on the reverse slopes of Mount Longdon and await further orders. At midday Thompson ordered the battalion to attack Wireless Ridge that night by hooking around to the north of Longdon rather than a direct assault from the direction of 3 Para's position. Later the attack was postponed to the following night to allow 5 Infantry Brigade time to reconnoitre their objectives.

Seizing Wireless Ridge on the night 13/14 June, at the same time as the Scots Guards assault on Tumbledown, was planned as the first move in the final push on Stanley by 3rd Commando Brigade; a series of attacks by 42 and 45 Commandos, 3 Para, and the Welsh Guards. Although there were measures in progress to persuade the Argentines to surrender, no one in 3rd Commando Brigade gave them much thought and fully expected to fight all the way

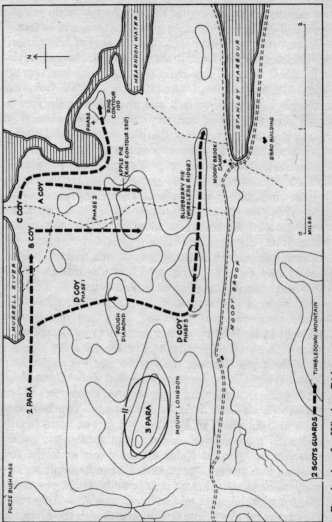

2 Para's plan for Wireless Ridge.

to the airport isthmus; after that the enemy might see the sense of giving in. Following 2 Para's experience at Goose Green, when they had been critically short of fire support, Chaundler had promised that this would not happen again. He asked for and was given the maximum fire support available. He had two batteries of 105s, *HMS Ambuscade* with her automatic 4.5-inch gun, the mortars of 3 Para in addition to his own, and for the first time a troop of Scorpions and Scimitars of the Blues and Royals. Keeble had persuaded the troop to come with them when the battalion left 5th Infantry Brigade's area. They left without asking permission. He told the troop leader to take as much ammunition as possible. They filled the CVRTs with about three times the combat load. On the start line they dumped the excess to allow the turrets to traverse. The Sultan armoured recovery vehicle was also brim-full of ammunition, and so heavy it broke the Murrell bridge, falling into the river, from which it was extracted with difficulty. Having decided on a plan earlier on 13 June, after a detailed examination of the ground, Chaundler made some changes. A feature north-east of Longdon thought to be held by 3 Para seemed to be occupied by enemy. A short altercation took place between 2 and 3 Para about who did hold the feature, and was settled by 2 Para having it comprehensively shelled without complaint from 3 Para! A hill (ring contour 100) on the left of the battalion's axis was held by the enemy. The hill (ring contour 250) north of Wireless Ridge was more heavily defended than he had thought, and finally, the enemy positions on Wireless Ridge extended further to the east than he had at first appreciated. Chaundler's plan was a framework, designed to be flexible and capable of amendment at short notice. The battalion was a worked-up team, they knew the aim of the operation and with the firepower at their disposal could 'cuff it' as they went along. In outline, he planned a four-phase noisy attack (ie with preliminary bombardment). In phase one, D Company would capture the feature north-east of Longdon (Rough Diamond). In phase two, A and B Companies would attack ring contour 250 (Apple Pie). In phase three, D Company would attack Wireless Ridge (Blueberry Pie) from the west, supported by fire from A and B Companies. In phase four C Company would attack ring contour 100. The registration of the fire plan was interrupted by what was to be the final appearance of the Argentine Air Force. Four Skyhawks bombed brigade headquarters and attacked the helicopters en route to lift 2 Para's mortar and machine gun platoons forward. Last minute adjustments to the artillery and mortar targets were made after dark, using illuminating rounds. In the forming-up position, just after last light, Chaundler was told that there was a minefield in front of Apple Pie and that Wireless Ridge was held by two companies, not one. He decided that it was too late to change anything at that stage and to press on. It started to snow.

At 9.15 pm on 13 June the supporting fire rained down on D Company's objective, Rough Diamond, and at 9.45 pm the company, supported by fire from the Scorpions, Scimitars and the machine gun platoon, crossed the start line. The company found a few dead, but the remainder had withdrawn. As the company reorganized, they were hit by enemy 155mm air-burst. Neame advanced about 300 metres to get out of the enemy defensive fire task. The phase two companies crossed their start line, Farrar-Hockley's A Company on the left and Crosland's B Company on the right. As they approached Apple Pie the enemy could be seen running away, shocked and terrified by the storm of fire. The battalion found several radios still switched on. Opposition was quickly silenced, but the main problem was the speed with which the well-handled Argentine artillery shelled their old positions, keeping it up for nine hours. At this stage, Chaundler decided to bring forward C Company's attack on ring contour 100, on the battalion's left flank. It was found clear. D Company moved to its next start line at the west end of Wireless Ridge, while the Scorpions, Scimitars, Milans and machine guns moved up to join A and B Companies on Apple Pie, to provide fire support. The first part of the ridge was taken unopposed, while suppressive fire was brought down on the eastern end. As D Company moved to assault the second part of their objective, they encountered considerable resistance by what is now known, was the regimental headquarters and nearly two companies. During the close-quarter battle for this objective a fire mission was called down, which landed directly on D Company, causing casualties. The enemy having conducted a fighting withdrawal from bunker to bunker, suddenly broke and ran, chivvied off the ridge by fire from the Scorpions and Scimitars, and pursued by D Company. Once again, as the company reorganized, enemy artillery and mortar fire came down. In the darkness the enemy could be heard regrouping further along the ridge and in the area of Moody Brook. As dawn broke on a freezing morning, about forty Argentines put in a counter-attack on D Company. The ammunition in the company had all but run out, and even 105mm gun ammunition was low, so the order was given to fix bayonets and prepare grenades. But a short fire mission from artillery and mortars and small arms fire from the company repulsed the attack. 2 Para had fought a model all-arms battle. The troop of the Blues and Royals had played a major part in victory achieved at low cost. Their excellent night sights had proved invaluable, acquiring targets despite the moon being obscured by falling snow. They were able to suppress enemy machine guns after the supporting mortars and guns had to lift.

Soon afterwards the battalion was treated to the sight of the enemy streaming away from Tumbledown, where the Scots Guards had defeated three enemy companies holding one of the strongest positions encountered in the campaign. The stream became a river as the enemy poured down the road into Stanley. The Argentine artillery kept firing even after the retreating troops passed the gun positions, and gave proof that they were still very much in the battle as Thompson was giving Chaundler his next objectives. At about 9 am the order for the whole brigade to advance was given. 2 Para was first into Stanley, with 3 Para hard on their heels. To everyone's delight, it was over. It had been a short war, and as wars go not particularly bloody, but had cost the two parachute battalions a total of 203 dead, wounded, sick and injured, the latter two categories mainly frost-bite, trench foot and fractures caused by the rough going. These casualties were borne mainly by the rifle companies and represent a heavy expenditure of fighting men; in each battalion about a third of those whose business it is to take the bayonet to the Queen's enemies. There would have been more dead but for the remarkable skills and co-operation of the Parachute Clearing Troops and the Naval doctors and medics of 3rd Commando Brigade. Between them, the two battalions were awarded two VCs, two DSOs, five MCs, five DCMs (one posthumous), 12 MMs (two posthumous), 34 MIDs (four posthumous), and one MBE.

EPILOGUE

This is the end of the book, but not the end of the story, which as far as the Parachute Regiment is concerned, continues. What the future holds, depends above all on Britain's defence policy, and the size and shape of her armed forces. Looking ahead, one thing is clear, there will be no more mass drops; the British do not have sufficient aircraft, and the vulnerability of fleets of air transports to modern air-defence systems, precludes large scale parachute operations in general war. In the light of this, it has been suggested that we no longer need parachute soldiers. However, the key to another crisis, or battle, outside the NATO context, unforeseen, as was the Falklands, might be a parachute operation. The unexpected almost always happens. The prudent commander keeps his options open, and ensures that his potential enemy is kept guessing. Abandoning the ability to insert even quite small parachute forces, removes a 'piece off the board'; one less threat for a potential opponent to counter.

Britain prides herself on the high quality of her soldiers. Excellence in battle is not inherent in any military organization, it is primarily the result of training and morale. The selection process, known as 'P' Company, and the experience of parachuting shared by all regardless of rank, produces a bonding and a spirit that few other training methods can match (the commando course is another). In Tunisia, Italy, Normandy and Germany, parachute battalions spent protracted periods fighting as infantry, establishing an enviable record for themselves. After the Second World War, there has been, up to now, only one parachute operation, Port Said. But always, the Regiment has borne out Brigadier Hill's dictum that a good parachute soldier can turn his hand to anything, living up to its motto, *Utrinque Paratus*, 'Ready for Anything'.

Glossary

Bandwagon   Tracked, articulated, oversnow vehicle consisting of a tower and trailer, built by Volvo. Highly successful on peat bog in the Falklands campaign.

Bangalore Torpedo   A length of piping filled with explosive, used for blowing a gap in a barbed wire entanglement.

Bren   The British light machine gun of World War Two.

Brigade Major (BM)   The senior operations staff officer of a brigade, and *de facto* chief of staff.

Chinook   Large twin-rotor helicopter with a payload of ten tons.

CSM   Company Sergeant Major.

CVRT   Combat Vehicle Reconnaissance Tracked – Scorpion or Scimitar. Both built by Alvis with the same hull, chassis and drive. Scorpion has a 76mm gun, and Scimitar has a 30mm automatic cannon.

DCM   Distinguished Conduct Medal, a decoration for gallantry for warrant officers, non-commissioned officers, and private soldiers.

DF   Defensive Fire – artillery, mortar or machine gun fire by troops in defensive positions against attacking troops or patrols.

Direct Fire   Weapons that have to be aimed directly at the target as opposed to indirect fire weapons such as artillery and mortars.

DSO   The Distinguished Service Order, a decoration for gallantry awarded to officers, usually where leadership was also displayed.

DZ   Dropping Zone, the area chosen for landing by parachute troops.

Eureka   A portable beacon carried by pathfinder troops, and used to guide aircraft carrying parachute troops to the DZ.

FOO   Forward Observation Officer, an artillery officer who directs artillery fire. Normally one with each forward rifle company from the battery supporting the battalion.

Flak   German slang for anti-aircraft fire from the German *fliegerabwehrkanone*.

FUP   Forming Up Position – the area behind the Start Line in which troops form up for an assault. Preferably in dead ground, i.e. out of sight of the enemy and therefore safe from direct fire weapons.

Gammon Bomb   Invented by Lieutenant Gammon of 1 Para in North Africa in 1942. It consisted of a stockinette bag with a simple igniter, into which each man could pack up to two pounds of plastic explosive.

GPMG   General Purpose Machine Gun – belt-fed 7.62 weapon, normally one per section in every battalion.

H-Hour   The time at which the first wave of assaulting troops crosses the Start Line.

LZ   Landing Zone, an area chosen for glider or helicopter landings.

LAW   Light Armour Weapon – a shoulder-held 66mm anti-tank rocket in a throw-away launcher.

MC   Military Cross, a decoration for gallantry, usually for junior officers.

Milan   A wire-guided anti-tank missile, very useful for bunker-busting.

MM   Military Medal, a decoration for gallantry for warrant officers, non-commissioned officers, and private soldiers.

NCO   Non-commissioned officer – lance-corporal to colour-sergeant.

OP   Observation Post – a small well-concealed position from which to observe.

OP Party   A gunner term to describe the FOO and his radio operators.

PIAT   Projector Infantry Anti Tank – a powerful spring, mounted in a tube which throws a hollow-charge projectile.

The hand-held anti-tank weapon of the British World War Two infantryman.

RV   Rendezvous, the point on or near the DZ or LZ where the unit rallies and reorganizes before moving off to the objective.

Sangar   A protective wall built of stones or peat blocks where the ground is too hard or too waterlogged to dig.

SP gun   Self Propelled gun – gun mounted on tracks, less lightly armoured than a tank but often mistaken for one. Designed with the necessary mobility and protection to provide artillery support for armoured units. A formidable adversary for lightly equipped troops.

Start Line   A line on the ground, usually a natural feature such as a stream, bank or fence, preferably at ninety degrees to the axis of advance, which marks the start line for the attack and is crossed at H-Hour in attack formation.

Stick   An aircraft load of parachute troops due to drop on one DZ in one run over it.

Strengths of Parachute Battalions   These vary through the years, but a rule of thumb strength is about 600–750 for a battalion, around 100 for a rifle company, and 30–35 for a platoon. These are all full-strength figures. The reader will note that on occasions parachute battalions fight on when reduced to less than a tenth of their strength.

Sources

Unpublished sources – War Diaries, State Papers and Reports in the Public Records Office, Kew

Formation of a parachute/glider force PREM 3–32/1
Employment of Airborne Forces WO205/669
HQ 1st Parachute Brigade War Diary Nov 42–Jun 43
   WO175,181
1st Parachute Battalion War Diary Nov 42–Jun 43 WO175/525
2st Parachute Battalion War Diary Nov 42–Jun 43 WO175/526
3rd Parachute Battalion War Diary Nov 42–Jun 43 WO175/527
Report on 6 Airborne Division – Normandy WO205/1119
5th Parachute Brigade operations in Normandy WO223/17
The story of the 7th Parachute Battalion 1943–45 WO223/18
8th Parachute Battalion (1947 Staff College Tour Account)
   WO223/19
3rd Parachute Brigade War Diary WO171/593
5th Parachute Brigade War Diary WO171/595
7th Parachute Battalion War Diary WO171/1239
8th Parachute Battalion War Diary WO171/1240
9th Parachute Battalion War Diaries WO171/1242
   WO171/5136
12th Parachute Battalion War Diaries WO171/1245
   WO171/5137
13th Parachute Battalion War Diaries WO171/1246
   WO171/5138
Number 3 Commando War Diary – Normandy WO218/65
Operation Market Garden reports and instructions WO205/693
1st Airborne Corps Report on Arnhem AIR37/1214
1st Airborne Division War Diary 1944 WO171/393

1st Parachute Brigade War Diary 1944 WO171/592
4th Parachute Brigade War Diary 1944 WO171/594
1st Parachute Battalion War Diary 1944 WO171/1236
2nd Parachute Battalion War Diary 1944 WO171/1237
3rd Parachute Battalion War Diary 1944 WO171/1238
10th Parachute Battalion War Diary 1944 WO171/1243
11th Parachute Battalion War Diary 1944 WO171/1244
156th Parachute Battalion War Diary 1944 WO171/1247
Arnhem War Diary SS Panzer Grenadier and Reserve Battalion
    16 WO205/1124
HQ 2 Independent Parachute Brigade War Diaries
    WO170/517/518 WO170/4410
4th Parachute Battalion War Diaries WO170/1341
    WO170/4971
5th Parachute Battalion War Diaries WO170/1342
    WO170/4972
6th Parachute Battalion War Diaries WO170/1343
    WO170/4973
Operation Varsity 6 Airborne Division Report WO205/947
Commander 2nd British Corps Report – Musketeer WO288/77
16th Parachute Brigade Report – Musketeer WO288/74
1st Guards Independent Parachute Company War Diary –
    Musketeer WO288/130

Other unpublished sources

A Brief History of the 2nd Independent Parachute Brigade
    Group
Operation Neptune June 1944 – Notes on the employment of
    6 Airborne Division
Short History of 1st Guards Independent Parachute Company,
    Airborne Forces Museum Archives
2nd Battalion the Parachute Regiment, Post Falklands Report
3rd Battalion the Parachute Regiment, Post Falklands Report
John Frost papers, Airborne Forces Museum Archives
Hackett papers, Liddell Hart Archives, King's College London

Warrack papers, Liddell Hart Archives, King's College London

General Sir Hugh Stockwell, personal papers, Liddell Hart Archives, King's College London.

2nd (British) Corps Report, Operation Musketeer, Liddell Hart Archives, King's College London

Personal diaries and accounts (rank at the time account was written or tape made; does not include tapes of interviews)

Lieutenant Bentham
Private Cook
Lieutenant General Sir Napier Crookenden
General Sir Kenneth Darling
Major General Dunbar
Brigadier Hackett
Brigadier Hill
Sergeant Johnstone
Signalman Jukes
Captain Kerr
Brigadier Lathbury
Company Sergeant Major Lawley
Lieutenant Colonel Luard
Corporal McConney

Dr Marquis
Private Miller
Lieutenant Colonel Parry
Brigadier Pearson
General Sir Nigel Poett
Major Sim
Lieutenant Stainforth
Major Taylor
Major Waddy
Lieutenant Colonel M J H Walsh
Colonel Warrack
Lieutenant Colonel Warren
Major Watson
Major Webber
Mr Woodcraft

Published Sources – books

Crookenden, Lieutenant General Sir Napier
    AIRBORNE OPERATIONS Salamander
    AIRBORNE AT WAR, Ian Allan
    BATTLE OF THE BULGE, Ian Allan
    DROP ZONE NORMANDY, Purnell Book Services Ltd
Deane-Drummond, Anthony RETURN TICKET, Collins
Dover, Major V, THE SILKEN CANOPY, Cassel

Fairley, J, REMEMBER ARNHEM, Pegasus Journal

Farrar-Hockley, AIRBORNE CARPET, McDonald & Co

Foxhall, R, THE GUINEA PIGS: BRITAIN'S FIRST PARATROOP RAID

Frost, Major General JD, AIRDROP AGAINST OUDNA, British Army Review, August 1982
  A DROP TOO MANY, Cassell

Gale, Lieutenant General Sir Richard, WITH THE 6TH AIRBORNE DIVISION IN NORMANDY, Sampson Low

Golden, L, ECHOES FROM ARNHEM, William Kimber

Golley, John, THE BIG DROP, Janes

Hackett, General Sir John, I WAS A STRANGER, Chatto and Windus

Hamilton, Nigel, MONTY THE FIELD MARSHAL, Hamish Hamilton

Hibbert, C. THE BATTLE OF ARNHEM, Batsford

Hill, Brigadier J, OPERATION TORCH, I PARA'S DROP IN NORTH AFRICA

HISTORY OF THE 2ND BATTALION THE PARACHUTE REGIMENT, short account of Battalion's activities 1942–45

Jefferson, Alan, ASSAULT ON THE GUNS OF MERVILLE, John Murray

de Klee, Captain M, A DROP WITH THE FRENCH Guards Magazine, Winter 1956–1957

Lamb, Richard, MONTGOMERY IN EUROPE. 1943–45, Buchan & Enright

Ministry of Information, BY AIR TO BATTLE, Official Account of the 1st and 6th Airborne Divisions 1945

Montgomery, NORMANDY TO THE BALTIC, Printing and Stationery Service BAOR

Newnham, Group Captain, M, PRELUDE TO GLORY, Purnell & Sons Ltd

Norton, Major GG, THE RED DEVILS, Leo Cooper,

Paget, Julian, LAST POST, ADEN 1964–67, Faber

Powell, G, THE DEVIL'S BIRTHDAY, THE BRIDGES TO ARNHEM 1944, Buchan and Enright
  MEN AT ARNHEM, Leo Cooper

Riley, N, ONE JUMP AHEAD, John Clare

Ryan, Cornelius, A BRIDGE TOO FAR, Hamish Hamilton

Saunders, H St G, THE RED BERET, Michael Joseph

Tugwell, Colonel, M A, ARNHEM, A CASE STUDY, Thornton Cox

ARNHEM, THE TEN GERMS OF FAILURE, RUSI Journal, December 1969

Urquhart, Major General, R E, ARNHEM, Collins

War Office, AIRBORNE FORCES, 1939–45

Wilson, Major General, R D, CORDON AND SEARCH, Gale and Polden.

Interviews and correspondence

Mr Cook

Brigadier Coxen

Lieutenant General Sir Napier Crookenden

Brigadier Crook

General Sir Kenneth Darling

Major General Deane-Drummond

The Reverend Downing

Major General Eberhardie

General Sir Anthony Farrar-Hockley

Mr Follet

Major General Frost

Mr Garret

Major Gourlay

General Sir John Hackett

Major Hargreaves

Major Hibbert

Brigadier Hill

Alan Jefferson

Lieutenant Colonel Keeble

His Honour Judge Lea

General Sir George Lea

Lieutenant-Colonel Lonsdale

Dr Marquis

Major Mitchell

Lieutenant Colonel Otway

Lieutenant Colonel Parry

Brigadier Pearson

Brigadier Pike

General Sir Nigel Poett

Colonel Powell

Nigel Riley

Major Sim

Major Taylor

Captain Timothy

Major General Urquhart

Colonel Waddy

Major General Walsh

Lieutenant Colonel Warren

Major Watson

Major Webber

His Honour Judge Sir David West-Russell

Lieutenant Colonel Williams

Mr Whitelock

Mr Woodcraft

Index

Abdiel, HMS, 112

Abdul Rahman, Tunku, 386–7

Aden, 359, 360, 361, 363, 373–85

Adrian IV, Pope, 406

Adsett, Private, 141–2

Airborne units *see* Parachute and Airborne units

Alanbrooke, Field Marshal, 50

Albania, 22, 273, 275–6, 278

Alexander, General, 112, 117

Alfrey, Lieutenant General, 85–6, 89

Algeria, 55, 91

Algiers, 55, 56, 57, 58, 64, 76, 90, 91, 125, 126

Ambuscade, HMS, 452

Amey, Sergeant, 159

Anderson, General, 56, 57, 59

Anderson, Lieutenant, 89–90

Antelope, HMS, 423

Arab League Army, 321

Ardennes operation, 281–7, 290

Ardent, HMS, 412

Arethusa, HMS, 143, 145

Argentina *see* Falklands

Argue, Major, 435, 444, 446–7

Arnhem, the battle for (Operation Market), 95, 99, 117, 194, 195–265, 288, 290, 321, 336

Arnold, Captain, 433

Arnold, CSM, 368

Arnold's Spur (Radfan), 367–9, 370, 372

Arrow, HMS, 426, 428

Ascension Island, 414, 416, 417, 420

Ashby, Lieutenant, 123

Ashford, Major, 69

Athens, 272, 273, 276, 277, 366

Atlantic Conveyor, 424

Augusta (Sicily), 97, 99

Awdry, Captain, 123

Bahrain, 363, 366, 373, 385

Bailey, Corporal, 445–6

Baker, Captain, 192

Bakri Ridge (Radfan), 367–9, 372

Bampfylde, Major, 182, 183, 184–5, 186

Barlow, Colonel, 235

Barnes, Major, 402

Barron, Captain, 256

Barry, Lieutenant, 218

Barry, Lieutenant, 432

Barton, Lieutenant, 397

Baskeyfield, Sergeant, 238

Batavia (now Djakarta), 310

Battle of Britain, 12, 25

Baughan, Corporal, 399

Begley, Captain, 331

Beale, Captain, 346

Beaufre, General, 356

Beckett, Brevet Lieutenant Colonel, 338

Beja (Tunisia), 58, 59, 60, 61, 62, 63

Belcher, Sergeant, 431

Bell, Captain, 95

Bell, Captain, 426, 434

Belsen concentration camp, 304, 318

Benouville (Normandy), 132, 155, 157, 158

Bentham, Lieutenant, 79, 80–81, 83, 88–9

Bibby, Lieutenant, 191

Bickerdike, Lieutenant, 445, 446

Birmingham, Sergeant, 87

Bittrich, Lieutenant General, 199, 201, 214, 254–6, 259

Black, Sergeant, 353, 354

Blacker, Brigadier, 366

Blackwood, Lieutenant, 262

Blair, Lieutenant Colonel, 410–11

'Bloody Sunday' (Northern Ireland), 409–10

Bluff Cove (Falklands), 438, 439, 440

Boca House (Falklands), 425, 426, 429, 430, 431

Bois de Bavant (Normandy), 130, 157, 168

Bols, Major General, 292, 301, 307

Bone airfield (Tunisia), 56–7

Borneo, 386–405

Boswell, Captain, 436

Boulter, Lance Corporal, 19

Brackpool, Corporal, 348

Brazier, Captain, 344

Bredin, Lieutenant Colonel, 357

Breeze, Lieutenant, 164

Brereton, Flight Sergeant, 2, 6–7, 8

Brereton, General, 195, 197, 199, 204, 209, 223

Bréville (Normandy), 133, 167, 176, 177, 179, 180–81, 182, 183, 184–7, 281

Brierly, Major, 377, 379

British Liberation Army (BLA), 309

Bromley-Martin, Lieutenant Giles, 79, 80–81

Brooke, Captain, 392

Brown, Lieutenant, 167–8

Browning, Lieutenant General, 31, 33, 36, 37, 41, 44–5, 47–8, 51, 53, 56, 90, 126, 129, 137, 196, 197, 198, 199, 203, 204, 205, 208–9, 212, 223, 257, 265

Brunei, Sultanate of, 386, 387

Bruneval (France), 33, 40, 43, 70, 74

Buchanan, Lieutenant, 66, 71–2, 74

Bucher, Major, 298

Bure (Belgium), 283–6

Bures bridges (Normandy), 130, 134, 164, 165–6, 167, 169

Burkinshaw, Lieutenant, 299

Burma, 310

Burt, Private, 446

Burwash, Lieutenant, 226

Butler, Major, 357

Butler, Brigadier, 336, 341, 344, 348, 350, 352, 356, 383

Cadden, Lance Corporal, 74

Caen Canal bridge, 130, 132, 134, 135, 149, 151, 153, 158, 161, 176, 207

Cain, Major, 259

Camilla Creek House (Falklands), 423, 425, 426, 431

Canadian Parachute Battalion, 1st, 127, 133, 140, 162, 163, 172–3, 181, 296, 307–8, 315

Canberra, SS, 414, 416, 421

'Cap Badge' (Radfan), 365–6

Carter, Corporal, 13

Cassino (Italy), 120–21

Cavanagh, Lieutenant, 344, 347

Celle (Germany), 304–5

Charteris, Lieutenant, 40, 41, 42, 43, 69–70

Château d'Amfreville (Normandy), 147

Château St Côme (Normandy), 177–9

Chaundler, Lieutenant Colonel, 439, 452, 453, 455

Chitral, P & O liner, 310
Churchill, Winston, 3, 23–5, 32, 272, 406
Clarke, Major, 284, 285
Cleasby–Thompson, Major, 61
Clements, Private, 345
Clements, Sergeant, 83
Cleminson, Captain, 239
Cluff, Captain, 392
Coates, Second Lieutenant, 345
Collett, Major, 436
Colley, Captain, 372
Collingwood, Major, 170, 177
Commando units *see* Parachute and Commando units
Conn, Captain, 397, 401
Connery, Private, 447
Cook, Private, 273, 274–5
Cooke, Colour Sergeant, 59–60
Cowley, RSM, 317
Cox, Flight Sergeant, 39, 40, 42
Cox, Lieutenant, 447
Coxen, Brigadier, xiii, 58, 59, 76, 77, 78, 82, 83, 84–7, 89, 91, 103, 118, 270–71, 272, 273, 274, 279
Coxen, Lieutenant, 402
Cramphorn, Major, 191
Crater (Aden), 380, 383
Crete, 25, 209, 346
Crook, Brigadier Paul, 332, 338, 342, 344, 346, 348, 351, 358
Crookenden, Lieutenant General Sir Napier, xiii, 28, 128, 170, 187, 189, 222, 286–7, 293–4, 301–2, 304–5, 306–8
Crosland, Major, 428, 430, 431, 437, 453
Cyprus, 324, 326–33, 337, 338, 340, 356, 357, 358, 386, 405

Daly, Captain, 16, 18, 19, 21
Darlan, Admiral Jean Louis, 58
Darling, General Sir Kenneth, xii, 135, 150, 151, 175–6, 243, 281, 288, 292–3, 297–8, 299, 310, 311, 314, 325, 393

Darwin (Falklands), 413, 417, 419, 420, 423, 424, 425, 426, 427, 429, 430–32, 433, 435
Darwin Hill, 425, 429–32
Davidson, Sergeant, 347
Dawes, Captain, 8
Dawes, Lance Sergeant, 2
Dawson, Major, 252
Dayan, Moshe, 319
Deane–Drummond, Major, 3, 9–10, 16, 17–18, 19, 20, 22–3, 210, 212, 213, 263–4
Deelan airfield (Holland), 197
Dempsey, General, 212–13, 265, 290
Dene, Lieutenant Colonel, 117–18
Dennis, Lance Sergeant, 16
Dennison, Major, 444, 446
Depienne (Tunisia), 64, 65, 67, 71, 91
Diedricks, Private, 242
Dieppe raid, 50, 51
Dives, river/valley (Normandy), 130, 147, 169, 171, 172, 174, 179
Dobie, Lieutenant Colonel, 76, 79, 135, 221, 226, 227, 232, 233, 235–6
Dorrien–Smith, Major, 235
Dover, Major Richard, 88, 101, 110–11, 195, 218–19, 320
Down, General, 28, 48, 51, 82, 117, 121, 204
Driel ferry (Arnhem), 231, 253, 255, 258
Dunbar, Brigadier, 383
Dutch Resistance, 199, 264, 314
Dyer, Major, 143

Eberhardie, Lieutenant Colonel, 393, 394–8, 399, 402
Eden, Sir Anthony, 335, 341, 358
Edgar, Corporal, 185
Egypt, 324, 375–6, 380; Suez crisis (1956), 332–58

Eisenhower, General Dwight D., 53, 332

El Aouina airfield (Tunis), 57

El Gamil airfield (Egypt), 338, 341–9

El Moguy, Egyptian commander of Port Said, 350–51

El Naqil (Pegasus Village), 365, 366

El Tina (Egypt), 356–7

ELAS and EAM (Greek Communists), 273, 276, 277–8

Elbe, River, 303, 305–6, 308

Empire Parkeston, LST, 355

England, Lieutenant, 296

Enosis (union with Greece), 327

EOKA (Greek Cypriot terrorists), 328, 329

Evans, Driver, 10, 12

Evans, Lieutenant, 123

Ewing, Piper, 41

Exercise Gordon, 320

Falklands war (1982), 113, 412–56

Farouk, king of Egypt, 324

Farrar–Hockley, Lieutenant Colonel, 366, 367, 369, 370–72, 373

Farrar–Hockley, Major, 428, 429, 453

Fearless, HMS, 416

Fearnby, Captain, 348

Federal National Guards (FNG, South Arabia), 360, 381

Federal Regular Army (FRA, South Arabia), 360, 362, 381

Feuchtinger, Brigadier General, 157

Fieldhouse, Admiral, 413, 414

Fitch, Lieutenant Colonel, 219–20

Fitzroy (Falklands), 437–9

Fitzroy Smith, Captain, 122–3

Flavell, Brigadier, 34, 75, 125

Fleming, Captain, 398

Fletcher, Guardsman, 339

FLOSY (Front for the Liberation of Southern Yemen), 376, 384

Foggia, 17, 21, 113,

Ford, Major, 190

Fouquières, Colonel, 347

France, French, 55; raid on Würzburg radar, 32–3, 37–45; invasion of Normandy, 125–94; invasion of South of, 266–71; Suez (1956), 331–58

Frank, Lieutenant, 101

Fraser, Lieutenant, 237

Frederick, Major General, 266, 267

Free Italy Movement, 17

Freer, Captain, 448

French paratroopers, 336, 349–50; 1 RPC, 340, 356; 2 RPC, 338, 340, 343, 356; 1 REP, 340

'Freya' radar, 32, 45

Frith, Sergeant, 178

Frost, Major General John, xii, 33–7, 40, 41–3, 44–5, 64–5, 67, 68, 69, 70, 71, 75, 81, 83, 88–9, 100–101, 105, 107, 108, 109, 110, 111, 113, 202, 213, 218, 219, 221, 222, 223, 224–5, 227, 233, 240, 246–7, 248, 250, 265

Fugelsang, Captain, 405

Fuller, Sergeant, 446

Gale, Major General Richard, 27, 28, 29, 33, 128–9, 130, 133, 136, 137, 147, 156–7, 161, 163, 180, 181, 188, 192, 204, 290, 292

Garrett, Sergeant, 126, 174

Gavin, General 'Slim Jim', 196, 199, 205, 209

Gibraltar, 56–7, 413

Gioia de Colle airfield, 113

Glider Pilot Regiment, 37; 1st Battalion, 46

Glubb, General, 326

Gombel Hill (Java), 312–13

Goose Green (Falklands), ix, 413, 417, 419, 420, 423, 424, 425, 426, 427, 432–3, 434, 435, 436, 437, 438, 452

Gotts, Tom, 79

Gough Major, 216, 219, 221, 247–8

Gourlay, Major, 268, 274

Gray, Captain, 171

Grayburn, Lieutenant, 248

Greece, 271–80, 327–8; *see also* Cyprus

Greek Mountain Brigade, 276

Greek National Guards, 276, 278

Greenhalgh, Captain, 438

Greenway, Captain, 143

Grivas, Colonel, 328, 329, 330–31

Groesbeek Heights (Holland), 209, 223

Gue Hill (Tunisia), 62–3

Guingaud, Major General de, 209

Gullan, Major, 431

Gunong Gajak (Borneo), 397, 398, 399

Gurkha Parachute Company, 393

Guthrie, Corporal, 80

Gwinnett, Padre, 147, 181

Hackett, General Sir John, xii, 93, 112, 197, 201, 205, 207, 209, 210, 218, 227, 229–31, 241, 243–4, 246, 249, 250, 251, 252, 256, 259–60, 321

Hagana, 319, 321, 322

Haifa (Palestine), 322, 323

Halliburton, Lieutenant, 146

Halstead, Lance Corporal, 173

Hamilton, Nigel, 202, 212

Hamminkeln (Germany), 292, 301

Happy Valley (Argoub, Tunisia), 79

Harding, Field Marshal, 327

Hardwick Hall camp, 33–4, 49

Hargreaves, Major, 269

Harris, Air Marshal 'Bomber', 50

Harzer, Colonel, 198, 219

Hawker, Private, 331

Heaps, Lieutenant, 233

Heathcote-Amory, Lieutenant Colonel, 250–51

Hermes, HMS, 414

Herouvillette (Normandy), 130, 157, 168, 175

Hewetson, Lieutenant Colonel, 169, 296, 319

Hewitt, Lance Corporal, 85

Hibbert, Major, xii, 202, 217, 219, 222, 225, 246, 248–9, 264

Hickinbotham, Sir Tom, 361

Hicks, Brigadier, 97, 197, 210, 229–32

Hill, Brigadier James, xii, 51, 53, 57–9, 60–64, 125–6, 127, 129, 133–4, 135, 137, 138, 139, 140, 141, 162–3, 164, 167, 170, 174, 176–7, 180, 181, 189, 288, 292, 295, 302, 304, 305–7, 456

Hiroshima and Nagasaki, atomic bombs dropped on, 309

Hitler, Adolph, 201, 282, 305

Hodge, Captain, 105

Hodgson, Major, 397, 401

Hogg, Second Lieutenant, 346, 348

Hollingshurst, Air Vice Marshal, 206

Hollingsworth, Corporal, 257

Hopkinson, Major General, 95, 117

Horrocks, Lieutenant General, 197, 265

Houghton, Corporal, 299

Howard, Major, 132, 134, 149, 154, 207

Hughes, Captain, 415–16

Hussein, King of Jordan, 326, 358

India, 309

Indian Airborne Division, 44th, 117

Indian Parachute Brigade, 89

Indian Parachute Division, 94

Indonesia, 310–16, 386–404

Intrepid, HMS, 419, 420, 421

IRA (Irish Republican Army), 319, 407

Iraq, 358, 363

Irgun Zvai Leumi (IZL), 319, 321, 322

Ismailia (Egypt), 336, 354, 356

Israel, Israelis, 361; Sinai War (1956), 340; Six Day War (1967), 380; *see also* Palestine
Ismay, General, 24
Italy, Italian campaign, 15, 94, 111–24, 204, 271, 276, 280, 290; raid on Tragino Aqueduct (1941), 14–23, 24; *see also* Sicily
Iveson, Squadron Leader, 425

Jackson, Lieutenant Colonel, 4
Jackson, Major, 372
Japan, Japanese, 93, 309, 310, 311, 312, 313, 314, 392
Java, 310–16, 317, 393
Java Sea, Battle of the, 45
Jebel Alliliga (Tunisia) 77–8
Jebel Bel (Tunisia), 81, 83
Jebel Haqla (Radfan), 370, 371
Jebel Mansour (Tunisia), 77, 78, 84
Jefferson, Lieutenant Alan, xii, 143–4, 146, 147, 295
Jenkins, Padre, 139
Jenner, Major, 432
Jerusalem, 323
Jewish Agency, 319
Jewkes, Captain, 365
Johnson, Lieutenant Colonel, 135, 181–2, 183–5, 186
Johnston, Lieutenant, 173
Johnstone, Sergeant, 69
Jones, Lance Corporal, 18
Jones, Lieutenant Colonel, 413, 415–16, 423, 424–5, 426, 429, 430
Jones, Sergeant, 121
Jordan, 326, 327, 358
Joubert, Colonel, 350
Juckes, Lieutenant, 167–8,
Jungle Warfare School, Johore Bahru, 393, 394, 396

Kabrit parachute school, 325
Kalamaki airfield (Athens), 272
Kalimantan (Indonesian Borneo), 386, 387, 391, 393

Keeble, Major, 415, 430–33, 434, 437–8, 439, 452
Kelly, Private, 398
Keneally, Sergeant, 317
Kent, Lance Corporal, 339, 349, 354
Kerr, Captain, 176
Kessel, Captain, 260
Khartoum airfield, 320
Kido, Major, 312, 313, 314
Killeen, Corporal, 159
Kindersley, Brigadier, 128, 133, 184
King, Captain, 228–9
Kingston, Captain, 357
Kippen, Major, 296
Kirby, Captain, 347
Klee, Major de, 338–40, 343, 349–50, 352–5, 405
Knight, Sergeant, 346
Koch, Oberstleutnant Walter, 74
Koepel (Holland), 231, 241
Korean War, 60, 366, 394
Kraft, Sturmbannführer, 215, 220
Kyrenia mountains (Cyprus), 328, 333, 337

Lagerern, Lieutenant, 283
Lamb, Richard, 204
Lamph, Private, 345
Lathbury, Brigadier, 101, 104, 105, 106, 107, 109, 125, 126, 135, 196, 210, 215, 218, 219–20, 221–2, 225–6, 227, 232, 233, 264
Lawley, CSM, 4, 12–13, 16, 17, 21, 115–17, 153–4, 161, 283–6, 299–300
Le Bas de Ranville (Normandy), 130, 151, 157, 159, 161, 180
Le Mésnil (Normandy), 134, 166, 167, 171, 173, 174, 175, 177–8
Le Muy (France), 266, 268, 270, 271
Le Plein (Normandy), 137, 147, 177, 182

Le Port (Normandy) 132, 159
Lea, Captain, 19, 22–3
Lea, Lieutenant Colonel, 230, 233, 234, 237, 238
Lebanon, 321, 358
Lee, Lieutenant, 448
Leese, General, 120, 122
Legg, Sergeant, 345
Leine, river (Germany), 303, 304, 308
Lewis, Major, 220
Lindsay, Lieutenant Colonel, 6–8, 93, 127, 129
Livingstone, Lieutenant, 428
Loch Fyne (Scotland), 38
Long, Colour-Sergeant, 144
Longstaff, Sergeant, 338
Lonsdale, Major, 100, 104, 106, 228, 238–9
Looker, Private, 345
Lord, Flight Lieutenant, 242
Lovat, Brigadier the Lord, 130, 147, 159, 161, 176, 184
Luard, Lieutenant Colonel, 153, 176, 189–91, 193, 284, 316

McCardie, Lieutenant Colonel, 232–3
McClelland, Padre Horace, 343
McConney, Corporal, 71–4
McCracken, Captain, 420
McDonald, Sergeant, 80
McDonald, Sergeant, 399
McElliott, Captain, 348, 351
MacEwan, Colonel, 163
MacGavin, Lieutenant, 68
McGeever, CSM, 295
McGill, Sergeant, 404
McGuigan, Corporal, 170
McIntyre, Private, 42
McKay, Lieutenant, 221, 247
McKay, Sergeant, 445–6
McLaughlin, Corporal, 446
McLeod, Lieutenant, 371
Mackenzie, Lieutenant Colonel, GSO1; 230, 261

McKinnon, Private, 220
McNab, Trooper, 339, 349, 350, 353–4
Madden, Major, 256
Maison Blanche (Algeria), 56–7, 58
Malay Volunteer Force, 310
Malaysia (Malaya), 309–10, 316, 393; East (Borneo), 386–404
Malta, 16, 17, 21, 99, 112, 340
Mansie, RSM, 2, 8
Marlow, Captain, 120
Marquis, Captain, 172–3, 290
Massu, General, 336, 356
Mediterranean, operations in the, 266–80
Medjez el Bab (Tunisia), 62, 64, 70, 74
Megara airfield (Greece), 272
Melfi, Giovanni, 117
Mellor, Lieutenant, 78
Melville, Guardsman, 339
Merville Battery (Normandy), 130, 133, 134, 136–7, 143–7, 174, 177
Metcalf, Captain, 298
Milburne, Sergeant, 160
Miller, Corporal, 402
Miller, Major, 382
Miller, Major, 416
Mitchell, Colour Sergeant, 316
Mitchell, Major, 83
Mitchell, Sergeant, 405
Model, Field-Marshal, 198, 201, 214, 259
Montgomery, Field-Marshal Bernard, 76, 97, 118, 129–30, 202, 209, 212, 265, 291
Moore, Major General, 437, 438
Morley, Captain, 346
Mortimer, Lieutenant, 268
Morton, Major, 379
Mottola, battle of, 113
Mount Kent (Falklands), 424, 435, 437, 440
Mount Longdon (Falklands), 440, 441, 443–50, 452, 453

Mount Tumbledown (Falklands), 444, 448, 449, 450, 454
Mountbatten, Admiral Lord Louis, 33, 38, 51
Murphy, Guardsman, 339, 349
Murray, Sergeant, 402
Murtagh, Private, 399

Nasser, President Abdel Gamal, 331–2, 351, 358, 361, 362, 375
Nastri, Private, 17, 20, 21
Neame, Major, 423, 428, 430, 432, 453
Near East operations, 326–58
Neder Rijn (Holland), 215, 218, 219, 253, 262, 265
Nelson, Lieutenant Colonel, 317, 324
Newall, Lieutenant, 347
Newnham, Wing Commander Maurice, 14, 26, 27, 28, 30
Nicklin, Lieutenant Colonel, 296
Nicosia (Cyprus), 329, 337
NICRA (Northern Ireland Civil Rights Association), 407
Nijmegen (Holland), 206, 207, 209, 214, 223, 247, 253, 317
NLF (National Liberation Front, South Arabia), 376, 384
Norland, MV, 416, 420
Norman, Air Commodore Nigel, 24, 41, 96
Norman, Major, 346
Norman, Sergeant, 430
Normandy landings (1944), 24, 98, 123, 125–94, 201, 205, 266, 281, 290, 292, 309, 383
North African campaign, 22, 51, 53, 55–92, 95, 99, 108, 110, 125, 134, 202, 213
North Kalimantan National Army, 387
Northern Ireland, x, 405, 406–11, 416
Norton, Major, 348
Norway, 309

Nott, John, 437
Nunn, Lieutenant, 431

Oosterbeek (Holland), 198, 201, 214, 217, 218, 219, 220, 233, 235, 238, 239, 240, 250, 253, 256
Operation Berlin, 260
Operation Comet, 207–8, 212–13
Operation Foxhunter, 337
Operation Lucky Alphonse, 329
Operation Market Garden *see* Arnhem
Operation Plunder, 290
Operation Sparrowhawk, 333
Operation Varsity *see* Rhine Crossing
Operation Zipper, 310
Orne, river, 129, 130, 133, 134, 148–50, 154–5, 176, 177
Otway, Lieutenant Colonel Terence, xii, 127, 136, 138, 140, 143, 144, 146, 147, 177, 179, 180, 181
Oudna airstrip (Tunisia), 64, 66–7, 68, 71, 75
Oued el Medene, river, 85–6
Owen, Captain Graham, 338, 350

Paisley, Revd Ian, 407
Palestine, 94, 280, 316, 317–24
Palestinian Arabs, 318, 319, 321–3
Palmach, 319
Panter, Lieutenant, 105
Paphos Forest (Cyprus), 328, 329
Parachute, Commando and Airborne units:
   1st Allied Airborne Army, 195, 199, 203, 256
   1st Airborne Corps, 196, 203, 212, 250
   8th Airborne Corps *see* US Airborne units
   First Airborne Task Force, 266, 269
   1st Airborne Division, 36, 47, 50,

Parachute, Commando and
Airborne units—*contd*
96–109, 110, 112, 113, 117,
176, 194, 196, 197–264, 290,
309, 315, 324
6th Airborne Division, 1, 94,
123–4, 125–94, 201, 203, 212,
222, 281, 282–315, 317, 318,
319–24
1st Airlanding Brigade, 47–8, 51,
97, 98, 108, 197, 207, 210,
223, 229, 235, 244, 264, 286,
292, 301
1st Parachute Brigade, 28–31,
33, 47, 48, 51, 53–92, 93, 96,
97, 99–109, 118, 171, 195,
196, 200, 202, 207, 210, 211,
213–27, 232–9, 246–9, 264,
315, 323
1st Special Service (Commando)
Brigade, 130, 147, 159, 161,
176, 188, 291, 305
2nd Independent Parachute
Brigade, xii, 118–23, 266–80,
315, 323, 324
3rd Commando Brigade, 356,
412–55
2nd Parachute Brigade, 28, 48,
51, 96–7, 99, 113, 117–18
3rd Parachute Brigade, 48, 125,
126–7, 130–48, 162–75,
176–81, 187–9, 192, 286, 288,
292, 295–6
4th Parachute Brigade, 93–5,
112, 113, 197, 202–3, 207,
209, 210, 211, 223, 227–31,
237, 240–42, 243–6, 249–52,
256, 264, 321
4th Special Service (Commando)
Brigade, 188
5th Parachute Brigade, 127, 128,
130, 132, 139, 140, 148–61,
174–6, 181–7, 189–94, 283–7,
292, 296–300, 303, 304,
306–7, 310–16
6th Airlanding Brigade, 128,

130, 133, 157, 171, 175, 186,
187, 189, 315
16th Independent Parachute
Brigade Group, 324, 331–58
Parachute Regiment, x, 324, 386
1st Battalion, The Parachute
Regiment, 4, 324; *see also* 1
Para
1st Parachute Battalion (1 Para),
4, 28, 33, 48, 117, 118, 125,
135, 324, 326, 327, 357, 358,
409–11; Aden, 373, 376–85;
Arnhem, 215, 219, 221, 222,
226–7, 232, 233–9, 262, 263;
becomes 1 (Guards) Para,
315–17; Cyprus, 329–32;
North Africa, 55, 57–64, 75,
76–8, 82–92, 134; Sicily, 99,
101–4, 105
2nd Parachute Battalion (2 Para),
29, 33–45, 53, 114, 115, 310,
315, 324, 331, 338, 356–7,
358, 410; Arnhem, 195, 213,
215, 217, 218–19, 222, 224–5,
248; Borneo, 393–404;
Falklands, 412–41, 448,
450–55; North Africa, 57,
64–75, 76, 77, 81, 82, 83, 85,
87–92; Sicily, 99–101, 103,
104–6; Würzburg radar raid,
34–45
3rd Parachute Battalion (3 Para),
29, 33–4, 320, 324, 326, 408;
Arnhem, 215–27 *passim*,
233–9; Cyprus, 326, 327,
329–32; Falklands, 413–14,
416, 417, 419–20, 421, 424–5,
435–52, 455; North Africa, 55,
57, 64, 76–81, 83, 85, 86, 87,
90, 91; Radfan, 363–73; Sicily,
99, 104, 105; Suez, 333–58
4th Parachute Battalion (4 Para),
48, 117, 120–21, 268–71,
272–5, 276, 279, 324
5th Parachute Battalion (5 Para),
48, 117, 119, 268, 273, 276–7,

5 Para—*contd*
316, 320, 324
6th Parachute Battalion (6 Para),
48, 112, 117, 121, 122–3, 268,
273, 276, 277, 279, 324, 366
7th Parachute Battalion (7 Para),
48, 127, 132, 134, 140,
149–50, 152, 154–5, 157–9,
161, 176, 189, 192, 193, 300,
316, 324
8th Parachute Battalion (8 Para),
48, 125, 127, 134–6, 140,
164–70, 171–3, 295–6, 304,
320, 383
9th Parachute Battalion (9 Para),
6, 49, 125, 126, 127, 128, 134,
136–8, 140, 144–7, 148,
163–4, 169, 171, 173, 174,
177–81, 187, 189, 192, 222,
286, 290, 293, 295–6, 305
10th Parachute Battalion (10
Para), 93, 94, 112, 229, 241,
242, 244–6, 251, 256
11th Parachute Battalion (11
Para), 93, 94–5, 228, 230,
233–9, 262
11th Special Air Service
Battalion, 13, 14–28
12th Parachute Battalion (12
Para), 127, 135, 138, 139,
150–52, 159–61, 175–6, 180,
181–7, 189, 192, 281, 294,
297–9, 316
13th Parachute Battalion (13
Para), 117, 127, 151, 152–3,
156, 161, 176, 190–91, 192–3,
283–6, 299, 316
17th Parachute Battalion (17
Para), 315–16
151st Parachute Battalion, 6,
93–5
156th Parachute Battalion, 93–4,
95, 113, 207, 240–42, 245,
250–51, 252, 261–2
No. 2 Commando, 4–13, 29, 49,
202

No. 3 Commando, 147
No. 6 Commando, 57, 182
No. 9 Commando, 276
40 RM Commando, 338, 357,
411, 414, 418, 419, 424
42 RM Commando, 324, 338,
341, 351, 357, 384–5, 414,
418, 424, 433, 435, 437, 439,
440, 450
45 RM Commando, 331, 348,
356–7, 360, 363–5, 370–73,
418, 424, 425, 436, 440, 441,
444, 449, 450
59 Commando Engineer
Squadron, 428
1st (Guards) Independent
Parachute Company, 324,
339–40, 356, 357, 386, 391–3,
404–5
21st Independent Parachute
Company 213–14, 254
22nd Independent Parachute
Company, 140
1st Independent Parachute
Platoon, 267
1st Parachute Field Squadron
Royal Engineers, 39
3rd Parachute Field Squadron
Royal Engineers, 164, 165,
167
9th Parachute Squadron, Royal
Engineers, 338
21st Reconnaissance Squadron,
210, 216, 219, 221, 222
parachutes, 5, 6, 10, 27, 30
parachuting: from balloons, 26–7,
34, 35; hole exit method, 8–9,
10, 11, 55; para roll, 29; pull-off
method, 5, 6–8, 9–10; Roman
Candle, 55
Parfitt, Lieutenant, 143
Parker, Colonel, 186
Parry, Lieutenant Colonel Allen,
xii, 140, 141, 143–6, 147, 188
Paterson, Second Lieutenant, 18
Patton, Major, 444

Peachey, Sapper, 167
Pearson, Brigadier Alastair, xii, 59, 60, 62, 64, 77–8, 81–3, 85–6, 87–8, 89, 91, 101–2, 106, 107, 125, 134–6, 140, 164–6, 167–70
Pearson, Colonel, 276
Pearson, Lieutenant, 121
Pearson, Staff Sergeant, 252
Penelope, HMS, 112
Penman, Squadron Leader, 433
Picchi, 17, 20, 21
Pickard, Wing Commander, 38, 41, 43
Pike, Lieutenant Colonel, 366, 367–8, 371–2, 414, 425, 440, 441, 443, 444, 446–9
Pine-Coffin, Lieutenant Colonel Geoffrey, 56–7, 127, 159
Plaman Mapu (Borneo), 396–402
Platt, Corporal, 84–5
Playford, Lieutenant, 68
Poett, General Sir Nigel, xii, 127, 132–3, 148–50, 155, 156, 189, 191, 192–3, 292, 297, 311
Polish Parachute Brigade, 207, 209, 210, 213, 223, 255
Pompforce, 273–6
Pond, Lieutenant, 146–7, 295
Pont du Fahs (Tunisia), 65, 71, 73
Pont l'Evêque (Normandy), 192
Ponte Grande (Sicily), 97–8
Pooley, Major, 147
Pope, Major, 171
Port Said, 335, 336, 338, 341, 344, 350, 351, 352, 353, 354, 355, 356, 357, 456
Port San Carlos Settlement (Falklands), 419, 424, 428, 435, 436
Powell, Colonel Geoffrey, xii, 94, 205, 207, 245, 250–51, 261
Priday, Major, 300
Primasole Bridge (Sicily), 97, 99, 101–8, 125, 197
Prince of Wales, HMS, 45
Prinz Albert, HMS, 38

Pritchard, Brigadier, 117, 121–2, 276–7
Pritchard, Major, 16, 18, 19–20
Provisional IRA (Provos), 407–11
Pugsley, Private, 345

Queripel, Captain, 245

Radfan, 359–73
Radfan Camp (Aden), 377, 380–82, 385
Radforce, 362, 365, 366
Rann, Captain, 101
Ranville (Normandy), 130, 132, 149, 150, 153, 154, 157, 161, 164, 176, 177
Raswa (Egypt), 338, 349, 355, 357
Read, Sergeant, 351
Repulse, HMS, 45
Rhine Crossing (Operation Varsity), 287, 288–308, 383
Rice, Major, 430
'Rice Bowl' (Radfan), 363, 365
Richards, CSM, 85
Richardson, Lieutenant, 351
Ridgeway, Major General, 204, 288, 290–92, 301, 306
Riley, Lieutenant Nigel, xii, 271, 276
Ringway, Central Landing School, 2–14, 16, 24, 25–30, 35, 49, 135
Ritchie, Major, 175–6
Robehomme bridge (Normandy), 130, 134, 172, 173
Robinson, Captain James, 163–4
Robinson, Warrant Officer, 348
Rock, Lieutenant Colonel, 11, 46
Rogers, Major, 183, 186
Rommel, Field Marshal Erwin, 56, 76
Roseveare, Major, 165–7, 174
Ross, Captain, 40, 42
Ross, CSM, 144
Royal Air Force (RAF), 1, 2, 14, 27, 28, 30, 32, 33, 35, 39, 46, 50, 110, 113, 129, 137, 139, 140,

Royal Air Force—*contd*
206, 210, 242–3, 293, 317, 323,
325, 326, 332, 363; PFIs
(physical fitness instructors),
27–8, 29
Royal Marines *see* Parachute and
Commando units
Royal Netherlands Army, 314
Russia, Russians, 32, 271, 272,
306–8, 351, 362

Sabah (Malaysia), 387
St Honorine (Normandy), 133,
175, 182
Sallal, General, 361
Salonika (Thessaloniki), 276
Salmon, Major, 126
San Carlos Water (Falklands), 412,
413, 417, 419
'Sand Fly' (Radfan), 363, 365
Sarawak (Malaysia), 387, 391–2
SAS, 317, 386, 391, 393, 405, 423,
424, 435
Scott, Major, 241
Seine, advance to the river, 188–9,
192, 290, 302
Sele, river, 15, 17, 21
Semarang (Java), 311–15
Sheikh Othman (Aden), 373, 377,
380–81, 383, 384
Shepherd, Guardsman, 404
Short, Captain, 69
Sicily, 46, 96–112, 197, 202, 204,
208, 218, 267, 290, 317
Sidi Bou Della ('Bowler Hat',
Tunisia), 85–6, 87
Sidi N'Sir (Tunisia), 61, 64
Sim Major, 128, 139, 150, 151,
152, 155–6, 159–61, 180,
182–3, 186–7, 294, 316
Sinai War (1956), 340
Singapore, 45, 310, 315, 386, 387,
389, 396
Sinn Fein, 408
Sir Galahad, LSL, 113, 440
Sir Tristram, LSL, 440

Six Day War (June 1967), 380
Skeet, Captain, 193
Slade, Lieutenant, 145
Smith, Sergeant, 115
Smith, Major, 143
Smyth, Lieutenant Colonel, 94, 251
SOE, British, 199
Sosabowski, Brigadier, 255
Souk el Arba (Tunisia), 59, 60, 91
Sousse (Tunisia), 64, 95, 96
South Arab Federation of, 359–85
South Arabian Army (SAA), 381–2,
384
South Arabian Police in Champion
Lines, 381–2
South Staffords, 2nd Battalion, 98,
230, 232–3, 239, 259
Spanish Civil, War, 4
Speidel, General, 157
Stanion, Corporal, 106–7
Stanley (Falklands), 417, 418, 424,
434, 436, 437, 439, 441, 450,
455
Starling, Major, 373, 384
statichutes, American, 9, 10
Steele Baume, Major Eric, 127
Stern Gang, 319, 322
Stevens, Major, 345–6
Stevenson, Lance Corporal, 166
Stockwell, General, 335, 341, 356
Strachan, Sergeant Major, 37–8,
41, 43
Strange, Flight Lieutenant Louis,
2, 11, 26
Street, Lieutenant, 79
Student, General, 201
Suez crisis (1956), 333–58, 361,
383
Suharto, General, 404
Sukarno, President of Indonesia,
386, 387, 392, 393, 404
Sulmona PoW camp, 22–3
Sussex Mountain (Falklands), 412,
419, 423, 425
Sweeney, Lieutenant, 150
Symonds, Colonel Loder, 254

Syracuse (Sicily), 97, 108

Tait, Wing Commander, 16
Tanner, Corporal, 379
Target for Tonight (film), 38
Tarrant, Major, 191
Tatham-Warter, Major, 247
Tatton Park, 5, 6, 16, 29
Taylor, Major Nigel, 127, 154–5,
  157–9
Teal Inlet Settlement (Falklands),
  425, 435, 436
Teed, Captain, 275
Teichman, Major, 34–5, 69
Tel Aviv (Palestine), 319
Tel el Kebir, 324
Telecommunications Research
  Establishment (TRE), 32–3, 45
Terrell, Major, 76, 167
Thomas, Lieutenant, 159
Thomas, Major General, 260
Thompson, Brigadier, 413, 416,
  417, 424, 431, 437, 439, 440,
  444, 449, 450, 455
Thompson, Captain, 397, 398
Thompson, Lieutenant, 166
Thompson, Lieutenant Colonel,
  238
Tilshead (Salisbury Plain), 35, 37,
  38
Timothy, Major, 40, 114–15,
  232–3, 236–7
Tindale, Corporal, 402
Tragino Aqueduct (Italy), airborne
  raid on (1941), 14–22, 24, 115,
  153
Transjordan Frontier Force, 321,
  322
Triumph, HMS, 17, 21–2
Troarn bridge (Normandy), 130,
  134, 164, 166, 167–8, 169, 170
Troodos mountains (Cyprus), 327,
  328, 337, 358
Tunis, 56, 66, 67, 75
Tunisian campaign, 55, 56, 57–92,
  93, 95, 108, 213, 317

Turkish Cypriots, 327
Two Sisters (Falklands), 441, 449

United Nations, 320, 321, 322, 376
Urquhart, Major Brian, 204–5
Urquhart, Major General, 196,
  202, 203, 204–5, 212, 213, 218,
  220, 221, 222, 226, 227, 229,
  231–3, 234–5, 243, 246–8, 250,
  253, 254, 255, 256–7, 259, 260,
  261, 264–5
US Airborne units, 75; 8th
  Airborne Corps, 288, 290–91,
  306; 17th Airborne Division, 1,
  288, 291, 294; 82nd Airborne
  Division, 112, 196, 197, 223,
  290; 101st Airborne Division,
  196, 197; 2nd Battalion 503
  Parachute Infantry, 53, 64
USAAF, 53, 56, 98–9, 100, 101,
  109, 110, 122, 206, 293

Varaville (Normandy), 130, 134,
  171
Vernon, Captain, 39, 43
Voeux, Lieutenant Colonel des,
  241, 250
Vokes, Sergeant, 348

Waddy, Colonel, xii, 207, 228–9,
  241–2, 257–8
Wadi Dhubsan (Radfan), 366–7,
  369, 370–73
Wadi Taym (Radfan), 362, 363,
  365
Walsh, Major General Mike, xii,
  326, 327, 331, 332–3, 337–8,
  343–4, 351, 357, 363, 366–7,
  373, 377–81, 382, 383–4
Walters, Major, 363, 365
Warcup, Sergeant, 184
Ward, Captain, 186–7
Ward-Booth, Major, 366
Warrack, Colonel, 216, 227, 257–8,
  259, 263
Warren, Major, 184–6

Warwick-Pengelly, Lieutenant, 182, 186
Watson, Lance Corporal, 18
Watson, Major, 152–3, 283
Watson, Private Jack, 368
Watts, Trooper, 12
Wavell, General Lord Archibald, 3
Webb, Captain, 398
Webber, Captain, 154, 158–9
Weeks, CSM, 446
Weiner, Sergeant, 261
Wesel (Germany), 290–91
Weser, crossing the river (Germany), 303, 304
Westerbouwing (Holland) 231, 253–4, 255
White, Lance Corporal, 339, 355
White, Lieutenant, 256
Whitelock, Captain, 62–3
Wilkinson, Private, 68
Willetts, Sergeant, 408–9
Williams, CSM, 398–400
Williams, Lance Corporal, 339, 353
Williams, Major General, USAAF, 206
Wilmot, Sergeant, 274–5

Wilson, Brigadier, 437–8
Wilson, Captain (MO), 299
Wilson, Corporal, 111
Wilson, Dr, 422
Wilson, Lieutenant Leslie, 81
Wilson, Major, 214, 254
Windy Gap (Falklands), 419, 421
Wireless Ridge (Falklands), 443, 444, 448, 450–55
Wismar (Germany), 306–8
Withers, Lieutenant, 98
Witzig, Colonel, 82, 88
Wolfheze crossing (Holland), 221, 244, 246
Woodcraft, Sergeant, 126, 177–9
Woods, Captain, 395
Woodward, Rear Admiral, 414
Würzburg radar, 32–3; raid on, 37–45

Yemen, 359, 361–2, 363, 376
Young, Lance-Corporal, 174
Young, Major, 171, 173
Young, Second Lieutenant, 382

Zwolanski, liaison officer, 255

The Raiders

The Army Commandos 1940–46

Robin Neillands

Churchill called them 'men of the hunter class'.

The Raiders is the story of the British Army Commandos, called to action in the dark days following Dunkirk to strike with mounting ferocity and ever-increasing skill in every theatre of war, from Norway to Syria, along the desert coasts of North Africa and in the jungle and swamps of the Arakan.

Told largely in the words of the volunteers who served in all ranks, this is an inspiring account of what it was really like to fight in one of the world's elite fighting forces, minute by minute, raid by raid. The fifty years that have elapsed since their formation have not dimmed these tales of triumph, of defeat, and above all courage.

FONTANA PAPERBACKS

Carve Her Name With Pride

R. J. Minney

Violette Szabo, a girl who before the war had led a quiet life in south London, was suddenly picked for special training so that she could go on a dangerous mission behind enemy lines in France.

When her mariage to a French legionnaire ended in tragedy with his death in Libya, Violette's desire to do something for her country became an urgent need.

As a secret agent she took a daring part in the plan to stop crack German reinforcements being put into action after the D-day landings. Tragically, this mission led to her capture and imprisonment, and after torture and weeks of rigorous questioning Violette Szabo was shot by the Nazis in the closing phases of the war.

Violette Szabo was posthumously awarded the George Cross – the first and only English girl to win this supreme award.

'From this book, detailed and documented, there springs the clear image of a vital, vigorous woman, brimming with fire and scorn.'   *Evening Standard*

'An exciting and moving story.'   *Daily Mail*

FONTANA PAPERBACKS

Fontana Paperbacks
Non-fiction

Fontana is a leading paperback publisher of non-fiction. Below are some recent titles.

You can buy Fontana paperbacks at your local bookshop or newsagent. Or you can order them from Fontana Paperbacks, Cash Sales Department, Box 29, Douglas, Isle of Man. Please send a cheque, postal or money order (not currency) worth the purchase price plus 22p per book for postage (maximum postage required is £3).

NAME (Block letters) _____

ADDRESS _____

_____

_____